THE WAY OF AN EAGLE

To Ruth,
for holding the fort.

The Way

of an Eagle

N. R. Phillips

Tykky-Dew
Press

Copyright © N. R. Phillips 2017

First published in 2017 by Tykky-Dew Press, Rosemorran, Clements Road, Penzance, TR18 4LL

email: tykkydew.press@gmail.com

Distributed by Lightning Source worldwide

British Library Cataloguing in Publication Data

A catalogue record for this book is available from the British Library

ISBN 978-0-9954574-0-9

Typeset by Amolibros, Milverton, Somerset

www.amolibros.com

This book production has been managed by Amolibros

Printed and bound by Lightning Source

There be three things which are too wonderful for me
yea, four which I know not:
the way of an eagle in the air,
the way of a serpent upon the rock,
the way of a ship in the midst of the sea,
and the way of a man with a maid.

Proverbs 30 : 18 – 19

Chapter One

Jack Pengelly's beard is streaked with grey now and he doesn't put that entirely down to age. Ever since the expedition there has remained a certain doubt whether it's all over and forgotten. Superficially, his life is far more tranquil than it's ever been, for he permits nothing to disturb the quiet routine of his life. There might be the occasional anxious moment out at sea, for the capricious ocean is both his ally and enemy, providing him with sustenance but ever eager to punish those who take its quieter moods for granted. Out there, alone, he's relaxed enough, yet his eyes are always alert, watching for the turn of the tide, fickle winds, a rising ground swell. For the seafarer, it was ever so.

It is events in distant parts that trouble him. There was a time when the Middle East seemed so far away that events there could never impinge on the lives of people at home. He knows that the knowledge he shares with the others, about those distant days of the disastrous expedition, might even now play a significant part in current conflicts.

There is always the niggling fear that they have not done with him but, with the passing of time, he's no longer quite so anxious that unknown enemies will seek him out, assuming that more momentous events in the Middle East have occupied their minds or, that for his own sake, they're sure he'll keep what he knows to himself. However, he would not forget the shiver of dread that the summons to London sent down his spine, fearful of being grasped in the long claws of the Establishment. He'll never forget that. It was more scary than all they'd gone through, holding that envelope.

He was certain that they were kept under loose surveillance, and didn't let that bother him. He had no objection to it under the circumstances, considered himself as patriotic as the next man, and had his country's interest at heart. After that interrogation in London there had been no further direct contact with those two. He had not even kept in touch with the other members of the expedition. After a few brief exchanges of letters – no email or cell phones then – they had lost touch. He had no idea where they were or how their lives had diverged but he assumed that they too had never divulged anything they'd learned in those last few grisly days. There remained the hope that one day, however long it took, he'd meet the expedition leader again, that he might, as he put it to himself, pay his debts.

Wars in foreign parts – there were always wars in foreign parts – were usually so remote that it was difficult to empathise with any of the combatants. It was not like that with the slaughter now being reported in Yemen. A war between peoples he had known and, indeed, loved. What had happened to Muqbel and his family? The suspicious clerk at that scruffy hotel? The old Sheik and the tribesmen in that remote village? The old couple at the caves, the beautiful children? All the other Yemenis who had been so kind to them? Were those lovely people now all engaged in killing each other, or already dead? He would never know. All this on his mind as a consequence of watching birds, he thought, as he looked yet again across the bay at the diving terns. A minor adventure to discover the migration route of eagles. So long ago. How could it have happened? It was bizarre!

Well, all adventures, and misadventures, have to start somewhere; yet, in recalling his Yemen experience, Jack's precise memory of its beginning still, after all this time, fails him. Despite having a vague notion in his head about going out there to look for the eagles, he could not claim that the expedition had been his own idea. He had mentioned the eagle migration to others, and speculated on it in his paper submitted to *Garzetta*, and awaiting publication. But he was forced to concede that the mounting of the expedition was entirely due to the efforts of Stanley Carter.

The thought of going had been in Jack's mind for months, so

there was no way of determining exactly when the madness of the Yemen began. He had no difficulty, however, in remembering the day he met Stanley Carter and took an instant dislike to him. It was soon after his return from two years working as a rigger in Saudi Arabia. With no commitments, and the girl he had left behind engaged to someone else, he had spent some of his high earnings on a boat of his own and resumed his old way of life, fishing out of St. Ives, Cornwall.

On that crucial October morning he went up to the headland because there was a gale blowing, driving foam-crested swells across the bay. Jack's boat had been hauled out of the harbour, big ships run for shelter, and thousands of sea birds driven before the stinging rain and the tempest pounding the western approaches. He was not the first one up there. His old friend, Julian, had beaten him to it, although it was still too dark to see much, and they stayed in the lee of the coastguard wall waiting for the light to improve. The wind seethed over granite and grass, the aerials on the mast behind them rattled and clanked, while across the eastern shore of the bay the dawn light fell upon an anchored trawler straining her chain in the rolling swells.

'Wind's veering,' Julian said. 'It'll soon be nor' west.'

More birders soon arrived and, by the time it was fully daylight, the wall was full of elbows steadying binoculars. When the wind finally drew into the northwest there was hardly space for anyone to stand in the shelter of the rocks. The rainsqualls died away. Clouds broke, and the intermittent sunshine soon became a continuous bright illumination of the spectacle before them. The colours, Jack thought, the colours. The greens, blues, reds and purple in the sea. The black and white of shearwaters and the yellow heads of noble gannets were clearly visible as the warm sun shone on the observers' backs. Flocks of kittiwakes, like swirling snow, were caught by the eddies and twisted into spiralling columns which strove to round the headland before plunging to the shelter of the wave-crests, low over the surface. The excitement was contagious as the passage of birds increased. Rising spray, from waves still pounding the headland, reflected brilliant rainbows from which flocks of auks emerged, as from pools of ethereal colour.

'The light's good,' Julian said. He had seen! They grinned at each other, sharing the understatement, and resumed their watching. 'A bit different from Arabia.'

''Tis a bit.' They spoke with their binoculars held up to their eyes, continually scanning the bay.

'Wouldn't you like to go out there again?'

'Sure. I'd like to spend a year out there. Just birding.' He stepped back to peer through his telescope at a distant speck which may have been… he hadn't seen one for three years… which looked like… yes!'

'Sabine's gull!'

The shoving and confusion, the searching and scanning as they all tried to see it, nearly knocked some of them off the headland.

'Where? Where's the Sabine's?'

There is always someone who arrives seconds too late, or leaves a minute too early, to see the rarity. This one was a bespectacled young man with quite handsome features surrounded by a short black beard and thick wavy hair. 'Was it verified?' he asked as he pushed his way to the front in the hope of getting a glimpse of the small gull receding into the troughs to the west.

Jack made a wry grimace to Julian. 'I must have a pump-ship,' he said. He squeezed his way out through the bird watchers and set out for the loo in the car park. He didn't want to miss a single minute of this gale, for it was the first since he had returned from those scorching days in Arabia. But there we are. When a man's got to pee, a man's got to pee. Looking across the bay, to where the rollers were crashing against the rocks, he saw the trawler steaming closer to the harbour, where there was still some shelter from the veering wind. She was plunging her bow into the seas, sending showers of green water along her decks.

Damn glad I'm not out there, Jack thought. He loved the sea, and was afraid of it, as he loved deserts and was afraid of them too; those great expanses of space where one could breathe fresh unpolluted air and feel exhilarated by the magnitude and mystery of nature. The rolling waves, reaching across the bay, were like the great dunes of Arabia, massive and beautiful in their splendour and power, these blue and cold, the others red and hot, both indifferent to the fate of those who dared venture into their fascinating undulations. There had been a time in Arabia when the desert almost claimed him. There had been a time when he had been caught at sea in such a gale... Yes. He was damn glad he was not out there. When he returned to the headland, the birds were still streaming by. 'What have I missed?' he asked.

'Another Sabine's,' said the newcomer without removing his eye from Jack's telescope.

'Did you see it, Jules?'

Julian looked round at Jack, shook his head slightly. 'No,' he said aloud, 'I could only find an immature little gull. A long way out.'

'Ma'lish,' Jack said, using a word of Arabic. 'Never mind.'

The man turned to look at him. His dark, almost black, eyes studied Jack intently, as if assessing his character and intelligence. 'You're Jack Pengelly,' he said, assuming so from that one word of Arabic.

'Oh, really?' Jack was used to people mispronouncing his name, with the accent on the first syllable, so let it pass.

There was something in the young man's demeanour which Jack disliked, a certain air of superiority, of ill-concealed arrogance, which tempted Jack to retaliate, for he was a man of quick response. In remembering the occasion now, and what followed from it, he wishes he had thrown the little bastard into the sea there and then, but there was something coming across the bay. He elbowed his way in to his telescope. 'There's a skua coming,' he said.

They could see what it was. They said nothing except to call, 'Skua!'

'Skua!' the newcomer cried. 'Juvenile arctic.'

As the bird approached, Julian corrected the identification with a cry of 'Long-tailed skua,' and was nearly capsized in the crush to see it.

'Who are you, then?' Jack asked the black-haired stranger when the excitement had died down. 'You seem to know me.'

'I'm Stanley Carter.'

Jack has never forgotten the tone in the man's voice. His voice implied that they should have heard of him, that he was *the* Stanley Carter, the famous ornithologist and author of papers on the birds of the Middle East and Central Asia. They had heard of him, and were astonished to see he was so young. Carter held out his hand, 'Peter Harvey said I would probably meet you up here.' The proffered hand was condescending, yet they accepted it, briefly, with nods.

Jack enquired about Peter Harvey, and Carter brought him up to date with progress in the Middle East. Harvey was writing a paper on the birds of Saudi Arabia.

'Did he tell you about the steppe eagles,' Jack asked. 'Those we saw in central Arabia, near Riyadh?'

'The winter visitors?'

'No, the migrants. The ones that move on.'

'He saw no evidence of onward migration.'

'But he left the country at the end of October! In another month most of them had moved on. Near Riyadh, the numbers dropped from well over a thousand down to a couple of hundred during the winter. I made regular counts.'

Carter dismissed the statement as no more than wild speculation. 'The general consensus of opinion is that they spread out over the central deserts. There is no evidence of onward migration.'

Jack found his opinionated tone of voice irritating. 'Well,' he said, 'I reckon they go over the Bab al Mandab into Africa via Djibouti.'

Carter dismissed Jack's theory with a derisory smile. 'So I believe. Peter mentioned something about your speculation.'

Jack allowed the implied insult, that his own observations and theory were mere speculation, to pass. 'The only reason,' he said, 'that there's no evidence of onward migration is that no one's been to look for it.'

'Until there is evidence to the contrary, opinions, however much one may stress them, will not stand up to scientific scrutiny and are, *ipso facto*, speculation.'

Carter spoke with an accent that Jack could not identify. He had an ear for language, and supposed that Carter was of mixed parentage or had been transposed in his youth. He was later proven right in both assumptions. Carter lived in Derby, the son of a Nottinghamshire miner and a Yorkshire mill-girl. He was in his final year at St.Catherines College, Oxford, which he had reached by reason of determination and intelligence. He prided himself in being inferior to none and in not suffering fools, gladly or otherwise. Jack absently checked a passing Balearic shearwater. He wrote with a laborious script in his notebook. 'Speculation is it,' he muttered. 'We'll see about that. I'm damn well going out there to check.'

'Going where?' Julian asked.

'Yemen.'

Later, Jack was to consider whether the madness began with that one impetuous word... Yemen. He had not, in fact, the slightest intention of going to Yemen or anywhere else at that time and, even as the word escaped from his lips, he realised his impulsive nature had got the better of him again. He was thirty years old and had travelled enough for a while... fishing, merchant navy, oilrigs and then Saudi Arabia. But, those eagles went over the Bab al Mandab. He was sure of it, although Carter was right in one respect. There was no evidence, apart from his own observations in Arabia. Why didn't they believe him? He could go and check. He should go, before the eagles were wiped out by human exploitation, both in Russia where they bred and in Africa where they wintered. He should go to Yemen, a country about which he knew almost nothing. 'I'm going out there,' he said, 'to look for the migration of those eagles.'

Carter smiled a brief, sour smile. 'There'll be no need. I'm organising a major expedition to Yemen next year.'

'You and who else?' Julian challenged. There was animosity in his voice.

'A competent team.' Carter's smile broadened. 'Peter Harvey and I have been planning it for some time.'

Jack was unable to conceal his envy. The Yemenis with whom he had worked in Saudi Arabia had described the mountains and green wadis with the tall stone-built buildings. They had also described the difficult terrain, the remote villages with tribal allegiances. Eagles over the jebels! He turned to the sea again.

During the morning some forty thousand birds flew by. As far as the distant horizon they could see flocks of sea birds: kittiwakes, auks, gannets shearwaters, a few fulmars, late terns, some petrels, scores of skuas, two more Sabine's, some scoter. Jack tried to forget about the eagles and concentrate on the birds flying before him, although it was impossible to count them all. The gale abated during the afternoon. As the wind died away, the numbers of birds began to drop with it. The trawler put to sea, glad to be clear of this lee shore. The migration tailed off to a few stragglers. Some twitchers began drifting away to the Hayle estuary in the hope of finding an American wader blown over in the storm.

As the evening shadows lengthened across the bay just few bird watchers remained at the wall. Yemen! Jack could not get it out of his mind. Arabia Felix, with Marib, home of Sheba, Jebel an Nabi Shuab, the mountain of the Prophet's uncle, the highest in all Arabia. And the birds... the endemics, red-breasted wheatear, little rock-thrush, Yemen accentor, if any remained. The eagles! They had to go over the Bab. He was sure of it.

'Who's going on the expedition?' he said at last, unable to restrain his curiosity.

Carter smiled as if he had been waiting for the question. Julian began dismantling his telescope tripod. He watched Carter closely as the latter replied to Jack's query.

'We're overwhelmed with applicants,' Carter said, 'but apart from myself there'll be only three, Peter Harvey, E. D. Manton and Brian Cook. A very competent team.'

There was a slight impediment in his speech. Apart from the stilted, academic delivery, which sounded incongruous with his accent, there was a sort of tick, or a click at the back of his throat, like a spasm of the epiglottis, which was accompanied by a slight inspiration of breath through the nose. A slight *sk, sk,* as an involuntary hesitation between sentences.

'Never heard of them,' Julian said, bluntly, as he retracted the legs of his tripod.

'I know Peter Harvey,' Jack said, 'and I've heard of E. D. Manton. He published something on aggressive behaviour among migrating dunlin, a bit obscure for me. Who's the other one, Brian Cook?'

A student, like myself. We're all very competent ornithologists.'

'Should have thought,' Julian said, pointedly, 'that any competent ornithologist would know the difference between an arctic and a long-tailed skua.'

Jack intervened quickly. 'When are you going?' he asked.

Carter was about to reply to Julian, but checked himself and answered Jack's question after the noises in his throat had ceased. 'Next September, for a month. The expedition will take a year to organise.'

The hitherto uncertain notion of going to Yemen was filling Jack with excitement. 'Who's paying?' he asked.

Stanley Carter was apparently irked by such an inane question. 'With a team like mine there'll be no difficulty in raising the money. This is part of the forward planning, which will occupy most of the next year. There are plenty of charities trying to justify their existence by giving away other people's money.'

'If the money's there, as you say it is,' Jack said, 'I'll apply for a few grants too. I've been thinking of going my own anyway. Why not?'

'Yemen,' Carter said, now thoroughly impatient with both of them, 'is no place for anyone to go mooning around on their own.' He took his old battered binoculars from his neck and shoved them in his pack.

'Mooning around,' Jack said, 'is not what I had in mind. The eagle migration won't be easy to find.'

'The eagle migration,' Carter said, 'will be impossible to find. It doesn't exist.'

'You can't say that,' Julian interrupted again, 'you have no proof. No data.'

'True,' Carter said, with a sudden change of temper and a smile.

'You're quite right. I withdraw the statement.' He lifted his pack onto a shoulder by one of the straps. 'Withdraw it... until next year! And now to the Isles of Scilly to find that American vagrant.'

He slipped his other arm through its strap and went off down the slope with the unsteady gait of a man carrying too much weight.

'Don't like that bugger,' Julian said.

Jack smiled. 'I'm not that keen, either, but I wouldn't mind going on the expedition to Yemen with him.'

'I wouldn't go on the bus to Penzance with him,' Julian said, cynically.

They had been friends too long, had spent too many hours birding together to argue over Stanley Carter. 'Perhaps you're right,' Jack said, 'but I'd love to go to Yemen. Apart from the eagles there are several endemics that haven't been seen for years. And there must be a massive migration through there. I saw some of it right in the middle of Saudi Arabia. Wouldn't you like to go out there?'

'Yes, but I can't go. You can. You know the language. You can even read and write Arabic.'

'Well, hardly. I keep telling people, I only know a bit. I can read it, that's true but you can read French, German, Italian and Spanish, that doesn't mean you can speak them.'

'You know enough to get by. Apply for a few grants and go on your own.'

They were the last ones up there. The wind had died to a gentle breeze and the low sun behind them illuminated the under-wings of the remaining kittiwakes with a rosy glow. The stubble fields over on the eastern shore were glowing yellow above the black line of cliffs where the remaining swell broke in a white frieze between land and sea.

'I think I will,' Jack said. 'I'll go on my own.'

Chapter Two

The city was among the mountains in the flat, highland plateau, hidden by haze. From the windows of the plane Jack could see bright green rectangles of irrigated alfalfa and clusters of stone villages, with plumes of dust following vehicles along sinuous tracks across a barren landscape. The old Boeing banked steeply, turning to starboard over the mountains, and the view was lost to him as it lurched back onto to an even keel and began descending steeply towards the airport. A murmur of apprehension arose from the passengers: prayers to Allah, from the migrant Yemenis returning from the rich countries of the Gulf and, from Stanley Carter, the leader of the four-man expedition setting out to study the birds of Yemen, an exclamatory 'Jesus Christ!'

'Salah ala Nabi,' said a softly spoken voice.

Stanley Carter turned his eyes from the window. The speaker was in a seat across the aisle. He was a young Yemeni, in European dress; check jacket, pale blue shirt and tight-fitting trousers over slim hips. His hair was sleek and wavy, jet black over his collar. Beside him sat a woman, older than himself, late twenties perhaps. The couple had boarded the plane at Sharjah and, since then, she had donned a black cloak-like garment which covered her European clothes, her head and most of her face. Only her dark, enigmatic eyes were visible. She clasped an expensive-looking leather shoulder bag on her lap. The man's eyes were unsmiling.

'What's he say?' Stanley Carter asked, anxiously.

'Pray upon the Prophet,' Jack Pengelly said with a stern look at Stanley.

Next to Stanley sat Mike Jenkin, a young civil servant with pale skin and fair hair. He smiled nervously, and tightened his seat belt.

Sitting across the aisle was Eddie Johns, the fourth member of the British expedition. Eddie was a big, muscular Londoner of twenty-five who had spent most of his life birding and worked at any job he could get to earn the money to pay for it. Both Eddie and Mike were reputed to be good field men, although Eddie was the more experienced of the two. In contrast to Eddie's cockney voice, Mike, who was rather short and plump, spoke with a middle-class region-less accent. He had told them very little about himself, however, deferring to Eddie's verbosity, Stanley's authority and Jack's jocularity.

As the plane descended they were met with a spiralling cloud of dust, dry leaves and sheets of paper, brought up from the ground in a violent, rising thermal. The old Boeing shuddered and fell in a peripheral air pocket. The jets screeched.

'What the hell is he doing?' Stanley muttered, 'If they can't fly the damn things why don't they employ European pilots? He's making the approach far too fast.' He also tightened his seat belt.

As Jack Pengelly glanced across the aisle, he felt some doubt as to whether he had done the right thing in joining Stanley Carter's expedition. More doubts were to follow.

The wheels hit the runway with a sharp squelch of friction, once, twice, and the jets roared a final protest as they bounced along the uneven concrete. An excited babble of conversation broke out among the passengers.

'It ain't the easiest of landings,' Eddie Johns said as he looked at the sky through the window, 'among these 'ills, at this altitude.' He was looking for the first bird. He kept a list of first and last birds for all the countries he had visited. 'Black kite,' he said, but the plane spun into the terminal and the bird was lost to view.

There were long queues at immigration control. Young men, little more than boys, stood about in military uniforms, casually grasping the straps of machine guns or rifles slung over their shoulders. The police at the passport-check examined everyone in meticulous detail, turning the pages with their thumbs, and looked from photograph to face with doubt and disbelief. They handed them back reluctantly, for fear they had missed something, and waved the people through with an indifferent flick of the wrist, resigned to the knowledge that they could not be expected to detect every infidel spy who might slip into their country.

The customs officers made a cursory search through their baggage, groping deep into rucksacks while chatting animatedly among themselves, chalked an obscure mark on the outside, and smiled them through. 'Welcome to my country. Welcome to Sana'a.'

'That was easy,' Eddie said. 'I thought they might make a fuss about so many cameras and binoculars.'

'You never know with Arabs,' Stanley said. 'Unpredictable lot.'

When they went outside into the bright sunshine, an hour after touchdown, the taste of the Middle East was already in their mouths. That mixture of dust and elusive flavours in the air, which is so striking on arrival in hot countries and which, so soon, becomes lost in familiarity. The air was hot, and the sun reflected brilliantly from the dusty ground. The brown faces of the taxi drivers, lined up along the convulsive kerb, were lightened by a thin film of fine powder, which also dimmed the windscreens of their vehicles. The Arab who had spoken on the plane came out to the road with his female companion where three ragged porters carried their luggage to the taxis and received generous payment with obsequious smiles. One of the drivers loaded them and their luggage into his car, and as they drove off, the man regarded the British bird watchers with disdain. An old man was led from the airport by a boy upon whose shoulder rested the old man's left hand. The right hand carried the slender cane of the blind, and his eyes were hidden by dark glasses. They were also driven off, leaving five taxis at the kerb. One of the scruffy porters tried to relieve Mike of the weight of his heavy pack.

'I can manage, thank you,' Mike said, politely.

'How far is it to the city?' Eddie asked.

'Ten kilometres,' Mike said.

The taxi drivers sat on the kerb. They wore long-sleeved shirts and skirts which came down to their calves. On their heads were wound cotton cloths, turban-like, with one corner hanging over a shoulder. Three were bearded, others with days of stubble. Their sandaled feet were coated in grime. One of them unwrapped a cloth and removed a bundle of bright green leaves, from which they selected pieces of leaf and began chewing.

'What the hell are they eating?' Eddie asked.

'Qat,' Jack said. 'A mild narcotic.' He dropped his pack to the ground. 'We might as well sit here until they've finished.'

The others also dropped their packs. Stanley told the porters to go away, with a wave of his arm. The drivers watched, then turned to the leaves. They selected choice pieces and stuffed them in their mouths until their cheeks became grotesquely distended, like small, overblown balloons, about to burst. Occasionally one of them spat, ejecting a disgusting spurt of green juice and saliva, which exploded in the dusty road.

'We can't waste time while these people become stoned on that stuff,' Stanley said. He went over to them. 'You taxi?' he said.

'Aiwa,' they agreed. 'Tax,' and continued chewing.

'Taxi Sana'a?' Stanley said. The other three came over to join him.

'Go Sana'a?' Eddie asked.

'Ingijh,' one of them said through a mouth-full of green herbage.

'Perhaps they don't like the English,' Mike said.

'Tell 'em we're Yanks,' Eddie suggested. 'After the troubles in Aden it's hardly surprising they don't like us.'

'How long do they go on chewing that damned stuff?' Stanley demanded.

'Couple of hours perhaps,' Jack said.

'Then what?' Stanley was getting impatient and was showing it. That slight catch in his throat was there again. *Sk sk.*

'Nothing you'd notice if you weren't looking for it. It's just a mild stimulant. Like having half a pint in the pub.' Jack looked about him. 'I could do with a skeet,' he said.

'Think I'd rather have 'alf a pint than chew that beastly stuff,'

Eddie said. He looked down at the Yemenis from his six-foot bulk. He was well built, with broad shoulders and big muscular arms. The Yemenis were like dwarves beside him.

'They're not allowed to drink alcohol,' Jack said. 'Mind you, lots of them do. It's not as strict as Saudi Arabia here. I think! Not sure, to tell the truth.'

A few sparrows pecked in the dust. There was an occasional lorry passing. Towards the city everything was lost to view in a distorting heat haze. Jack looked to the sky. 'Look,' he said, 'brown-necked ravens.' They were wheeling high above them, three together, in loose circles, with their glossy plumage glistening in the sun. 'Makes you realise you're in the Middle East, eh Stanley.'

'I don't need brown-necked ravens to remind me where I am. Wait until you see chanting goshawk, then you'll really know you're in Yemen. But at this rate we'll see bugger all.' He turned to the qat chewers.

'Go Sana'a?' he said. 'Sana'a. Taxi. Four.'

He held up four fingers and pointed to the others and their rucksacks. 'Four Sana'a?' The Arabs looked at him as he pointed to the city, muttering among themselves, and ignored him. He began to raise his voice. 'You driver?' he said. 'You driver?' pointing at them in turn.

'Cool it, Stanley,' Jack said.

'You driver? Taxi? Go Sana'a? Today, not next week. Get off your arse and go Sana'a. Eh?'

Mike Jenkin was twenty-seven years old, though he looked older. A graduate in humanities, his inherent tact and courtesy were sorely tried in his professional life, but he had learned to cope with people under stress. Even the most belligerent antagonism could be resolved, he believed, if people could be persuaded to see reason. Stanley was overwrought. They had had a long and tiring journey. He said, 'Take it easy, Stanley, old man.'

'I'm not your old man,' Stanley snapped. He turned to Jack. 'And how long are we to cool it? I thought you knew how to deal with these bloody people.'

'For God's sake, shut up,' Jack said under his breath. 'You'll have the army out here in a minute.'

'Shouldn't upset them actually,' Mike said, still smarting from Stanley's rebuff.

We might as well start walkin' now,' Eddie grumbled, 'they'll never take us after insults like that.'

'They don't speak English,' Stanley said. 'They wouldn't know an insult from a knighthood.'

Eddie looked down at him. Stanley was the shortest of the four, yet, with his bustling personality, he dominated the group. His mind was never at rest, his eyes always darting from here to there, like an impatient sparrow, as he shifted his weight from foot to foot. Eddie was slow, laconic, but equally outspoken. 'I know,' he said in his cockney drawl, 'when I'm being insulted, in any language, and I expect they do too, mate.' He picked up his rucksack. 'Come on. It's six miles. The walk will be good trainin'. And we might get a lift.'

Stanley ignored him. 'I thought,' he said to Jack, 'that you knew the bloody language.'

Jack fished in his pocket for cigarettes. 'I told you! I only know a little. Their accents are different from Saudi Arabia. I have to listen hard to understand anything.'

'If you can't interpret the language, you may as well have stayed at home,' Carter told him.

Jack lit his cigarette. He blew a long plume of smoke into the air and sat on the frame of his rucksack, fighting his temper. He got up and moved over into the shade of the airport wall. He watched the road, his three English companions and the group of Yemenis, and quietly smoked his cigarette. Yemen, at last, after all the months of anticipation. Stanley Carter might be an arrogant little twit, but he certainly seemed to know how to touch up the charities for money. Apart from expenditure on personal equipment, the expedition was financed wholly from grants and sponsorships. Stanley appeared to have much of the more expensive sponsored items about his own person, however. His new 10 x 40 roof-prism binoculars were certainly a recent acquisition. What matter? Jack did not begrudge him the rewards for his effort in organising the expedition, although he did think that such perquisites should have been disclosed. He rose from off his haunches, stepped on the cigarette end, and said 'I must have a skeet.'

There was a lorry, a big Mercedes truck with one wheel missing and its axle perched on a pile of rocks, just past the line of taxis. He walked over and went behind it, past the chewing Yemenis, and pee'd into the dust. The Yemenis were looking at him. He grinned at them on the way back.

'Marhabah,' he said. 'Qat quais?'

'Marhabtain,' they replied, and yes, it was very good qat. The youngest and tidiest of them held out some leaves for him, smiling. He declined the offer with a raised hand and joined the others. 'Come on,' he said, 'let's go.'

They hoisted their heavy packs on to their backs and walked towards the city in silence. As they passed the Yemeni drivers there was a murmur of hoarse laughter, 'Like donkeys,' Jack heard one of them say, and nodded in agreement. 'Masallamah,' he said. Be with peace, the courtesy of departure.

'Masallamah,' they said.

With bent backs they walked in single file towards the town. Passing drivers tooted horns at them. Veiled women turned their heads in the back seats of cars. There was no shade and the dust from passing trucks accumulated in their throats. Too late, they realised they had no water. After one mile along the hot road, a Toyota Land Cruiser came from behind and pulled in beside them. The driver leaned out.

'Sana'a?' he inquired.

They stopped, looking at each other in disbelief. The driver emerged from his vehicle. He was thin, with shiny black hair and a narrow moustache. There was a couple of days' stubble on his chin and his teeth were white, unstained from qat. His skirt was patterned in tartan and his shirt was green, clean and pressed. He was the one who had offered Jack the leaves.

17

'Sana'a?' he said again, as they stood looking at him under the weight of their packs.

'Ask him how much,' Stanley said.

'B'kam?' Jack said. 'Kam fulous?'

The driver shrugged his shoulders and smiled apologetically.

'He probably thinks we're desperate,' Stanley said. 'How much, mister?'

The driver pursed his lips around a smile, directing it from one to the other of them, 'Ayah kidmak,' he said.

'What's that mean?'

'At your service.' Jack grinned at the Yemeni who opened the tailgate and indicated that they load their gear.

'Come on,' Eddie said, 'we can argue about the fare when we get there.'

They piled their rucksacks in the back and climbed into the vehicle. Stanley sat in the front, next to the driver. The car was elaborately decorated, with coloured postcards, brightly tasselled frills around the windows, embroidered cushions, photographs of Arab girls, and texts from the Koran in elaborate calligraphy. There was a smell of stale perfume and the sweat of many bodies. The driver sang as he drove, a monotonous warble in quartertones and discord, and steered erratically, swerving to avoid obstacles in the road and oncoming traffic, which passed in clouds of dust and blaring music from transistors in the cabs. The road into the city was broad, badly surfaced, with dry hillsides and barren, rubbish-littered desert on either side. There were some small villages off the road, tight clusters of square, stone-built buildings among small fields enclosed in dry-stone walls. There were many rectangles of dark green qat shrubs, planted in lines, among the ripening corn and patches of alfalfa. Herds of goats, tended by children, browsed among the sparse vegetation and wind-blown rubbish. Although so near the capital, the villages had an air of isolation and hostility, with their high walls and small windows. Numerous watchtowers with narrow slits in the walls, for the use of firearms, dotted the plain, which shimmered with heat in the distance and was totally bird-less. They observed the passing scene with unspoken misgivings.

'In Saudi Arabia,' Jack said, 'I saw buildings five stories high, built entirely of mud.' The response was scornful glances and silence.

They passed several wrecked vehicles, mangled and bent, blackened by fire. A dead dog at the roadside, split open and putrid, scented the air for a mile. Paper and plastic hung from stunted shrubs along the route.

'Typical,' Stanley spat.

'You should see the beaches at home,' Jack said, 'when the tourists leave them every evening. Dead badgers at the roadsides and fly-tipping in the countryside. If our country was as bare as this, there'd be rubbish seen everywhere.'

As they approached the city there were more people: truck-loads of labourers with their head-cloths blowing in the wind, merchants from the provinces wearing white skirts and daggers at their belts, tribesmen carrying machine guns or rifles.

'They're a wild-looking lot,' Eddie said.

'I expect they're all right, actually' Mike said nervously as he peered through the dusty window. 'Quite friendly, actually.'

The driver kept one hand hovering near the horn, and blasted loitering pedestrians out of his way with an apologetic smile.

'Maffi muk.'

'Maffi muk,' Jack agreed. No brains.

Soon, there were people everywhere, in and out of the shops, crowding the pavements, running between the traffic, sitting at the barbers, arguing with each other, and the deafening blare of music came from all directions, as the traders turned up their transistors to full blast in every shop. A young traffic-cop, standing on an island in the middle of a road junction, lashed out indiscriminately with his stick, striking cars and drivers alike with little effect, for the drivers laughed good-naturedly and ignored him.

'What a place!' Eddie said.

'Typical Arab chaos,' Stanley muttered.

'Anyone thought where we're going?' Mike asked.

'Ask him where we're going,' Stanley ordered.

The driver turned and spoke to Jack. 'What's he say?'

'Do we want the hotel?'

They turned into a wider street, where they saw a Union Jack hanging limply from a pole in the garden of a building on the corner. They stopped outside a new, modern hotel, swathed in reflective glass. It looked ostentatious amongst the dust and chaos of the street. Three large Europeans went inside.

'Yankee oil men,' Stanley said. 'We can't afford to stay here.'

Jack spoke to the driver.

'What did you say?' Stanley demanded.

'I asked him to find us a cheap hotel.' He held Stanley's eye, and added 'Please.'

The driver eventually took them through a maze of streets to a hotel in the old part of the town. It had been a palace of the emir, he said. It was tall, and beautifully proportioned, with an ancient, heavily studded wooden door of immense weight. Small windows in the stonework of the walls were outlined in white. The taxi driver helped them with their gear.

'How much do we owe you?' Jack asked, trying his Arabic again. 'Kam fulous?'

The driver shrugged helplessly, as if to indicate that such calculations were totally beyond his mental powers and in any case such a matter was trifling, and of no importance. 'Allah kareem,' he smiled.

'What's he say?' Stanley said.

'God is kind. Pay him.'

'We don't have any small denomination notes,' Stanley said.

'Fulous k'teer,' Much money' the driver said as he eyed the expedition money in Stanley's wallet, indicating that he was a rich man.

'Allah kareem,' Jack told him, God is kind, and they smiled in appreciation of this little exchange. Jack gave him a five-hundred-riyal note, which he selected from the bundle in Stanley's wallet, and the driver shoved a fistful of change into his hand and took him by the sleeve.

'My name,' the driver said, 'is Muqbel Amin Qasm. Tomorrow I come take all men tourist place.'

'You speak English,' Stanley informed him.

'A little.' He smiled apologetically to Stanley and turned again to Jack. 'Where you go after tomorrow? Tomorrow tourist office, sign paper. I take. Nine o'clock I come. He got into his car and drove away saying 'Masallamah' with a broad smile.

'Masallamah,' Jack said to the back of the vehicle.

'You paid him too much,' Stanley said.

They checked into the hotel. The interior was cool and quiet and there was a room available on the top floor. As there were only two beds, Stanley argued a reduction in price which put him in a more amiable mood. There was a narrow, winding stairway up the centre of the building, with old, creaking wooden doors leading off to rooms and passages on each floor. The walls were covered in white plaster, made from powdered alabaster, and the ceilings were decorated in intricate stucco-work with patterns of flowers and twining stems. The windows were made of gypsum, with panes of alabaster cut in arches and diamonds. Stained glass threw bright sunbeams onto the carpeted floors. From the top storey a final narrow stairway led up to the roof. The reception clerk invited them to go up. When they had settled themselves in and cleaned up in the primitive bathroom, they went aloft to see the view. The hotel was one of the tallest buildings in the original city. From the parapet at the top they looked out over the flat-roofed houses and minarets and domes of the mosques. The houses in the old quarter were clustered together in tall blocks, separated by the medieval streets with central gutters to take the rains away from the ancient doorways.

'Yemeni architecture,' Mike mused, 'must be the most beautiful in the world. Some of these houses are hundreds of years old, all built of stone and mud bricks.'

Looking down onto them was like looking into the shadows of the past. The new hotel, shops lining the main streets, some blocks of modern flats all spreading out from the new centre, heralded the beginning of the end for the old city. Such houses, as had served the inhabitants for a thousand years, would soon be built no more. The old ways were as doomed here as they were at home, Jack thought. The whole world was on the change, like people getting on in life, not knowing what their future would be.

Two saker falcons flew overhead, calling to each other among the wheeling kites, and there were squat, fan-tailed ravens perched on the higher rooftops, reminding them of the purpose of this crazy trip.

'Look,' Eddie suddenly cried, 'in the trees of that garden. That pigeon.'

'Bruce's green pigeon!' Mike said. 'My first life-tick for Yemen.'

The bird flew across into tamarisks in another garden. A hoopoe flew out. Stanley followed it with his binoculars.

'I should be careful about using them in town, if I were you,' Jack said. 'Somebody is sure to think we're spies.'

Stanley ignored him, and kept scanning the gardens below. 'There's that girl,' he said, 'the one we saw on the plane.'

'Where?'

'Down there. On that roof. She's hanging out some washing. I'm sure it's her.'

'Well, why not? She has to live somewhere.'

'Are you sure it's her?' Mike asked. He adjusted his spectacles. 'I thought she was quite attractive, actually. Hmm.'

'Here, have a look.' Stanley passed over his new binoculars.

'Oh yes. That's her. She's still wearing the same clothes she had on under that black thing.'

'Let's have a look,' Eddie laughed. 'We might as well all get deported while we're at it.'

Their movements on the skyline had attracted the girl's attention and, as Eddie focused on her, she looked up at them. Eddie knew better than to duck out of sight. He kept the glasses to his eye and slowly panned them away from her, saying, 'She's seen us, I fink!' lapsing into his cockney accent.

The girl was joined by the man who was on the plane. She continued to hang the washing without looking again at the foreigners, but her companion stared up at them until Jack said

'We'd better get off the roof. Peering at a bint through binoculars! You could lose your head for that in Saudi Arabia.'

'The sooner we get out of the city the better,' Stanley declared. 'We should be able to go north tomorrow.'

'I doubt it,' Jack said. 'By the time we register with the immigration authority and see the British Embassy people, the day will be gone.' He led the way back down to their room.

Mike sat on the floor by the low window. He could see down into the street. A truckload of soldiers went by, slowly making headway through the crowd, like a boat in a current, and they saw a tall man rushing through the crowds, pushing people aside. He carried an automatic rifle slung from his shoulder and a large dagger at his waist. Occasionally he glanced back and they could see he was smiling grimly as he weaved his way in and out of the thronging traffic. They then saw that he was chased by two policemen with pistols drawn, who struggled to catch him but soon gave up as he disappeared amongst the crowd.

Then Mike saw the man they had seen on the roof come into the street and walk towards the hotel door. He was lost to sight. 'I think he's after us,' Mike said.

'Probably come to find out who we are,' Jack said. 'What we're doing here.'

'Jittery kind of place,' Mike remarked, with an apologetic smile.

'We'll be all right when we get out of the city,' Stanley asserted. 'There's never any trouble in the country. All we have to do is keep away from people and villages.'

Jack looked at him with incredulity, 'Do you know,' he asked, 'how many people there are in this country, Stanley?'

'Six million?' Mike offered.

'Right. In an area the size of England and Wales. And there's nobody in three quarters of the country over to the east, where there's no water. We'll find it very difficult to get away from people.'

'I know,' Stanley exploded indignantly, 'how many people there are here. Do you think I embarked on a venture like this without thoroughly researching the project? I'm not entirely without brains.'

23

Jack wished that Mike had not offered the information. He found himself wanting to catch Stanley out. 'Where there's water, there's people,' he said, irritably. 'And we'll certainly need water.'

The evening sky was darkening and the mountains to the east became warm and clear in the evening light. Mike remained by the window, writing notes. Bright mosaics of colour from the stained glass spread across the floor towards the walls. He was disconcerted by the animosity between Stanley and Jack and attempted to clear the atmosphere by changing the subject to the purpose of their visit. 'I suppose we'll be writing up a daily log when we get organised,' he said cheerfully. 'I've seen fifteen species today.'

'We start the log tonight,' Stanley said. 'Observations in the cities are no less significant than those in the countryside. I don't have to remind you that this country is ornithologically unexplored and every observation we make is of significance, however trifling it might appear to the unscientific mind. We are scientific pioneers, exploring entirely new ground, and I want every scrap of data we can gather.' He produced a large loose-leaf folder and laid it on the low table. 'I have a tentative species list here, compiled from the literature, such as it is. No doubt it is full of errors. Some of the nineteenth century stuff is very dubious and Colonel Meinertzhagen is not much better. Pompous old duffer must have pulled rank to get half of it published.'

There was an embarrassed silence as the other three deferred to Stanley's position as leader and allowed him to state his opinion without opposition. Both Jack and Eddie suspected that Mike came from a similar social background to the late Colonel, as his voice indicated a public school, although he had not mentioned it.

'Come on then,' Eddie said. 'Get on with it!'

Stanley began writing. 'Day one,' he said as he wrote. '*The Stanley Carter Ornithological Expedition to Yemen*'

Eddie winked at Jack and they grinned disrespectfully behind their leader's back. The light faded quickly as the sun dropped into the haze in the west. Eddie rose from his recumbent position on the floor and dropped the switch on the wall beside the door. The bulb, hanging from a fly-spattered flex in the centre of the ceiling, flickered indecisively and then settled down to emit a dull yellow glow.

'Even the bleedin' 'lectric has dust in it,' Eddie said.

Stanley adjusted his spectacles again, moving them around his nose until they settled in the original position. He ignored the chuckles of Mike and Jack and waited for Eddie's guffaws to fade away before continuing with the first entries in the daily log.

Chapter Three

Achmed Ali Ghanem lounged on the cushions bordering the walls of the mafrahj, the elegant living room at the top of the house. From the low windows he could see down into the street that, in his grandfather's time, had been one of the busiest thoroughfares in Sana'a. Now, it was too narrow for modern traffic, and a few bicycles and the leaking cart of the old water seller, with his ancient donkey and dying trade, were the only vehicles to penetrate its cool shade.

'Damned foreigners,' he said, 'why can't they leave us alone.'

His sister, Nadirah, crossed the carpeted room and came to the window. She placed a brass coffee jug on the low table beside her brother. He turned to her. 'Why not?' he demanded.

She filled two glasses with coffee and smiled at him. 'There will be many foreigners. Now that they have found the oil.'

'Aiwa!' he said. 'Yes. They will all be our friends now. Ha!'

She sat beside him and looked around the mafrahj. Being on the top storey, the room was above the noise and dust of the streets. The architecture was similar to that of the hotel where the Englishmen had been seen on the roof. The six low windows, rising with clear glass from the floor-line, and finished in an arched frame of stained glass at eye level, allowed the light to enter but prevented the high summer sun from bringing its heat into the house. They also allowed a rifle to be used effectively against anyone in the street below. The room was some seven metres long and four wide; a tall, well-proportioned room with the decorative plasterwork, the walls and ceiling all spotlessly white. There was little furniture, just a low table, and two large wooden chests, intricately carved, and no chairs. The cushions around the walls were covered in carpet. They were some two metres long and firm, while another row of smaller, softer cushions leaned against the walls. They were deep, dark red. At intervals, other cushions were arranged to divide the seating and provide armrests. The rugs on the floor had been brought in by the Turks in their grandfathers' time, and abandoned when they fled. Shod or sandaled feet had never trod their weave, for all footwear was discarded before entry to this room. It was an austere, cool room, yet restful and welcoming. An embroidered scroll of text from the Holy Koran, in elaborate calligraphy, hung from the end wall above the largest chest.

Nadirah was too happy to worry about a few foreigners on the hotel roof. Tomorrow they would be at Wadi Bana, and reunited with their father. 'You may speak in Arabic,' she said, 'I have not been away long enough to forget my own language.'

'I want to practise English. We will have to speak with these people.' He sipped his coffee, with the smoke from a cigarette curling around his fingers. 'Who speaks Czech in Yemen?'

Nadirah laughed. 'Not me. I wish to speak nothing but the language of the Holy Koran.'

'Why are they at such a hotel. Are they so poor? That fool of a clerk said they are tourists, come to see birds! Who can believe? Not me. They are spies! I shall see they are watched.'

'Oh, forget them. Tomorrow we see our father. Tomorrow we see our home.'

'Our home. And now our oil. Our riches. This will be the danger for us. All the foreigners will be here. They say we need them to protect us from our enemies. Who our enemies?' He spread his hands in interrogation. 'The Americans said the Ruskis our enemy. The Ruskis said the Americans are not to be trusted. In Prague I met students who hated the Russians. In England they are afraid of crazy Americans with too much of the big bomb.'

'Atomic.'

'Yes yes, I know atomic! Now they are all good friends. I tell you one thing, my sister. They better not come to damn-well Yemen. Yemen is for Yemeni. We make for the sure.'

Nadirah spoke to him in Arabic, 'Yah saqeeq. O, my brother let your mind sleep.'

'Yah saqeeqi,' O my sister.

They were using the most intimate term, for siblings of the same father and mother, for their father had taken but one wife and remained true to her even after her death during what should have been the birth of her third child. There had been few mourners at her grave, for she had been only a woman, but the whole village had been saddened at the death of one so young and healthy. Their father had looked down at the little dead thing in his arms and watched helplessly as the blood and life flowed from the only woman he could ever love. Then he had driven the midwife and women from her bedside in an uncharacteristic frenzy of rage, which had terrified them all with fear for his sanity. He returned to the room, and saw it through alone. 'I loved her,' he said, when it was all over, and never spoke of her again.

'Lah tinsah,' Achmed said. 'Do not forget, my sister, that we have been one of the poorest countries in the world. This oil is for the people. We will have no kings going whoring in London and Rome while women die having babies for want of a doctor, and the children who survive grow up in ignorance.'

'Be careful, Achmed,' his sister implored.

'You see! I must be afraid to speak in my own country. Have we spies in our own mafrahj? Bism Allah, In the name of God, we have spies in the hotel. That clerk, he said they have more cameras and binoculars than he has ever seen outside of Khalid's photo shop. I told him to spy on them also. Ha!'

'They are tourists. Yemen is so interesting to them.'

'Interesting! They will go back and tell their friends about the dirty Arabs who shit in the street and have four wives to wait on them. They will tell about the stinking rubbish in the back streets, and the flies and the sores in the children's hair.'

'And the Kalashnikovs and the daggers at the waist,' she said, laughing. 'But believe me there is stinking rubbish in the back streets of many English towns.'

28

'The khanjar at the waist is part of our national costume,' Achmed reminded her. 'Like the Englishman's umbrella.' He could not suppress a smile at the comparison.

'And the Kalashnikovs?'

He shrugged, and was silent for a while. Then he said 'But we drove the sons of camels out of Aden.'

'That was South Yemen.'

'There is only one Yemen,' he said vehemently in English. 'and I tell them in their own language, we will unite and be prosperous again after long.'

'Before long.'

'Aish hathah?' What is that?

'You do not say after long, it is before long.'

He gazed at her in doubt, saying, 'Before long, after long, before long. Crazy language.' He laughed, 'Crazy language for crazy people. Why did they fight us in Aden? Why? They are stupid. Majnoon. Crazy.'

'Oh Achmed, forget them. When are we going home?'

He replied absently, still wondering what four Englishmen were doing with so much spying equipment in his country. 'After tomorrow.'

She smiled to herself at this literal translation of the Arabic, 'Ba'ad bukrah' the day after tomorrow. In fact, his English was more fluent than his Czech, and he had found it difficult to study at the University of Prague. Her brother was a civil engineer, for he considered good roads and water supplies more important in the long term than oil wells and refineries. Nadirah suspected that his studies would have been easier if he had spent less time involved with politics, but declined to mention this in her letters from England. Discretion was taught them by their father, who said nothing, but by his example they had become aware that certain topics were never discussed before strangers, and rarely before friends. The old man had let wars and civil wars rage about him, kept his counsel and survived. There was death enough in the world, he reasoned, without risking his family through allegiances with passing regimes.

They were all Yemeni, he told his son. That was all that mattered. He would have died, gladly, in defending his country from outsiders but he was unsure where outsiders began. His wife's family in South Yemen had been deprived of their land and tenanted houses with the coming of the revolution, yet her brothers' sons, who sometimes walked through the mountains at night to visit him, said that life was better there afterwards, with cheap rents and food. Were his children's cousins then their enemies, and now their friends again? He did not know. The Saudis were outsiders, guraba, he had no doubt of that, for his nephew from Ta'izz had worked there and returned with enough money to buy a house and a car, and a bitter resentment at the way he had been treated by the arrogant sons of ignorant, lazy Bedouin. Yet his cousin in Sa'dah, in the north, told him that the Saudis were the same as Yemenis and historically the countries were one. The people on the Tihamah, on the shores of the Red Sea, were black men, sons of slaves, habashi who lived in houses of grass like kaffirs; were they foreigners? He supposed not, but the old Imams had been obliged to use force to subdue them. He kept quiet about these matters and quarrelled only with his neighbour, over water. He was ignorant, but he knew it. He was intelligent, and knew that too. He knew that he had been deprived of knowledge and he made one decision in his life, which overrode the fatalism of his own faith that abandoned all to the will of Allah. His children would not be ignorant! He would see to that. He had sent them to school in Kitab when other men put their children to work in the fields. And, when they were watching their sheep and goats, his own children took their books in their hands, and each night he asked to be informed of what they had learned, listening to them read from their text books as well as Holy Koran. They had gone to college in Sana'a and then, to his consternation, abroad; Achmed to Prague, wherever that was, and Nadirah to Britain. He ignored the criticism of his neighbours and cultivated more qat to pay for what the government did not. The whole business of scholarships and foreign travel was beyond him, so he left it to those who understood these things – his children. But a girl, to

Britain, his neighbours said, having no idea how difficult that had been. The man is mad.

'Why can't we go tomorrow?' Nadirah asked her brother. 'It has been a long time. Our father will be waiting.' Her voice was low and melodious, always restrained, unlike his, which tended to rise from its deep soft tones whenever he was excited.

'We will go home, after tomorrow. Tomorrow, I have business,' he said, 'In Sa'dah.'

Nadirah concealed the chill of fear that numbed her. Sa'dah, that town in the north, was the centre of firearms trading. In the market there one could buy, or sell, any weapon in the world if the cash was shown, and traders dealt openly in the streets with guns of every calibre and ammunition to match. From there it was but a short drive to Jebel Urf and the Saudi border, or east by camel into the unknown territory of the Bani Kitaf. It was a dangerous place. 'Sa'dah is a long way,' she said, 'how will you get there, do your business, and return in one day?'

'Maybe two days.'

Nadirah sighed. Her brother was younger than she but, as the oldest son, he demanded her obedience and acquiescence in things women did not understand. Yet she knew that he deferred to her opinion and admired her in so many ways. He was always too proud and stubborn to concede these feelings and she was too self-assured to assert herself. 'Will you go to the ministry about your appointment? They will want you to begin work immediately.'

'To begin what?' he gestured helplessly. 'There is so much to be done. Water, sewage, roads, houses. Where do I begin? Shall I go to the ministry and tell them what to do, all the cousins and sons of ministers who know nothing and have done nothing, for I, Achmed Ali Ghanem, have returned?' He had risen and was striding about the mafrahj. 'Shall I go to the hospital in Ta'izz and tell them the musryeen may go back to Cairo for my sister is now a great nurse who will cure all the ills of Yemen?'

She tried to calm him by taking his hand. 'Our father is old, and there is a harvest to gather. Shall we not go to him and forget politics

31

and strife? For a little while, until we settle our minds, for we have both been away too long. We are home now, Achmed. We have time. Have you forgotten the letters you wrote to me, reminding me of the clear waters of Wadi Bana and the call of the hudhud[1]* in spring? We shall go to our father in the clean air, away from this dust and noise. I am tired of cities, cars, and aeroplanes. Have you forgotten that you said you loved your home more than you could love a woman? That was in your first letter from Prague. Of course, I did not believe you.' She was relieved to see his eyes relax in a smile.

'I would not have gone to Prague if the British offered me the same help.' Here was the politics still. 'Thank God it was so.'

'Why?'

'Because now you know the West and I know the East,' he laughed. 'Neither can fool us. She made no comment and they sat silently, listening to the noises of the city, each absorbed in their own thoughts until there was a banging on the door below, voices, and the plod of sandaled feet on the stairs.

'Yah Achmed!' An approaching call rang out, 'Yah Achmed, where are you my friend?'

Nadirah draped her black shawl over her head and wound the fabric around her face, leaving only her black eyes uncovered. She knew that voice. She gathered the coffee, pots and glasses onto a brass tray as the man entered. He had kicked off his sandals and now he removed his head-cloth. It was dirty. His white skirt was dirty. His brown legs were dirty, coated in dust, and his shirt and jacket old and worn. At his waist he wore a heavy dagger with a curved blade and a rhinoceros-horn handle. The scabbard was encrusted with semiprecious stones. The belt, from which it hung, was of thick, embroidered tapestry. From his right hand hung a Kalashnikov rifle, held indifferently by the barrel. He leaned it against the wall.

Achmed greeted him enthusiastically, uttering the three welcomes, 'Ahlain. Ahlain. Ahlain,' as he took his hand and led him to the cushions at the head of the room.

'Salaam alaik,' the man said to Nadirah, formally, yet casually. She

1 * The Hoopoe

32

replied with a deferential nod of the head and a polite, 'Marhabbah,' before leaving the room. The two men looked at each other in silence, smiling happily.

'So, you are home.'

'I am home.'

'It is well timed. We are needed.'

They took each other's hands in a spontaneous gesture of friendship and laughed aloud together. Achmed called to the door, 'Nadirah! Bring coffee,' and to the man beside him, 'We have no servants here. Only the watchman.'

'He is trusted?'

'Have no fear. He was with my grandfather in the old days.' He offered cigarettes and they both lit them. They were silent again. It had been long time since they had met, in Prague. Nadirah brought in the coffee. Her brother looked at her, she at him.

He poured the thick liquid into the glasses. 'Have you forgotten Abdullah, Nadirah?'

'No. I have not forgotten Abdullah.' She looked directly at the man for the first time. The scar at the corner of his eye had healed well. He was very tall for a Yemeni, near fifty years old, but looking fit. There were streaks of grey in his beard, his face was lined and his eyes were as cold as ever. Even in laughter there was a chilling appraisal as he looked at her and said, 'And I have not forgotten you, sadiqa.'

Nadirah turned from him and sat on the cushions. She was not so sure that she was his friend, or that he was hers. There was an innuendo of irony in the way he had said it... sadiqa... as if he had not forgiven her for a past transgression. One that none but they were aware of. She had refused his offer of marriage.

'So,' she said, 'you have also returned. I thought you were in Moscow.'

'Be quiet, woman!' her brother snapped, for there was a sarcastic tone to her voice.

Abdullah laughed. 'Moscow was too cold. The winds among the unbelievers there have turned bitter.'

'Prague is also cold,' Achmed said.

'Yes. I went to warmer climates, where my language was understood, for I can speak only Arabic. Benghazi and Baghdad are warm cities, with friendly people.' He turned to Achmed. 'Very generous.'

Nadirah glanced sharply at her brother, to catch his reaction. There was his usual open smile, giving so much away. She feared for him at the hands of Abdullah and his devious eyes. She knew them both, so well. In another age she would have married Abdullah and loved him for his audacity and his bravery. Not now.

'I saw four foreigners,' Abdullah said, abruptly, 'on the roof of the Old Palace. I could not stop to speak to them, for the police were looking for me at the time.' He laughed. 'They said that my papers were not in order. Ha! Papers to enter my own country. To hell with them.'

'Abdullah,' Nadirah interjected. 'What do you want with us? You have always been in trouble. We have work to do. We have so much to do now, so much work for united Yemen.'

Abdullah looked at her with his eyes frowning in irritation. 'Work for Yemen! I was working for Yemen when you were but an infant and women knew their place, when the tanks from Egypt overran our country. And when we defeated them I was hunted down by Yemenis because I was too powerful, too dangerous for my own good, eh? Little more than a boy! Now I am wanted again by Yemenis and I must sneak into my own country like a thief in the night. You will work and I will work, for Yemen. Each in our own way. What is the matter with you?'

'So they know you are back?' Achmed asked.

Abdullah ignored the question for a while, still staring at Nadirah, but eventually he turned to Achmed and said, 'They know everything. The country is full of spies. They would shoot me. They would like to shoot me but I still have too many friends. They are being very careful.'

Nadirah didn't know who he was talking about. They, they, all the time. Some enemy or other. Poor Abdullah, one part of her thought, still living in the past, looking for old enemies, looking for a fight, a fight with anyone, for fights were action, yet she knew that his way was outdated, obsolete in the modern world, and could only hinder progress in the long run. Abdullah was an anachronism but her country was full of them. Ignorant, dangerous, courageous men.

'Did anyone see you come here?' she demanded.

'Who knows?' Abdullah shrugged. 'Perhaps the English spies on the roof.'

'Oh!' she said in exasperation as she turned to her brother. 'In the name of God, Achmed, send him away.'

The two men laughed as she flounced in anger from the room. 'Women!' Achmed said and, in a subdued voice, asked, 'You have arranged for us to see our friends in Sa'dah? We need the money from the transaction.'

'I have been to Sa'dah. The fair one was there. Our friends await the shipment and the money is waiting. Pay on delivery.'

'They do not trust us?' Achmed asked.

'In these times, my brother, nobody trusts anybody. It is very difficult and we are too important to be involved directly. So we need help. Help can be bought, but help can betray.' Abdullah looked across the roofs to the hotel. 'The British spies,' he said, as if suddenly distracted, 'will need a vehicle and a driver.'

Chapter Four

The four bird watchers were wakened at four thirty next morning by the prayer calls to the faithful, suddenly emanating from the loudspeakers lashed to the minarets throughout the city. *Bism Allah ar rahman ar raheem*. In the name of God the Compassionate, the Merciful, ... there is no God but God, and Muhammad is his prophet...

'I'd forgotten the prayer calls,' Jack said, looking down through the window, 'You get used to them after a while.'

'Doubt it!' Eddie said. 'I never did at home.' He slipped his shirt on over his muscular torso as Stanley emerged, clad in pyjamas, from his sleeping bag. Stanley was grumbling at the noise. 'These people always seem to put modern technology to the wrong use,' he said testily.

'No worse than the electronic bells in some of our churches,' Jack said.

Mike Jenkin lay on the other bed, with his arms behind his head. Today, he said to himself, will be a day of frustration. Today, I shall not take offence at anything Stanley might say. He leaned toward his pack and picked up his field guide with a sigh.

Two hours later they were in the hotel entrance after sampling an excellent breakfast of eggs and tomatoes, which the establishment provided. They sat in the small lobby, killing time. Stanley took out their map, champing at the delay. 'You'd think,' he complained, 'that the embassy would open at a reasonable hour.'

'Do we have to go to the embassy?' Eddie asked. 'They won't be a lot of use, in my opinion. We might as well not bother with them.'

'All we want is a few introductions,' Stanley said, 'just to know if there are any British firms working in remote areas. They've got bugger all else to do in a country like this.'

'I thought you could have found out about that before we left,' Eddie said. He wasn't really listening to Stanley but was looking through the window, watching the people in the street outside.

Stanley glared at his broad back. 'I did try,' he said. 'The only company that I knew for certain were here was Wireless and Telegraph, so I wrote to them, the great communications experts. They didn't reply.'

It was his first joke. They dutifully laughed.

The clerk, who emerged from a door behind the desk, saw Stanley looking at the map and came out to see it. 'You have map my country. Where you go?' He took the map from Stanley, who was obliged to relinquish it or risk tearing it in half. 'I show,' said the clerk. 'I show all best place for see tourists. Go Kawkaban? Very beautiful. Naquil Sumarah you go. Oooooh!' he closed his eyes in ecstasy. 'You see all place.'

'No,' Jack said. 'We go to Dhi Bin.'

'Dhi Bin?' He was horrified. 'Dhi Bin! Why you go Dhi Bin? Mush quais, Dhi Bin. No good, Dhi Bin.'

'We want to go down Wadi Attaf.'

'Wadi Attaf? Where Wadi Attaf? No Wadi Attaf.' He shoved the map back at Stanley contemptuously. 'No good, this map.'

'It's the only map there is, mate,' Eddie said, turning from the door with a laugh.

'We want to get to Wadi Jauf, actually,' Mike said.

'Wadi Jauf. Wadi Jauf?' The idea was preposterous. He laughed at them. 'You no go Wadi Jauf. Mush quais, Wadi Jauf.'

'Laish mush quais?' Why no good? Jack said. The clerk seemed not to notice that Jack spoke in Arabic but replied in the same language.

'What's he say?' Stanley demanded.

'He says that the people are bad in Wadi Jauf. They are thieves and heathen. There are no roads and no water. We will never get there.'

'Harrami. Harrami,' the clerk said. 'Mush quais.' He considered for a moment. 'You go Kawkaban, very beautiful.'

Stanley picked up his rucksack. 'Come on,' he said, 'we can't hang about here all day. We'll go to the embassy and then to the immigration authority to get our passports stamped.'

The clerk said, 'Many people, office. Leave all things here. Come back.' He began pulling a rucksack to the back of his desk. It was big Eddie's.

'Leave it alone,' Eddie said. The clerk shrugged and left it.

'We might as well leave the stuff here, actually,' Mike said, 'there's no point in lugging it around the city all day.'

'I have no intention,' Stanley grumbled, 'of taking all day over announcing our presence to the British Embassy and registering with the immigration office.' He lowered his voice and went on, 'When you have had a little more experience with Arabs you will realise that they are all a bunch of money-grubbers. This clerk,' he flicked his eyelashes in the direction of the reception, 'is merely intent on getting us to stay for another night, or else to make an exorbitant charge for the privilege of leaving our equipment in this so-called hotel.'

Mike turned to the clerk. 'How much?'

'What how much?'

'To leave our things.'

The clerk thought for a moment. 'You friend, no money.' He began dragging the rucksack again, but Eddie lifted it and dropped it behind the desk. The others followed suit. The clerk beamed at them.

'After one hour,' Stanley said, 'we come back.'

The clerk shrugged with a slight inclination of the head and a faint smile, a gesture which indicated that all was at the will of Allah and one that was to become very familiar to them over the ensuing weeks.

The British Embassy proved to be the dingy building with the Union Jack they had seen the day before. The garden was surrounded by a wall with jagged glass set in the concrete capping. It was a rather sad and dowdy building, built in the modern Yemeni style from cut stone, with iron grids protecting the windows. Yet there was an air of quiet dignity about it, with a mass of bougainvillaea straggling from the far corner of the garden wall, and the flag hanging limply from its pole.

At the gate a Yemeni guard examined the four suspiciously, surmised that they were British and indicated a small door to the right of the main entrance, pointing with his stick and saying nothing. Inside they found a large clerk, probably Egyptian, Jack thought, sitting at a desk in a corridor. They told him their business and he retired with their passports through a large door, indifferently, without a word. There was a long wait before he returned and led them to an office along the dim corridor.

A middle-aged, pink-faced man sat behind a large, paper-cluttered desk that almost filled the room. He glanced up from the confusion. 'Ji… ffy,' he sang as he wrote something on a form, and then he ignored them as he shuffled through several sheaves of paper, comparing one with another. He scribbled a few lines and then rose to greet them, extending his hand over the desk. His greeting was formal, without smiles.

'Courtenay,' he said. 'Now what can I do for you?'

He did not ask their names as he shook hands with them. They assumed he would have known them from their passports. After a rambling statement from Stanley, telling him the purpose of their visit; to study birds and look for the migration route of steppe eagles, that they had come to register their presence, as advised, and that they would appreciate any help he might offer in the way of introductions or the addresses of any expats working in remote areas, he returned to his chair and leaned back heavily on its arm.

'Now, look here,' he said, with an expression of tolerance, like a schoolmaster addressing a wayward class of adolescents. 'You chaps must realise that the expats in this country are here to do a jolly hard job of work under jolly difficult conditions. They have little time to spare in helping tourists who get into trouble. And we at the embassy are in the front line, in a manner of speaking, under fire, in diplomatic terms, as you might say. I hope you have sufficient funds. We can't be expected to fish you out, you know. Do what we can... advice and the like... but take my tip, stay on the beaten track, so to speak. Don't go wandering orf into the bush, as you might say. We had no end of problems with jolly D.B.S.s in India, don't-you-know. We don't want that kind of thing happening here.'

'D.B.S.s?' Eddie queried. 'What are they?'

'Distressed British Subjects. Frightful problem. Awful people going about the world letting the side down.'

Stanley was gathering his wits to protest and ask what was the point of spending a small fortune on an ornithological expedition if they were not to go into the bloody bushes but, by the time he had made a couple of indignant 'skuks' in his throat, Mike forestalled him with, 'We had rather hoped to meet Cecil Hayward, sir.'

Courtenay glanced at the form where his Egyptian clerk had copied the information on their passports. He appraised Mike anew, obviously resisting a temptation to ask how Mike might know of Cecil Hayward, the third secretary, and his junior in rank but social superior, to whom he would eventually be subordinate. Mike answered his unspoken question.

'Balliol connections, sir.'

'Ah! Ah yes. Splendid. Splendid.'

Courtenay was evidently astonished that any of these scruffy bird watchers should have connections at that institution, yet he now thought he heard the same connotations of long-standing authority in Mike's voice that he heard daily from Hayward.

'Now there I can help you,' he said, and drew a map on a scrap of paper. 'He's at home today. I'll give him a buzz while you are registering with immigration. You've seen the note in your visas? Yes? Register within five days? Good! Good fellows. Not quite as informal as the holiday brochures imply eh? Do it right away, take my tip. It's a frightful business.'

He rose from his chair and came to the front of the enormous desk, squeezing between its hard edge and a dusty filing cabinet, with his flaccid stomach and protruding backside straining at the confines of his shirt and crumpled trousers. 'Take most of the day, no doubt.'

'All day?' Stanley demanded.

'Afraid so. Ha ha. That's the way things are here. Sort of difficulty we cope with every day, take in our stride, as the saying goes. Immigration will be packed now with all the foreign teachers coming in for the autumn term. We're obliged to employ a 'fixer' for that sort of thing, pay a few small gratuities, shall we say. Saves a lot of our valuable time.' It was implied that their time was of no particular value and might as well be spent in the queues at the immigration office as anywhere else. 'Fixer away at the moment,' he said. 'Can't help you there. I'm afraid.'

He was dismissing them and came to the door, handing each a passport which they accepted in silence, aware that they were not their own. 'Well, good luck with your, ah, expedition. In the tradition of the great British explorers, what? Footsteps of Doughty and all that. Splendid show! Glad to offer all the help we can. Though you must realise,' he said, 'that should you have reason to visit me again, I shall not be free to devote as much time to you as I have today.'

'Oh yes, sir,' said Mike, 'we do appreciate that. Goodbye, sir.'

The others went out without a word. They had been in the office of Harry Courtenay, second secretary, consular section, of the British Embassy, Sana'a, for less than ten minutes. Balliol connections, Jack was thinking. What did that mean? I know almost nothing about the other members of this expedition. He had noted Stuart Carter's inclusion of the eagle migration as one of their objectives, but decided to let it pass.

Back at the hotel, they found the same Land Cruiser which had brought them from the airport. The driver greeted them enthusiastically, 'Sabah al kier.' Morning of health.

'Sabah al noor,' Jack replied. 'Morning of light.'

With an appreciative smile, the driver added, 'Muqbel Amin Qasm. Aayah kidmak.'

Jack shook hands with him. 'Muqbel Amin Qasm,' he said, repeating the driver's name. At our service.'

'Tell him to bugger off,' Stanley said.

'Go makatib wazarat?' Muqbel asked, ignoring Stanley. 'Go offices of the ministry. I take.'

After some argument, between Stanley and Eddie, they went with the driver to the offices, which were on the northern outskirts of the city. Scores of vehicles were parked in a walled compound and on the road outside. Hundreds of people were milling around and a queue, leading off to somewhere in the interior, reached the door.

'Good God!' Stanley said. 'It's bloody chaos.'

'Where do we begin?' Eddie said.

'We could ask,' Mike said, looking hopefully at Jack.

'I'll try,' Jack said. 'My Arabic is not very good, you know.'

'Looks like five or six different officials we have to see,' Stanley said. 'Probably don't trust it to one. Typical!'

'And the same rigmarole to get our exit visas stamped when we leave,' Jack said. 'We'll lose two days, at least, and on the way out too, by the look of it.'

The taxi driver had left them in the entrance hall of the building and returned after thirty-five minutes. 'Give passport!' he said, holding out his hand. 'Give hundred riyal.'

They handed them over.

Stanley reluctantly handed over the money. The Yemeni disappeared among the crowds.

After ten minutes waiting, Stanley said, 'That was a damn silly thing to do. We'll probably never see him again. I've never actually paid anyone to rob me before.'

Two hours later, after brief glimpses of the driver going from office to office, they were outside sitting in his vehicle. He gave them their passports and they passed them around until each had swapped another for his own. The entry visas were all duly stamped. 'I have friend,' said Muqbel Amin Qasm.

By the time they returned to the hotel, cleaned up and had a meal, it was early evening. They walked through the city to the house of Cecil Hayward, the third secretary at the embassy and friend of a friend of a friend of Mike Jenkin. It had, in the garden wall, like most of the others, a door fashioned of sheet-iron welded on to an angle-iron frame. It was painted in once bright, but now faded, colours in a geometric design of total incoherence. From somewhere beyond its security there came the hiss of running water. There was a button attached to a couple of wires which dangled through the masonry. Stanley Carter pressed it, at the risk of electrocution and little hope of response but, to their amazement, they heard the distant ringing of an unenthusiastic bell and the immediate cry from the garden of, 'Co…ming.'

Cecil Hayward was much younger than they had illogically expected, thirtyish perhaps, or even younger. He had a slightly tanned, boyish face and light brown hair, which gleamed in the sunshine. He was dressed in an immaculate pair of light fawn slacks and a sparkling white shirt, with a red and white cotton scarf knotted loosely at his throat. He held the nozzle of a hosepipe, carefully directing the reluctant dribble of water from splashing his polished leather sandals.

'Oh. Do come in,' he said, as if delightfully surprised at their arrival. His accent was unmistakably public school; even with the utterance of this one short invitation he had revealed his plutocratic background of position and influence. He did not offer to shake hands. The bird watchers may have considered this a slight, especially Carter, but no slight was intended. Indeed, such was his command of social delicacies, the lack of handshake intimated at his expectations of a more personal relationship than the purely formal demanded by his office.

As they entered the garden he closed, and locked, the door behind them. He turned off the water supplying his hose.

'I'm Stanley Carter,' Stanley said, holding out his hand. 'The ornithologist.'

Hayward shook the hand politely. Stanley introduced the others, 'Mike Jenkin, Eddie Johns and Jack Pengelly.'

'Pengelly,' Hayward observed. 'A Janner, no less. More of a Cousin-Jack now, presumably.'

'That's right.' Jack noted the correct pronunciation of his name, and was a little intrigued to know how Cecil Hayward should know the nickname of Cornishmen abroad, but presumed, rightly, that he had encountered many such in his travels. Hayward led them into the house up a flight of marble stairs to a large, sparsely furnished room on the first floor. He indicated that they should make themselves comfortable in the several armchairs and disappeared into the kitchen to make them tea, which he wheeled in on a trolley laden with fine china and cakes. He served them graciously, enquiring as to the exact amount of sugar and milk.

'Powdered, of course,' he said, 'but the tea is the best Indian.' He had an effeminate way of pursing his lips and a delicate movement of the hands with cups and plates.

'Well, Mr Hayward...' Stanley began.

Hayward interrupted him. 'You might call me Cecil, I think.' He smiled with a quick raising of the eyebrows. 'Considered to be rather a cissy name these days perhaps. But there has been a Cecil in the family for generations, so that's what it had to be. Only son, you see.' He shrugged, with a slight toss of his wavy hair. 'I don't mind, really,' he said, 'what you might call me as long as it's not Cess.' He sat in a chair, thoughtfully holding his cup and saucer.

'We're hoping to go to the north,' Stanley said. 'Do you think we'll have any problems?'

'Oh yes. Lots!' He turned to Jack. 'At prep-school they called me Shit Pit, you know.'

Jack spluttered and coughed over his teacup.

'Yes,' Cecil mused. 'Went from Ces you see. That's why I don't like it. From Cecil to Ces. From Ces to Cesspit, and then eventually to Shit Pit.' He glanced over their cups. 'More tea?'

They helped themselves, avoiding eye contact.

'I was known as 'Pity' for years. In fact I believe I still am, behind my back. Very cruel... Boys!'

He thought about it for a while, with his head cocked to one side. 'Girls are worse, mind you.'

He turned, at last, to Stanley. 'Yes, you'll have problems going north. Very tribal still, despite the new road to Marib and the discovery of oil. No one will admit it but, off the main road, the tribes still control the countryside in remote areas. Some people from the agricultural project went to see the ruins at Marib. Took

44

two nurses from the aid programme. They had a Yemeni Toyota with a Yemeni driver they'd hired. What an experience! Tribesmen held them up and stole everything they had. Thought they were going to rape the women at one point, and the men too shouldn't be surprised. And what could they have done about it, my dear? What could anyone do about it with a Kalashnikov in the ribs?' He took a sip of his tea. 'They were going to take the Land Cruiser too, but the driver convinced them it was his own, and that his livelihood depended on it, so they let them keep it. Very considerate, I'm sure. Took everything else of course, money, cameras, clothes... Any problems, you ask!'

'Did they inform the police?'

'Shouldn't have thought so. Wouldn't have achieved anything. The police are not likely to venture off the roads out there. Could tell the army. They might risk a quick visit to shoot a few of them. But that would only stir up more trouble for the government. 'Spect the tribesmen only saw it as a form of toll. Have to realise that these people have been exacting tolls from travellers for thousands of years. The whole economy of the country depended on it at one time.'

He chose a cake from a plate with great deliberation. 'Please help yourselves. They won't keep.'

They heard the distant ringing of the bell at his gate.

'That'll be Alison,' Cecil said. 'I'll let her in. My watchman's on holiday. Always is.'

They were silent in his absence, deliberating on the wisdom of venturing into the unknown, seeking the unseen. He returned with a tall, fair girl in her early twenties, well built, with broad, athletic shoulders. She wore a long cotton dress with sleeves to the wrist. He introduced them, remembering first names, Jack noted, despite the perfunctory manner of their own introduction. Cecil went to make fresh tea for Alison, who sat beside Stanley Carter and listened to his explanation of what they were doing in the country. Stanley made it clear that he was the leader of the expedition. 'I intend to go north... I shall explore the possibilities...'

Jack, ever conscious of his own accent, listened to the girl and tried to categorise her background. English girls' high school, modern, regionless. Somewhere in the south of England. She would be of the kind who described themselves as 'cosmopolitan'. A perfect match for Cecil Hayward, he thought, if he was interested.

Eddie passed her a plate of cakes, using the gesture as an excuse to look directly into her pale green eyes and divert her attention from Stanley.

Mike was asking her what she was doing in Yemen, and had been told that she was visiting her parents, when Cecil returned and the discussion reverted to the difficulties of travelling in remote areas of the country.

'What about going south?' Jack asked, with his mind on the eagles making for the short sea crossing at the Bab al Mandab.

'South's not so bad, as long as you keep well away from the border with South Yemen. Up north, and to the east, no one knows where the country begins and ends. Loyalties tend to change according to who can pay the most, don't y' know.'

He glanced briefly at Alison, almost as if he had said something untoward. She was interested in the cakes.

'In the past, the trouble in the south has been from the south,' Cecil went on. 'The Peoples Democratic Republic of Yemen, or South Yemen as it's known. There was a bloody skirmish this spring. Some in the north wished to take over the south, especially when more oil was discovered, and both see the strategic value of the port of Aden. One lot backed by Russia, the other by Saudi Arabia and the USA. The place is like a tinder box. There is some talk of unity, but that's a long way off .' He fussed over the girl's tea. 'Just as you like it, Alison.'

'If the two halves do come together,' Jack asked, a hint of irony in his voice, 'with the oil and the strategic port of Aden, they would be a force to be reckoned reckon with, surely?'

'Quite,' Hayward said. Jack noticed that he avoided elaborating on the consequences.

'Then,' Hayward continued, 'there are the old royalists who backed the Imam Yahya and still own considerable amounts of land and wealth. They fear the modernists who want more Western liberalism, and most of all they fear the communists. On top of all this, or underlying it, if you like, there are ancient tribal loyalties and squabbles, not to mention disputes between neighbouring villages over water rights and wells. And we don't mention the tension between Sunnis and Shias.' He shrugged his shoulders and smiled. 'A right old hotch potch. Have to tread very carefully here.'

Stanley was not interested in the politics of the country, 'What about British companies working here,' he said, 'anyone out in the remote areas?'

Hayward leaned back to reach toward a low table. There was a brief hesitation, as if of doubt, before he handed Stanley two sheets of embassy notepaper. 'Letter for you,' he said. 'In English and Arabic, explaining what you are doing here, just in case. The other is a list of names and addresses which might be useful to you. Actually, I suggest you first go north, to Wadi Attaf, just east of Raydah. The Department of Overseas Survey has a team of surveyors out there working under Fred Stirling.'

Stanley shuffled the sheets, showing a reluctant smile as Eddie said, 'That's exactly where we want to go. Great!'

'The surveyors are camped at the head of the wadi marked 'Ataf' on the map. No use asking the Yemenis how to get there. They've never heard of some of the names on the maps. Now, going south should be easier. I suggest you call on the chaps at the British agricultural project in Ta'izz. Apart from anything else they may be able to put you up for a day or two. They also have a house at Hudaydah, on the coast. They all know you're here, of course.'

Jack was noting Cecil Hayward's precise pronunciation of the Arabic place-names, and guessed that he was fluent in the language.

'How can they all know about us already?' Eddie asked. 'We've only been here a day.'

'Everyone knows what's going on here, never fear. Nearly all the expats have short-wave radios and keep in touch at specified times, to keep up with the news and spread the latest gossip. There are no telephones in remote areas you know, even in town they are unreliable. The radios are illegal, of course, but everything is illegal if the president says so. Small things I mean.'

Stanley could not hide his delight. 'There seems to be somebody British in all the big towns,' he said.

'Hardly big, some of them.' He turned to Mike, who had said little, and addressed him, personally. 'Now, I'm going off for a while, so, if you care to use this house as a base in Sana'a, you may do so, with pleasure.'

'We don't intend to spend much time in the city,' Stanley said, implying that it was he who would decide whether or not they stayed here, 'but we appreciate your offer.'

Hayward continued speaking to Mike. 'I'll give you a key and tell Hamid, my watchman, you'll be staying.'

Mike thanked him and said they would come on their return from the north. Stanley said they might be grateful to call in, just for a clean up, after spending some time in the mountains.

'I'm sure you will,' Hayward said with an air of certainty that irked Stanley as implying that they did not really know what they were letting themselves in for.

Alison, who had been listening without comment, suddenly interjected.

'May I come with you?'

They looked at her in astonishment and doubt, all thinking that they would have problems enough without a woman trailing along. Cecil came to their rescue, however, and suggested that perhaps she might prefer to wait and go south with them and visit the coral reefs of the Red Sea after they were more used to the country.

'All right then,' she said.

Outside, the dusk was enveloping the city. Calls for evening prayers drew the faithful to the mosques, and the smell of cooking wafted from the roadside cafes preparing the meals of workers leaving the building sites. The room was growing dark but Cecil made no move to put the light on. He cleared away the teacups, refusing help from Alison. Conversation lapsed. Eventually Cecil returned from his kitchen with another tray of confectionery. He produced a bottle and glasses from the sideboard. 'Now,' he said, 'to celebrate the beginning of your expedition, a teeny drop of whisky.'

'Thought it was illegal,' Mike said with a laugh.

'It is. But *everybody* drinks it.' He passed the tray around. 'And you must try some of these. I made them myself.'

'What are they?' Eddie said, always interested in food. 'Scones?'

Cecil gave each of them one of his delicacies. When it came to Eddie's turn he nudged his muscular arm and said, 'Hashish patties. Oops.'

They stayed talking about the country and the objectives of the expedition until late at night. Alison asked about their itinerary and when they expected to visit the coast, explaining that she had seen little of the country, unlike Cecil who appeared to be familiar with all but the remotest areas. He was, as Jack had surmised, fluent in Arabic, and something of a bird watcher himself. He suggested they visit certain areas near the city where there were groves of walnut trees and he had seen amethyst starlings. He had seen eagles, he said, but could not identify them. Their enthusiasm for the venture was revived, especially as they now had a base and contacts in the country. Stanley, despite his prejudice and inverted snobbery, found himself mellowing towards Cecil Hayward as he drank his whisky and, as they were leaving and Cecil and Alison came out into the warm, moonlit garden to let them out, he thanked him for his help.

'Very kind of you, old man,' he said with a tipsy wobble of his dark head. 'Can't say the same for your colleague at the embassy though. Harry Courtenay! The pompous bloody git.'

'He's my father!' Alison said.

Eddie couldn't stop laughing until they reached the hotel.

Chapter Five

When they emerged into the bright sunshine next morning, the Toyota Land Cruiser was parked outside the hotel and the driver was leaning against the door.

Stanley sighed. 'Looks like we're stuck with him.'

They piled their gear in the back of the vehicle. The driver stood aside and allowed them to stow it as they wished but, when all was ready, he said 'Moya, yani? Water? No water?'

'Of course we have water,' Stanley said. 'In the containers.'

These were collapsed plastic wine boxes, which he had insisted on bringing as being the most efficient method of transporting water, saying that when not in use they folded flat and were easy and light to carry.

'Water, lazim,' the driver said, combining the two languages as he climbed into the drivers seat, lifting his skirt as he did so, a subconscious movement, like a man hitching his trousers before sitting in a chair. He waved a cheery, 'Masallamah,' to the hotel clerk who watched them go with a suspicious frown.

'How much petrol?' Stanley asked. He was in the front passenger seat, and leaned over to look at the dials.

'K'teer. Benzine k'teer.'

'What's he saying?'

'Too much,' the driver said with a smile. 'Petrol too much.'

He jerked his head in a quick, expressive movement with the eyes momentarily closed, followed by a fleeting smile, almost regretful in its brevity. It was an Arab gesture of apology for his efficiency.

'Me, Muqbel,' he said, in case they had forgotten his name, which they had. They went out through the new sector of the city, past

50

the embassies and ministry buildings. They saw the Russian flag and the Chinese while, over the buildings inside a walled compound, an immaculate Stars and Stripes billowed in slow, confident motion.

'Everybody's here,' Mike said.

Muqbel drew in beside a shop displaying an array of bright plastic artefacts hanging from the walls. He chose three heavy-duty jerry cans with screwed tops.

'We take,' he said. 'Water.'

Stanley reluctantly paid for them and, after a further stop to buy food, they at last made for the open road. They were following a Datsun pick-up full of women and children as they reached the first low hills half an hour from the city. Stanley, who had again taken the front seat, opened his pack and took out a map which he spread across his knees. Muqbel glanced at it and spoke in Arabic to Jack.

'Woss he say?' Eddie asked.

'Put the map away.'

Muqbel looked again at the map and fluttered his fingers over it, muttering to himself.

'How,' Stanley asked in an even voice, 'can we identify the landmarks and localities for the daily log if we don't know where we are? Just keep your eyes open for any birds and leave the navigation to me.'

'Hardly necessary at the moment, actually,' Mike said, 'while we're on the main road.'

Muqbel slowed down and pulled in to the thin scrub at the verge. He turned to Jack, in the back, and then to Stanley. 'Askari,' he said.

'Soldiers,' Jack translated. 'On road, one kilometre.'

Muqbel flicked Stanley's map with his finger, 'This paper! No good, this paper.'

'It must be a road-block,' Eddie said.

'Well, why didn't he say so?' Stanley said irritably.

'Why not do as he says,' Jack grumbled, 'and put the map away? He knows the country better than we ever will.'

Stanley twisted around to look the others in the face. 'We'd better get something straight right now,' he said. 'I'm responsible for this expedition, and I'm the one who makes the decisions. We are not taking orders from some bloody taxi driver.' He stared at each of them in turn, and there was a prolonged silence. He had spoken too rapidly for Muqbel to follow or understand anything but he obviously realised they were discussing him and he looked at Stanley blankly.

Eddie looked at the mountains in the distance and said, 'Oh, for Gawd's sake!'

Mike said, 'We don't want any trouble, Stanley.' And they could see the temper rising in Stanley's face.

Eventually Jack said, 'Well, get on with it!'

'Get on with what?' Stanley demanded.

'Make your decision. Are you going to hide the map, or will you ride up to the road-block with the bloody thing on your lap like General Montgomery at El Alamien and get us all arrested as spies?'

Stanley looked at him with something akin to hatred in his eyes but he said nothing. Muqbel looked straight ahead at the dust following the Datsun. Stanley turned back to sit squarely in his seat. He folded the map and put it in his pack. He jerked his head towards the road and Muqbel pulled out, accelerating to catch up with the Datsun. 'If they search us, they'll find a dozen maps,' Stanley muttered.

'They won't search us,' Eddie said. 'We're foreign tourists.'

As they rounded the next bend, between two high embankments where the highway had been cut through a low hill, they saw the roadblock ahead. There was a small corrugated iron hut and a long pole across the road. The pole was counterbalanced by an old oil-drum, full of rocks. At the verge was a large cut-out silhouette of a soldier with its hand held high in the signal for 'Halt'. It was made of plywood and painted like a giant pop-up picture from a children's book and it swayed slightly in the breeze, rocking its flimsy stand.

'Do you think he's in charge?' Eddie asked, but the poker-faced soldiers dissuaded them from any inclination to laugh. They were armed with automatic rifles, clean and gleaming, which contrasted incongruously, ominously, with their shabby uniforms. Some wore boots and others open-toed sandals or plastic flip-flops. One seemed no older than fourteen or fifteen and he carried an automatic rifle carelessly slung over his shoulder as he sauntered from the hut. His uniform was too big and hung like a sack from his slender frame.

They had stopped the pick-up and ordered everyone out. They were searching the cab and opening crates in the back. The family were lined up at the roadside and were silent as they watched the search, equally poker-faced as the soldiers.

'What are they looking for?' Stanley said. No one replied as the Yemenis were ordered back into their vehicle. A little girl sucked her thumb as they drove off. As Muqbel drove very slowly to the barrier they saw the barrel of an armour-piercing gun protruding from the turret of a tank, partly hidden by a camouflage net, on the hillside to the left.

'All window open,' Muqbel said.

They opened them and felt an irrational sense of fear, with their stomach muscles tightening, as the soldiers turned their attention to this wagonload of foreigners. One, who had three stripes of a sergeant crudely stitched to his shirt sleeves, put his head through Muqbel's window and looked carefully around the rucksacks, boxes of food and jerry cans of water. He spoke to Muqbel without looking at him. Muqbel handed him a document printed on poor quality paper, yellowing and stained with sweat. The sergeant gave it a cursory glance. 'Passports!' he said. The four took them from their pockets and handed them over. He shuffled them through his fingers. Compared the photographs with the faces.

'Ingaleze!' he said.

They agreed with him: 'Yes, British,' Jack said.

The sergeant turned the pages, speaking to Muqbel in subdued tones. Jack could not catch what they were saying but heard the word 'ingijh' that they had heard at the airport and 'tourists' and 'Amran' the name of the next town on the road.

The sergeant handed the passports back, one at a time, to the wrong owners, and they said nothing as they put them away in their pockets. He stepped back and waved them on. The young soldier banged the side of the vehicle with his fist, another one smiled as they passed and spat out a stream of green juice from his cheek-full of qat.

As they drove on, Muqbel shrugged his shoulders in acceptance of circumstances he was powerless to alter. They wound up the windows to keep out the hot wind as they sped along the road, each engrossed in his own thoughts. Mike took the passport from his pocket and the rest followed suit, returning them to their rightful owners, a routine they were getting used to. A sense of relief gradually overcame them as they watched the vast, barren landscape falling behind them and they scanned the hillsides for birds. They began singing… 'I was boor-orn under a wa-ndring star…'

'This is the life,' Stanley said.

They drove northwest for forty kilometres and passed through the old town of Amran, which had been the provincial capital. The original walled city was over to the left, standing like a stone citadel at the junction of the road to the west, down the escarpment to the depths of Wadi Mawr and the Red Sea. Black cones of lava, long cooled and dead, rose incongruously from the bright glare of the limestone plain. Fields of crops bordered the road and the horizon was forever mountains, blue in the distant haze.

Twenty kilometres or so past Amran they reached the straggling town of Raydah and Muqbel pulled over to the dusty heaps of rubble bordering the tarmac. 'Five minute,' he said, and left them.

They were parked at the end of the street, just past the last building. Swallows swooped over a shallow pool, picking insects from the ripples around a wading ruff. Yellow wagtails strutted about the perimeter, snatching flies from the mud.

'They've had rain,' Stanley said.

'I could do with stretching my legs,' Eddie said.

They got out and walked back through the rubble of the main street, looking at the souks, oily garages and workshops. Most of the people ignored them. Some of the traders smiled and a group of older, white-bearded men eyed them suspiciously while a group of boys jeered, 'Nazranee. Nazranee.' Which, Jack said, was like calling a Muslim, 'Mohammedan' or 'Mecca-ite'. They went back to the vehicle.

'Where's that driver?' Stanley muttered under his breath. 'I don't want to stay here for long. The sooner we get away from people, the better I'll like it.'

'Me too, actually,' Mike concurred, happy to find himself in agreement with Stanley.

Over to the east, where they were about to venture, they could see vast areas of black landscape where ancient volcanoes had spilled their violence over the land. The wide plain and the mountains beyond were piebald, lava and limestone, barren, without vegetation; the prospect appeared threatening and inhospitable. Way over among the hills they could see a couple of dust clouds following vehicles along tracks that led to nowhere.

'Looks wild enough out there,' Eddie said, 'even for you, Stanley.'

'Probably not that wild,' Mike said. 'I think I can see villages along the hills and ridges.' He glanced along the road and took his binoculars from their case. 'Well, what do you think of that? Black villages on the black hills and white villages on the white ones. They're all made of stone from the immediate area.'

'Let's have a shufti.' Mike handed his binoculars to Eddie.

'Yeah. Nice touch, the way they've used the opposite colour stone in some of the quoins and lintels.' He returned the glasses. 'Wonder how old they are.'

They tried to ignore the local boys, who were clamouring for a look through the binoculars, crying, 'Shoof, ashoof.'

'If your mate takes much longer,' Stanley said, looking at Jack, 'it will be too damned dark to find the survey party.'

Jack declined to comment but he noted that Stanley was not so keen to camp out in this area unprotected and alone. He wondered just how much roughing it Stanley had done in the past. Not much, probably. 'See that building there,' he said, indicating a long, low, stone-built shed on top of an incline alongside the road, 'that's the public convenience, if you want it.'

The stone building was cleverly cantilevered, so that at its rear the floor was over-hanging, some six feet above ground level. A series of holes in the floor were lined up over a corresponding series of heaps of excrement, which had grown so high as to become a mass as tall as a man, with little pinnacles thrusting towards the holes above.

They looked at it in silence. 'No, thanks all the same,' Mike said. 'I can wait. Very interesting, actually. I've read about these things. They used to have slaves to clear them in the old days. It was burned as fuel to fire the public baths. In this climate it dries very quickly. The houses used the same system, a projecting chamber in an upper storey with a hole in the middle. It was called the long-drop system. Actually, it's exactly the same as that used in medieval European castles. You can imagine what it was like in a warm, wet summer in England.'

They imagined.

'They all seem to have enough money for guns,' Jack said. 'Look at this one.'

They all turned, and caught the dark eyes of the man approaching them. He was dressed in an old army pullover and a white Yemeni skirt, the futtah, from below the hem of which appeared his bare brown legs. They were strong, muscular legs, with good skin, though coated in the inevitable film of dust. On his feet were leather sandals. He wore the Yemeni head-cloth, with a corner trailing down over his neck and shoulder. The khaki pullover was held about the waist by an embroidered belt with a dagger. His shoulders were criss-crossed by a double band of ammunition for the automatic rifle he carried over one shoulder. A magazine was ready in the clip. He was a man of about fifty years, with a lined but handsome face, and deep-set eyes. His beard was trimmed to a point, in the Arab fashion, but now the shaven cheeks and neck were darkened by a growth of stubble.

His stride was long, firm, with a swinging ease, and his shoulders were held high, despite the weight of metal hung about them. The local boys stood in silence as he passed, though he ignored them. Men in the street looked furtively over their shoulders and turned to their business. The British bird watchers were disconcerted by the cold stare from his expressionless eyes and turned away in embarrassment as he studied them intently while passing. They watched him retreating along the road leading from the town. There was a nervous giggle from the boys, who suddenly turned and fled. The man turned from the road and strode off to the east, towards a gap in the mountains, far in the distance, where Wadi Attaf led on down to the great Wadi Jauf, Saudi Arabia and the Empty Quarter.

'That's an AK47 he's carrying,' Mike said, 'a Kalashnikov.'

'Wouldn't know a Kalashnikov from a Rachmaninov, myself,' Eddie said, 'but I wouldn't fancy meeting him on a dark night, even if he was only carrying a bottle of Smirnoff.'

'Especially then, perhaps,' Jack said, 'did you see his eye.'

'Didn't feel like looking at him long enough to see anything,' Eddie said as he watched the retreating figure striding confidently into the distance. 'What about his eyes?'

'Just the left one. There was a small scar beside his left eye. On the temple really. As if he's been in a fight.'

Stanley said, 'You're letting your imagination run wild. Typical Celt, if I may say so. No doubt we'll see plenty of wild-looking tribesmen carrying guns in this country. It's all part of the experience.'

They didn't answer. The retreating figure diminished in the distance as it headed for the gap in the mountains. A passing black kite was joined by a couple of brown-necked ravens and together they settled on a pile of rubbish at the roadside.

In Europe there would almost certainly be a movement of birds through that gap in the mountains but here there were so many mountains, so many gaps, so many jebels and wadis, that it might take years of searching before the right gap, on the route of migration, was found. They could wander round these vast empty mountains for weeks and miss the migration route of the eagles, if it existed, by a few miles or a few days. They could disappear out there, be robbed, or murdered, and no one would ever know what had happened to them.

'If we can't find the eagles,' Eddie said, 'I think we ought to go down south and investigate the coast and Tihamah,'

Stanley turned back to them and said, 'The purpose of this expedition is to study the ornithology of the whole country. We are not returning to say we gave up after seeing one man walk past us with a gun three days after we arrived.'

Jack acepted that Stanley was no longer denying the possibility of an eagle migration. He gazed at the distance in silence.

'I just want to make sure we do return,' Eddie said. 'That's all, mate.'

'If that bloody driver doesn't return soon,' Stanley grumbled, 'we won't go anywhere, much less get back.'

But Muqbel was already approaching the Toyota, with several flat discs of unleavened bread, 'naan', in his hand. He climbed into the driver's seat with a happy smile and drove on. He soon turned off the road and they drove into the black landscape. Ahead, they could see a massive cliff of limestone with a black spew of solidified lava pouring down and spreading over the plain like a petrified river of gloom. It was a barren, threatening prospect. As they drove into it they passed a small village built of pale limestone, perched among the cliffs, and they could see the silhouettes of other villages straddling the tops of cones and ridges to their right. They were black, like their surroundings, forbidding and hostile in their appearance, apparently deserted, for there was no sign of life about their walls. Muqbel pointed over to the centre of the plain. 'Asdiqa'ak.'

'Fain?' asked Jack

Muqbel stopped the vehicle at the top of a small rise and pointed again. 'Hunaak,' he said.

'Wha's he say?' Eddie asked.

'Our friends are out there.'

'I can't see anything,' Mike stated doubtfully. 'Looks barren and empty to me.' He looked through his binoculars, panning the distant scene. 'Ah! There they are. Right in the middle of the lava!'

The cluster of dark green tents, two Landrovers and a water bowser were like a natural irregularity in the topography, unintentionally camouflaged but glaringly obvious when once discerned. There was no concealing the relief that any of them felt as they drove across and parked among the tents. Muqbel exchanged greetings with several Yemeni porters and the flap of a tent was withdrawn to allow the emergence of a tall, slightly stooping Englishman. He was dark skinned, from the sun, and dark haired, though balding. Tanned legs, thin and sinuous, emerged from a pair of baggy khaki shorts. His shirt hung loose and unbuttoned from his lean shoulders. His brow was wrinkled from a perpetual frown. 'Hullo,' he said casually, as if to old friends he was perplexed at meeting here of all places.

'You're Fred Stirling,' Stanley told him.

'Yes.' His voice was gruff, very deep and throaty. He shook hands with them all as they introduced themselves, with a curt nod of the head to each. 'Get yourselves settled in,' he said, 'I'm due to call up Sana'a in five minutes. I'll tell them you're here'

They erected their one-man tents or, in Muqbel's case, prepared a bed in the back of the Land Cruiser, and cooked their first meal in the open. It was all from tins. A soggy stew which, with the bread Muqbel had bought in Raydah, tasted delicious and induced a mood of contentment, comradeship and optimism. As dusk fell the prayer calls from the mosques in the villages reached them and Muqbel lined up with the porters and faced the Holy City to participate in prayer. In the name of God, the Compassionate, the Merciful... Soon after, the Yemenis were all in their beds.

Fred Stirling came over and asked the bird watchers to his tent where there was another Englishman, who proved to be Irish as soon as he opened his mouth and introduced himself. Patrick Donovan, a huge, broad-shouldered man with massive arms and thick thighs which strained the seams of his shirtsleeves and shorts. Fred was filling a huge teapot, which he then covered in a bright hand-knitted tea cosy and placed on a box, surrounded by mugs, a tin of evaporated milk, sugar and a bottle of whisky.

'Pat's morale booster,' Fred said, prosaically. 'He's had a bit of bother today.' He carefully poured the tea, tipped a tot of whisky into each and passed the mugs around. 'Tribesmen stopped him going down the wadi. Threatened to shoot the whole party if they didn't clear off. We never argue with locals, especially when they're armed with guns.'

'Tis impossible to work in this country,' Pat said. 'My driver said the tribesman told him we had to get permission from the Sheikh. Yet how can we meet the Sheikh if they won't let us in.'

'They're very suspicious of foreigners.' Fred said, 'and they don't believe the government, no matter what they say. We try to explain that we are making maps so that they can have better roads for taking crops to market. They say they grow only enough for themselves and that the roads will allow the government to come in and tax them.' He shrugged his scrawny shoulders. 'We only want to get on with the job we're paid for. Their squabbles are nothing to do with us. I'll go and speak to the Mudeer, that's the governor of the province, tomorrow and sort it out, if I can find him. We'll still have to get permission from the local Sheikh. Another day wasted.'

'Where do you boys want to go?' Pat asked.

'That's the problem,' Mike said. We don't know. We're exploring the country, checking resident birds and looking for migration routes.'

'They'll never believe that. They'll probably suspect you of spying. Half of them believe the maps we produce are for our own military.'

'Well, aren't they?' Stanley asked.

Jack thought that was a tactless remark for Stanley to make, and he saw the furrows deepen on Fred Stirling's brow.

'If they want to make roads, open up the country and increase trade, then they must have maps,' Pat said, with one eye on Fred.

'Maps are for everyone,' Fred said, 'including bird watchers.'

'I thought,' Stanley said, apparently oblivious of his gaffe, 'that maps were made from aerial photographs these days.'

'That's what everybody thinks who's never been involved with it. But in fact aerial photography is still too inaccurate and needs triangulation on the ground.'

'Are you using radio telemetry?' Mike asked. His three companions turned to him in astonishment, not knowing what he was talking about.

'Yes,' Fred said, his thoughts elsewhere. 'We'll probably have to arrange a raffeeq. That's a sort of guide and guarantee of safe conduct – with the Mudeer, the Governor. We only want to go about thirty kilometres down Wadi Attaf and up Jebel Yanur. It's not the end of the earth.'

'Might just as well be,' Pat said, as he poured more whisky.

'Is there any oil down there?' Stanley asked. 'Seems more than coincidence that they found it at the end of the new road to Marib.'

'I don't know anything about oil,' Fred said. He drained his tea and poured neat whisky into his mug. 'And I don't usually drink when I'm in the bush.'

Jack found himself falling asleep on his feet. 'I thought whisky was prohibited in this country.'

'So it is,' Pat told him. 'The best things are prohibited in every bloody country.'

They had just wriggled into their sleeping bags when the firing began. Short bursts, from machine guns of some sort, and irregular single shots from rifles shattered the quiet of the night. They stuck their heads from their tents and listened. The firing lasted for some five minutes and then stopped, as abruptly as it had begun.

'What the hell was that all about?' Eddie said. They heard Muqbel speaking to the porters.

'What was that, Muqbel?' Jack called.

They heard the creaking of Fred Stirling's camp bed as he turned over. The light went out in Pat's tent.

'Maybe wedding!' Muqbel said.

Jack withdrew his head and began laughing quietly, uncontrollably to himself. Oh, how wonderful to be here, he thought, simply to be here. In Yemen, the land of Sheba. He felt as if he had returned to the very foundations of his own culture and identity. He had returned to an age when countries and their people had character and individuality, as had his own before the progress towards that total uniformity which was called the Western World. He was glad he had come on this trip, Stanley Carter notwithstanding. He must not, would not, allow the little twit to ruin the thrill and excitement of being here, looking for eagles.

Chapter Six

To their surprise, they all woke feeling remarkably fresh and rested. They credited it to sleeping in the clear mountain air. The first thought that occurred to Jack was that they had not filled in the daily log last night.

Fred Stirling left early to go in search of the Mudeer at Amran. Pat said he was taking a Landrover down the wadi to survey the low hill-range they could see, in the hope of finding a way into the territory of the Sheikh. He offered to take two of them with him and they decided that Mike and Jack should go, while Stanley and Eddie stayed to explore the immediate area of the campsite. While eating breakfast they saw small parties of short-toed larks flying, very low over the ground, from the direction of the distant gap in the hills. Some birds, at least, evidently used the passes between the mountains. 'What was all that gunfire we heard last night?' Mike asked Pat when they were on their way, crammed into the Landrover with three Yemeni porters.

'You never know. Could have been a punch-up. On the other hand it could have been high spirits at a wedding or something. You just never know.'

They went fifteen kilometres down the wadi, passing on their way a symmetrical cone of lava which was topped by an ancient fort, black and crumbling. From the summit there would be full command of the whole pass, the approach from Wadi Jauf, and the whole tribal area from the east. In the old days a few well-positioned men could have held back an army from here. They felt as if they were driving into the battlefields of yesterday. They kept a lookout for birds; saw some unidentified wheatears on the slopes, a few house buntings, and a bulbul in the scrub, but the area was still barren, with just a few succulents growing precariously among the stones. Then, as they passed through another area of black lava, they saw two red-breasted wheatears, which delighted them, for the species was the first of the endemics they had encountered.

Pat ignored both birds and birders for most of the way and kept his eyes on the track ahead or scanned the ridges of the hills, which closed in upon them as the wadi narrowed. He held a map-case on his knees and referred to it whenever a new feature of the landscape came into view. 'High time these maps were brought up to date,' he said 'they're very vague.' He eventually drew off the dirt track they were following and turned south along the tyre-marks of other vehicles, too few to have cut a definite route to the hills ahead. 'Jebel Yanur?' Pat enquired of his porters.

They professed ignorance and doubt with a shrug of the shoulders. Body language; it was universal. They were very quiet, Jack thought. Young Arabs were usually so garrulous. He hoped that Pat knew where he was going; all the mountains looked the same. 'They don't like it up here,' Pat said. 'Mush quais, eh fellahs?' he asked them, using one of his few phrases of Arabic. 'Mush quais!'

'Aiwah!' they readily agreed. 'Yes. Mush quais. No good here.'

Pat laughed. 'Up here, they feel just as foreign as we do, and they're only a couple of hundred miles from home, in their own country. They're worse on the Tihamah, where they can't stand the heat. They're mountain men. Tihamah mush quais!' he said.

'Aiwah. Tihamah mush quais.'

'Every bloody where mush quais.' Pat said and lurched the Landrover around a hairpin bend. The tread-marks led them on, up into the hills.

Half an hour of steep climbing and they were astride a broad ridge. Ahead was a sheer drop down a precipitous cliff, to their right a fairly shallow wadi, some five hundred feet deep, with a village perched on the cliff opposite, and to their left a wide view of the country to the east.

'This will do,' Pat said. 'I can make a few checks from here.'

His porters set up his equipment on a small hillock and he seemed to forget the birders, as he peered through the lens of the radio telemeter.

'I'm bouncing signals off those hills over there,' he explained, but they decided to leave him to it and wandered along the ridge toward the cliff.

By watching the sun, Jack realised they had travelled over a wide semicircle to reach the high ground above the cliff and were, in fact, not all that far from the camp. The sun was brilliant, reflecting from the ground in shimmering waves, though the air was cool. The area was even more barren, almost pure limestone. Nothing could grow in this contortion of rock. Splinters of limestone clinked like glass underfoot and the sound echoed about them, amplified by silence. There was no one to be seen about the village, which was no more than three or four tall, flat-topped houses. There were no animals and not a bird to be seen. Near the bottom of the wadi a squat tower stood in sentinel, a few stones dislodged and fallen from the parapet. They sat on a rock to scan the skies and saw that the rock and the boulders hanging on the slopes were embedded with fossils. Jack picked some from the ground, remarking that he had seen similar types in the desert pavement in Saudi Arabia. 'They lived under the Jurassic sea.'

'The oil's not far away, then.' Mike said, 'We're probably sitting on a lake of it.'

Jack said 'Yeah!' and imagined the skyline and the surrounding hills spattered with wellheads and slashed by roads. 'Great!'

There was no life to be seen. No eagles. No sound. The survey party was out of sight, back along the ridge. The sun rebounded from the pink-tinged rock. Jack dropped the fossils and they fell with a brittle tinkle to the ground. A blue lizard raised its head from behind a boulder and regarded them with a dispassionate eye. They watched its throat pulsating as it ventured into the sun and cautiously flattened its body against the top of the boulder to absorb the heat, with its flicking tongue tasting the air. They kept still and watched it scuttle forward and settle in an eroded cavity. The eyelids drooped to shield the pupils from the sun. Why did Stanley Carter have to be so disagreeable, Mike was thinking to himself, and spoil the enjoyment of the trip for everyone. He would get far more work done from a willing team, yet he seemed determined to dampen their enthusiasm with derogatory comments. The most advisable response was to ignore it, but Eddie was not likely to suffer too much of it without retaliation and Jack was as quick-tempered as Stanley, in his way.

'What's that?' Jack said. 'A warbler or something, flitting among those boulders.' They both put their binoculars to their eyes. They could see nothing.

Suddenly, the lizard was gone and the echo of a single gunshot reverberated from the wadi. The distorted sound seemed all about them and had no direction.

'Where the hell did that come from?' Jack said, as he eased himself down behind the rock, thinking that there was probably someone hunting... something.

Another shot. From somewhere in the boulders on the other side of the wadi. The whine of a ricochet.

'That was a bit close,' Mike said, looking around. 'Where the devil is he? Whatever does he think he's doing?'

'He's firing at us, for Christ's sake!' Jack screamed. 'Get your head down!'

And another bullet. This one struck the ground over to their left. The whine of its ricochet passed over their heads and Mike fell beside Jack, behind the rock. Jack found himself shaking with fright; it was a violent internal trembling which, strangely, left him with steady hands and head. They dropped to the ground and lay behind the boulder which had been their peaceful seat a minute before. Jack saw that Mike too was trembling slightly and felt absurdly reassured.

'I think we ought to go,' Mike said.

'So do I.'

They arose to a crouching position and, feeling somewhat foolish at first, ran back towards the Landrover. Immediately two more shots rang out and they heard the bullets strike the ground behind them. They threw themselves behind a rock. Silence! They waited.

'We can't stay here for ever,' Jack said.

'Where are they?' Mike groaned. 'Why shoot at us?'

They heard Pat shouting. They could not distinguish the words, but he was evidently calling them in some alarm. Mike raised himself to his knees.

'Get down,' Jack said, as he grabbed Mike's trouser leg. 'They'll blow your bloody head off.'

Mike shook off his hand and stood up. 'Come on,' he said.

Jack stood also, with his shoulders hunched, and together they took a couple of hesitant paces out into the open. Then they ran over the clinking limestone and raced for the Landrover.

The Yemeni porters were throwing the last of the equipment into the vehicle, yelling, 'Yallah! Yallah!' Hurry! Hurry! Two more shots followed on the heels of the birders as they reached the vehicle, and then there was a further shot, a whining ricochet and a cry from one of the Yemenis. He fell to the ground.

'Be Jaysus,' Pat cried. 'They'll kill us all!'

He picked the man up, shoved him in the back of the Landrover and slammed the door. He jumped into the driver's seat and turned the ignition key. They heard another shot before the engine fired but the bullet went they knew not where. There were two hundred metres of open ground before the track led down behind the ridge and out of the sniper's sight. Two hundred metres in which they were sitting ducks as the vehicle rumbled over the stony ground. But there were no more shots. Jack turned to the injured porter. The man was clutching his leg, from which a stream of blood flowed through his fingers. He smiled an apology for getting hit.

'Let's have a look,' Jack said. There was a splinter of limestone chipping embedded deep in the muscle of his calf.

'First aid in the rack.' Pat said.

Jack gripped the chipping between finger and thumb and drew it out. He placed antiseptic on the wound and bound it up to check the bleeding as the Landrover bounced over the stones and slewed around the bends of the steeply descending track.

'Bani Arhab mush quais,' the porter said, and his companions agreed. What had they ever done to their own countrymen to deserve this? Yet, as the Landrover sped away and reached the bottom of the hill and Pat drove up the wadi towards their base, slowing down to spare his instruments and the bruises of his passengers, they all found themselves laughing.

'Quite exciting,' Mike said, 'actually.'

★ ★ ★

Stanley Carter had watched the Landrover drive away from camp in the clear, cold air of the morning. The sun was rising above the distant mountains and casting deep, black shadows across the lava on the plain. The dust from the wheels rose behind the vehicle and hung suspended over the track as if reluctant to spread its pollution wider. There was a bird singing somewhere, a plaintive, apologetic warble from among the black stones and barren fields south of the camp.

'What's that singing?' Eddie said, more of a statement to draw attention to the sound than a question requiring an answer.

'Why don't you find out?' Stanley said. 'That's what you're supposed to be here for.'

Eddie took his binoculars from the pole of his tent, where he kept them hanging ready for instant use, and strode off across the lava without a word. He was glad of the excuse to leave Stanley behind in camp and had intended to do so without this provocation, so he went off in search of the hidden singer. He could see nothing, but the thin song was issuing from somewhere over towards the black drystone walls to the south. Squat, brown lizards scuttled through the walls and watched him pass. He found the singing bird and walked on, for he had no intention of returning to spend the day alone with Stanley.

He strode on towards a small village. It was settled among a large outcrop of rock at the top of the hill and looked poor, of six or seven dwellings randomly set along the track which widened to form a main thoroughfare, or square, in the centre of the cluster, where a wrecked car lay on its side. No longer recognisable as to make or design, it had been stripped of wheels, engine, doors and windscreen. A tangle of old oil drums and rusty corrugated iron lay heaped against it. Several goats rummaged among a pile of rubbish. The place reminded him of smallholdings he had seen in Wales and Cornwall, and he smiled to himself at the annoyance Jack would show should he tell him so. He wondered if he should proceed through the houses. Surely that would be OK. Just to walk through. The children saw him, two little girls who peeped through a doorway and ran back into the house, crying aloud. Eddie hurried on, to be clear of the village before anyone else emerged. He could return, he observed, by skirting the village and clambering down the hillside.

'Yah,' someone called.

Two men were standing in the road at the other side of the village. They beckoned him over. He had no option but to comply. He wished Jack were with him as he approached them. How could he communicate without the language? They looked unwashed and unshaven. One was old, with a double row of gold teeth, like miniature pears, set crudely into his gums. The other was younger but, like his companion, was deeply lined and hollow-cheeked. Both wore skirts which had once been white, loose shirts and tightly bound head-cloths. The younger had a rifle hung from a strap across his shoulder. He spoke directly to Eddie, looking into his eyes with an unblinking, questioning gaze.

'I'm sorry, mate,' Eddie said, 'I no speakee Arabee.'

The man beckoned him to sit, and they sat among the rubble at the trackside where a fall of rocks edged the path. He reached and took Eddie's binoculars away, lifting the strap from around his neck. He looked through them and made noises of approval and passed them to the older man who grinned a golden grin and squinted towards the camp. The young man called to the houses. A female voice answered. He pointed to the camp, just discernible as faint green pyramids in the black distance, and back to Eddie.

'Yes,' Eddie said, 'from the camp.'

'Ingalize?'

'Yes. London.'

The rifle lay against a rock. It was an old Lee-Enfield, Eddie noted, like his grandfather had used in the war. Wherever had that come from? And the ammo? He doubted he would ever get his binoculars back. The two men took turns peering all about them, pointing out familiar landmarks, appraising the instrument, speaking in low, calm voices. The young man called again to the house. The woman shrieked a reply and emerged with a large modern Japanese vacuum flask and a fistful of glasses. She set them on the ground, grumbling. The old man scolded her and the young one dismissed her with a flick of the wrist. He poured hot, sweet, tea and offered a glass to Eddie who accepted with laughter and relief.

When the tea was all finished – the Yemenis would have none of this nonsense about it being impolite to accept more than two cups – they rose from the ground, the binoculars were handed back, and the two men walked over to a broken section of dry-stone wall. It had been swept away, they made Eddie understand, by water from a flash flood running down the hillside. They began manhandling the fallen stones back into place, grunting and breathing heavily, with great intakes of breath which they exhaled forcefully with puffed-out cheeks. Eddie bent to help them. Soon he was gasping for breath. Altitude! he thought. It's the lack of oxygen. He began puffing and blowing like the Yemenis to feed the oxygen to his lungs and, between them, they had the wall repaired in an hour. Eddie enjoyed working with them and communicated by signs and gestures. They admired his size and strength but he had no doubt that they could have worked him into the ground, had they wished. They were all muscle and sinew, the old man as fit as the young, and they had not an ounce of fat between them.

He left them after drinking more tea in the afternoon and made his way back through the village. What a load of rubbish, he said to himself, they had been told about the tribesmen.

'Hi hi hi,' came the voices of the children, now emboldened by their father's acceptance of the foreigner. They took him by the hand and led him to a block of limestone leaning against the wall of a house.

'Hamyar,' they said, 'Hamyar Hamyar,' and showed him the inscriptions carved into the stone.

'I'm sorry. No speak Arabi.'

'Hamyary. Hamyary,' they said. 'Malika Bilkis,' and turned to the direction of the gunshot. There was nothing to be seen. It was a long way off, somewhere in the hills. There was another shot. A pause and then a few more.

'Bunduk!' said one of the children, sighting along an imaginary rifle.

★ ★ ★

Stanley watched Eddie go striding towards the village and the hills in the distance with a satisfied smile. He could see that if these amateurs were to produce any return for all the effort he had invested in this expedition then clearly they would need prodding from time to time. He prided himself in knowing the requirements of an efficient leader... see a job that needs doing and get someone to do it! As leader, he himself had enough to do in ensuring that their efforts were co-ordinated and the observations recorded in a scientific manner. He could not afford to let the expedition degenerate into a carefree bird-watching holiday, which was what would happen if Eddie Johns had his way. The world of ornithology is a small one, and word soon spreads when expeditions fail and the leaders prove to be incompetent scientists. Stanley Carter knew that his future career depended on the results of this expedition, and a successful conclusion, with papers published in the right journals, would lead to further offers of money from trust-funds and charities anxious to further their images as patrons of the sciences. Their benevolence may as well benefit Stanley Carter as anyone else.

The porters remaining in camp spoke no English except for a few words they had learned through familiarity; *come here, go there, wait, tomorrow*. Fred Stirling had worked in too many countries, had dealt with too many languages and dialects to bother with learning Arabic. In a few months it might be Sindebele, or Amharic, he had to contend with. No man might know everything, so he employed interpreters and hoped that there was not too much misunderstanding in translation. The porters respected him and never approached him directly, only through his Number One. He had found it the only way to work. In his absence the men were now sitting about outside their tents, talking quietly. They were willing workers but a day off is not to be scorned. Allah Kareem, God is kind. Muqbel sat with his countrymen and watched the tall figure of Eddie diminishing in the distance. He mentioned it to the porters. They looked after Eddie and shrugged.

Over to the west a dark cloud rose above the horizon and some rain fell in a compact shower from its horizontal base. It drifted towards the plain and evaporated without sullying the clear blue sky overhead. Muqbel rose from the ground and went to his Toyota. He checked the oil, fuel and water. He wiped the windscreen and placed a cassette in the stereo player. He was on to a good thing, Stanley decided. Getting paid for hanging around in camp. A few short-toed larks were still flying up from the wadi, in small, loose flocks. Stanley looked at them through his binoculars, then at the distant horizons, high cliffs and flat-topped mountains. All ornithologically unexplored, he thought to himself. He was making history. The first man to lead an expedition into what was virtually virgin territory. Great things could follow this. He went over to Muqbel.

'How far to those mountains?'

Muqbel shrugged, 'Not too much,' he said, glancing at the indicated escarpment.

These Arabs, Stanley swore to himself, would never give one a direct answer to any question, however trivial. 'How far?' he said, 'How long? One hour? Two hours?'

'Maybe one hour.' Muqbel spoke to the porters in Arabic. There followed a lengthy exchange. Stanley's eyes went from one to another, understanding not a word.

'Bad place!' Muqbel said.

'The whole damned country is a bad place. I want to go over there and have a look. What do you think you are getting paid for?' He spoke too quickly and Muqbel had difficulty in understanding his accent.

Muqbel spoke to the porters again. They laughed at some joke among themselves.

'OK,' he said. 'Go to mountain.' Followed by a disarming smile.

Stanley's anger subsided. One only needed to be firm with these people. After twenty minutes of driving they were at the base of the escarpment. The cliffs rose from the plain in an impenetrable wall of sheer rock. High up on a wide ledge Stanley saw patches of white bird-droppings and the overhanging sticks and twigs of a large, untidy nest. He leaned on the hot bonnet of the Toyota to steady his binoculars. No birds were at the nest. He saw two barbary falcons swooping after rock doves and, among some thin acacias at the base of the cliff, a large, dark pigeon which he identified as a red-eyed dove. He laughed to himself, and Muqbel nodded in appreciation from the driver's seat. He passed a flask of water to Stanley. It was decidedly warm, but Stanley drank it, as he had brought none himself. As he tipped his head he noticed two large birds in the sky above his head.

'Eagles!'

He raised his binoculars. He saw the pale bases to the primary feathers, the white backs as they banked against the cliff, the massive wingspan. 'Good God!' he said, and steadied his elbows against the bonnet. 'Verreaux's eagle. What a bird!' He reached into his pocket for his notebook and began scribbling. He barely heard the gun shot.

'We go!' Muqbel said. 'Yallah. In car, Mister Stanley.'

Stanley ignored him. Continued writing in his notebook. Muqbel started the engine. The vibrations made it impossible to write with the notebook on the bonnet. Stanley swore aloud. Muqbel turned the Toyota around. 'No good place,' he said. 'Yallah, Mister Stanley.'

Stanley was forced into a run to catch up with the vehicle. 'Wait! You stupid bugger, wait.' He opened the door and clambered aboard as the wheels bucked against stones lying in their path. 'What the hell do you think you're doing?'

Muqbel smiled. 'We go now.'

They heard a few more shots before the noise of the Land Cruiser, bouncing along the track, drowned all other sounds and Muqbel headed back to base.

★ ★ ★

Fred Stirling drove back into camp with his frown still in pretty good shape. He had found the Mudeer and arranged for a guide to take them to see the Sheikh. That was the way he had become accustomed to doing business; see-somebody-about-seeing-somebody… one got there in the end. But what a waste of time. Doing the job was difficult enough, but trying to explain to the fat-arses in the UK why it took three days to complete one triangulation was even more difficult. His frown deepened when he saw Pat's Landrover back in camp so early. He checked the leg of the wounded porter while Pat related the events of the day.

'So, they were not firing at you, then?' He looked at Jack and Mike, whose faces registered doubt, and then back at Pat. 'Seems to me they were warning you off. They could have picked you off, one by one, if they'd wanted to, and no-one could have known who did it.' He went into his tent and put his kettle on the portable gas-stove. He told them of the arrangements he had made. He warmed the teapot. He covered the pot in his hand-knitted tea cosy and placed one mug on an upturned box. They left him alone.

When the expedition members gathered outside his tent that evening to fill in the daily log, Stanley Carter sat listening to them discussing the day's events.

'Couldn't understand a word,' Eddie was saying, 'but they were very friendly. They gave me tea and the kids showed me an inscription on a stone. Said something about a kiss, sounded like.'

'Bilkis,' Mike said. 'Queen of Sheba. Lived at Marib, about a hundred kilometres south east of here. Probably a Hamyaritic inscription. I should like to see that.'

'I expect the villagers would be delighted. The kids were obviously very proud of it.'

'I'll get some photographs. See if I can get the inscription translated.'

Jack was still a little shaky from the events of the morning and was irked to find Mike taking it so coolly. He had never been out in

73

a shower of lead before and wanted to go over it and talk about it and relive the experience in relating it to others. What a yarn to tell when he returned to Cornwall. He heard again the whining ricochets and described them whistling overhead. Poiinnnng. Tweeennnngg. Two more shots! We hid behind a rock…

No! Fred was right. They had not been firing at us. It was an accident that the porter had been hit by a chip of rock. However, it was an experience. Mike is OK, keeps his cool in an emergency. 'Do you fancy going down the wadi again tomorrow?' he asked him.

'Actually, I'd quite like to wander up and see the inscribed stone, while I have the opportunity.' Mike was apologetic in declining to accompany Jack but, nevertheless, there was something of the shared experience still in his voice, as if they were now closer than the others. Jack decided to bring them into the conversation to prevent the team splitting into factions. 'You heard the shots, then?' he asked Eddie.

Stanley interrupted. 'We all heard the shots. But unlike you lot, who seem to have spent the day sight-seeing, I was forced to abandon a very important ornithological observation due to our brave driver deserting in the face of a few bangs in the distance.' He was working himself up to give them a good dressing down and get it into their thick heads that this expedition was here to study the birds of Yemen and nothing, absolutely nothing, was going to prevent it from doing so. He glared at the grin spreading over Eddie's face.

'The bloody bangs,' Jack retorted angrily 'were not so damned far-in-the-distance from where we were standing. You ought to try having hot lead whistling around your ears sometime.'

Stanley regarded him dispassionately. For a man so many years his senior Jack was inordinately volatile. For the expedition to succeed, all of them would need manipulation and the full exploitation of their limited talents. Jack was the easy one, and Stanley foresaw no difficulties in controlling him. 'All right!' he said. 'I grant that you and Mike were more or less forced back into camp by circumstances beyond your control. Eddie, however, has been wandering about in quest of the Tablets of Moses and drinking tea, which was no doubt very pleasant, but hardly likely to contribute much to the ornithology of Yemen. With which,' he continued after an awkward silence, 'this expedition is exclusively concerned.'

'Get stuffed!' Eddie said. 'Who do you fink you're talking to, you arrogant little git.'

There was that *'sk sk'* catch in Stanley's throat. A nervous tic when he was angry or on the defensive. Eddie laughed aloud, flung the dregs of his tea onto the ground and made as if to move away.

'Not to an ornithologist,' Stanley said.

Eddie's smile faded to a look of animosity. 'Oh? What then?' he demanded.

'Am I not right in believing that you set off this morning to identify a bird-song which has probably never been recorded before, and abandoned the objective in order to cavort with the villagers and work as a common labourer?'

Mike had been following the exchanges with some anxiety, lest Stanley pushed Eddie too far. The day had not been easy. 'Perhaps,' he said, hesitantly, 'if we were to fill in the daily log we might discover just what has been achieved today.'

Stanley looked at him with drawn lips. This one was the difficult one. But upper middle class assuming the right of leadership was not going to take over this expedition. He would see to that. 'Right!' he said. 'Let's get on with it. It will not have escaped you that we have two days to record. You will not allow another such lapse.'

He opened the log and began reading down the list of all those species recorded or likely to be recorded in the country, beginning...
'Persian shearwater, brown booby, white pelican...'

It was the only way to do it, recite the whole list, so that nothing should be overlooked, but the likelihood of seeing sea-birds like shearwaters and boobies in this desert landscape was remote, to say the least. Eddie winked at Jack as Stanley read down the list. He stopped at Verreaux's eagle, looked up at them with a self-satisfied smile. 'Breeding pair near Dhi Bin,' he said.

One of the most spectacular birds of prey in the world and they had all missed them except for himself, his smug expression told them.

'Where did you see them?' Eddie asked, his animosity overcome by curiosity. 'One of the birds I've always wanted to see.'

Jack said, 'Did you see the nest? Any eggs or young?'

'I said, a breeding pair.' Stanley's voice was condescending, implying that he was exasperated at the necessity to explain everything to some people.

'Can't see how you can record them as breeding without evidence,' Eddie said. 'Not if you want the log to be a scientific record.'

'The ledges were plastered in droppings. They were obviously a breeding pair. And why not? They breed in Ethiopia and Oman. We are within their range. If it were not for that bloody Arab panicking I would have marked them down to the nest. It was obvious that they were about to settle on it.'

'Can't help that,' Jack said, with a grin at Mike. 'You'll have to record them as "one pair seen," or, to be quite accurate, "two birds seen" because you've got no evidence that they were, in fact, paired.'

Stanley saw this as an attack on his scientific integrity. 'You may not be aware,' he said, 'that Verreaux's eagle, like all the large raptors, is solitary while not breeding.'

'You can't,' Eddie insisted, 'record them as breeding. If you want the glory of being the first to record Verreaux's eagle breeding in Yemen you'll have to go back there tomorrow and damn well get proof.' Eddie was not smiling. 'And you'd better take Mike wiv yah.'

'Are you suggesting that my observations are unreliable?'

'I'm saying the same as you, mate, that such an important record needs corroboration, that's all.' They stared at each other.

Mike said, 'Perhaps we'd better get on. We all have our own notes to write after the log is complete.'

Stanley adjusted his spectacles with a co-ordinated distortion of his eyebrows, ears, forehead and nose '...booted eagle,' he continued, 'Bonelli's eagle, osprey, lesser kestrel...' the list went on, '...desert wheatear, red- rumped wheatear...' Mike and Jack informed him of the birds in the wadi '...mourning wheatear...'

'Breeding pair near Dhi Bin,' Eddie interjected.

Stanley raised his head, 'Ah!' he said. 'A contribution from our tea-drinking archaeologist friend.'

'Male in song,' Eddie read from his notes. 'Female seen feeding fledgling out of nest. Other singing males together with females in the vicinity, suggesting loose colony or concentration in favoured locality.' He was parodying the accepted terminology.

Stanley wrote studiously in the log, speaking as he wrote. ' ... Pair-said-seen-breeding-Dhi-Bin-Eddie-Johns...'

'You little berk!'

'Is it not accurate?'

'You know damned well that "said seen" in the record is a bloody euphemism for an unreliable observer.'

'Perhaps,' Mike interrupted again, 'we can get proof of both Verreaux's eagle and mourning wheatear breeding tomorrow, but we really ought to get on.'

No one answered, and Stanley continued reading down the list. The entries under Verreaux's eagle and mourning wheatear had been made, he thought to himself, recorded for posterity. Tomorrow, he would obtain the proof himself.

'...Yemen serin, Yemen linnet, house bunting, African rock bunting...'

'Hang on,' Jack said. 'Not so fast! House bunting, several flocks seen. Probably breeding. Six males in song.'

Stanley looked at him and dropped his pen. 'And the proof?' he asked.

'Just listen.'

From the short scrub among the dry-stone walls, a little way to the north of the camp, they heard a short, jangling song-phrase, like a chaffinch or a cirl bunting opening up.

'Go and check them for yourself if you don't believe me. I have a tape recording too, if you want to hear it. We haven't all been idle this afternoon.'

Stanley wrote in the log and continued reciting... 'cinereous bunting, ortolan.' The list was complete. 'You must all be quite clear...' he began.

Fred Stirling came over to their tents. Expeditions were his life. Every day he was obliged to deal with truculent personnel and uncooperative locals in one country or another, and he needed no more than a cursory glance to discern the acrimony among the bird watchers. He had sufficient problems of his own, without shouldering any more. Nothing in his manner indicated any awareness of the trouble brewing, except for a momentary deepening of his frown.

'I thought one of you might like to come with me tomorrow,' he said, 'to see the Sheikh.'

One of them! When they all wanted to go.

'Yes. I'd be...' Stanley began.

'You speak a bit of Arabic?' Fred spoke directly to Jack.

'Yes, but it is only a little. Half the words they use I can't even find in my dictionary.'

'Might help if I had someone who could say the odd word to the Sheikh.' His frown foresaw the difficulties. 'My interpreter is pretty good, but it always helps to have someone else to ease things along.'

'Well, sure, if I can help. Be delighted.'

Chapter Seven

The morning was cold. Before Jack was properly dressed Muqbel brought him a cup of tea. Their breath condensed in the still air. 'You going to the Sheikh, Muqbel?'

'I stay. Maybe go Jebel Mister Stanley.' Muqbel was not happy at the prospect. He returned to the porters' tents.

Fred Stirling passed with a box of equipment and offered a gruff, obligatory, greeting. Not at his best in the mornings, Jack decided. 'The raffeeq is here,' Fred said and Jack was astonished to find that, standing among the porters, was the same wild-looking tribesman who had passed them in Raydah. He was dressed as before and his stubble remained unshaven, with his head-cloth wound beneath his chin as protection from the morning chill. His Kalashnikov was slung carelessly over one shoulder, and a bandolier of ammunition hung from the other. The Yemenis were standing before him in deference to his authority and direct questioning. He spoke to the man with the wounded leg and laughed dismissively. He interrogated Muqbel, looking at Jack as he did so. He smiled, and his teeth shone absurdly white in his dark, scruffy features. Jack nodded at him but did not return the smile. If this man was to be their assurance of safe conduct he hoped he was more reliable than he appeared. Jack would not have trusted him an inch. He asked Muqbel about him. 'He OK,' Muqbel said, doubtfully. 'Yimkin. Maybe! His name Abdullah.'

The journey to the Sheikh took them all of three hours. They went down the wadi until the bare fields gave way to a dry, boulder-strewn scree tumbling down the steep slopes on either side of them. Jack had no idea of the actual distance they travelled, for the going was difficult, in places necessitating the negotiation of boulder-strewn water-flows and sand-blown slopes, and their speed was impossible to judge. At one place, where the wadi widened out, they saw the ruin of a modern concrete building and, scattered about it, were the burnt-out remains of military vehicles. A little further on they passed the hulk of a tank, with its paint blistered in the heat of fire and sweltering summers. Fred's stern glance told Jack not to mention it.

After that the wadi narrowed again to a narrow defile between high cliffs, and Jack was disconcerted to see tangles of debris high in the branches of acacia trees overhanging the track.

'Flash floods,' Fred said and concentrated on his driving.

The final hour shook them all together like dice in a cup. They climbed in an interminable, jolting rumble over solid rock, and it took all of Fred's skill as a driver to follow the directions of the raffeeq, who sat beside him with the loaded Kalashnikov between his knees, apparently unaware of any discomfort. Fred was thinking privately to himself that the man could be taking them anywhere, but occasionally he turned and said, 'All right back there?'

They came, at last, to a solitary house standing on an outcrop of rock in a small side-wadi, where a few crops were growing in a miserable area of shallow soil. The house was of three storeys, built of black volcanic stone with white plaster outlining the windows. A thin camel stood tied to a rock, with half a dozen even thinner chickens scratching at her feet. Several children with ragged clothes and running noses shooed a hump-backed cow from the way of the vehicle. The animal was reluctant to move, as if death at the hands of the children or the approaching vehicle was preferable to its wretched existence on this barren, grassless mountain. A couple of single-storey extensions formed an open courtyard in front of the house, which had originally been built on a square foundation, and they all alighted there, relieved to be free of the vibrations in their bones. Three men met them, two of whom were carrying automatic rifles; all had daggers at their waists. All of the Yemenis exchanged the formal greetings. Peace be upon you. And upon you be peace.

And called the blessings of Allah upon each other. 'Salaam alaikum,' they said to the foreigners.

'Wa, alaikum salaam,' Jack said.

Fred Stirling said, 'Good morning.'

One of the three, a young, fine featured youth with clear skin, held his Kalashnikov with his right index finger hovering eagerly near the trigger. He did not smile, despite the greetings, but regarded the strangers with open hostility. Jack had no doubt that it was he who had fired the shots on the previous day. They were led into the house and up a narrow stairway to the mafrahj. The Sheikh awaited them. He was a small, emaciated man with a thin white beard and a wizened eye. He bade them welcome and indicated that they be seated on the cushions. Jack had a feeling that he had seen him before. Abdullah, the raffeeq, embraced the old Sheikh warmly and hung his gun on a hook in the wall as casually as a man hanging an umbrella. He was smiling broadly, showing his white teeth, in contrast to the sullen youth, and seated himself next to Jack. The youth sat on Jack's other side and kept his gun beside him. Fred sat beside the Sheikh, in the honoured place, and Khaled the interpreter sat next to him. The old man spoke quietly to a man, perhaps a son, who left the room. Khaled spoke with evident respect to the Sheikh, answering questions with care and consideration, translating now and then for the benefit of Fred, whose deep voice rumbled about the room like distant thunder in the mountains.

Other men arrived, were greeted and hung up their guns. They sat around the room, some talking and laughing with Abdullah, others eyeing the foreigners with suspicion. There had been no unbelievers here before. The son returned with cinnamon flavoured tea and Abdullah passed a glass to Jack. The talk continued and Fred explained what they were doing and why they wished to work in the area. The old man nodded in understanding of Khaled's translation but made no effort to conceal his doubts. Abdullah kept looking through the window at the approach to the house and the hills beyond, as if he expected someone. He offered more tea but Jack refused, less from politeness than fear of filling his bladder.

'Chai zayada?' Abdullah said.

'Shukran. Kafayah.' Thank you. Enough.

'Kallem Arabi quais,' Abdullah said, and Jack smiled at the compliment which was sheer flattery, for his Arabic was anything but good.

'I no speak...' Abdullah began. He continued in Arabic, 'I try to learn English. We have no school here when I was a boy... You teach me English.'

He was commanding, rather than asking, yet there was a simple desire to learn evident in his sudden smile. He was unpredictable, Jack feared, intelligent enough to be aware of his ignorance and frustrated by it. The type who could be dangerous if antagonised. Jack said again that his own Arabic was not very good. Abdullah dismissed this. 'What is this?' he asked, indicating the room, 'Al mafrajh, al quorfah?'

'The room,' Jack said.

'Throom.' His teeth flashed again.

'The... room. Quorfah... room. Al quorfah... The room.'

'The... room,' Abdullah said.

'Quais,' Jack said. 'Quais k'teer. Good, very good.

The sullen youth with the Kalashnikov had been listening to this. 'Why,' he demanded, 'do you learn this heathen language?' He obviously had no fear of Abdullah and was equally as fiery.

Abdullah's anger matched his own and his eyes blazed at the youth's insolence.

'We must learn everything,' he cried, 'if Yemen is to progress. Do you wish to live in ignorance all your life?' He turned to Jack in apology for the youth's outburst.

'First we learn their language,' the boy insisted, 'then we wear their clothes. We forget we are Arab. Then we forget our God. Make them learn Arabic if they wish to come here exploiting our country.'

Jack felt a degree of sympathy for the boy's apprehensions. What he was saying had the ring of truth, but their neighbours had been unable to resist the Westernisation of their country, despite draconian, yet well-intended, restrictions placed upon the people. He glanced at the men now filling the room. He could not see these people becoming nine-to-five office workers, which is what would be required of them when the country caught up with the rest of the world on the profits of oil. At least they should make an attempt to retain their identity and the independence of their country. He remembered that his own language and culture had been overwhelmed in a similar manner. 'He's right,' he said.

The raffeeq considered this. 'Will you,' he asked in an ominously quiet voice, 'become Arab if you speak Arabic?'

Jack was searching for the words to explain that they could not compare the two situations, that it was all different for him. He was in too deep. His Arabic was inadequate. He looked to Khaled, Fred's interpreter, who was studying the carpet.

The boy cried, 'It is written! Who speaks Arabic... is Arab!' There was no denying the scriptures. All other conversation ceased. The youth was about to continue. 'These foreigners...' he was saying, 'Gurabah, kawajah...'

The voice of the Sheikh checked the young man's anger with a word. Abdullah's eyes flashed angrily. These old men and foolish boys, he was obviously thinking, will keep us in the past forever, but he deferred to his elder.

Fred Stirling frowned at Jack from across the room and wished he had brought only Khaled as interpreter. He had understood none of the exchange; saw only the animosity, and permission to work in the area receding like a tide. All eyes in the mafrahj were travelling from the Sheikh to Abdullah, the angry youth and Jack. They waited for the old man to speak as he adjusted his skirt around his crossed legs.

'Where did you learn the Holy Language, my brother?'

Jack felt all eyes on him. They were intelligent, interrogating eyes. Involuntarily he glanced, for a second, at the armoury of weapons hanging about the walls, and he prayed that his Arabic was adequate for the questions about to be asked of him.

'The Kingdom of Saudi Arabia,' he said.

'What city?'

'Riyadh.'

'What was your company? Who did you work for?'

'Al Mustashfa Malik Faisal.' At the King Faisal Hospital.

'You are a doctor?'

'I am an engineer.' It was the nearest he could get. 'Anna muhandis.'

The Sheikh regarded him in silence.

'Muhandis zait!' the boy said. Oil engineer!

The Sheikh silenced him with a gesture. He was so thin, his shoulders shrunken, his beard white and his skin deeply fissured with age, but there was no questioning his dignity. He considered the situation and, after exchanging a knowing look with one of the older men beside him, he said, 'Before three months I was in King Faisal Hospital. On two eyes I had cataracts. I was blind. A British surgeon restored my sight.'

Jack understood what the old man said, just. He remembered the blind man led from the airport. Had he been the Sheikh? The operation must have cost him something. Plus the journey to Riyadh. You could never tell with these people; how wealthy they were. The old man could have been passed by as a beggar in the streets of Sana'a. What could he say? In the hope that it would not be considered a blasphemy, coming from an unbeliever, he said. 'Allah kareem.'

'Without progress, Yemen will remain blind,' the Sheikh said. He turned and whispered to his son who left the room and returned with the women of the family, who remained outside the door and passed in trays of food which were placed on the floor in the centre of the room, in reach of all.

'Eat!' said the Sheikh.

The decision had been made, permission to work in the area granted. Abdullah would be their guide and safe conduct and, at times, the youth also. He accepted the decision of the Sheikh with good grace but would not be convinced of the benefits to be gained as a result. When they had finished eating, Abdullah, who had retained his watch on the approach to the house during the conversation, suddenly grabbed his gun threw and open the window. He aimed at the hillside and let out a short burst of gunfire, which filled the room with grey smoke of cordite. There was a scream. A woman's scream. Then a stream of female invective from the courtyard. Abdullah's bullets had cut her clothesline.

'I thought I saw somebody,' he said, indifferent to the jeers and laughter from the men.

Jack laughed too and Abdullah clasped him round the shoulders. He thrust the AK47 into his arms and told him to fire through the window. Have a go! He showed him how to release the safety catch and how to set the gun for single or repetitive shots. Jack aimed and, by some incredible fluke, hit the top of the flimsy clothes pole, sending the line flying and the remaining washing to the ground. There was a roar of approval in the room. Jack apologised. He didn't think he could hit it. No one believed him.

On the return journey, back to base-camp, Abdullah was silent, as if in deep thought, and merely pointed the way now and then when the track forked or disappeared as they drove over solid rock. Whether the silence was the effect of the qat or the difficulties in trying to converse through Jack's limited Arabic they did not know, but they were all relieved when he ordered them to stop and he alighted from the Landrover. He said he would see them the following morning. There was only one track now, up the wadi past the burnt-out tanks. They could not get lost, he said, as he insisted on shaking hands all round. They left him standing on the track, apparently in the middle of nowhere.

'This man, no good!' Khaled grumbled.

Fred nodded in agreement but was not particularly worried about the raffeeq as long as permission to work in the area had been granted. They had a free hand, more or less, in the province, and the bird watchers too could wander about at will.

'Due to your eye surgeon in Riyadh,' Fred commented, by way of thanks.

85

They remained in the area for two weeks, during which time they saw little of Fred or Pat except for an hour or two in the evenings when they compared notes. Stanley had hoped to scrounge lifts in one of the survey party's vehicles, but Fred would have none of that and they were obliged to retain the services of their own driver, Muqbel, who agreed to work for a daily fee plus petrol. He was delighted, refrained from pointing out that there was no other vehicle or driver in the area that they could have hired, and seemed to regard the whole venture as a paid holiday and an opportunity to practise his English.

They became known in the area. Villagers waved as they passed and invited them to share tea in the fields where they worked. Occasionally Abdullah forced his company on them and, through Muqbel and Jack's inadequate Arabic, grilled them about the expedition and its purpose, evidently, it seemed, believing not a word of it. However, they used these occasions to venture into more remote districts in the hope that his presence guaranteed some security. They travelled west of Raydah one morning, towards Wadi Shamin and a totally different landscape. The terrain lay before them in a contortion of mountains and deep wadis, vast and at first sight empty but, through the heat-haze rising with the advancing day, they could discern village after village, perched on peaks and ridges, scattered like a random smattering of inaccessible fortresses. The whole country was populated, with villages on every prominence or perched like eyries on the very edge of precipitous cliffs, yet they saw few people. All the mountainsides were terraced into fields on all but the steepest, impossible slopes, and the terraces rose, tier after tier, for thousands of feet, wherever the ground was sufficiently level to gouge a small, tillable plot. The land was ancient, parched with age and exhaustion. In the far distance they could see the massive, squat formation of Jebel Shaharah with its cliffs white with the droppings of vultures while, at their feet it seemed, Wadi Shamin held a thin trickle of water, two thousand feet below.

'What a country,' Eddie said.

They saw griffon vultures soaring below them and then rise on the hot, ascending air and drift away to Jebel Shaharah. House martins were sweeping about the escarpment on which the bird watchers stood gazing into the depths as if into a model. They checked the cliffs rising from the wadis. Some were irregular and strewn with outcrops supporting a thin vegetation, while others rose unbroken from the wadi floors for hundreds, thousands, of feet, with their faces slashed vertically and horizontally and splashed with the droppings of birds.

'There could be bald ibises breeding here,' Jack said.

They went back to base early, for Abdullah was not interested in bald ibises and was impatient to return. They never argued with him.

Each evening they heard Fred's radio when he tuned in to Sana'a and then, after a brief exchange of assurances, he returned to the BBC World Service. The birders sometimes went to his tent to listen to the news, but he never invited them to stay. He was a solitary man. He informed them in good time of his return to Sana'a, saying that he would be glad to leave as the people in Raydah were complaining that his party were taking too much water from the well and had limited them to half a bowser a day. They had to pay for the water, but that was not the issue; the water table was dropping and there was none to spare.

'Best clear out,' he said. 'We've finished the survey. And you'd better come too.'

'We haven't finished our survey,' Stanley said. 'We're staying here.'

Chapter Eight

As a professional diplomat, Harry Courtenay found it incumbent upon himself, as he put it, to be aware of events in his parish. It was, therefore, with a sense of duty rather than idle curiosity that, in addition to the sophisticated equipment at the embassy, he listened to conversations by means of a radio frequency scanner concealed in the spare bedroom that he called the Home Office. It was, he explained to his wife, a joke.

'Home Office. Rather good, eh?'

His wife said, 'But it hasn't got a desk, dear.'

He listened to Fred Stirling informing his own office in Sana'a that he was returning to base, and that the British bird watchers had decided to stay up north on their own.

'Knew it,' he said, as he switched off the receiver. 'They'll be nothing but a damned nuisance all the time they're here.'

Harry had little time for such minor irritations. There was daily news of much activity in the Middle East. Portentous events which might necessitate the mobilisation of the full resources of British diplomacy and, incidentally, promote Harry's career. The general unrest, together with the uncertainty regarding Yemeni sympathies and their oilfields, were changing the whole relevance of our presence in this backwater of a posting. The problem, as Harry saw it, was that it was so difficult to obtain information as to what was actually going on. He was so pressed with office work that he was forced to rely on others for information.

Fred Stirling, on the other hand, was in a position to obtain intelligence, both from personal observation and from his men. Harry had hinted that the interests of their country might be furthered by such gleanings, but Stirling had insisted that he never saw anything of significance and in any case he was not paid to be a 'bloody spy.'

Harry felt that Cecil Hayward also had an unfair advantage over him in that he was fluent in the filthy language. The only Arabic Harry learned was during his short stay in the army, when he had picked up all the barrack-room obscenities, and he assumed that Arabs were as profane as the common soldiers with whom he had been obliged to consort. Harry studied Russian in his enthusiastic youth, with the hope of a posting to Moscow, and had forgotten it in middle age when that expectation remained unfulfilled.

On the afternoon of Fred's return to the city, Harry found time, by rearranging his busy schedule, to commiserate with him over the shooting incident in the north.

Fred was tired. He was supervising the unloading of the vehicles and the sorting of equipment in the dusty compound of the Department of Overseas Survey when Harry, 'Just dropped in to see how you are, old fellow.'

Fred was in no mood for the diplomat's sympathy, which he saw as thinly veiled interrogation.

'What should I have done?' he demanded testily when questioned on the advisability of dealing with the governor of the province, 'Left fifteen men and three vehicles lying idle for a week while reams of paper were shuffled about the country? I have work to do on the Tihamah as soon as the weather cools. You seem to forget that I am accountable to London for expenditure of time and money.'

Fred Stirling had the contempt of all field men for office-wallahs. He suffered fools enough without this desk-bound pedant interfering in matters of which he knew nothing. 'Water is short up there,' he said by way of additional reason for getting on with the job as quickly as possible. 'The tribesmen were complaining that we were taking too much from the well.'

Courtenay had no sympathy. 'We are all accountable to London, my dear chap.'

Fred ignored the comment as Harry had ignored his explanation. It was none of Harry's business anyway. He went over to the truck and climbed over the tailgate. Harry followed him, resenting this dismissal.

'I have been led to believe,' Harry said, 'and I think you should take note...'

Fred threw a folded tent to the ground, and a cloud of dust exploded at Harry's feet, smothering his neatly pressed slacks and polished shoes. Harry's pink face became suffused with a glowing red. 'I have been led to believe...' he said again, through tightly drawn lips.

Fred placed his foot on the tailgate and leaned his elbow on his knee as he turned to listen. He guessed that 'led to believe' meant that Courtenay had been playing the earwig again and listening to his private conversations on the radio. That in itself was not important, for he and his wife had developed their own codes over the years.

'I have been led to believe that you abandoned four United Kingdom citizens in an unstable tribal area where your own men have come under fire from hostile elements.'

Fred looked at him blankly, assessing the smug smile. He realised that he could be in trouble if things went wrong up there and Courtenay foisted the blame on to him. He had merely allowed the bird watchers to camp at his base and had given them water and security. He was not responsible for them, or their safety, but Courtenay could misconstrue his actions should they come to harm. Momentarily, he cursed Stanley Carter's obstinacy; the others seemed willing enough to return. Courtenay was waiting for his comment.

'They'll be OK,' Fred said. Was this fool unaware that Cecil Hayward had sent the bird watchers to him? If he wished, he could pass any bucks right back to the embassy. He was no longer concerned with anything Harry might do. 'Abdullah will look after them,' he said.

'A taxi driver? Come come!' Harry's smile broadened in derision.

'Not the taxi driver,' Fred said in exasperation. 'The raffeeq, our guide and guarantee of safe conduct. They still have them, you know.' He took his teapot from a box in the back of a truck and jumped to the ground. He cradled the pot in his arms, lovingly adjusting the woollen cosy. He wished to take it home, fill it with the large leaves of Chai Rhabia, which his wife would have bought from the souk, pour on water brought exactly to the boil, wait three minutes, and drink the finest tea in the world.

'Raffeeq?' Courtenay said. 'What raffeeq? I know nothing of a raffeeq.'

Fred had had enough. He wanted to get this stuff put away and go home. 'The bloody raffeeq who led us into the hands of the rebels or the royalists or the communists or the cannibals or whatever the hell they were. Abdullah, the scar-faced bandit.'

'I see,' Courtenay said, suddenly thoughtful. 'Tell me, this Abdullah. Fiftyish? The scar small, near the left eye?'

'Friend of yours?' Fred said sarcastically. Courtenay waited for an answer. 'Yes,' Fred said eventually, wondering how Courtenay could possibly know of the villainous tribesman who had been their guide in the remote mountains of the north. 'Who is he?'

'Oh, nobody important. Don't know where he's living, I suppose?'

The question was too casual, and too fatuous, they both realised, Courtenay with regret, Fred Stirling with ill-concealed contempt. The two men stared at each other.

'Well,' Harry said, 'I dare say our bird watchers are in good hands... if you say so.'

He left Fred unloading the last of his equipment and walked briskly through the wide streets of the new part of town to his own modern villa. He admitted to himself that Fred Stirling had got the better of him but, on the other hand, he prided himself that he revealed nothing of significance regarding Abdullah. Best that Stirling should remain in ignorance of affairs beyond his brief, so to speak. The damned insolence of the man. They called it dumb insubordination in the services. He was a dangerous by-passer who refused to observe the niceties of protocol in the mistaken assumption that these things were simply administrative restrictions. He did not follow channels, he let things slip, which led to too many complications. Perhaps a word with the Old Man was called for. Take the business of visiting this bloody Sheikh without consulting the Ministry of the Interior... the

Ministry of Development, or whichever Ministry was involved. It simply would not do. Bound to lead to ramifications. That was it... ramifications! As well the corps were not here if these people were to conduct their own negotiations; and what if things went wrong? Dammit, they had gone wrong, with this shooting business. If that Yemeni porter had been killed there would have been interminable diplomatic squabbles. There may even have been compensation, blood money, to pay, and God knows the questions that would raise.

Definitely time for a word. Just a quiet word before things got out of hand. Couldn't do him any harm. Moscow or Washington were only a step or two in the right direction. Harry entered his house glowing in the knowledge that only he was aware that the most dangerous Yemeni terrorist rebel was back in the country and hiding somewhere in the north.

Alison Courtenay was suspicious of her father's jovial greetings. Normally he came in and flopped into a chair complaining of the heat, or the dust, or overwork. Her mother greeted Harry with gushing enthusiasm and asked Alison to pour a drink for her father, adding, 'And I dare say you could do with one too, darling.' Alison was not deceived. Her mother had been hovering around the whisky bottle for the last hour, but that was understandable, being stuck in this Godforsaken dust hole of a country. Her mother was still slim, thin in fact, and did daily battle with the climate over her skin, noting the growing lines and creases with despair. Like Harry, she wanted Moscow or Washington, or Paris would be rather fun. Harry had dutifully struggled with his Russian and never been given the opportunity to use it. Languages were not his forte, poor dear. She knew, and refused to admit that Harry knew too, that he had been overtaken in the promotional race by people like Cecil Hayward. This was his last opportunity, at fifty-seven, to make an impression and be recommended for a step up. The alternative was an eight-year wait for retirement and a lawn to mow in Surrey.

'Those bird watchers are still up north somewhere,' Harry told them, 'God knows what mischief they'll get up to.'

'Hardly your responsibility, darling,' his wife said with sympathy he had long believed to be genuine. 'Leave them to Cecil Hayward. He sent them up there.'

'Hayward's gone on leave,' Harry said. He prided himself on being a man of few, carefully chosen words, the significance of which he implied by intonation. 'Not an ideal time to go.' The round face crumpled into a smile of resignation.

'Pour another drink for Daddy, darling,' Mrs Courtenay said, as she set her empty glass on the coffee table. 'We may as well use it after all these months of waiting.'

As Alison poured more whisky for her parents, Harry said, 'I have received certain intelligence...' and sipped his whisky. 'Abdullah has returned.'

'Who's Abdullah?' Alison asked indifferently as she passed her mother a glass.

'Alison, dear, you should not ask your father questions which he may not be free to answer.'

'Then why mention it? Abdullah could be the houseboy, for all I know.'

'Alison, darling, how could you?'

'It's quite all right, dear,' Harry said expansively. 'I know I can rely upon the discretion of my family. The information is not classified, as you might say. Not yet.'

Harry lounged back in the armchair and tried on an expression of grave solemnity as he spoke, decided it was inappropriate and settled for amused concern as befitting one who had matters under control.

'Abdullah,' he said, 'if that is indeed his name, has been a bit of a thorn in our side for some time. All began in Aden when he was just a boy. Mad Mitch said at one point that he was the most dangerous of them all, for he did not hate the British. Find that hard to believe myself. Damned fanatic, if you ask me. After we came out, Abdullah disappeared, went to ground in a manner of speaking. We don't know which side he was on following the death of the Imam, but during the civil war he was with the royalists. No doubt of that. He was responsible for the massacre of an Egyptian armoured battalion near Dhi Bin. I have it orf the cuff that the British were involved with him at that time. Supplied him with a few popguns, not enough to determine the outcome, don't you know, but enough to sweeten him for future use, if you follow me. He didn't fall for that. Ha ha. I have it that a few rockets hurtled about the F.O. But there were no names, of course.'

He was implying that there could never be 'names' after any attempt to further national interests, however misguided. Harry was not resentful that there should have been a 'papering over the cracks'. He would not refer to such interior decorating as a cover-up, however. After all, none of us are infallible. Nevertheless, he was glad that he had never made such a blunder.

'But why should it concern us if Abdullah is in Yemen?' Alison said. 'It's his own country, after all.'

'Ah,' said her father, 'but he has been out, don't you see?' Been out. And where? That is the point. It is all a question of apple carts, my dear.' He thought this frightfully funny and would be drawn no further. 'Question of apple carts,' he repeated.

'But these bird people, darling,' his wife said. 'Surely they can come to no harm. Seems an innocent enough pastime for young boys.'

'Not so young,' he said. 'One of them must be thirty-odd. Old enough to know better than to come bothering busy embassy staff with trivialities in a sensitive area like this. Besides, we want no bother with tourists going about getting themselves lorst, or running out of funds and needing to be shipped home at our expense. Saw enough of that with the blasted hippies in India, dammit.'

Alison twirled the glass in her hand. She was sure her father was exaggerating, and she wanted to go to the coast with the four men, so to take his mind from them she said, 'I'm never sure whether alcohol is permitted in this country. Why have you been waiting for it?'

'More protocol,' Harry said. 'There's been a shipment impounded in the docks at Mukha for weeks. They've been holding it as part of their protest against one of their aeroplanes being held at Heathrow for non-payment of dues. All sorted out now. Ha ha. Place is suddenly awash. Officially of course it's not allowed. Muslim law and all that. But unofficially they allow expats to import a drop, mainly, it seems to me, so that their own people can siphon it orf.' He thought that perhaps he had been indiscreet in telling Alison all this, so he said, 'Not easy for their government don't you know. They have to placate the fundamentals...' He tailed off. 'Difficult. Damned difficult.' He slumped in his chair, his exuberance exhausted.

Mrs Courtenay said, 'You look tired, darling.'

Harry always took this observation as a compliment. 'Yes,' he said. 'It's been another of those days.'

'Why don't you take a break, Daddy?' Alison said, brightly. 'Why don't we go down to the coast for a while? I want to see the coral reefs in the Red Sea; I've brought my mask and snorkel. You could have a go.'

Her father was about to make excuses but she persisted. 'You said, the last time I was here, that we could. I've seen nothing of the country but the streets between here and the embassy. It's always been the same. I've travelled the world with you and Mummy and seen nothing of it. The people at home just could not believe how ignorant I am about Yemen. There was nothing I could tell them. I haven't seen anything. Please!'

'Your father is not on holiday, dear.'

'It's this business of Abdullah and the uncertainties in the South,' Harry said, while thinking, God... The Red Sea. The heat of the Tihamah. His skin could not stand it. He would blister and peel. 'I have to be on hand. Don't you see?'

'No. I don't see. Everyone else has time off. I haven't even been to Kawkaban, or even to the old souk, which is five minutes from this house.'

'Alison, dear, please don't get excited,' her mother said. 'But that is true, darling. You have promised to take us to the Bab al Yemen souk.'

'Yes I know,' he conceded, 'but it is difficult. Hayward's gone on leave, and the Old Man expects me to be on top of everything, indeed I expect it of myself, and I don't like the idea of you both being jostled in that crowd.' The very thought of it was depressing. Hundreds of Arabs pushing and shoving in those tiny streets. Pickpockets, half of them. 'You must be aware,' he said, 'of the dangers of two attractive European women in such a crush of Arabs.'

'Oh really, darling,' his wife protested.

Alison said, 'The Yemeni women that I've seen are stunners. They must be the most beautiful women in the world. I can't see that their men would be very interested in us.'

Harry Courtenay observed that he could never have made such a remark. Alison was unaware of the implied insult to her mother. To suggest that she might be less attractive than an Arab indeed! His was, he thought, a diplomatic mind, always aware of the minor gaffes. His wife had once been something of a beauty. Not too bright, in the intellectual sense, but capable of making the most of her charms in furthering his career. His daughter, alas, had none of her mother's assets. She was blunt and indiscreet. She had also inherited his own big bones, which made her something of an athlete now, and might well run to fat in middle age. His own corpulence was due to the sedentary nature of his occupation and unavoidable in a man of his age. 'You don't understand the Arab mind,' he said.

'I shall ask Cecil to take me to the coast,' Alison said, seeing her parents' minds working.

'He's gone on leave. I told you.'

'Why not ask the bird people to take her?' Mrs Courtenay said, and Alison knew she would get her way. To have asked would have been denied, whereas if it was her parents' suggestion that she go with the scruffy bird watchers, she could go with their approbation. She stifled a smile as her mother continued, 'They are almost sure to go and see the Flamingos.'

'Flamingos!' Harry exploded. 'We are not on the shores of Lake Naivasha, for Heaven's sake.'

'Well, Cecil Hayward said there were some.'

'Cecil Hayward.' Harry snorted indignantly. 'Bloody Hayward.' A very uncharacteristic explosion, Alison noticed. 'What does Hayward know about birds? People assume, for reasons totally beyond my comprehension, that the man knows everything under the sun.' He laughed derisively. 'Flamingos! They are supposed to be looking for eagles!'

Just an excuse to wheedle money out of some charity in order to have a long holiday at other people's expense. He had met with such before. And now they were traipsing around somewhere up north, completely out of touch and likely to get lorst, or robbed, murdered even. They were behaving totally irresponsibly. He had enough on his mind without being troubled with such people. Might be a good idea if Alison did go down to the blasted sea again and kept the whole lot of them out of mischief for a day or two. He was sure there was trouble brewing in the country, and it was absolutely imperative he be at hand to keep tabs on it. Too many comings and goings these last weeks. Always a sign of unrest – comings and goings and that blasted Abdullah back in circulation. If only I could discover what he's up to. Put a word in the right ear. Good God, young Hayward simply did not realise how fortunate he was, not having the encumbrance of a family with daughters visiting at a time when he could ill afford distractions from the job in hand. Free to go haring off and relax when his leave came round. Disappearing at weekends to go diving under the Red Sea or traipsing up to Kawkaban with his silly little pack on his back. Harry's most important commitment at the moment was to keep tracks on Abdullah, and he simply could not do it under water or shopping in the souk. He quite simply did not have time to go to the coast. 'I'll have a word,' he said 'with these bird-watching fellows. Doubt they'll stay up north much longer.'

★ ★ ★

On Stanley's insistence, the bird-watching fellows stayed up north long enough to visit a small side-wadi where they had seen a flow of water. Among other things they saw a small party of Lichtenstein's sand-grouse, which vindicated his imposition but, after a couple of nights alone and little water to wash in when the plastic wine boxes split, the others persuaded him of the desirability of returning to Cecil Hayward's villa for a few days' rest.

Travelling back to Sana'a was uneventful. Dusk was falling as they approached the roadblock, where the soldiers examined their documents again and waved them through. In each of their minds was the memory of that vast, tumultuous landscape and the improbability of their ever finding the migration route of the steppe eagles. Which pass, bluff, col, peak or escarpment would they use? They could be streaming through that bewilderment of mountains on a narrow front and remain unseen from a mile away. The shimmering haze distorted the images of whole mountains. Eagles, or any other birds, would be impossible to distinguish at a distance.

They arrived back in Sana'a late at night. Muqbel dropped them at Cecil Hayward's door. 'Come back? Tomorrow come back?'

'No!' Stanley said.

Cecil was away. His house was in the charge of his servant, Hamid, a wizened ancient with but a single tooth, which he hooked over his upper lip while interrogating them with his beady eyes. He spoke no English, and they assumed this was one of the reasons that Cecil had employed such a decrepit individual. Hamid let them in after Jack explained who they were, talking through the merest gap between the iron door and the wall topped with splintered glass. He cooked them a meal while they spent time in Cecil's shower, and seemed to take a liking to Eddie, who towered over the little man, with his massive arm around his shoulders.

'Fanks, 'amid,' Eddie said when they'd finished eating, 'that was great.' Adding in an undertone, 'Whatever the hell it was.'

After bringing their notes up to date, they slept. Next morning they were somewhat disconcerted when Hamid announced the presence of the pink diplomat from the embassy, Alison Courtenay's father. They expected to be censured for some unwitting misdemeanour but Courtenay was all solicitation and obsequious smiles. They made him a cup of coffee far too strong for his delicate stomach, which he sipped occasionally, like one drinking tar. He asked about their trip to the north. They had an adventure to relate and told him of the shooting, the Sheikh's house and the sinister Abdullah.

He listened with interest, advised them to keep to the main roads and not to place too much trust in Arab taxi drivers. 'Seems you chaps have set yourselves a formidable task. Over a week of your time gone already.' And, with a condescending smile, 'I must say, I've never seen an eagle.'

'We intend to get our visas extended,' Stanley said. 'We're staying for at least another month.'

'My dear chap, that will not be easy. Most unlikely.' He attempted another sip of the black potion. 'Most unlikely.'

The bird watchers were visibly crestfallen. Over a week gone with not a single migrant eagle. True, they had recorded observations on other species, which were valuable contributions to the ornithology of the country, but their prime objective, to which Stanley now tacitly agreed, was to track the migration of the steppe eagle, and they had seen not a single one.

'Our sponsors have put up a lot of money,' Stanley said. 'I'll go to the Ministry and explain that the expedition is very important and may change a whole concept of trans-Arabian migration.'

'Shouldn't mention expeditions if I were you. They don't like them. Believe it shows up their ignorance about their own country, don't you know.' He let them consider the prospect of returning to the UK with nothing seen of their absurd eagles. 'You've seen the visa department,' he said. 'Chaos. Absolute chaos. Besides, they'll probably suspect you of spying. You have already given them reason to deport you.'

Mike said, 'Whatever for, sir?'

'Visiting a prohibited area.' Harry shrugged his heavy shoulders. 'Everywhere is a prohibited area unless you have permission to travel there.'

'But there are tourists here now and then,' Eddie interjected. 'Where the hell do they go?'

Courtenay forced a smile. This one was definitely not One Of Us, he decided. 'The average tourist sees enough of interest on the main road between here and Ta'izz, with perhaps a quick swim in the Red Sea at Mukha. They are not travellers, in the same sense that you and I are travellers.'

'So there's no chance of getting our visas extended,' Jack stated.

Another one, Harry concluded after a brief glance at the Cornishman, no breeding. He had long remarked on the superiority of the stable Anglo-Saxons over these hysterical Celts on their fringe. 'Quite,' he said. 'May I use Cecil's lavatory?' They were here on sufferance, these people. As well to remind them.

When he was out of the room Jack said, 'We'd better set off early tomorrow and make the most of our time.'

'Can't do much in three weeks,' Eddie grumbled.

'It will be less than that,' Mike reminded them. 'We'll have to be back in Sana'a to make plane reservations, get our visas stamped and all the rest of it. Could take days, actually.'

'We'll do nothing of the kind,' Stanley hissed at them to ensure that Courtenay did not overhear. 'We'll damn well stay here until we've found the eagles or the migration period is over. If our visas run out they'll only make us pay a fine. And if our money runs out the bloody embassy can get us home.'

'I say,' Mike said. 'We can't do that. Lead to all sorts of trouble.'

'We are bloody well staying,' Stanley insisted, 'to do what we set out to do. Find the bloody eagles.'

'You speak for yourself, mate,' Eddie said. 'I ain't spendin' months in a Yemeni jail just for your bleedin' glory.' His Cockney accent was becoming more evident every day, Jack noted.

'What did I tell you...?' Stanley began.

Courtenay returned, seeing with satisfaction the sullen animosity, which was evident among the bird watchers. His ploy had worked perfectly. He proved to himself time and again that he was a born manipulator of men. 'Tell you what,' he said. 'Been thinking. See what I can do. Can't promise anything. Nothing official you understand, but sometimes there are ways and means. Yes, ways and means.'

'That's awfully kind of you, sir,' Mike said.

Jack winced at the 'awfully kind'. Why were these people of the Establishment always creeping up each other's arses, he thought? Mike changed his attitude completely when speaking to this pompous fool.

'Question of strings,' Courtenay was saying. 'Question of strings, what? Now tell me where you plan to go on these adventures of yours. So that we can keep an eye on you. Glad that the old British spirit of adventure is not dead, eh? Shades of Thesiger and the Empty Quarter. Charles Doughty, remarkable fellow.' He had forgotten saying this before.

'Philby...' Stanley added. Courtenay blinked.

'We're not sure where we are going...' Mike began, but Courtenay said, 'Not sure? But you must have a plan. Must have an itinerary. Work out the logistics in advance. Save yourselves no end of problems. Take my advice.'

Jack thought that Stanley might say something antagonistic, or Mike make some further ingratiating remark so, to forestall them, he said, 'Well, we've been north, so presumably we'll go south.'

'South, south. Yes. Go south. Have a look at the Sumarah Pass. See Ta'izz. Go to Mukha. I say... you're not planning to visit the coast, are you?'

'We had hoped to visit the coast,' Mike said, 'but time may be against us, sir.'

'Yes yes. Well, let me worry about the time, young man.' His smile of confident reassurance gave them hope. 'But if you are going to the coast, there is a little something you can do for me...'

He was implying that the favour was owed. A reciprocal gesture in appreciation of a service rendered. They could not refuse.

Alison Courtenay came to see them the next day. They were in the throes of an argument about where to go and how to get there. Jack was for hiring Muqbel again. Stanley said they should go by one of the taxis making the normal run to Ta'izz, or even by bus, and save money. Eddie said he didn't give a damn how they went as long as they got out of the city and began birding again. The arrival of Alison took their minds from the squabble for a while. She was a tall girl, taller than all of them except Eddie, and fair-haired, like her father, but with her mother's darker complexion. She was wearing a skirt and a loose shirt. In jeans she would have been too provocative for the Arabs, her father had insisted. Either she had forgiven Stanley his *faux pas*, regarding her father, or she found it expedient to forget it in order to be taken to the coast. A woman on the expedition was the last thing any of them wanted, they had agreed, but Courtenay had them by the balls. They could hardly refuse his request after his offer of help with the visas. There had been plenty of female undergrads at university who had asked to come on the expedition, but Stanley had refused them all. He did not know how to dominate women, especially one like this, a middle-class, over-privileged, self-confident stalwart who made him aware of his own short stature. He preferred girls from his own background, the ones who thought he was so clever to get to Oxford. Mike took charge of her. Observed the niceties. Made tea. Her going with them had effectively delayed their departure by a day. They were now to leave on the following morning.

'Early,' Stanley insisted.

'If we go by taxi or bus,' Jack said in resumption of his argument, 'we'll be unable to stop when we see something interesting. I say we should find Muqbel and hire him for the rest of the trip. We should have more than enough money according to my sums.'

'There'll be five of us now,' Mike observed. 'With all our gear the taxis may not take us.'

'They'll take twenty if the price is right,' Stanley insisted. 'You've seen how they overload their vehicles.'

'Exactly,' Eddie said, 'I don't want to be killed on a hairpin bend. Even with Muqbel's Land Cruiser we'll be crowded enough.' He was not an impetuous man, but now was the time for decisions and action. 'Why don't we hire him and have done with it?'

'I'm prepared to pay my share,' Alison said.

The offer of extra money mollified Stanley somewhat: 'We can ask what he would charge, I suppose, if we can find him.'

'He'll be at the taxi rank, by the Bab al Yemen souk,' Jack said. 'He told me. I'll go and find him.'

'May I come with you?' Alison asked. 'We can have a look at the souk while we're there.'

She's like her father, Jack thought, thinks it's an honour for people like me to do them favours.

Chapter Nine

They found Muqbel squatting on the ground among the taxis at the bus terminus, just as he had been doing at the airport on the day of their arrival. It seemed so long ago.

'Tomorrow,' he said, and ejected a stream of green qat juice into the dust, 'I no come!'

'No come? Why?'

'Mister Stanley, Mush quais.'

Jack laughed, and agreed with him. 'But tomorrow we take Miss Alison,' he indicated his companion, 'to Mukha. We need a good driver. We can pay for two weeks.'

Muqbel looked her over. He was not impressed. Big European women always treated him like a servant. Ordering him to carry this, be careful with that. He could earn more money ferrying American oilmen from the airport to the new hotel. And in any case he intended to go home and see his family.

'I very busy,' he said. 'Sorry, Mister Jack.'

There was no persuading him. Stanley would have his own way, it seemed. They left him sitting there chewing qat with the other drivers who watched them depart along the road, grinning broadly among themselves.

Jack was disappointed and angry with Stanley. They could go by one of the crowded buses, or hire another taxi, but a driver as helpful and obliging as Muqbel would be hard to find. He led Alison away from the terminus, thinking that half the problems with this expedition they had brought upon themselves.

'I hate the way these people look at me,' Alison said suddenly. 'They are so repulsive.'

'What do you mean?'

'The way they leer at one. I hate it.'

Jack looked at her; she was an inch or two taller than him, and he suspected that she was not being absolutely honest with herself. Men of her circles leered with elegance and called it charm.

'Come on,' he said. 'Let's go to the souk.'

Among the old streets there was little traffic and few people, for some were too narrow for cars, and others rose up and down over flights of shallow stone steps. They wound and twisted in angular and spontaneous confusion, in deep shade at ground level, like chasms, or cracks in sun-baked mud. They opened out here and there, unexpectedly, to bright squares and open spaces where, it seemed, a house, or cluster of houses had collapsed. Time itself was trapped in the maze. In one alleyway they stood pressed into an entrance, with its carved wooden door split and disintegrating, to allow the passage of a water carrier. His donkey was a sad creature, with a faded cloth harness and unshod hooves, which drew the dust of the ground in a reluctant mist behind her. Her old master sat on the empty butt, which had been ingeniously attached to the axle of a small car and fitted with a pair of shafts. He appeared to be asleep and his bare legs, hanging from the hem of his mud-spattered skirt, swung to the rhythm of the animal's trot as the tread-less tyres rolled silently by. One would have thought, in the distant days of his youth, that the demand for water-carriers would ensure prosperity for generations of his family, but nowadays there were pipes and pumps, and even whole rooms for bathing, in people's houses and the world had gone mad. There was no longer the satisfaction of seeing men quench their thirst with the sweet water from the deep, cool well dug by his grandfather. They drank from tin cans; sugar-water and dye that would kill them all, while he carried undrinkable horse piss to building sites for masons to mix concrete. Sleep. It is the will of Allah.

The Bab al Yemen, Gate of Yemen, Souq was a labyrinth of narrow alleys hardly wider than a man's height. The entrance was a tall, ornate gateway beside which traders had set up their stalls and an armed policeman stood picking his nose. There was a shirt seller, a man selling bright squares of silk, a heap of suitcases for men travelling to work in Saudi Arabia, a higher construction of handmade tin chests decorated in bright patterns of gaudy paint. A group of enthralled listeners had gathered round a storyteller.

Inside the gate the crush of people almost obstructed progress but, by good-naturedly pushing and shoving with the best of them, Jack led Alison into the pandemonium. Each shop in the souk is little more than a box in which the proprietor sits surrounded by his wares. The spice seller, the coffee seller, the vegetable seller, watchmaker, cobbler, tinsmith, saddler, gunsmith, all greeted them cheerfully and asked them to buy. The music makers used the most modern of instruments... transistors and stereos.

'They're all very small people,' Alison said, as she hung on Jack's elbow.

'All hill men are small: Ghurkhas, Yemenis, Welshmen, Cornishmen.' He led her on, secretly revelling in her trepidation, until they came to the antique souk, which was quieter, with few customers and slightly larger shops into which four or five people might accumulate among the artefacts. There was a silversmith and a goldsmith where two veiled women haggled over the price of bangles and rings. The street widened into a small square at the junction of several others, like the hub of a buckled wheel. They stopped at an antique shop and looked at the guns, swords, pots, pieces of carved alabaster, soapstone, the Yemeni dagger. 'How much? Kam fulous, khanjar?'

Jack whistled at the price, asked if it was rhinoceros horn, was not understood. Did not know the Arabic for rhinoceros. They did not see Abdullah squatting in a silversmith's shop. They examined some alabaster, some intricate silver filigree jewellery.

'Made by Yehudi,' the proprietor said.

To the next shop. More antiques.

'I dare say they are all fakes,' Alison said.

'Salaam alaikum,' said the trader. He sat among his dusty antiques as though he, and they, had been thus for centuries. He was big for a

Yemeni, broad of shoulder and fat of belly, with a full white beard and calm, smiling eyes. He was old, yet still a handsome man, and his skirt, shirt and head-cloth were spotlessly clean. His large toes protruded from leather sandals. Silently, he picked up this and that, guns swords, daggers, returning them to the shelves and boxes after Jack's shrug of indifference, offering his choicest pieces without a word. He rose from his bundle of carpet and looked about the square. The women were leaving the goldsmith's. Abdullah watched Alison and Jack from among the silver jewellery.

From beneath a pile of carpet the shopkeeper produced a section of carved limestone coping. Maybe some thirty centimetres long, by fifteen wide, it bore the same characters as Jack had seen when Eddie took him to see the stone in the village. Alison showed some interest, turning the carving over in her hand.

'It's heavy,' she said.

'Yes, too heavy to take home.'

The trader had dealt with foreigners before, knew what they wanted. The world was full of criminals. He came forward again, looked furtively about the souk and then, taking them by the hands, led them to the shadowy depths of his shop. He opened a tin chest, the like of which they had seen piled at the gate. He removed some rags, followed by a clean and gleaming pistol that Jack thought he was offering for sale. But the gun was laid aside and, from the bottom of the chest, was taken another bundle of clean cloth concealing a further hidden object. The trader went to the door, looked about, came back and, with his back to the sunlight, unwrapped the heavy bundle. His fingers moved slowly, delicately, until, lying on his hands, they saw an elegantly carved alabaster plaque of a bull's head, in bas-relief, with the horns standing clear of the square-cut base.

'Himyari,' the man whispered. The ancient Himyaritic civilisation of the country. He was behaving, they thought as they glanced at each other, like a ham actor or a caricature of himself, the archetypal Arab trader of false sincerity and cunning.

Jack took the piece in his hand. Beautifully carved, with some inscription in the same ancient alphabet, it invited touch and intimacy.

He ran his fingers over the smooth surface and passed it to Alison.

'How much?' she asked.

The trader smiled. It was beyond value.

'Probably a fake too,' Alison said. 'The sale and export of all antiquities is strictly forbidden.'

'Fake or not, it's a superb piece of work. It's exquisite.' It was too beautiful to dismiss with indifference. He turned it over in his hands with admiration. 'I've a good mind to buy it.' How much? Jack asked in Arabic, 'Kam fulous?'

Abdullah was suddenly in the doorway behind them. He was wearing European clothes, with trousers and shirt; he had shaved the stubble from around his beard and was clean and tidy, with gleaming black hair. Jack might have passed him by unrecognised had he not made his presence known. His shadow darkened the door. He spoke to the old man and there ensued a rapid exchange during which both appeared to be expressing opinions as to whether or not the carving should be sold to the foreigners. From the gestures, and odd word understood here and there, Jack gathered that, in Abdullah's opinion, the thing was part of Yemeni heritage and too valuable to be sold to a foreigner and that it should have remained hidden. The older man was angry, but eventually deferred to the arguments of Abdullah, with whom he was evidently well acquainted. He took the bull's head from Jack, with an apologetic shrug, and folded it back into its cloth. Abdullah expressed his contempt with a quick flick of the head and a click of the tongue.

'What was all that about?' Alison whispered.'

'I'm not sure. They were speaking too fast for me. My Arabic's not very good.'

Abdullah, with a quick smile, indicated that they were to follow him, into the tangle of streets. 'Ta'al, ta'al,' he said. Come, come.

They had no wish to follow Abdullah. Such men are best avoided. They stepped from the shop with apologies to the dealer, who dismissed the incident with a shake of the head, and looked at each other doubtfully, undecided. There was a sudden metallic clatter as the goldsmith drew down the iron rollers and closed the shop.

There was another clanking as his neighbour followed suit. Abdullah looked about him like a wary gazelle, and the two foreigners backed away from him. The street was empty except for traders hurriedly closing shutters. Abdullah flicked his fingers to indicate they should go back into the antique shop.

'Is it prayer time?' Alison asked, as they backed away.

'Too early.'

Then there were two policemen, or soldiers, emerging from an alley and Abdullah had a pistol in his hand. It appeared there as if such a thing was part of him, like some growth or deformity previously unnoticed, and he shouted at the soldiers, a warning or challenge. They hesitated and reached for their holsters. One explosion put a hole in the ground at their feet and they sought shelter back in the alley from where they came. Abdullah ran for a lane without shops that led for a hundred paces in a straight line before turning round a corner, sending another shot slicing into the masonry over their heads as he entered the vulnerable, but only, way of escape. One soldier ran to the alley, pointed his gun around the corner and fired blindly, while the other stepped out to the entrance and took careful aim, holding the gun in both steady hands. As he fired, he spun around like a dancer, with his arms spread wide, before crumpling forward to the ground where a red stain spread into the thirsty dust on his uniform. He was very young.

'Jesus Christ!' Jack said.

The second soldier looked around the corner and fired the last of his ammunition up the street, but no one was there. Abdullah had gone.

Alison was pale as death and stood immobilised by shock. The soldier knelt briefly over his comrade and then ran up the street, angrily reloading his gun.

Jack's initial impulse was to grab Alison and run, but the main gate would be sealed within minutes and they knew of no other way out from this maze of alleys. If they had been seen talking to Abdullah they would be arrested as sure as God made little apples. The antique dealer could betray them. Jack turned to look at him.

The man was folding the oily rags around the pistol he had taken from the tin box. There was no mistaking its outline. The little shop was filled with the faint blue haze and the smell of cordite. As their eyes met they heard shouts in the souk and the noise of a car crashing through the merchandise as it approached. There was a hardening of the jaw beneath the white beard and a hand slipped into the folds of the rag. Their eyes were unblinking... Jack's wide with incredulity, the Arab's calm and expressionless; he was leaving all the decisions to the foreigner, the kawajah.

Jack turned away to Alison who was still staring in horror at the body in the dust. She knew that the soldier was dead, but his limbs still moved, slowly, with his hands clawing the ground and his jaws closing on a disgusting mixture of blood and filth, while the dust settled on his wide-open eyes. She had not seen the shopkeeper's gun. Jack dragged her into the shop as the old Arab wrapped the gun in the rags. He thrust the foreigners roughly aside as the police car slewed to a halt. He pointed to the street where Abdullah and the soldier had gone, crying, 'That way, that way. Hurry! Yallah. Yallah!'

The car went after them with its wings scraping the walls on either side of the narrow thoroughfare. A boy, twelve or thirteen years old, emerged from the direction of the main gate, dashed to the fallen soldier, pulled the pistol from beneath the body and was gone, back into the labyrinth.

Jack's mind refused the evidence of his eyes as the minutes passed. He could not believe what he had just seen, but there was the dead soldier, there was Alison standing speechless in the shop, watching the dead soldier being carried away. There was the goldsmith opening his shop with a clatter of rollers, and others following suit as the square filled with people. There was the white-bearded old trader waiting for Jack's reaction, with the concealed gun still in his hand and a barely perceptible shrug of the shoulders.

Jack nodded a resigned acceptance of the situation. The man hid the pistol back in the box, slammed the lid and went out into the sunshine.

Jack clasped Alison by the elbow and propelled her from the shop, with its ancient and modern instruments of death, and pushed her toward the street leading to the gate without looking at the soldier or the shopkeeper, but he glanced at his own fly-front when he saw the wet stain spreading at the hem of Alison's skirt.

They stole some of Cecil Hayward's whisky. Jack's hand shook as he poured it from the bottle before flopping into one of Cecil's deep, comfortable chairs. Alison had regained her colour and, apparently, her composure. To his annoyance she sat on the arm of the chair and, with her arm lying across his shoulders, kissed him. 'Thanks,' she said. He offered her a brief smile, and his own arm fell to her hip. He suspected that she was patronising him, for there was not a tremble in her body, while his hand refused to be still and his own body felt cold, as of a chill. He sipped the drink. The house was empty apart from themselves, and he assumed the others had gone out for supplies, in preparation for tomorrow's journey. Stanley would not have let them idle for long.

'I suppose it was self-defence,' Alison said abruptly. 'That man could have shot the soldiers before they drew their pistols, if he'd wanted to.'

That man! She didn't know, Jack realised, who that man was. There had been nothing in their conversation to indicate previous acquaintance, so she had assumed that Abdullah was as much a stranger to Jack as to herself. His hand stroked her absently. He was barely aware of the movement or that he was relaxing in the comfort of her human proximity.

'He didn't do it,' he said. Their voices were subdued, as if they were mourners at the poor man's funeral.

'But I saw it,' she protested, 'the soldier stepped out from behind the corner...'

'It was the old man. The antique seller. He shot the soldier in the back.'

'What?'

For the first time there was a tremor in her voice, as if this new knowledge superseded her acceptance of the incident and forced her to reassess her reaction to a death, which was now murder.

'Oh God!' she said. 'These people. When I tell my father...'

'Alison.'

'Yes?'

A slight movement of the head would have pressed his cheek into her breast. The drying sweat in her armpit mingled its musty fragrance with a faint remnant of cheap Arabic Attar of Roses which she had bought somewhere in the city. She had made no mention of the stains on her skirt and either did not know or did not care about them.

'Do you think we could keep this to ourselves?' Jack asked. 'Not tell anybody?'

'If you want.'

He thought her answer was too immediate, impulsive and unreasoned. She obviously intended to tell her father as soon as she saw him. Why not? she was thinking. He had to convince her of the folly in divulging this terrible thing.

'It's just that... your father... I mean, no one knows we saw anything, or that we know anything about this murder. If they did we'd be held for questioning or something. Our birding would be finished. At best we'd be deported. At worst we could be arrested as accomplices in murder. It's nothing to do with us. Just say nothing.'

'And my father?' She could not see his eyes.

'He's been very good to us,' Jack lied. The softness had gone from her. He felt the muscles harden against his hand. 'We don't want to cause him any trouble and,' he felt slightly deceitful in continuing, 'you might not be allowed to come to the coast with us.'

She rose from the arm of his chair and took her glass to the low window, where she stood looking down into Cecil's dry garden. 'And?' she said, evidently not satisfied with his reasons for secrecy.

Jack finished the drink and laid his head back against the chair, letting the spirit burn the chill from his blood.

'Look,' he said, 'it's all right for you. You've got diplomatic immunity.' He remembered the cold stare in the old trader's eyes. 'That old bloke let us go because I saw nothing. Understood nothing.

Neither of us saw a bloody thing. Can't you understand? If we tell anyone, anyone at all, they'll kill us.'

'Kill us?' She turned to face him.

His eyes were closed. He was thinking of telling her that Abdullah had probably killed more men than she had played games of hockey, but declined to do so on remembering that she was unaware that he knew Abdullah. If she didn't know, she couldn't tell.

'They are not Boy Scouts, for Christ's sake,' he said wearily, with his eyes still closed.

She considered that. He was right. It was none of their business. Her father had told her that these people were a murderous, untrustworthy bunch, always brawling and killing each other at the slightest provocation. Now she had proved it for herself. It was not important and no concern of hers. Probably happened every day. 'I was brought up to keep secrets,' she said.

Jack opened his eyes. 'Thanks.'

He felt like crying. It was the shock. 'Let's go off tomorrow and try to forget it.'

He wished that he had pissed himself too and got the shock out of his system. How could these people of the British Establishment keep their upper lips so bloody stiff?

'I shall stay here tonight,' she said. He shrugged. 'So as not to delay you in the morning.' He nodded. 'I'll go home now and get my things.' He nodded again, pursing his lips, and said, 'I'd better come with you.'

She would have none of it, she said she preferred to go alone and that it was not far.

'As you wish.'

He went to the window and looked down at her as she came into the garden. She greeted the watchman, Hamid, as he stirred from his hut and let her through the gate with an obsequious, single-toothed smile, as if this was a perfectly normal, uneventful day in her life. How many secrets did these watchmen keep, who were their masters and what their price, Jack thought as the door was locked behind her. Was old Hamid 'positively vetted'? There was no certainty of safety anywhere now. Nevertheless he felt secure in the cool spaciousness of Cecil Hayward's mafrajh with the evening sun slicing through the windows and illuminating his rugs and Arabic ornaments. The room was unmistakably expatriate British, with the portrait of the Queen on the far wall and its aura of sparse simplicity and authoritative precision in the positioning of the furniture. It was a room of confidence. He turned from the window and picked up Alison's unfinished drink. No point in wasting it.

I don't even know, it suddenly occurred to him, whether the soldier was shot to protect Abdullah or to implicate him. He did not know whose side the shopkeeper was on, or whether Abdullah was now alive or dead. What matter? Jack Pengelly tried to convince himself that he had seen nothing, knew nothing. He didn't know and didn't care. He heard the others arriving, with Eddie greeting the watchman.

''ello 'amid.

'Ma'lish,' Jack said, and drank the whisky. What does it matter?

Alison had serious doubts about withholding the incident at the souk from her father, even though his indifference had induced her to keep practically everything of importance from him all her life. His mind was already full and he had never seriously listened to anything she had told him before. She was still undecided as she let herself in to their villa, despite her assurances to Jack. If she considered it her duty, she would tell, as the only honourable course to take. The truth was, she admitted to herself, that she could not drive the incident from her mind and she looked into the eyes of the dying soldier each time her mind wandered back to those unacceptable seconds. She finally understood why her parents had prevented her from mingling with the populace in the various countries they had lived in over the years. She had heard many stories of violence and death and had experienced vicarious thrills of horror, but the reality was unbearable. She had, however, proved her mettle and kept her head. She had not screamed or panicked, nor let Jack Pengelly see how terrified she had been.

She wandered through the rooms in search of her parents, hoping that they were not there. The place was empty, her father at his office and her mother probably gone visiting some equally bored expatriate wife. The houseboy was asleep in his concrete shack in the garden. She opened the secret alcohol store. No, not that. She went to her own room and sat on the edge of the bed, trembling slightly from the unpurged adrenalin still exciting her muscles. She kicked off her shoes and sat with her arms spread out behind her and her head thrown back. She gazed at the cracks in the ceiling while the fan turned slowly in long, sweeping swathes with a hypnotically regular rhythmic creak as some irregularity in its mechanism repeatedly came full circle. It was the most exciting thing that had ever happened to her. She was ashamed to admit that she was glad she had lived through such an experience, but the excitement was too intense to bear alone. In leaving Jack at Cecil's she had somehow left the emotion of the incident ungratified. She should have stayed and talked it out with him. Gone over it in detail, instead of which he wanted only to forget it, pretend it had never happened. He should have put his arms around her as they sat on the chair. He should have understood what she needed.

There was the old trader, there was the bull's head, there was the pistol, the tall bearded Yemeni, shots, blood. Like stroboscopic pulses of unacceptable truth, the images throbbed in her mind. Then the comfort of Jack's hand feeling the uncluttered contour of her hip. A hesitant, gentle touch which had probably not detected that she never wore anything under her skirt in this climate.

She must wash, but there were scents about her body she had never previously known, and they told of secret, subconscious emotions undetected in herself before, as if for the first time she was totally aware of herself. And she would have liked to keep them around herself forever. But, she must wash, stand in the shower and remove those taints of the unacceptable. The fear, the sweat. Sweet sweat. She removed her clammy shirt and let her head fall back again beneath the slow, creaking revolutions of the fan. Alone, always alone when her emotions revealed their secrets. Even her sweat betrayed her secret and her need of affection so long denied. She slipped the skirt from under her hips and dropped it to the floor and laid back on the bed and let the tears flow unchecked down over her grimy cheeks.

And the shower of warm, hard water washes away the grime and turns to a thin brown stream swirling the dust of the souk from your hair and arms and the fur, and the water swirls over the uneven tiles and the scents and terrors of the day are gone down a hole in the floor. And a little sleep. A warm, drowsing sleep under the slow, rotating fan creaking overhead, and the falling sun spreading the colours of the window glass about the room, like the fragments of a shattered rainbow, and the call to prayers from the mosque as from a distant dream or obliterated memory, and wake to your mother and father entering the house with theatrical laughs and terms of endearment caressing as fog.

She dressed in a khaki shirt and a loose cotton skirt and packed a few changes of similar clothes, together with her jeans, skin-diving gear, light boots and a wide-brimmed hat.

'Ah,' her father said, 'all set for the great adventure?' As usual they had gone straight to the drinks when they came in. 'You can join us in a pre-prandial resuscitation. Just about ready for a little pick-me-up,' he sang. 'Another one of those days. Never mind. Everything under control. Had a good day, my dear?' He was not expecting answers to his questions and poured Alison a drink which he passed to her with a forced smile. 'And how are the eagle seekers? Eh? Ready to soar? Splendid. Splendid. There you are, my dear.' He passed a drink to the eager hands of Mrs Courtenay. 'Do wish your mother and I were coming with you, Alison?'

A lie, to which her mother added, 'We would love to go snogging on the reef.'

'Snorkelling.' Alison said.

Her father sighed a wistful smile of apology, but her mother was absorbed in the siphoning of soda water.

Why should she tell them? They had not the slightest interest or concern regarding the events of her day. She would not tolerate the repression of her excitement by their indifference or condescension.

'Tell those boys,' her father said, 'not to worry about the visas. I'll get Muhammad on to it.'

'One cannot approach higher authority than that,' Alison said, but her father was not amused. He tended to regard all humorous remarks as facetious irrelevancies.

'Muhammad Karim,' he said, coldly, 'our fixer.'

'Sorry, Daddy!'

'So many of them seem to have the same names,' Mrs Courtenay said. 'Rather sweet.'

Harry glanced sharply at his wife. He could never understand why she was so popular. There were times when only his diplomatic training precluded an explosion of wrath at her inane statements.

Outside, in the garden, the houseboy was cooking his meal over a portable gas stove. A moth fluttered at the bare electric light bulb over his bed. Harry drew the curtains. Distant traffic blew horns and the music of many cassette recorders mingled in the sudden night. Alison rose to leave them, the incident at the souk a secret, still.

Harry wrote some addresses, unaware that they had already been given to the bird watchers by Cecil Hayward.

'The agricultural project in Ta'izz, a vet in Dhammar and another in Hudaydah. Not that you'll get that far. They all have radios. Keep me in touch. Mention my name. Tell 'em who you are, my dear. You might mention that we have had word about stirrings. Things going on. In the south. Can't broadcast it. Too many ears.'

'What's going on in the south?' Alison asked bluntly.

'Darling, please,' her mother said.

Alison ignored her. She knew that her father would not have mentioned the politics of the country unless he had some information to impart to his listeners. She looked at him expectantly.

'Damned trouble is,' Harry said after some deliberation, 'we don't know. I certainly don't know, but I get the impression there is something stirring and that Hayward is fully informed and keeping it under wraps. Jolly unprofessional if you ask me. However, due to your father's initiative, we have confirmed that Abdullah Ismail is back in the country and up to no good.'

'Isn't he the foreign minister, or the president or someone?' Mrs Courtenay asked. 'I'm sure I've heard the name before.'

Harry visibly quailed at the idea that anyone in the government might be one and the same as the ex-terrorist from Aden. He quickly recovered his composure. 'No, darling,' he said.

'I shall stay at Cecil's tonight,' Alison said, 'so that we can make an early start in the morning.'

'As you wish, my dear,' Harry said, and went in to his 'Home Office' to listen-in to his scanner for a while before dinner. It was the least he could do, to keep tabs on things.

Chapter Ten

Nadirah Ghanem could not restrain her excitement as she and her brother were driven along the last dusty stretch of road leading to home. She took her brother's hand in her own and gazed lovingly at the familiar landmarks. She saw the villages on the hills, homes of their neighbours and, in the distance, perched in isolation at the top of a cliff, the tall house of her own family.

They left Sana'a after a longer delay than she had anticipated, for Achmed's repeated promises of leaving 'soon', or 'tomorrow, maybe' had both exasperated her and persuaded her not to leave alone. He had gone to Sa'dah, way up in the north, near the Saudi border, and had stayed for a week, though she was relieved that he had not returned loaded with weapons. Then he had spent days seeing people in the capital. 'Business,' he told her, 'Nothing to do with you.' The road from Sana'a wound south through the undulating country along the spine of the central highlands, through Dhamar and Yarim, along the plain of the Qa al Haql, and down to the lowlands through the Sumarah Pass. They turned left before the pass and drove along an unmade road to where the vast plain extended like a wide arrow into the ring of mountains ahead. As the flat fields about them narrowed and the hills rose abruptly on either side, they seemed to be driving toward a wall of solid rock. The low, afternoon sunlight glistened on the golden stubble in the wheat fields. Set in rising terraces among black outcrops in the limestone, they were like rich, glowing fire-pits on the slopes, where wild flowers bloomed in crevices among the rocks, yellow and green contrasting with red limestone, the black hills and the golden corn glowing in the sunshine all about them. Workers in the fields waved in answer to their driver's toots upon the horn.

The taxi skirted a low, boulder strewn, conical hill which stood isolated in the flat fields between the cliffs at the end of the plain. The track petered out and they drove over grazed grass where children tended small, hump-backed cattle, and they halted at the base of the cliff where a flight of irregular stone steps led up to the house. The children came running from the fields, crying shrieks of joy. Nadirah leapt from the car and hugged them all, laughing and crying.

'Oh Joharah, Oh Zana, how you've grown. Mustafa, you little urchin. Has your nose been running for a year?'

The boy submitted to having his nose wiped. Unsmiling, he said, 'Haad marreed.' Grandfather is sick.

They all called him Grandfather, all the children of the villages, though their relationship was more of a distant uncle, brother to their own fathers or grandfathers. He was a much-loved man, old Ali Nasser Ghanem. Like most of the hill men he had left home from time to time. He once worked for the British in Aden, carrying bags of imports to waiting camels, but that was a long time ago, when his own father was anxious for his sons to see the world outside their secluded highlands.

Nadirah rushed to the steps and came breathless to her father's side. There was nothing she could do. He slipped away from them a week later. She was not even sure what he died of. Perhaps it was tuberculosis finally beating him. Perhaps it was the exhaustion of a long hard life. Perhaps it was the will of Allah. She had no means of telling. They buried him among his ancestors in a flat acre among the hills and placed a piece of stone at his head. The same stone might have lain at other heads in times past, who could tell. The sun, the wind and the seasonal rain would soon obliterate the signs of disturbed earth. Achmed was now the head of the family of which Nadirah was the only other member. It was time for both to marry.

She did not chide her brother for the lost days which she could have spent with their father. It was not necessary, Achmed knew how she felt. He tried to console her, but only time would heal her grief. They wandered over the farm, where women and boys from the village gathered the last of the crops and spread the stalks of sorghum on the roof to dry. Nadirah went to Ta'izz, down to the hospital where she was to work. They told her of the medical advances in the country and where the new clinics were, one in Dhamar, one down in the wadi at Medinat al Abid. Everything was improving.

When she returned, Abdullah was in the house. He was lounging on the cushions in the mafrahj, smoking cigarettes and drinking coffee with Achmed. A Kalashnikov and bandoliers of ammunition lay in an untidy, careless heap by the door. Nadirah's consternation amused Abdullah, who laughed aloud.

'What do you want here?' she demanded, their old familiarity entitling her to this impetuous question.

Her brother scolded her for her insolence, for Abdullah was an old friend, he said, son of their father's friend, and was to be welcomed. He was merely resting for a few days after travelling in the north, and would soon be leaving for the coast, on business. He was, Achmed reminded her later when they were alone, a man of influence and some wealth. He would make a good husband for someone. Nadirah smiled. If that was all he wanted she could cope with him for a few days of polite refusal. She suspected, rightly, that her brother had already given approval but had not consulted her for fear of her wrath and predictable protests. She would say, 'I am a modern woman (from whom Allah protect us, he would reply), and will choose my own husband.'

A few days later they saw the trail of dust drifting off the road in the wake of Muqbel Amin Qasm's Toyota Land Cruiser. The dust, together with the dust of other vehicles, settled on the vegetation bordering the road. The leaves and stems were lightly coated in a film of brown which would thicken and suffocate them all unless the autumn rain fell soon and washed them clean. In centuries past, the soft pads of camels had never created such turbulence.

Achmed Ali Ghanem passed a pair of binoculars to his friend and smiled ruefully. 'They come,' he said. 'Just as you said. Are they such fools?'

'Not fools. One from Oxford University.' He laughed at such intelligence. 'But, you know I never underestimate the enemy.'

'And the driver?'

Abdullah looked down at the vehicle nearing the cone in the plain below them. 'He is from Ta'izz, At Turbah. I know it well. One can see the lights of Aden from the cliff top, did you know? It's a thirsty climb, to reach such heights.' He handed the binoculars back. 'Don't worry, he knows nothing and will do as he is told. All taxis are for hire.'

Achmed took his turn at watching the approaching foreigners. 'It's a hazardous venture. Is the consignment ready? Does Hamid know they come?'

He adjusted the focus. The Toyota stopped and the passengers alighted before Muqbel pointed ahead and drove on out of sight behind the hill. The others followed him on foot.

'They have a woman,' Achmed said. 'You said nothing of a woman.'

Abdullah looked more closely at the foreigners. 'Ah,' he said. 'She is the daughter of Courtenay, the pink one. He must have sent her to watch these people. He is a devious camel, that one. He would risk his own daughter.'

Achmed looked quickly at his friend. That deceptive smile. 'You said there was no risk,' he said. 'You know I would not agree to harming them. Apart from anything else it would be counterproductive. Secrecy is our ally. You say it yourself.'

'Don't worry,' Abdullah laughed. 'I would not harm a hair of her British head.' Achmed doubted that. Abdullah had reason to hate all British.

They watched the party of five walk after the Land Cruiser and disappear behind the hill. Achmed was doubtful about Abdullah. He took too many risks, simply because he had nothing to lose. He had no land, no house, no family and tended to regard the more cautious of his compatriots as weak and indecisive. He was a leader, but one who should be followed with prudence. One attribute he had in common with Achmed was his unwavering suspicion of foreigners.

Achmed called to his sister. 'Nadirah. We have visitors.

Foreigners. He winked at Abdullah. 'Let's go down and welcome them.'

Abdullah moved to the door. 'Yes,' he said quietly to Achmed. 'You must extend to them our traditional Arabic hospitality.'

They laughed and smashed their right hands together in a grasp of brotherhood and conspiracy.

★ ★ ★

Stanley Carter had been spitting with anger all day. Despite his insistence on an early start, their departure had been delayed for more than two hours by what he considered to be trivial procrastination. He had walked out at dawn to find a taxi or, if no such were available, to ascertain the times of the buses. Jack had offered to go, for his Arabic may have been useful, but Stanley had suspected that his intention was to hire Muqbel again and insisted that he would do the hiring and go alone. Muqbel, he decided, had become too complacent, insolent almost, and should be replaced.

None of the drivers would accept him. They were either too busy or could not understand English. As to bus timetables, they laughed in his face... what about punctures, breakdowns, sandstorms, flash floods, boiling radiators? Timetables? In the name of Allah, the man was mad!

Stanley returned to Cecil's villa in a vile temper, which was aggravated by seeing Muqbel's Land Cruiser parked outside the rickety sheet-iron gate. So he thinks he can pick and choose to take us according to his whim, does he? Well we'll see about that. They damn well would not hire him, even if it meant walking to the coast with their packs on their backs or riding on a camel. He smiled grimly in anticipation of the imminent confrontation, grasped the bell button dangling from the wires in the wall and had his arm thrown back in a convulsive jerk by 240 volts, more or less, depending on demand and the output from the power station. Hamid found him doubled up, with tears streaming from his eyes as he grasped the aching ligaments of his elbow. Obscenities streamed through his clenched teeth and black, curly beard.

'Karharabah mush quais,' Hamid said. Electricity no good. Stanley pushed past him, not understanding Hamid's sympathetic words. He found his expedition drinking Mukha coffee with the sacked taxi-driver and Alison Courtenay. They were admiring a bull's head plaque, carved in alabaster.

'Who gave it to you?' Jack was asking.

Muqbel was very vague, evading the question, as if it embarrassed him. 'I not know, Mr Jack. I saw man who bring it only. He same-same like servant.'

'Messenger?'

'Aywa. Yes, messenger.'

Stanley stood watching them, allowing his simmering temper to come quietly to the boil. Mike turned the object over in his hands. The workmanship was undoubtedly exquisite, with fine detail about the eyes and flaring nostrils. He said it was either a very good copy or else a genuine Hamyaritic antique and worth a lot of money. Eddie said it looked like a lot of old bull and dug Stanley in the ribs with his elbow. Jack, fearful of consequences, denied knowing why anyone should send him such an artefact. Alison said nothing, but glanced anxiously at Jack as he wrapped the carving in cloth and placed it among the belongings he was to leave at Cecil's villa. He wished to minimise the significance of the gift. 'Perhaps it's from the Sheikh, at Raydah,' he said, and turned to Stanley. 'Have you hired a vehicle? We're all ready to go.'

Faint clicks echoed from the spasms of Stanley's epiglottis... *sk sk sk*, as they looked at him expectantly and he looked at them. What a diabolical shower, he thought. Eddie, the stupid great lout; no sense of responsibility or commitment. Mike, an intellectual dustbin, smatterings of information on every irrelevant subject but no ornithologist. Jack, a typically rebellious Celt needing to be manipulated like a child. And now the expedition was lumbered with Harry Courtenay's daughter, out for a joy ride. None of them had the slightest dedication to the expedition or their leader, but they would learn that he was not a man to be trifled with. The time would come.

'No,' he said. 'I have not hired a vehicle. Neither have I ascertained the departure times of the buses.' He did not miss the smirk on Eddie's face. 'We'll go to the bombsite they call a terminus and wait until a bus departs for Ta'izz. We will all be on it.'

'That's ridiculous,' Jack said. 'Muqbel's decided he can take us and is here. He'll take us and stay with us and bring us back. What's the matter with you?'

'Seems the sensible thing to do,' Mike offered. Stanley turned on him and exploded in anger. 'The sensible thing to do,' he spat, 'is to go on my own and leave you lot here in the comfort of Hayward's lounge. I could do better alone. You are diverted from our objective at the slightest excuse. You are proving to be the most incompetent shower of imbeciles I could possibly have recruited. I remind you that I control the finances of this expedition and that I have it in my power to dismiss any one of you at will. You could be abandoned and forced to finance your own return. My expedition is not obliged to carry passengers.'

There was a prolonged silence. Mike realised that Stanley was venting his anger at being frustrated by the Yemeni drivers but felt it unreasonable to be expected to tolerate such personal abuse. He decided, however, that Stanley would have to be placated if the expedition was to proceed and took a breath to speak. Eddie beat him to it.

'Go on then,' he said.

'Go on what, you lumbering great moron?' Stanley had completely lost control.

'Sack us, and fuck off on your own.'

Of course, he could do no such thing. Eddie laughed at him but Jack, noting the contempt in the laugh, knew that Eddie could be pushed only so far. Stanley seemed to think that Eddie would accept any personal insults, but he was wrong. Big Eddie would turn violent if provoked beyond his limit and the violence would be sudden, without warning. Stanley was playing a dangerous game.

Alison was beginning to think that it had been a big mistake to accompany these people. She could wait and go to the coast with Cecil when he returned from leave. The difficulty would be explaining her decision to her father. She knew that her parents were glad to see her off their hands for a few days and she did not want to tell them about the incident at the souk. 'If we're going,' she said, 'we'll have to get a move on. It's a long way to Mukha.'

Stanley had no choice but to concede that they were obliged to hire Muqbel again. He turned to Jack in a final attempt to save face. 'All right,' he said. 'We'll hire him on the same terms as before. But I hold you personally responsible for his behaviour. You seem unable to grasp the basic avarice of these people. Can't you see that there's a conspiracy among his mates to ensure that we hire him and no other for the rest of our stay? Normally they would jump at the chance to take money off a bunch of ignorant foreigners, and there's no way he would hire himself and the vehicle for what we can offer him. We'll be damn lucky if he doesn't disappear with all our gear one night or leave us stranded at the roadside having a piss.'

The image of the vehicle disappearing with all their gear while they stood with their cocks in their hands induced the opposite of Stanley's intended reaction.

They burst out laughing, although Jack watched Muqbel's face, searching for some clue as to why he had changed his mind after being so adamant that there was no way he'd hire his vehicle to Mr Stanley. Muqbel was laughing with the rest of them, enjoying their hilarity, although having no idea what it was about. 'Come on, then,' Jack said. 'Let's get loaded up.'

'Good idea, actually,' Mike said, happy to leave the quarrel behind them.

Two hours later, about a hundred and twenty kilometres along the road, the Land Cruiser broke down. They had stopped for petrol in Yarim, a straggling town with shops and garages along the main street which passed between the old buildings on either side. Muqbel suggested they go in to a mutbakh for coffee, and they left the vehicle at the garage while they sat in the little eating-place with a crowd of other travellers. Alison was uneasy at first, to be in such close proximity to so many grimy Arabs, but Jack and Mike enjoyed the break, Jack in particular using the opportunity to practise his Arabic away from any threat from Abdullah or the old shopkeeper. They climbed back into the vehicle refreshed and happy to be on their way but, after fifteen kilometres in which the engine spluttered and stalled several times, they finally came to a halt in the centre of a plain, just a few kilometres before the Sumarah Pass and the long descent down the escarpment to the head of Wadi Zabid. They had climbed another five hundred metres since leaving Sana'a and were some two and a half thousand metres above sea level. The additional altitude and the advancing autumn brought a noticeable chill to the air, although the sun was still an unobstructed brilliance in the clear sky. Muqbel turned the ignition key. The engine fired and stopped again.

'Benzine wasikh,' Muqbel said.

Stanley chewed on his lip with exasperation. 'What did he say?' he asked, with an effort of self-control.

'Dirty petrol.'

'Bloody hell,' Stanley said.

The engine fired, Muqbel pulled out on to the road. After a few splutters and convulsive jerks as he accelerated, the engine died. He smiled apologetically, tried again. By driving very slowly he kept the vehicle going but the slightest acceleration caused the fuel-starved engine to stall. He coaxed the vehicle along the road and eventually came to a small village.

'Maybe stay here?' he said.

'We are not staying here,' Stanley said, looking at the crowds gathering about them. 'And that is final.'

None of them wished to stay in the village. Where could they wash, cook, do their business, without a crowd of children and other curious spectators pestering them? They also told Muqbel that they could not stay there. He explained that it was quite common for dirt to get in petrol pumps. It was not his fault. If they would be patient he would enquire as to where they could camp. He left them and returned after talking with some people who were threshing corn on a stone-paved area just outside the village.

'Find good place,' he said, and eased the vehicle forward. He turned left off the main road and drove slowly along a dirt track until they came to the small, conical hill in the plain below the house of Achmed and Nadirah Ghanem. The passengers alighted and Muqbel drove a little further and parked on the raised ground to the north of the hill from where they had a good view of the country around them. There was no doubt that it was a good site. The hill sheltered them from the view of a solitary house perched high on a cliff, while before them the plain stretched far into the distance. To their right, the east, was an area of reeds and a small stream, which meandered around the cone to the cliffs after passing beneath an ancient stone bridge. Stanley admitted that it was an ideal campsite but, 'That's not the point,' he said. 'We're losing a day at the coast because of the incompetence of that bloody driver. If he finds a good campsite that does not compensate for the loss of a day.'

'Not his fault if the petrol's full of dust, Stan, everything else in the country is.' Eddie laughed at his own remark. He had evidently forgiven Stanley his earlier, insulting comments, or was making conciliatory gestures for the sake of harmony. 'In any case, we were all late this morning and you were the last up, remember?'

'Last up I may have been, but if your mind can recall the events of a few hours ago, you will remember that I was also the first one ready to leave. And, don't call me "Stan".' He climbed back into the vehicle, muttering to himself, and passed out the gear. 'We'd better get this stuff unloaded if we are to prepare a meal before dark. Then our friend can take his Japanese scrap-heap to the nearest garage, wherever that is, and get it fixed.'

As if setting an example, he unloaded all the gear and set it on the ground, but Mike and Jack were looking around at the scenery with Alison. They were at the southern edge of a vast area of cultivated plateau surrounded by jagged outcrops of rock and peaks of mountains way off on the horizon. The whole of the flat area was cultivated yet there was no one to be seen in all the land before them. They had seen these sudden bursts of energy from Stanley before. After setting an example, he usually found some reason to abandon the more arduous tasks. They were getting to know him and let him get on with it.

'Odd thing about this country,' Mike said. 'There never seems to be anyone in sight, outside of the towns, yet one invariably feels under surveillance. It's odd. Though one becomes used to it.'

'How clear the air is,' Alison said, 'and how colourful everything looks. The black rocks seem to emphasise the shades of the fields and the blue of the sky.'

'It's the altitude,' Stanley said, brusquely. He had the cooking utensils out and was setting up the stove with a noisy clatter. 'I suggest,' he added, 'that we cease admiring the scenery and get some work done.'

'Right,' Eddie said. 'If you're doing the cooking, we'll set up the tents and find some water.'

This had not been Stanley's intention. He hated cooking, wangled his way out of it whenever possible, but saw that he was now obliged to do it. As an indication that he was still in charge, however, he said, 'And where do you think we can get fresh water here? Use the water in the containers.'

'Yours are busted. Muqbel's are empty.'

'There seems to be a tremendous number of swifts flying over the plain,' Mike said. 'Can you see them?'

'Company,' Jack said. 'We have company. They all turned to see two people approaching.

'Gawd,' Eddie said under his breath. 'It's that bloke and that bint again, the ones we saw on the plane. I hope they don't chuck us out.' They waited until the two Yemenis approached them.

'Salaam alaikum,' said Achmed.

'Wa alaikum salaam,' Jack replied.

Achmed looked them over. There was an uneasy silence. Nadirah stood behind her brother, glancing at Alison, who smiled awkwardly. Achmed spoke to Muqbel, who replied politely in deference to Achmed's authority. Jack thought he had better attempt to explain their presence and was searching for words when Stanley said, 'I suppose he's the local squire. Can't you say something to him?'

Achmed went to the car. He looked inside. He looked at the folded tents lying on the ground. He was wearing a long skirt and a check jacket. His headscarf trailed over his shoulder. A heavily embroidered belt around his waist held an ornate dagger against his stomach, the traditional khanjar. He was spotlessly clean, whereas the birders were grimy with the dust of travel. Although he was the smallest man present, he commanded respect by reason of his bearing and innate dignity. There was a lively glint in his dark eye. His beard was neat, his teeth white. He turned to his sister, who was wearing a full, long-sleeved dress of dark red and green and a scarf over her hair and shoulders. He spoke to her so softly that Jack could not understand a single word. Muqbel laughed.

'What's he saying?' Stanley demanded. Muqbel shook his head to indicate that he could not repeat such a remark.

'My brother,' Nadirah said, in her faintly accented English, 'is making a joke. He said the Bedouin usually bring black tents and camels. He has forgotten his manners.'

Achmed's face broke into a smile. He went to Stanley and held out his hand. 'Welcome. I am Achmed Ghanem.'

'Stanley Carter. You speak English.'

'Just a little.'

They made the formal introductions. Alison shook hands with Nadirah, the one so tall strong and blond, the other so frail and dark. The bird watchers explained what they were doing.

'How interesting.'

Could they stay here?

'As long as you wish.'

Was it all right to wander around the area with binoculars?

'Of course. Go where you wish.'

Was there a shop?

In the nearest village, a cluster of houses in the flat plain in the distance. A garage? Best to go back to Yarim. It was not far.

'We will be leaving tomorrow,' Stanley said.

Achmed spread his hands before him. 'Inshallah,' he smiled. God willing.

Was there fresh water?

'I will show you,' Nadirah said, and Alison took one of their water containers and followed Nadirah to a spring of sparkling clarity near the bridge where Nadirah filled it by carefully lowering it below the surface and allowing the water to flow in without clouding. 'It looks very clear,' Alison observed.

'Have no worry. We have been drinking this water for generations. I have sample tested, just for the sure. It is hard of the limestone, but contains no harmful bacteria.'

Alison thought the fact that the water had been drunk for generations was of little assurance, but was impressed by the prudence of getting the water analysed. She was about to make a congratulatory remark and ask where it was done when Nadirah said, 'Tell your friends not to make dirty, this water, and to be careful where they drop the excrement.'

A red flush of embarrassment and anger spread over Alison's face. The idea! That this Arab should admonish the daughter of a British consul officer on the niceties of personal hygiene was sheer effrontery.

'You are not allowed the tenting at the roadside in Britain,' Nadirah said flatly. 'By the law, yes? I have seen the... tayeed, notice, mush kiddah, isn't it? Here we have no law. It is unnecessary but, if your friends do not wish to offend my people, they must remember such things.' She smiled.

This advice is for me too, Alison thought. She means no offence and is being helpful. Her directness is merely the limitation of a foreign language. 'I will tell them,' she said.

'Shukran.' Thank you.

'You speak very good English.'

Nadirah acknowledged the compliment with a smile. 'I have been working in Britain. I am a nurse.'

Alison was forced to admit that this 'Arab bint' was probably her intellectual superior. The revelation was somewhat disconcerting. Her father's attitude, that the British were superior to all foreigners, had pervaded her life and, despite her travels, she had met very few, except on formal occasions. It suddenly occurred to her that, apart from a smattering of French, which she never used, she knew no other language. Hardly a word of Arabic had she learned.

Nadirah told her more about living in the country. 'The water is pure, but we often have to carry it to the house for drinking. We have a...' another pause for the right word ' ...cistern up there, we call it barikah, which fills with rainwater. When the barikah is empty we know the value of water, believe me. It is hard work to carry water and the women do it, this hard work. My father said I have become soft and corrupted by Western ways because I want a water pump and a bathroom.'

'Will he do it? Install a pump?'

'He is dead. One week. Achmed, my brother is head of the family now. Perhaps I can persuade him, inshallah.'

'I am sorry, about your father.'

'Thank you.'

Your house is very beautiful.'

'Yes,' Nadirah said. 'Picturesque, you say. I know. But how can we provide them with water, electricity, roads, when every village is on a mountaintop? Achmed is an engineer. I leave it to him.'

'An engineer?'

Alison was astonished that this brother and sister from this remote village in such an apparent backward country should have achieved so much. 'Did he also study in England?'

'He was in Prague.'

'Prague?'

Jack came over for the water. Alison asked if she should come and help. He told her to stay where she was. Stanley was no cook and would have her do it all if she offered help. He hoisted the water-container on to his shoulder. It was heavy.

Nadirah watched his return to the camp, where Achmed was regarding the preparations with amusement. Alison turned again to the scenery and the intense colours in the clear air.

'You are very fortunate, living here. It is very beautiful.'

'Yes. Very beautiful.'

'So peaceful.'

She suddenly recollected the incident in the city and the utter contrast to the tranquillity of their present surroundings. She remembered the noise, the crowds, the dirt, then the convulsions, the blood, and the dust settling on those open, staring eyes. She recalled the terrifying helplessness of witnessing murder as if in a dream, a nightmare. She shivered involuntarily and felt herself trembling from the effects of shock, long delayed.

Nadirah immediately perceived the change of mood. 'You are cold? No? You are sick?'

'No. I'm all right, thank you.'

She was cold. The sun was going down. She wanted to go to the loo. Where? Oh God, this was going to be an awful week. 'I'm just a bit scared,' she said.

'Scared?'

'Frightened, worried. I am afraid of some things in your country. I'm sorry.'

'It is a little strange for you. I was afraid in Britain, at first.'

'Yesterday,' Alison said to justify her fears, 'we saw a man killed in Sana'a. He was shot.'

She heard Jack's insistent voice... We know nothing. We saw nothing... but, with her eyes misting over, she said, 'He was so young. A policeman. Or a soldier. I don't know.'

'Where you see this?'

She told Nadirah what had happened. With a shake of the head she controlled herself sufficiently to prevent the flow of tears and did not see the look of consternation pass over Nadirah's eyes. 'Ah well, we have murders in England. I must try to put it from my mind.'

Nadirah regarded her sympathetically. Such a soft heart for a big, strong woman. 'All cities are dangerous,' she said. 'But you are safe here.'

The long fingers of shadow crept over the plain as they returned to the camp. Nadirah and Achmed went to their house, climbing the long stone stairway up the face of the cliff in animated conversation.

Stanley's meal was eaten in silence. The darkness was upon them before they had finished clearing up his devastation among the cooking pots. They filled in the daily log by the light of the portable gas light and this caused Stanley more annoyance, for there was little to record, just the birds they had seen at the roadside or perched on telephone wires. Another day wasted, he grumbled.

Muqbel, as usual, was to sleep in his vehicle. The others had pitched their tents in a semi-circle, with the flaps towards the gaslight, stove and boxes in the centre. They could see lights from the villages atop the mountains in the distance, while along the main road, to the west, there was a continuous stream of headlights from traffic too far off to be heard. The night was utterly silent, yet there were people all about them.

'Are we safe here?' Alison asked.

The men looked at her, doubtfully. They had forgotten their own fears on the first nights of sleeping out in this country. They had become used to the occasional bursts of gunfire. 'It's only a wedding,' or 'Probably the Sheikh's birthday,' but Stanley was not to let her off lightly.

'Probably as safe as anywhere in this country,' he said as he crawled into his tent. 'They're an unpredictable shower.'

'Here, very safe place,' Muqbel said. 'Dhi Bin no good. Raydah mush quais. Here, same-same sleep in own garden.' He climbed into the vehicle, saying, 'Masa al kier.'

'Good night,' Jack said.

The cab radio was soon tuned in to the vibrant music of Arabia. A woman singing.

'Bloody cacophony,' Stanley said.

'I like it,' Jack told him.

'So do I.' Alison found herself siding with Jack for fear that Stanley order Muqbel to turn it off.

'It sounds like Oum Kalthoom,' Mike said.

'What the hell is Oum Kalthoom?' Stanley could not forbear from asking.

'The singer. Oum Kalthoom. She was a very popular Egyptian singer. She's dead now.'

133

'Bloody know-all,' Stanley said under his breath.

Mike exchanged grins with Eddie.

'Some of us did our homework before coming on this trip,' Eddie said. Stanley did not hear. He was crawling into his tent.

'Are you warm enough?' Jack asked Alison.

'Yes. I brought plenty of clothes. Don't worry. Aren't you going to turn in?'

'No. Not yet.'

Stanley was closing the flap of his tent. Mike was getting into his. Eddie was putting on another pullover.

'I hope,' Stanley said, 'that you are not intending spending half the night chatting.'

Alison checked her watch. It was just after eight.

'Some of us have had a busy day,' Stanley said as he ran the zip fastener up the tent flap.

'Sorry,' Alison said.

Jack rose and beckoned her with a nod of the head. She followed him out of the circle of lamplight into the darkness.

'Stanley sleeps ten hours a night,' he said, 'when he feels like it.'

'That's a lot,' she said, as she picked her way through the dusk.

'Too much. With twelve hours of darkness at this latitude I find that turning in too early has the effect of inducing a restless night, so I get less sleep, not more.'

He led her to the dark shapes of boulders at the base of the hill. 'Mike often reads for an hour in his tent. Must be costing him a fortune in batteries.'

He walked on, passing among the boulders before climbing up the slope. She followed close behind him and he registered the fact that she did not get out of breath, despite the altitude. She was fit. They climbed to the top of the cone, which took no more than five minutes, and rested against an outcrop from where they could see all about them. The night was lit by stars in the inky sky and the campsite, with the central gaslight, was shooting arms of yellow light between the tents. Someone was moving about and his shadow leaped away, returned and slipped into the tent beside him. 'Eddie,' Jack informed her.

She nodded. 'Ah.' She could see his eyes sparkling with the light reflected from the camp, or was it the stars?

'You must be tired,' he said. 'You probably slept as little as I did last night.'

'No, I'm not tired. In fact I slept very well.' She slipped her hands into her pockets. 'Shock, I think.' She laughed nervously. 'Do you really believe we're under threat, Jack? I keep thinking about the bull's head.'

'So do I. But I've come to the conclusion that we must accept it as a gift of gratitude, rather than a threat. But we should remember that they could be equally as vindictive as they are generous. It is, perhaps, a warning, to keep our mouths shut.'

'Oh Jack.'

'Yes?' He turned to face her, anticipating her reply.

'I told Nadirah, the Yemeni girl, about the soldier.' He did not reply or respond in any way. She felt nervous of him. 'Please understand,' she pleaded. 'I don't know why I told her. I just feel she can be trusted.'

'Yes. Well, let's hope so.' He was obviously very angry.

'Oh, I'm sorry. But I'm sure she is genuinely friendly towards us, really.'

She was being over-emphatic, began trembling slightly, shivered and hunched her shoulders against the cold, although her shivers were induced by more than the temperature.

'I hope you're right,' Jack said.

He was standing before her, with his own hands in his pockets, and she sensed the sudden indifference in his voice, as if he had lost interest in her and had become preoccupied with something he was watching. He was staring past her into the night. 'Can you see the swifts?' he said.

She turned to see that the moon was rising over the distant mountains like a huge ball of red light. Two dark strands of cloud bisected the disc, which was ascending into the clear black sky of hanging stars. A long, involuntary breath of awe whistled though her lips in appreciation of the scene before her, and they watched in silence as the moon rose clear of the mountains and glowed, as if incandescent, with warm orange light. The crisp, black silhouette of the skyline beneath the moon melted into misty obscurity to their left and right, where the low hills rose in darkness and distance undefined. Alison eventually turned to see Jack's reaction to the scene and saw that he was almost oblivious of her presence. His eyes were looking unblinkingly at the plain below them, and she turned again to the moon. Somewhere, among the low hills bordering the plain on the other side of the marsh, there was a stretch of water and the moon was becoming reflected on its unruffled surface in the windless night.

'That's a barikah,' Jack said at last, as the water became red, glinting in the black shadows among the hills. 'The water. It's a reservoir. A barikah.'

'I see it,' she said.

She looked at him again. He was smiling at her. The moonlight was becoming trapped in her fair hair, although her features were in darkness. 'Probably good for birds,' he said, vaguely.

'I see.'

'Have you ever slept under the moon? No? You should. No one knows Arabia until they've slept under her moon.'

She thought he was taunting her, implying that she would never know, or love, this country as he did.

'It's too cold,' she said.

'Not on the coast.'

He was still smiling at her. In this dark landscape he had become her superior, because he was unafraid of it, while she was still nervous. He came close to her side and leaned over the boulder with her. Their shoulders touched.

'Sorry,' he said.

'That's all right.' She studied the rising moon.

'I'm going down,' he said. 'If there's anything you need to do in private, go among those boulders, over there. And mind the snakes.'

Their heads turned to face each other. She looked at him and grinned. They were very close, their shoulders touching. Their smiles and grins dissolved into frank, searching stares as they scrutinised each other's eyes. Jack turned until his body faced her. She continued looking at him for a while and then looked away and spread her elbows on the boulder, with her chin on her arms. 'Snakes?' she laughed and the moonlight lit her hair in a halo of gold as she turned her head, moved closer and smiled at him.

After gazing at her for a minute, his features blank, Jack suddenly turned away. 'See you in the morning,' he said quietly, and began the descent to the tents.

Alison remained motionless, without replying, and watched him go. He went down slowly, occasionally glancing at the moon, where black silhouettes of swifts could be seen moving towards the Sumarah Pass. His slight, almost slender form was soon lost in the darkness and she heard stones clinking under his feet.

She turned her head and laid her cheek on her arm. What was the matter with him, she thought, do I have to unzip his bloody flies, or something?

Chapter Eleven

There was a tinkling of ice as a sheet of frozen condensation fell from the flaps to the stony ground when Alison opened her tent. She could not believe that the temperature had fallen so much in the night, for she had slept completely unaware of it in her sleeping bag. However, with the first rays of sunshine spreading over the plain, the sun was already melting the ice and warming the air, and the bird watchers were sitting around the stove drinking tea as the shadows receded to the east. They had their binoculars hung around their necks or close at hand, ready for immediate use.

'Cup tea?' Jack asked.

'Yes please, but I'll come and get it.'

Before she had emerged from her tent, however, Muqbel brought a cup over to her, saying, 'Sabah al kier.' Morning of health.

'Oh, thank you, Muqbel.'

He smiled happily at her. 'Today, very cold,' he said. 'Some more cup tea, Mr Mike. This very good tea. I buy from Bab al Yemen souk.'

'Are you intending to spend the day serving tea?' Stanley said. 'Or are you taking this car to the garage?'

'Go after half hour. Mumkin I mend sayarah here. Mush kwais garage. Fulous k'teer hunak.'

'What the hell is he talking about?' Stanley turned to Jack, who grinned at Muqbel. 'The garage is too expensive,' Jack said. 'He wants to repair it here.'

'We're going to a garage to have the job done properly. I want no more breakdowns on this trip. We leave for the Tihamah this afternoon, no matter what. It shouldn't take more than an hour to drain and clear the fuel system.' He was speaking calmly, with authority, as a leader. The others made no comment. 'I shall go with you to the garage, Muqbel, to see the job done properly.'

Muqbel evidently saw that Stanley meant to have his way but, instead of objecting, he said, 'All men come, laish la. You see Naqil Sumarah. I go Yarim b'sayarrah.'

'What is he saying?' Stanley said with great forbearance. 'It would help if he spoke English.'

'He suggests that we all go to see the Sumarah Pass and wait there while he takes the car to Yarim for repair. Then, presumably, he'll pick us up on the way back.' He was getting fed up with Stanley's refusal to try to understand Muqbel's broken English.

'Seems like a good idea,' Eddie said. 'All the swifts are going towards the pass, and there are some raptors above the hills over there which will probably follow them.' They all rose to their feet and scanned the sky with their binoculars to see the birds Eddie had found.

'Buzzards,' Jack said.

'And kestrels,' added Mike. 'I say! Just look at those swifts.'

The sky overhead was full of them, thousands of them, all moving towards the pass.

'A few hours at the pass might well prove productive,' Mike said in mock understatement.

'Damn right,' Eddie said, enthusiastically.

'I'd quite like to go,' Alison said, catching the enthusiasm of the others.

Stanley considered the proposition. 'I shall stay with the vehicle,' he said.

He was implying that this was a duty rather than a desire and that he would far rather spend the time sitting at the Sumarah Pass watching migrants. 'And someone must stay here and watch the gear.'

'All thing OK here,' Muqbel said. 'Harramy mafish.'

Stanley simply looked at him while waiting for Jack to translate.

'No thieves here,' Jack said. But, as he alone had not actually expressed a desire to see the pass, he suggested that he stay behind while the others went as soon as possible, leaving the camp chores to him. When they had gone, he cleaned the campsite, put the kettle on the burner and went to the spring for water. As he was returning, he saw Nadirah walking round the hill and heading for the tents. Seeing him alone, she hesitated, but Jack waved and she came on. They exchanged the formal greetings and he placed a box for her to sit upon. She declined to accept, as she did his offer of tea, looking doubtfully at their cooking facilities.

'I wish to speak with Miss Courtenay,' she said.

Jack looked at her sharply. For some inexplicable reason, he thought she was lying. 'She's gone to the Sumarah Pass with the others,' he said, thinking it highly unlikely that any of them could have left the site without it being known to those in the house perched over the plain.

'Why Sumarah?'

He explained about the vehicle and the others' departure. 'The pass may be a route for the birds too. They often use the same way through mountain ranges as we do. And the views from the top of the pass are quite spectacular, so we've been told.' He doubted if she would understand 'spectacular' but if so she gave no indication of it.

'Here is the more beautiful,' she said. 'But why to stay here alone and not see also?'

'Somebody has to guard the camp.'

He said it without thinking, without anticipating the implied insult to her people, and he flushed with embarrassment as her spine stiffened with annoyance. 'I'm sorry,' he spluttered. 'I didn't mean...'

'You did not mean the wogs are not to be trusted. I understand. From a country where there is so much crime, you have learned to be careful. I was also always very careful in Britain.' She relaxed and smiled slyly at him, relishing his discomfiture.

'Yes,' he mumbled. 'Yes, well, you're right. Yes...'

She allowed him to recover his composure and continue with... 'I mean, there's good and bad everywhere. At least...' He was going to say we don't have to live in cliff-top fortresses, but desisted. Given the history of the country, the statement would have born no relevance to the present day.

'At least? What at least?' she asked.

'Oh, nothing.'

There was a long silence. He thought she considered it improper to stay with him alone, yet was reluctant to leave. He searched for conversation which might delay her departure. 'Alison will be back at mid-day,' he said.

'Inshallah.'

'You and your brother speak good English.'

'I speak English superlative. My brother is fair only,' she said indifferently, as if she had made the observation many times. 'He speaks better the Czech.'

Her vocabulary was more extensive than her familiarity with the idiom, Jack noticed. A condition with which he himself had long been acquainted. But Czech, indeed.

'Does he, be damned.'

'And what will you do? Your work today?' she asked.

He told her: check the marsh, look through the reeds, bring his notes up to date and, if there was time, climb the hill behind them to have a better look at the plain.

'You see my house,' she said.

'Now?'

'From the hill. You do not look with the durrbeen... what is this?'

'Binoculars.'

'Yes binoculars.'

'Why not?'

'It is the bad manner.'

'Ah. Yes, I see. OK. I'd really like to go over there, but I won't have time.' He pointed. 'There is a barikah among the hills. Apart from the marsh, it is a bit bare for birds just here.'

'What do you mean? Bear or bare?' She was demonstrating her command of the language, and laughed. 'Wild animals, or naked?'

'Naked. Barren. There is no life.' He thought it prudent to mollify her resentment of any implied criticism of her country. 'I mean Yemen is a little barren compared with Britain.'

'Nadirah smiled, enigmatically. 'You think?' she said. She rose

141

to her feet. 'I shall come at twelve o'clock, to see Miss Courtenay. Goodbye Mister...'

'My name is Jack. Masallamah.'

'Masallamah.'

By noon he had checked the surrounding area and was waiting for the others to return. It was hot in the sun. He climbed the hill to escape the heat and sat among the boulders in the shade. He thought about the Arab girl. There seemed no reason for her visit to the camp that morning and he was sure she had not forgotten his name. That she was perfectly aware that Alison had gone off with the others, he had no doubt; it was as if she had come to ask something, or determine something, but had changed her mind. A light breeze cooled him. The air was crisp and clear. He could see far into the distance. He checked the skies for eagles. There were buzzards soaring over the distant peaks. He heard the cries of children from behind him, over the rocks. He climbed a little further, to the top of the cone, from where he found he could see into the house of the Ghanem family, perched on the edge of the opposite cliff. He could see into a courtyard formed by a drystone wall surrounding the building. The house was soundly built and well maintained, with the windows of the top floor outlined in white. The children were shooing goats from the massive, ornately carved door, which was weathered to a timeless, silver grey. Nadirah was with the children. Near the gate into the yard he could see the entrance to a cave, or chamber, cut into the cliff, and from there stone steps led down the cliff to the level of the fields. As he watched Nadirah and the children, Jack saw her brother, Achmed, emerge from the cave. He was followed by another.

Jack's hands rose to his binoculars. It couldn't be. But it was! No, he changed his mind. It couldn't be Abdullah. Not here and, besides, it is the bad manner. The two men went to the house. Jack moved to where he was not silhouetted against the sky. He was looking south, but the sun was too high in the sky to be in his eyes. He could see it glinting on the surface of the barikah over to the left, in the east. The house before him could be overlooked from the cliffs in that direction too. The stream below trickled through rich, close-cropped grass and seemed to run into the solid rock of the cliff below the Ghanem's house. Nadirah looked once in Jack's direction, but he was sure she had not seen him. He was about to sneak away when Achmed came from the door. He and Nadirah seemed to be quarrelling and the children stood watching in apprehension. She grabbed something from the stone wall and began running down the steps. Jack dodged back among the boulders and scrambled down the slope to the dismantled tents and boxes of equipment in time to greet her again with the formal welcome, but she forestalled him.

'Come,' she said without preamble, 'I will show you Arabia Felix as she is.'

'What do you mean?'

'Come.'

Jack picked up his light pack and followed her around the base of the conical hill, walking on the track which was used by the animals as they were driven out to pasture on the plain in the early mornings. She was barefooted, carrying her sandals by the straps in one hand. She walked before him, carefully choosing the spots to drop her footprints in the dust between the stones. She was very slender and small, like a child on the track in front of him, but with a sensuous woman's curves as she skirted the limestone outcrops jutting across the path. He found himself avoiding her footprints in the dust, placing his boots between or to one side of them, for they seemed so delicate and perfect that it would have been sacrilege to destroy them. It was absurd. In a few minutes they would fill with dust and in as few hours be obliterated forever by the hooves of goats or the feet of men, gone into oblivion with the thousands of others which had similarly left their impression on this land. He scuffed his boots through the prints in front of him and deliberately placed his feet over several more, to expunge them completely as he walked behind her. He took his eyes from the track as they rounded the base of the hill and came towards the stream. She trod on a hidden thorn and limped a few paces, swearing softly.

'Why do you not wear your shoes?' he said. 'You will cut yourself.'

She turned to him, laughing. 'You can see I am not used to it. My feet have become soft but I want to feel the soil of Yemen under my feet. I do not expect you English to understand.'

Jack took a breath, to tell her, as he had told so many others, that he was not exactly English, but deferred. What point?

'I think I do,' he said.

She shrugged, 'Mumkin.' Possibly. She dropped her sandals and slipped her feet into them. 'Come,' she said, and led on to the cliff.

Her house was high above them and, as they followed the stream and approached the shadows of the cliff, he saw that it was cleft in two. A narrow gorge, some twenty metres wide, twisted abruptly out of sight after penetrating the sheer wall of rock that rose on either side of it. A donkey grazed, untethered on the narrow strip of grass beside the water. It was in deep, cool shade.

The gorge narrowed until the path where they walked was the only level ground between the water of the widening stream and the towering rocks, which loomed over them in precarious stability. There was an eerie silence, as if outside sounds could never penetrate these cool depths. They had to scramble over boulders in the water as the defile narrowed to no more than the width of the stream. Nadirah led him on and her own silence became as oppressive as the towering rocks above them. He felt constrained to silence also and glanced uneasily at the narrow wedge of blue sky overhead. They turned another bend in the tortuous river bed and suddenly the gorge opened out into a deep, widening wadi where the stream sparkled in sunshine as it trickled over rocks and spread out into clear pools between green tree-clad slopes where wild flowers bloomed among grasses and scree at the base of the cliffs. It was a scene of rare beauty, with the vast cliffs rising and sheltering the wadi, while the wadi itself sloped away till it narrowed again and disappeared, it seemed, into the very face of the massive cliff in the distance. Jack stopped, overawed by the unbelievable scene before him. The intense colours of the red cliffs and brilliant greens were so unexpected in this reputedly barren land, that he could hardly believe his eyes.

'God,' he said at last. 'How lovely! How beautiful!'

He fumbled in his pack for his camera but Nadirah gave him no time. 'Come,' she said, and walked on down the wadi. 'This place called Wadi Bana.'

He stumbled after her, gazing all the while at the massive cliffs and the pools of clear water where shoals of fish swirled as their shadows fell upon the surface. She led the way down to where the steam entered another narrow gorge in the apparently impenetrable cliffs before broadening out again into yet another, wider, greener expanse of colour, even more spectacular than the first.

'It's fantastic,' he said. 'It's incredible.'

She said nothing but led him a little further before leaving the course of the stream and climbing the right slope to where a large acacia tree spread shade over a green patch among the boulders.

'Here,' she said, 'we shall see when they come.'

'Who?' he said, suddenly alarmed. 'Who is coming?'

'I do not know. Somebody. Maybe nobody. From here we see.'

Jack acknowledged her choice of vantage point, they could see a long stretch of the wadi, up and down, but assumed that it was only her brother that she might be wary of. He would chastise her for being alone with a man, especially a foreign, unbelieving man.

The wadi was resounding with the cries of birds. High along the cliff edges he saw red-rumped swallows and a long-legged buzzard. There was a griffon vulture soaring overhead, while among the trees he saw flocks of white-eyes and brown woodland warblers. Bee-eaters called, and a night heron, disturbed by their voices, flew out from the cover along the stream. He saw some little rock-thrushes, glimpses and shadows of several shapes which would take time to identify. 'God, what a place,' he cried. 'What a place!'

Nadirah ignored him and glanced frequently at the narrow bend in the wadi from where any followers would have to emerge.

Jack kept his binoculars to his eyes while butterflies and dragonflies drew his attention as they flitted beside the stream and among the trees. Then, as his hands tightened on his binoculars, he felt a tremble of excitement. It would not show itself, but he was sure it was one. Was it? Yes. One, two of them. He could see the streaked bodies and the black marks on the heads. Yemen accentors. They were here. He watched them for several minutes in silence, oblivious of Nadirah's glances to the top of the cliff and the entrance to the wadi. 'Those little birds down there,' he said at last, 'are of a species that have not been seen by an ornithologist for more than seventy years.'

She glanced at the bushes. 'Asfoor,' she said indifferently. 'Asafeer. Sparrows.'

'They are very special. They are very rare and found nowhere in the world but Yemen.'

She shrugged. 'We have many special things in Yemen.'

He was exasperated by her indifference. 'Then you should take interest in them,' he insisted. 'Try to cons... save them.'

'I know the meaning of conserve.'

'Yes. I'm sorry. I find it hard to believe your English is so good.'

'Bism Allah!' she cried angrily. 'Why must you always think that Arabs are stupid? You and your kind have been coming to Arab countries for centuries, telling us what to do. And we have to learn English to be told. Hmm? Why don't any of you take the lesson in Arabic?'

'I am trying. I can speak some Arabic, you know.'

'Ha!' she said. 'I can speak some Arabic. I can speak some Arabic.' She mocked him. 'Maybe you can ask the time, or the way to Sana'a. How would you like to study for a degree at an Arabic university, eh? How many English can do this, eh? How many?'

He knew that she was indisputably right, yet found her volatile diatribe disconcerting. He was not to blame for the shortcomings of his compatriots, past or present. He could have told her about the disappearance of his own language in face of the universal, aggressive speech of the Anglo-Saxons, but felt bound to defend those she saw as his own kind.

'I suppose Cecil Hayward could do it,' he mused, yet not too sure even of Cecil's fluency.

'Cecil Hayward,' she conceded, 'yes, he could do it. He has done it. But it was the language, Arabic, that he studied.'

How, he thought, could she possibly know that? How could she even know of the existence of Cecil Hayward? 'Oh?' he said as casually as possible. 'Where?'

'Qahirah. Cairo. He studied Arabic at Cairo to become a spy.'

Jack burst into laughter. 'A spy,' he protested. 'Really! Cecil Hayward a spy?' While thinking to himself, Cecil is hardly the cloak and dagger type.

Nadirah was silent while his laughter spent itself. 'All diplomats are spies,' she said.

He thought it best not to rise to that challenge and did not answer. One, two of the Yemen accentors were venturing out into the open, hopping onto a patch of sheep-nibbled grass, just as dunnocks might on an English lawn. He took out his note book and scribbled hastily before they flew once again into cover. Nadirah was suddenly amused at his absorption and he caught her laughing at him.

'That's better,' he said. 'We don't have to quarrel. Please remember that I am only an ignorant kawajah.'

'I am sorry. Please continue your working.'

'They really are special,' he said. She shrugged indifferently and he attempted to explain their significance. 'They are relics, left in isolation here in the mountains after the retreat of the last glaciation. Their nearest relatives are in the mountains of Iran. They are of great interest ecologically. You understand?'

'Of course.'

'Yes. Well, no one knows much about them, their song, nesting, food, distribution, or how many are surviving. They may be among the rarest birds in the world. Sorry if I'm boring you, but it is very exciting for us to find something like this. I ought to go back and tell the others.'

'Tomorrow they see.'

'We are going to Ta'izz this afternoon.'

'Inshallah,' she said. God willing.

The others returned after dark, just as Jack was becoming seriously worried about them. As they alighted from a vehicle that was evidently not Muqbel's there was no doubt that Stanley was in a foul temper. He was cursing the incompetence of all Arabs and their language and, in particular, he cursed Muqbel as a stupid, bone idle idiot, not fit to drive a wheelbarrow, much less a Toyota Land Cruiser. Jack had difficulty in extracting a rational explanation of the day's events from Stanley and it was Mike who eventually explained what had occurred to delay them and cause Stanley such exasperation.

It appeared that Eddie, Mike and Alison had been dropped at the Sumarah Pass, as planned. Stanley had gone to Yarim with Muqbel to get the fuel line cleared. Muqbel had said that this was unnecessary now, for the engine had run as smooth as silk on the way to the pass. Stanley had insisted, however, and they drove off, having arranged to return in two hours. Mike said that he and Eddie had then explored the top of the pass with Alison and had seen thousands of swifts pouring through, with a few buzzards and kestrels. Fifty griffon vultures were soaring on the rising air currents sweeping up from the coastal lowlands, far below. They saw a lammergeyer at close range, and Mike thought he had some good photographs of it in flight. They had been so enjoying themselves that the return of Stanley had been temporarily forgotten and it was only when he was an hour overdue that they became anxious and settled themselves in a position where they could watch both the road and the birds flying through the pass. Mike described the incredible views from the clifftops, with the foothills falling away below them like billowing waves rolling into mists of shimmering heat over the Tihamah.

'It's going to be jolly hot down there, old man.'

As the afternoon wore on they had realised the folly of being left without food, water or money. There was a continual, if light, flow of traffic along the road and they considered hitching a lift to Yarim or the turnoff to the campsite. It was with some vexation that they realised that they did not know the name of the area in which they were camped, so could not even ask directions. None of them spoke Arabic, anyway. Despite that, they would probably have returned to the camp eventually. Stanley, however, might return and find no one waiting. The rule of survival being 'stay put and wait', they hung on until late afternoon, when darkness threatened to envelop them. Then Eddie volunteered to hitch-hike to Yarim and look for

Stanley while the other two watched the road in case he meanwhile returned. They could pick up Eddie, who would wait in Yarim. If Muqbel had been involved in an accident and could not be found, then they were all to make their way back to base at midnight as best they could.

Eddie set off walking and was some time in getting a lift. He reached Yarim and could not find the garage or anyone who spoke English. Unwilling to change an agreed plan, he sat on an oil drum at the southern edge of town to wait, with increasing anxiety as a gathering of locals tried to communicate with him in Arabic. It was well after dark when Muqbel drew into the side of the road in a different vehicle and from the wrong direction, with all of the others aboard. As the car stopped, Stanley leaned from the passenger window and said angrily, 'Get in. You stupid great sod.'

Eddie, Mike said, had opened Stanley's door and dragged him from the car with one hand. He held him by the shirt front against the rear door and threatened to thump him into oblivion. Mike had to get out of the other side, after bundling Alison before him, and separated them with some difficulty, using force of reason rather than physical strength, for he was no match for Eddie's powerful muscles. The gathered crowd demanded an explanation from Muqbel, who placated them with some inspired fiction and then implored his passengers to return to the vehicle so they could depart before the arrival of the police.

It seemed that Muqbel's garage had proven to be a shack in the dust at the end of a side alley in town. Stanley had complained at this, ignoring Muqbel's insistence that the mechanic was very competent and a personal friend of his. He refused to go anywhere else, and the mechanic stripped the fuel lines, which proved to be clear. Then, just as he was putting the final components back in place, he had dropped the union to the filter in the road. It had rolled in the dust under the vehicle and was never seen again. There was not another in stock, and the apologetic mechanic was obliged to traipse from garage to garage in a futile attempt to find one that would fit. Muqbel went with him and left Stanley impatiently sitting on the immobilised

Toyota, nursing his frustration. Hours later, Muqbel and his friend returned with the news that such a part, or anything like it, was not to be obtained in Yarim. They had sent for one, which would be coming up from Ta'izz during the night.

Evidently delighted with their competent arrangements, they then said that they had every confidence that the part would arrive as promised and, furthermore, they had also arranged for Muqbel to borrow another vehicle in order to take Mr Stanley and his friends back to their campsite

Stanley was almost apoplectic with anger but could do nothing. The smiling Muqbel went to fetch another vehicle, similar to his own, and then drove back to the Sumarah Pass. They must have missed Eddie just as he was entering the narrow streets of Yarim so, after picking up Mike and Alison at the pass, they were obliged to drive all the way back to Yarim again, with Stanley ranting at them for being the most incompetent bunch of imbeciles he had ever had the misfortune to associate with in his whole life. Alison cowered in the back of the car, fearing that he would burst a blood vessel or go completely mad with temper. Neither of the two argued with Stanley, for the only one who might retaliate was Mike, and his placid nature and self-control precluded any likelihood of confrontation. His silence merely added to Stanley's exasperation however and the result of these tribulations was that, by the time they found Eddie, Stanley was ready to explode, but so too, after his anxious hours of waiting, was Eddie.

'I thought he was going to throttle him,' Mike said. 'Most unpleasant.'

'If he starts on me, I'll throttle him myself,' Jack said.

When Jack had realised that whatever had happened to his companions there was no possibility of them proceeding to Ta'izz that day, he had set about preparing a meal for their return. So now he had merely to put the pots on the burners and, while waiting for them to heat, he brewed tea. He had nothing to say in reply to Stanley's grumbles about the food, noted that there was not a scrap left over and waited until the comparatively relaxed atmosphere of the daily log, filled in by the light of the gas lamps, before informing them, as calmly as he was able, of his discovery of the day. Stanley was listing the species as usual... 'red-throated pipit, yellow wagtail, grey wag', white wag', black-capped bulbul, Yemen accentor, black bush-chat ...'

'Hang on. Jack said. 'Yemen accentor. Two.'

Despite the cries of jubilation from the others, Stanley said, coldly, 'Where? May we ask?'

'Down in the wadi.'

'What wadi?'

'Behind the hill,' Jack gasped. 'It's fantastic, man. Like the Garden of Eden. You have to go through a narrow gorge... I'll show you tomorrow. It's beautiful, unbelievable, absolutely incredible.'

'Are you telling me that you left the camp unattended and went wandering off like an impatient child, all by yourself? Against my specific orders.'

Mike watched Jack exercise an effort of self-control, for which he was duly grateful. He had no wish to disentangle Stanley from any more team members today. Jack accepted that he was the only one who had not previously felt the lash of Stanley's tongue today and blandly ignored the outburst. He continued addressing Mike and Eddie, turning occasionally to Alison, that she might share in his excitement. He described the birds he had seen, the wadi with its luxuriant vegetation and told of the Yemen accentors in detail. Like dunnocks, he told Alison, with a black head and white eye-stripe. But she had little idea of what a dunnock might be. There was a choking catch in Stanley's throat, and he eventually found his voice.

'I'm speaking to you, Pengelly!'

Jack might have not heard him. He rose to his feet, slipped his anorak on and walked out of the camp to the hill. Half an hour later, Alison joined him and they watched the moonrise in silence, as he smoked several cigarettes in succession. 'I'll pack 'em up soon,' he said. 'Fags.'

As usual after one of Stanley's outbursts, he made no mention of the day's events next morning, and none of the others felt inclined to do so. They all hoped for an amiable day. Muqbel went off to get his vehicle. All declined his offer to take them to the pass, for Jack was to show them the wadi and the accentors. Stanley ordered Muqbel to return by noon, so that they could depart in time to arrive in Ta'izz before dark, as had been their intention the previous day.

Mike pointed out that as they had seen no eagle migration whatsoever and there might well indeed be none. They might as well explore one area as another, so what was the hurry? They could stay here and study the area for a few days if they found it interesting.

Stanley's reaction to this was to remind them that they had promised to take Alison to the coast, which convinced no one of anything except that he was trying to re-establish his authority.

Jack led them down the wadi to the tree where he had sat with Nadirah. None of the Yemenis had been seen today and he wondered if her brother had forbidden her so speak to the foreigners alone. They settled themselves down and were awaiting the emergence of the birds from the scrub when Stanley said, 'You realise that should Jack's tentative identification prove correct, we cannot publish such an important observation without a specimen.'

Jack pretended he had not heard. The others were remarking on the beauty of the wadi, with its flowers and butterflies, but Stanley had been silent, as if preoccupied. There had been the temptation to suggest that Stanley remain in camp alone, to guard the gear, but Jack had decided to say nothing to antagonise him further when they had left the camp unoccupied for the second day in succession.

While they waited, Eddie tried to engage Alison in conversation, chatting her up, but she was somewhat aloof. A snob, Jack thought, deriding Eddie's cockney accent. She tried to bring Mike and Stanley into conversation, in an attempt to dispel any animosity remaining from the previous day, although the men were essentially concentrating on the scrub, in anticipation of sighting the birds, with no wish to speak to each other. Just after Alison had checked the time and found it almost noon, Mike said quietly, 'There! Below the thick acacia.'

The two little birds dropped on to the bare ground among the fallen thorns, with their wings and tails flickering and quivering in the dappled sunlight. Jack was doubly elated that his observation should be confirmed and, while the others watched he remained silent, waiting their reaction.

Eddie said, 'What a tick!'

Alison said, 'They're very drab little things.'

Mike said, 'They are bird-watcher's birds, as we say.'

Stanley said, 'We need a skin.'

There was an ominous silence, until Jack said, very quietly, almost whispering, 'If you skin one of them, I'll skin you and throw your carcass to the vultures.'

Alison looked to see what effect this considered statement had on Stanley, for she sensed that Jack meant it, that he would do it if Stanley so much as laid a hand on these drab little birds out in front of them. She was anticipating an outburst and was even more disconcerted to see merely an expression, a smirk of satisfaction, cross Stanley's features.

'I knew,' Stanley said, 'that at some point in this expedition we would sort the men from the boys.'

Jack lowered his binoculars and looked at Stanley in expectation.

'The ornithologists,' Stanley continued, 'from the bird-lovers. With your attitude to scientific research, you should have stayed at home to hang bags of peanuts outside the kitchen window.'

To Alison's relief, Jack's response was merely a smile. His sense of humour had superseded his anger, yet, when his smile had died away, he said, 'To the vultures, *Gyps fulvus*, OK?'

They continued to observe the birds and take notes for an hour or more. Mike very reluctantly refrained from approaching nearer to take photographs, for fear of scaring them away. 'Perhaps we can come here again, on the return journey,' he said.

Sudden shots of gunfire echoed through the wadi. Close. Very close. They could see no one. Mike took Alison by the arm and indicated a cluster of nearby boulders. She crawled among them, and the men followed, all trembling with fear. More shots. Then they saw a baboon, leaping and scrambling up the cliff opposite. Another burst. Chips of stone flew from the rocks behind the fleeing animal which climbed into a hanging -gully and was lost to view.

'Baboon,' Mike whispered.

'Here's another one,' Eddie said.

It was Achmed who came walking up the wadi. He had not seen them and, for reasons which they were afterwards unable to justify, they hid away from him by lying still, among the boulders, until he had passed, with a gun held casually over his shoulder by the barrel. They waited for more shots, but none came. Eddie attempted to rise and Mike whispered, 'Not yet.'

Alison was terrified, deathly pale. The shots had revived the horror of the souk. Jack, against his will, found himself looking at the hem of her skirt and was relieved to see it dry.

'We must wait,' Mike said, 'until he's gone up the wadi and hopefully to his house, or he will know that we saw him.'

'What if we did?' Eddie said, sarcastically. 'It's a free country ain' it?'

'He may take offence,' Jack said.

After several minutes of silence, Stanley said, 'You should have called out to him, instead of hushing us up.'

Mike was becoming well used to Stanley evading his responsibilities as leader until after decisions had been made, so he ignored the implied chastisement. 'I was about to say,' he continued, 'that he may well have not wished us to see his gun.'

'Why not?' they queried. 'Hundreds of them carry guns.'

'Because, unlike the many Kalashnikovs we have seen, his is a NATO issue weapon. It's a Heckler and Koch sub-machine gun, as used by the SAS. One of the latest and best.'

'So?' Eddie asked.

'So how did he acquire it?'

Stanley sat up with an air of boredom. He was still hidden from the track, owing to his short stature. 'For once,' he said in a condescending tone of voice, 'you amaze me, Mike. Presumably one so knowledgeable in matters military will be aware, considering current events, that our armaments manufacturers will supply anybody with money to pay, and the Saudis have plenty of that. It would surprise me if some of the weapons didn't go astray from time to time among these people.'

'I don't know about that,' Mike said doubtfully. 'They're very expensive weapons.'

'I'm sure,' Alison said, 'that our government would have taken every precaution to ensure that the weapons remained in friendly hands.'

For once, Jack found himself laughing, however cynically, with Stanley. 'Oh yeah,' he said. 'You can be sure of that!'

Stanley, in his self-satisfied way said, 'If our friend has gone, we'd better move. We can still be in Ta'izz before dark.'

Chapter Twelve

Since Alison had departed with the bird watchers, Harry Courtenay had given the current situation considerable thought. This thought had been aided by fair amounts of the liquid cargo recently impounded at Mukha. Here too was reason for self-congratulation. Whereas most of the shipment was still aboard, Harry had seen to it that the consignment allocated to the embassy staff had been released immediately after the international negotiations had been concluded. He had been congratulated by all concerned, and quite rightly too. What happened to the rest of the cargo was no concern of his. No doubt the captain, who was as dour a Scot as he had ever met, would dump it on the jetty and put to sea as soon as possible. Harry imagined the whisky bottles exploding in the heat and permitted himself a rare laugh.

Harry had decided that the time was ripe for revelations. He set out for his office in the embassy building with a jaunty step. Truth was, he never felt himself properly dressed without his umbrella but he had been persuaded that it was 'not quite the thing' for this country and carried instead a slender walking stick with which to measure his stride. The difficulty was that these unobservant little people kept getting under his feet. No sooner had he begun a reasonable stride than one of them got in his way, or a whole crowd of them strung themselves out in the road and completely obstructed his passage. He was obliged to shorten his step and dodge through the crowds with his stick held close to his body like a redundant shepherd's crook. He arrived at his office and pressed himself between the desk and wall cabinet with a grunt of irritation. He placed a clean sheet of paper before him and wrote, *Action to be taken on intelligence received.*

He was not entirely happy with that heading, but decided it could be changed later. The most important thing was to organise and co-ordinate his course of action.

Abdullah, he wrote, **Reported movements**. Here he paused. Unfortunately, there was little to report but there was no doubting, on the other hand, the significance of what there was. Harry leaned back with his hands behind his head. Perhaps a word would suffice? Harry was a man who normally believed in protocol and that, in his estimation, meant the written word. There was no substitute for it in its unambiguity but, in a case as delicate as this, perhaps a word in an ear might be more appropriate. Keep it informal...

The knock on Harry's door, followed by his sonorous 'Come,' preceded the entry of Cecil Hayward. Harry crumpled the paper in his large, soft hand. 'Ah,' he said, 'come in, dear boy. How lovely to see you.'

Cecil was wearing his informal clothes. He was still on leave, he said, but there was something Harry ought to know. Harry quailed at this. There had been memorable occasions in the past when he ought to have known things, things which other people should have told him.

'Can you spare an hour?' Cecil said.

'An hour?' Harry's mouth dried up. 'One can listen to rather a lot in an hour,' he croaked with an attempt at humour he did not feel.

'Not so much listen,' Cecil said, 'as look. Can you come to my villa?'

Harry followed him through the streets as best he could. Cecil dodged through the crowds with ease, swaying his slender hips around the obstructing Yemenis as Harry blundered along behind him. When they arrived at Cecil's gate Harry was quite out of breath and patience. 'Can't see, dear boy, why you could not have brought it to my office,' he said, 'whatever it is.'

'Best not,' Cecil said, as he led him up to the mafrahj. 'Sensitive business.'

Harry flopped into one of Cecil's chairs. On the coffee table in front of him there was a bull's head carved in marble or something.

Another of Cecil's acquisitions from the souk, Harry thought, in his usual doubtful taste.

'Perhaps I'd better make some tea,' Cecil said.

Harry was left alone in the mafrahj while Cecil went to the kitchen. He was getting annoyed. He was wondering whether to pull rank on Hayward and ask him why he had called him away from important work to drink tea. The man, Harry thought, can do nothing without a bellyful of the stuff. Cecil returned at last and placed the tray on the table. He poured with his customary precision, while Harry, in his thoughts, was constructing the order of words to be had with the Old Man.

Cecil sat opposite him and sipped his tea. He indicated the bull's head with an inclination of his eyes.

'What do you think of that?'

Harry had no idea what to think of it. He thought there must be something more than an ornament to induce Cecil Hayward to drag him from his office at this time of day, but feared that Cecil was employing talk of trivia in order to prepare him for something more fearsome.

'Rather nice,' Harry said, although the thing was definitely not to his own taste. He preferred the oriental style of decoration and remembered for a moment the Chinese carpets he had stored at home in anticipation of his retirement.

'It's priceless,' Cecil said.

'Oh really?'

Harry studied the carving with new interest. Like many others, he could see the beauty in artefacts of known high value. 'Rather well done,' he said. 'Looks Cretan or something. Minotaurs and things. Where did you get it? On leave?'

'It's not mine.' Cecil ran his fingers over the bull's smooth contours. 'Indeed I wish it were.' He sighed. 'Because I'd then know where it came from, as well as its value.' He passed it over to Harry, who held it awkwardly in both hands.

'Unless I'm very much mistaken,' Cecil told him, 'this is a pre-Hamyaritic votive plaque, probably Qatabanian. And a very fine piece of workmanship it is.'

'Ah,' Harry said. 'I see.' Which he evidently did not, although he was beginning to see that it was this plaque he had been invited here to discuss. 'But if it's not yours, then whose is it and, furthermore, why should it be of interest to me?' His intention was to imply that he saw no point in wasting official time on irrelevancies.

Cecil said, 'I found it among the equipment the bird watchers left here. It apparently belongs to Jack Pengelly. The point is that the export of all such antiquities is illegal, that the Yemenis are extremely proud of their heritage and they enforce the law regarding such artefacts very severely.'

Harry was aware of all this and was glad it was nothing to do with him. The thought passed through his mind that it was unlike Cecil to search his guests' belongings in their absence.

'Do you suppose they stole it?' he asked hopefully.

'No. I don't. Neither do I suppose they could have possibly bought such an expensive item. They may have found it, which I doubt, or they may have had it given to them.'

'Given to them?' Harry said. He was thinking that if they had not stolen it or bought it or found it, there was really no alternative, which Cecil Hayward should see. He placed the carving back on the table, wondering what Hayward's true intention in dragging him from his office had been. 'Given by whom?'

Cecil picked up the head. He turned it over. 'I'm sure it's genuine,' he said. 'What's-her-name, the American archaeologist at the museum would know, but I daren't take it to her, or any one else in the country.'

'Why is it so important?' Harry asked, impatiently. 'People are always dealing illegally in antiquities. Nothing to do with us, old chap.'

Cecil thoughtfully returned the figure to the table, as if reluctant to relinquish such a treasure from his hand.

'You know,' Cecil said, 'that there was a terrorist in Aden known as Abdullah?'

'Abdullah?' Harry said, suddenly very hoarse. 'Yes, of course.' And in order that his intelligence should not be pre-empted, added, 'He's back in the country.'

'You knew?' Cecil said, for once astonished at some announcement from Harry.

'I make it my business to know,' Harry said. 'It is a prerequisite of the job, old fellow.'

Hayward passed his fingers through his fair, wavy hair and said, 'How did you know?'

'Fred Stirling. Seems he employed the fellow as some sort of bodyguard while surveying in the north.' Harry enjoyed the look of consternation that registered in Hayward's beautiful eyes. He considered it permissible to economise with the truth in circumstances where the whole truth might distort the facts. In furtherance of this, he added, 'Altogether untoward, if you ask me.'

'He told you this?'

'After some questioning, yes.'

We would see now, Harry thought, where Mister Stirling's insolence would lead him. It was high time the fellow learned some home truths of foreign service.

'So,' Cecil mused, 'the bird watchers will also have met Abdullah?'

'Exactly. They're nothing but a damned nuisance, just as I predicted.'

The tea in Cecil's fine china cup was untouched but for the first sip. A brown stain was forming on the translucent glaze. He stared at the plaque on the table while the silence between him and his superior lengthened interminably. Harry began to suspect that he had omitted, or forgotten, some vital item of intelligence, or that Cecil was deliberately withholding information from him.

'Where are they now?' Cecil asked.

'Gone to look for flamingos,' Harry said, 'at Mukha.' He laughed nervously. 'That should keep them out of mischief for a while. Rather there, where they can be chaperoned, as you might say, rather than blundering around up north in the tribal areas near the border.'

'Do they know anything about Abdullah? His past? Who he is?'

'Should think it highly unlikely. I certainly did not disclose such information. They won't know anything about him, unless Alison tells them.'

Harry could see, from the sharp glance that Hayward darted in his direction, that he had blundered, although he was not sure where, unless it was in revealing classified information. 'One feels obliged to reveal a certain amount to one's family,' he ventured.

'Indeed,' Cecil agreed. His voice was less than reassuring. 'But Alison is hardly likely to tell them anything,' he said, 'if they're down on the coast.'

Harry knew, he heard with foreboding in his head, Hayward's response to his next, obligatory, remark even before it was properly formulated in his mind. He saw no way out of it.

'Alison is with them.'

'Is that wise, do you think?'

Obviously it was not wise, although Harry could not see for the life of him why this should be so and why Cecil should be so concerned abut it. 'Well,' he said defensively, 'I can't see them coming to any harm. As long as they stay in that area.'

'Quite,' Cecil said. He picked up the alabaster head and turned it over in his finely manicured hands. 'This thing is worth thousands, you know. Not the sort of thing that's given away for nothing. If is a gift, I'd like to know what Pengelly did to warrant such generosity. Let's hope he's not mixed up in anything subversive.'

'Subversive?' Harry croaked. 'Perhaps we ought to go down to Mukha and find out. If Abdullah has anything to do with it we ought to know. Damned Pengelly fellah should have told us. We'll have the hosts around our necks, apart from anything else. Perhaps we should tell them, drop a word, of warning as you might say, about Abdullah. Mention the carving. Keep it in the channels, so to speak.'

'We can't do that,' Cecil insisted.

'I don't see why not,' Harry told his wife that evening. 'Seems the desirable thing to do.'

'Perhaps it's one of those knees to nose things,' Mrs Courtenay said, trying to follow her husband's reasoning.

Harry looked at her with his mouth drooping. 'If,' he said when he realised what she meant, 'you mean needs to know, then may I simply state that I, of all people, need to know, and know I do not.'

He threw the contents of his glass down his throat in disgust.

'There's something going on,' he said. 'Something big. And I mean to discover what. That bloody Hayward is keeping me in the dark and I don't like it. It's unprofessional and damn well underhand. I have a good mind to have a word.'

'I do hope Alison is all right,' Mrs Courtenay said, not really listening to him.

'Alison, my dear, is up to her neck in hot water.' And seeing her look of dismay, which he secretly relished, added, 'The hot water of the Red Sea, and is perfectly safe at Mukha.'

Alison was, in fact, still at the campsite near Wadi Bana, for Muqbel did not return with his vehicle in time for them to leave that day. When it became apparent that there would be no time for the journey to Ta'izz before dark, they spent the rest of the afternoon checking the area in the immediate vicinity of the camp, with Stanley becoming ever more frustrated and angry. Jack took Eddie to the reservoir he had seen from the hilltop. Alison volunteered to do the cooking, saying it would be 'rather fun.' Mike went off with his camera and Stanley went alone down Wadi Bana for another look at the accentors.

The reservoir was over a hundred metres long, by half as much wide. There were some whiskered terns flying over it. On the muddy shore at the western end they saw a flock of waders and settled down to check them. At their backs the ground rose steeply to the cliff-top that overlooked Wadi Bana.

'We could see into Wadi Bana from up there,' Eddie said. 'And right into the bint's house, if we wanted to.'

'She asked me not to. Said it was bad manners.'

The waders came closer. They saw green and wood sandpipers, a marsh sandpiper, and a flock of stints. 'Some of them are looking odd,' Jack said. 'I reckon they're long-toed stints, you know. Some of them might even be red-necked.'

'You'll never get the mad scientist to accept that,' Eddie said, 'unless we can trap some.'

Eddie was joking in his reference to Stanley, but Jack had begun to wonder himself if there was not something disturbed in the mind of their leader.

Muqbel returned late in the evening with his vehicle repaired and running well, he said. He withstood a tirade of abuse from Stanley with indifference, explaining or attempting to explain, that he had done his best and had gone personally to Ta'izz to get the union when it did not arrive as promised. While there, he had gone home for a few hours to see his family. Why not?'

They drove to Ta'izz without incident next morning, after Achmed and Nadirah came to see them off. She waved to them all, while looking straight into Jack's eyes.

"ow the 'ell did they know we were goin'?' Eddie said.

The others had no idea and didn't care. They went through the pass and down over the winding road into the warm wadis and luxuriant growth of banana trees and tall euphorbias clustered like candelabra on the dry hillsides. They saw hornbills among the acacias.

'What a country,' Eddie said.

They found the villa of Cecil Hayward's friend in Ta'izz without difficulty and let themselves in after finding the key where he had indicated. There was a note on the table which said, *'Back Thursday, Dave.'*

They indulged themselves in the bathroom in turn before completing the log. After they had filled in their own records Jack sat out on the balcony in the warm evening air. Alison joined him. He offered her a cigarette, saying they had better not smoke inside or 'His Lordship,' meaning Stanley, might object. She declined. 'I don't smoke. It's nice out here,' she said. 'Much warmer than in the mountains, but not too warm for comfort.'

The villa, as all modern houses were somewhat pretentiously called, was perched on the slope of the hill rising to the south of the city. Such was the angle of ground on which the house was built that the rear of the building was set into the hillside and protected from rock-falls by a high wall, behind which towered the crags and outcrops of Jebel Sabir. At the front a balcony projected from the living room over a garage and store room at street level below. It was a perfect vantage point from which to view the city.

Muqbel came out into the courtyard below the balcony, opened the wide gate in the walled garden and drove the Toyota inside, off the unsurfaced street before the house.

'He's being very particular,' Alison said.

'He's OK. Probably going to sleep in it later.'

Muqbel closed the sheet-iron gates and went off in the direction of the city, an untidy sprawl spreading over a wide hollow in the mountains. Beyond, the foothills dropped away, becoming less contorted, then lost in the dark. The still night echoed sounds arising from the distant streets, like the murmur of oceans.

Jack was content to let his mind rest, enjoying the night until Alison said, 'You're an oddly assorted lot. What made you organise a trip, sorry, expedition, to Yemen?'

'I came because I had this hunch about the eagles. I couldn't afford to come on my own, and all the ornithologists with experience of the Middle East pooh-poohed the idea, including Carter. They said there was no raptor migration over the Bab al Mandab.'

'Raptors?'

'Birds of prey. Their wing-loading's so great that, when they make a sea crossing, they have to use the shortest ones, like Gibraltar and the Bosporus. They're too heavy to maintain long flights over water. They rise high in the air, with the assistance of thermals rising from the land, and glide over. Stanley maintained the purpose of the expedition was to be a general study of the country's birds and prove, incidentally, that there was *no* raptor migration through Yemen. He was just not prepared to stick his neck out and agree with me. He was afraid of his professional reputation but, once we got here, there was no way he could hide the fact that his true objective is to find the third route of raptors from Europe and Asia to Africa. The only thing wrong with this expedition is its leader, but he raised the money, you have to give him credit for that. He's a clever bugger.'

'I can't stand him,' she said. 'He's so arrogant and presumptuous, it's a wonder you don't hit him.'

Jack had not expected her to express such a strong opinion. He looked at her afresh as she leaned back in her chair, looking him in the eye. 'Eddie's the only one who's likely to hit him. He seems easy going but can stand only so much. I'm afraid Stanley will push him too far. Mike, on the other hand, is one of the most placid men I've ever met.' He glanced at her. 'One of your sort.'

'What do you mean?'

'Now, don't take offence. I mean... that there are some people, like Mike and your father, you too I think, whose character enables them to hide their true feelings, never giving anything away. I wish I was the same. I know I'm too volatile.'

She was quiet for some time, looking at the lights of the city. Then she said, 'So you think you know me, do you?'

'No. I don't. That's my whole contention. People like Stanley Carter, Eddie and me, are manifestly obvious, but I feel I could never really get to know Mike... or you. I wouldn't know where to begin.'

Over among the hills behind the city they saw lights rising into the air, and they heard the rotors of a helicopter. Not everything in the country was backward, Jack thought, the military everywhere have the most modern equipment. 'That must be the airport,' he said.

Alison glanced briefly in the direction of the rising lights, which receded, blinking confidently into the night. She decided that this Jack Pengelly was very immature for a man of his age. 'You could try,' she said, 'to get to know me.'

Jack didn't answer. Perhaps, he thought, I don't want to do that. He wondered where Muqbel had really gone off to. Why he had taken so long to rectify a simple fault in the vehicle. It was out of character. Puzzling...

Chapter Thirteen

A sakari here,' Muqbel said as they left the outskirts of the city on the following morning and drove west, down the road between the foothills, to the coast. They had made an early start and even Stanley was in a joyful and enthusiastic mood. Alison sat in the front next to Muqbel, so that she could have the best view of the scenery, and the others piled into the back with all their gear. There was the roadblock in front of them. The barrier was down, and several vehicles were waiting to be examined.

'What are they looking for?' Alison asked.

Muqbel smiled, although he was obviously tense, as always when stopped by the military. 'I not know,' he said. 'Maybe bunduk, the guns. I don't know.'

Alison was reassured. 'At least we have no guns.'

Muqbel turned to her. 'Maybe whisky,' he said, suddenly laughing. 'Maybe Yehudi.'

'What's Yehudi?'

Muqbel grinned. 'I not know Englisi. Yehudi.'

'Jews,' Jack said. They laughed. The soldier waved them to the barrier. A sergeant asked for their credentials, and his eyes scrutinised Alison carefully as he examined her diplomatic passport among the others. He spoke quickly and quietly to Muqbel, who answered in a monosyllable, and waved them through.

'What's he say?' Stanley demanded.

Muqbel shrugged. 'It is nothing. Ma'lish.'

He swerved to avoid a couple of goats that wandered into the road. 'Ta'izz OK,' he said. 'No good Khamir. Dhi Bin no good.'

His assurance alleviated the tension that inevitably built up at the checkpoints, and they drove happily on, glad to be out of the city and birding again.

Alison said, 'Diplomatic passports always cause trepidation. They never seem to accept they're genuine.'

After some five kilometres they passed a fork to the left, where the tarmac road led off into the hills. A battered signpost announced that the road led to A'Turbah. Muqbel waved towards the road. 'I live,' he said.

'You live at A'Turbah?'

'No A'Turbah. Near. In the mountain. Jebel Sami. Very nice.'

As the road followed a broad wadi down to the Tihamah, the temperature rose with every metre they dropped in altitude. Clouds gathered along the peaks and from time to time a few heavy drops of rain fell upon the road, where they quickly evaporated and rose as vapour to rejoin the clouds and fall again on the cool terraces in the mountains. The road was good and soon they passed the villages of Hajdah and Khuzayjah and, by midday, had reached the dry sands of the arid coastal lowland. Hot air came through the window as from a furnace. They began to sweat profusely, and their shirts stuck to their backs against the seats. Swirls of dust rose over the millet fields here and there, rising quickly, from nowhere and as quickly dispersing. They saw camels, with their long legs distorted by a shimmering haze over the ground.

'STOP!' Stanley suddenly cried as they were driving along a straight stretch of road. 'Stop! Stop! STOP!'

Muqbel pulled the Toyota over, off the tarmac, as Eddie strained his neck to look through the window saying 'What have you seen?'

'Chanting goshawk,' Stanley said. 'Back there, on one of the acacia trees.'

He leapt from the vehicle and all but Muqbel followed suit. They looked back along the road, where another vehicle was pulling off the tarmac in the distance.

'Why did he take so damn long to stop?' Stanley grumbled as Mike and Eddie exchanged brief expressions of exasperation. 'It's way back there. Bloody Arabs. They'll never do as they're told.'

'It's up,' Mike said. 'Coming this way.'

The bird flew over several roadside telegraph poles and alighted on another, close to where they stood.

'Oh,' Jack said. 'What a beaut.'

'Oh, ace,' Eddie said, turning to Alison. 'Good 'ere innit?'

'What's that beside it?' she asked. 'Along the wire?'

A momentary silence.

'Abyssinian roller…' Eddie shrieked. ' …Yeeh haah!'

'I can hear bee-eaters,' Jack said. 'Overhead somewhere.' He turned his eye to the blue glare above. 'I expect they're migrants.' He put his binoculars to his eyes.

'Yallah,' they heard Muqbel shouting from the car. 'Sadiq. Sadiq!'

'I thought I saw a raptor then,' Jack said. 'Way up. There's another!'

'Sadiq. You come.'

'Oh shut up,' Stanley said.

'I can see some raptors too,' Eddie said. 'They look like eagles. Keep losing them in the haze.'

The five of them stood in a cluster, looking at the skies.

'My,' Alison said. 'Isn't it hot?'

'Sure I saw them,' Jack muttered.

'Me too,' Eddie said. 'But I can't see a damn thing now.'

They heard the Toyota come roaring back towards them in reverse. They leapt out of its path. Muqbel had his head out of the window. He braked and jumped out. The car up the road seemed to have gone off into the scrub.

'Sadiq. Mister Jack. All come in car.'

They took no notice until Jack lowered his glasses in frustration. 'I don't know. Perhaps it was just dust,' he sighed. 'Wait a minute, Muqbel.'

Muqbel was insistent. He took Jack by the shoulders and turned him, pointed down the road.

'Mister Jack, all man come in car.'

Some five hundred metres away, a great wall of dust towered a thousand feet into the air and spread to the left and right as far as they could see. It seemed solid, stationary, like a permanent barrier, but at its base, scrub and thorn trees disappeared into a vortex as the very earth appeared to be drawn into its maw. It was advancing inexorably towards them.

Jack said, 'Bloody hell.'

Eddie said, 'Christ almigh'y.'

Alison said, 'My God, look at that.'

Mike said, 'A dust storm.'

They heard the clicking from somewhere in the throat of Stanley Carter, as if he were anticipating a horrible, breathless end and had completely lost his voice. 'People,' he eventually croaked, 'have been know to choke to death in one of those.'

'All man in car!' Muqbel cried as he climbed back into the driver's seat. He engaged the gear and was driving towards the brown, swirling mass almost before the others were aboard. They closed all the windows as he accelerated towards the dust.

'Go back, you bloody fool,' Stanley shouted. 'What the hell are you doing?'

Muqbel ignored him, drove on and swerved off the road onto the hard surface beside an abandoned ruin just before the storm overwhelmed them. 'Drivers no good,' he said. 'Big truck no see on road. No stop. Mush quais.'

He switched the engine off and wound his head-cloth around his face. 'Ten minute. All gone.'

Eddie looked at the great wall of dust. He twisted his neck to see the top of it. 'See all the swallows,' he said. 'There must be thousands of them flying before the storm.'

The others saw only a few, skimming low over the ground, and then the dust was all about them. A violent wind rocked the vehicle and the air became full of flying leaves, bits of paper and plastic as the fierce, yet strangely silent, flurries blew in all directions around them. The sun was completely obliterated and the dust adhered to the windows in a thickening film. It was as if night had fallen inside the Toyota and outside they could see nothing.

They covered all their optical equipment and put it in their packs. Jack wrapped a towel round his face and decided to buy a proper Arab head-cloth as soon as they stopped at a souk. 'It'll get everywhere,' he said.

Like brown flour, or the finest snuff, it came through every gap in the vehicle's bodywork. It adhered to the inside, as well as the outside of the glass. It covered everything and they could taste it in their mouths. They felt it accumulating in their noses and throats.

'I reckon they *were* steppe eagles,' Jack said. No one replied.

Alison was seized with a fit of coughing. Muqbel shrugged in sympathy. 'Not long time,' he said, and they waited for the storm to pass.

After some ten minutes, the dust moved on, followed by a hot and steady wind, which spattered large, exploding raindrops against the windscreen. The shower passed and the sun emerged, almost overhead for it was nearly noon, and beat down on the roof. Sweat ran in beads and trickles through the grime on their faces. Muqbel got out. He took some water from a jerry can into his cupped hands and drew it into his nostrils, then he blew his nose between two forefingers, ejecting the dust with the water. He had a drink.

'Dirty devil,' said Stanley

'Seems like a good idea to me,' Jack said. He got out, followed by the others, and also drew water into his nose. 'That's better,' he said. The others washed the dust from their hands and faces.

'It's everywhere,' Alison complained. 'I'm filthy.'

After they had driven a further twenty kilometres along the road, Muqbel pulled in beside an agglomeration of ramshackle buildings. 'Mafraq al Mukha,' he said. 'Good place stop.'

One of the buildings was a sort of shop and rest house, with two enormous refrigerators visible inside the rickety door and a variety of signs, stuck, nailed or tied to the outside walls, announcing the presence of cool, refreshing drinks.

'There's progress for you,' Mike said, with no trace of humour on his face.

Beneath a flimsy veranda of palm fronds, some benches were placed along the walls. A group of men sat drinking and smoking, some on the benches, others lolling or sitting cross-legged on the floor. They regarded the Europeans with indifference.

'I'm about ready for a cold drink,' Eddie said. 'What about you lot?'

'You'll have to buy your own,' Stanley stated. 'Expedition funds do not run to the purchase of that rot-gut. We have plenty of tea if any of you cares to brew up.'

Eddie went in and bought five bottles, intending to hand them around to all but Stanley, but when he came out Muqbel was gone, so he included Stanley in the share-out. No point in causing a row, he thought. 'Where's Muqbel?'

'God knows. Went off round the back, somewhere.'

'Probably gone for a piss,' Jack said, forgetting Alison until it was too late. He thought he might have embarrassed her, with her fastidious manners. He glanced at her. She was looking at the flat landscape rolling away to the coastal dunes and the sea, somewhere over the low horizon.

'Tell him,' she said, 'to have one for me.'

They joined Eddie under the canopy of palm fronds on the veranda, where they were sheltered from the sun, the wind and the sand, although still in the heat reflected from the bright desert and dusty road where the shadeless surface shimmered in the heat. They sipped their drinks, now watched with open curiosity by the men on the benches. They saw a soldier approaching. Young, with his uniform crumpled as if slept in for many nights. He came on to the veranda, bought a drink, leaned against a fridge and said something to the men, who all laughed and looked at Alison.

'What did he say?'

'Don't know. Couldn't understand him,' Jack said. And to distract their attention from the gaze of the Yemeni men. 'We're only twenty kilometres from the sea. I could do with a dip.'

'So could I,' Alison said, looking at her grimy arms, 'if only to wash this dirt off.'

Stanley looked at them with impatience. 'One must expect a little discomfort on trips like this,' he said through his coated beard. His

171

eyebrows were grey, the furrows across his forehead damp with grime and sweat.

The drinks were consumed. There seemed little doubt that the amounts in the bottles had been carefully calculated by the American manufacturers to ensure that no-one's thirst was ever quenched by a single bottle. Mike bought five more. Alison held the cold glass against her cheek, wondering where Muqbel was. There were sweat stains on her shirt, at the sides of her breasts. There wouldn't be a ladies' room here, she thought, and smiled to herself.

There was little traffic in the road: a few cars and another Toyota Land Cruiser, which stopped to pick up some of the men from the veranda. The driver called, 'Any more for Ta'izz?' and drove off, with the roof rack piled high with boxes and bundles tied in cloth. The vehicle swayed violently as it skidded on a heap of accumulated sand spilling across the road. What had happened, Jack wondered, to the car they saw behind them before the dust storm? The soldier finished his drink and walked off in the direction of the coast. Then they noticed the low, clustered buildings of a military camp huddled among the hills a couple of kilometres away. There would be difficulty in explaining the use of cameras and binoculars in this area, although the wind-blown scrub was almost devoid of birds, so there was little call for them. A few bleached sparrows pecked among the rubbish, and a brown-necked raven flew overhead, calling. They heard bee-eaters overhead, but from the veranda they could not be seen.

Stanley was becoming visibly impatient with Muqbel's absence, but said nothing, as he could see the others also becoming concerned. Occasionally he rose and looked along the road, with that *sk sk* in his throat revealing his annoyance. A jeep left the military camp and drove towards them, slowly, as if going nowhere in particular. It stopped beside the walking soldier, who pointed back, and then came on.

Muqbel came from around the back of the shop, followed by a man with his head-cloth wound tightly around his face as if to protect his mouth from the wind-blown sand, but there was no mistaking the small line of scar tissue beside the left eye, and they all regarded him with misgiving. Although the other three had not seen him since he'd been their guide, up north, and were unaware of his presence at the house of Nadirah and Achmed, Jack could sense the apprehension in their eyes as they looked at him settling down in a vacant space on the bench beside them. Alison also regarded him, with fear in her eyes. She looked to Jack for guidance. The other three had not been told of the shooting in the souk, and Jack indicated, with a brief negative shake of his head, that she should say nothing as Abdullah greeted them with smiles.

'Salaam alaikum,' he said, and called to the shopkeeper, who hurriedly brought more drinks for them all.

Stanley rose to lead them out. 'We do not have time to sit here all day drinking expensively flavoured water,' he said with ill-concealed annoyance, assuming that Abdullah was intending to impose his intrusive presence on them yet again.

'For God's sake,' Jack hissed at him, 'sit down and shut up,' and was relieved when, for once, Stanley acquiesced.

They watched Abdullah's eyes following the progress of the approaching jeep and his apparent indifference as he turned his back on it, raised one foot to the bench where he settled himself down, unwound his head-cloth and produced a packet of cigarettes. He offered them around, an unusual gesture. All declined except for Jack, who noticed that Abdullah's eyes were still surreptitiously watching the jeep as he half turned with the lighted match.

'Shukran,' Jack said. Thank you.

'Afwan.' You are welcome, Abdullah laughed.

The events at the Bab al Yemen souk might never have happened. Jack had a fleeting notion that they had not happened, that the heat was inducing hallucinations or his memory defective. After she'd recognised him, Alison's eyes never left Abdullah's. The jeep passed and drove towards Ta'izz. Abdullah called to the shopkeeper, speaking rapid Arabic. The shopkeeper answered from somewhere, out of sight. Abdullah clicked his tongue in indifference. He was not a big man, though taller and considerably broader than the average Yemeni, yet he undoubtedly had a dominant personality. He had spoken to the shopkeeper with the authority of a man used to giving orders and of being obeyed. All eyes were on him, yet he was apparently absorbed in his own thoughts, quietly smoking his cigarette as he lolled on the bench. They wanted to communicate with him, to discover and understand him, but he spoke no English. He smiled at the men in turn, although ignoring Alison. A lorry, laden with armed soldiers, came along the Tihamah road and turned off towards the barracks. He watched its progress with contempt.

'Askari k'teer,' he said.

'Soldier too much,' Muqbel volunteered.

'There seems to be soldiers everywhere,' Mike said.

'We're quite near the old border,' Alison explained, unnecessarily. They all knew where they were.

Abdullah then said something to Muqbel who translated as best he could with help from Jack.

'No go Mukha. Askari too much. No can use durrbeen.' Binoculars. 'Many people. No tuyoor.' Birds.

Abdullah spoke again. Muqbel translated. 'We go Al Fazah. Good place. Much bird. No people. Only habashi.'

'Sounds OK,' Jack said.

Stanley exploded in anger. 'We are going,' he said, 'to Mukha. All the Europeans go to Mukha. It is also the nearest we are likely to be allowed to get to the Bab al Mandab, where your eagles are supposed to cross into Africa. Let's get back into the car and be on our way, OK?'

Abdullah listened to this outburst of indignation with interest, understanding all of it from Stanley's voice and gesticulations, then he swung his feet around, placed his hands upon his knees and, for two whole minutes, spoke earnestly to Stanley, who understood not a single word but could not divert his eyes from the intense gaze of the Arab.

'No good, Mukha,' said Muqbel when Abdullah had finished.

There was an uneasy silence. The lounging Yemenis waited for some reaction. Abdullah added something further.

'Two waters,' Muqbel said. And then, when his English failed him, 'Al bahr wa barikah.'

'The sea and a lake,' Jack said.

'Wa asjarr.'

'And trees.'

'Shade,' Eddie said. 'What more do we want?'

Stanley considered the proposition. The military would obviously curtail their activities in this area. It was a bit much to expect to get right down to the Bab, which was probably prohibited anyway.

'How far?' he asked, reluctantly.

Muqbel asked Abdullah, who said it was only about one hundred and twenty kilometres, and only forty five of them off the tarmac road. Much better than Al Mukha for birds, he said.

'We go Al Fazah?' Muqbel enquired eagerly. 'Two hour, finish.'

'You been there before?' Stanley asked.

'Before, I not go.'

'Oh come on!' Eddie suddenly cried. 'Are we going to explore the bleedin' country or ain't we?'

They all rose to their feet, and Stanley was obliged to assent to the general enthusiasm. There was still a lingering doubt in Jack's mind. He turned to Abdullah. 'Are you going to Al Fazah?' Abdullah guessed what Jack had said and declined with apologies, much to Jack's relief. For a moment he thought the crafty devil was simply trying to manipulate them to scrounge a lift. The others were all aboard. He climbed in beside Muqbel. The army jeep was returning along the Ta'izz road, hidden from the veranda. There was a barrel of a gun protruding from the passenger's window. Muqbel drove around behind the shop and called back to Abdullah who leapt from the veranda, ran to the Toyota and climbed in beside Jack in the front seat. Muqbel lurched the vehicle back on to the road, and Jack was made painfully aware that the lump under Abdullah's jacket was a handgun. Abdullah flashed his white teeth in a quick, apologetic smile. They dropped him among a clump of acacias twenty kilometres along the road. He strode off without a wave or a backward look.

'Bloody glad to see the back of him,' Eddie said.

Jack turned and caught Alison's eye. She smiled at him briefly, wordlessly agreeing with Eddie.

The wind died as they drove north, but the blown sand from the dunes to seaward had covered the road in several places, and they were obliged to get out and push where the road dipped to pass a wadi bed, or sand had gathered in soft drifts in the shelter of outcrops of rock. The delays, and shoving in the heat and sweat, induced a general irritation among them. Even Muqbel was silent and made no attempt to play his noisy tapes. They passed the towns of Hayss and Zabid, from where they would turn off for the coast. The journey had taken them nearly four hours, not the promised two. They could not blame Muqbel for the wind-blown sand. He filled the tanks with petrol in the town, replenished the water and drove west towards the track across the wilderness of dunes and, somewhere on the other side, the sea.

There had once been a hard-core surface on the track. Now it was broken into potholes and bone-shaking corrugations and, for many stretches, completely lost under the shifting sand.

'Do you think this is advisable?' Mike said.

It was too late now to retract, so they went on. They passed through a couple of small villages with clusters of grass huts enclosed in fences of thorn. Groups of palm trees rose from some succour far below and were the last casters of shade before the dunes rose before them like rolling waves. The only indication of a route was a line of wheel tracks heading off into the sand. Muqbel asked directions from a black man in a tall straw hat in the last village. He had never heard of Al Fazah, he said. A companion emerged from behind the thorns, pointed to the tracks and said, 'Follow those,' with a toothless laugh.

'Habashi,' Muqbel said. 'Mush quais. Maffi muk.' No good. No brains.

They threaded their way between the dunes, keeping the Toyota to the hard-bottomed depressions between the soft, shifting slopes of slithering sand. They could see nothing else but the towering dunes on either side of them and the faint tracks leading them on.

The thought suddenly occurred to Mike that no one knew where they were, and he felt very vulnerable. He could see Muqbel's face in the driving mirror, and it was apparent that he too was becoming anxious. 'Abdullah mush quais,' he said once. The tracks suddenly disappeared under dunes as the hard depression came to an abrupt end at a barrier of blown sand. There was no space to turn. Muqbel stopped the Land Cruiser. They all got out and climbed the slope before them.

'We'll have to get over it,' Mike said.

'It's too steep.'

They could see that once over the top there was a clear run to the hard surface beyond. The sand had accumulated in the recent storm and could move again, cutting them off from the road. In the distance they could see the haze which was the sea. 'We'll never do it.'

An isolated palm tree was buried up to its fronds in the desolation all about them. Behind them was the distorted vision of other palms and an impression of green, shimmering somewhere back towards the road. The sun was descending into obscurity behind a horizon of dust, high in the sky.

'You stannah,' Muqbel said, and Jack translated, by now spontaneously. 'Wait here.'

They climbed the slopes on each side of the obstructing sand while Muqbel reversed as far back as he could on the solid ground.

'If he doesn't make it, we're stuck here for the night,' Stanley said. 'Be damn lucky if the bloody car isn't buried by morning. There must be another way in, the bloody fool.'

'Well,' Eddie said as Muqbel put the vehicle into four-wheel drive, 'if it's that easy, why didn't you find it?'

They all clambered out of the way as the heavy vehicle came roaring along the depression and up the dune, with sand flying like spray from its wheels. It reached the top and slid askew down the other side. Everyone cheered except Stanley. 'That was damn lucky,' he said.

Muqbel drove carefully down the shifting sand to the hard base. 'Not too much,' he said.

There were no more tracks before them, so he drove carefully along the depressions among the dunes, heading vaguely towards the sea.

'Where did the other tracks go?' Alison asked.

Nobody knew but, rounding a dune, they suddenly came across the vehicle that had made them. It was a laden pick-up, stuck in a slight depression with its wheels spinning uselessly in the sand. A young Yemeni was being showered in sand as he tried to push the truck from behind while the driver, swathed up to his eyes in a head-cloth, was struggling with the steering wheel. The truck was down to its axles and going deeper with every touch of the accelerator. There was space for Muqbel to drive past, which he did, and then stopped, produced a rope from his vehicle, made it fast and pulled the other clear. The swathed driver accepted such help with indifference, it seemed to the birders, for he was so anxious to be on his way that he scarcely expressed his gratitude. However, after Muqbel had spoken to him, he led the way slowly through the remaining dunes. They were almost clear, with the sea in sight and a hard surface to drive on, when the pick-up became stuck again. It was leading the way through a narrow gap between two high dunes when the wheels began spinning in a patch of blown sand, and the truck settled into the sand like a hen on eggs. Muqbel could not pass so there was no alternative but to dig it out.

'Why didn't he put his blasted foot down?' Stanley said, and for once, everyone agreed with him.

Within sight of the sea, they all dug and shoved and fetched hard palm leaves to lay under the wheels, with the sweat gluing salted sand into their bodies like a layer of coarse mud. The driver of the pick-up remained covered in the head-cloth. They could see only his eyes, but he was evidently old, wizened and rather frail, for his perfunctory efforts at digging left him breathless.

'Don't these Arabs ever sweat?' Eddie said, as he etched a line through the grime on his belly with a fingernail.

Muqbel heard him and said, 'Pepsi too much.'

Half an hour later, by which time they were all thoroughly

exhausted, they reached he beach and watched the pick-up go off to the left in the direction of a small promontory of rock jutting into the sea. In the opposite direction along the beach a clump of palm trees loomed black against the darkened sky, and the five exhausted British climbed wearily back into their vehicle for Muqbel to drive the half kilometre or so in their direction and find a campsite.

The sun made a brief reappearance in the narrow strip of clear sky between the high dust clouds and the horizon and then faded into a mist, exchanging one obscuring veil for another before passing on to heat the vast expanses of the Sahara.

Muqbel drove along the beach to the trees, where he pulled in close beside them and stopped. There was a clearing with enough space for them all to sleep. There was dead wood and palm fronds for a fire. There was the sea in front of them and, a little farther along the beach, was the glinting surface of a small lagoon. The calls of waders rose from the shore but, apart from that and the slight murmur of breaking surf, there was silence. They sat in the vehicle, listening to the calling birds, almost too tired to get out and prepare the meal they desperately needed.

'They invented algebra in Zabid,' Mike said. No one was interested in algebra.

They brewed tea, the usual saucepan of stew and opened tins of fruit.

'I have bread,' Muqbel said, and produced two loaves of flat khubs that they spread with butter and ate with both stew and fruit. It was a meal without argument. They washed the dishes. They sat on their camp beds as the night darkened around them, each reluctant to initiate conversation lest it precipitate a quarrel. Muqbel was asleep minutes after lying down in the back of the taxi. There was the daily log to enter. They heard shufflings amongst the palms behind them. What was that? All listened. Jack looked about him for a weapon.

Crabs! Emerging from the cover of the fallen fronds among the trees, hermit crabs dragged their shells from where they had hidden during the heat of the day, and hurried through the campsite to the shore, to scavenge along the tide line.

'Aren't they funny?' Alison said.

'Hilarious,' Stanley said, and poured water from a jerry can into a bowl.

Mike wondered if there was enough fresh water for them all to wash. Eddie flopped onto his bed, saying, 'To hell with washing. I'm too bleedin' tired,' and as one who had done most of the digging he was entitled to that.

Alison said she was going down to the sea and this was what Jack had been looking forward to for hours. They took towels and left the camp.

The sand on the beach was coral, coarse and light. It stuck to their feet. The crabs scurried in the surf, burdened by the whelk-shells on their backs.

'It's very dark, already,' Alison said.

'Yes,' Jack said absently. 'Abdullah had a gun again.'

'I know that,' she said. 'But I don't know how the others knew him. They recognised him as soon as I did.'

'I didn't tell you, but he was the guide and safe conduct, a raffeeq, for the surveyors when we were up north. He seemed more keen to spend time with us when we went off on our own. Then, he carried a Kalashnikov, but he always has a gun of some sort, it seems. He can be very friendly, charming in his way, but I don't trust him, and thought it better you didn't know about him. Knowledge can be dangerous, and sometimes it's hard to keep to ourselves.' He thought it best to tell her but not to mention Harry, her father.

They walked along the shore. There was a tree trunk, bleached, half buried in the sand. They sat beside it. They were both wondering if anybody ever told anybody about anything deeply personal and important.

'I'm going in the sea,' Jack said.

'So am I.'

They took off their clothes from their grimy bodies. She took his hand and led him toward the water.

'That man,' she said, 'in the pick-up. The old one, the driver.'

'Yes?'

'He's Hamid.'

'Hamid...? Cecil Hayward's watchman...? Are you sure?'

'No. Not absolutely. But I think so.'

Jack was thinking that if only he were not so exhausted he would identify the waders calling on the lagoon and be interested in the naked body beside him. He was also wondering how she had managed to recover so readily from the events in the souk, a matter which they were both, it seemed, reluctant to raise. The events seemed remote, the memories of another age, vague and retrospectively unbelievable. He began to feel that the days and weeks here were extended to embrace more events than they could normally accommodate, and were somehow elongated into another extrapolation of time, which had overtaken his mind. He was trying to catch up on his own life.

'He can't be Hamid,' he said.

They reached the quiet sea and stood in the turbulence of the lapping, diminutive waves with sparks of phosphorus extending along the shore to the darkness on either side of them.

'It's warm,' Alison said.

'Yes.'

There was no intimacy in the touch of his hand and he had not looked at her body. She glanced at him and saw that he was not aroused by her. He was preoccupied, as if numbed, or exhausted, staring out to sea. She could not reach him.

'What's the matter, Jack?'

'I'm suspicious.'

'Of what?'

'Oh, I don't know. Just... things. Abdullah, Achmed, Hamid.' He was going to say Courtenay, forgetting for a moment that the diplomat was the father of the naked girl standing beside him in the sea. 'We seem to be completely out of control, manipulated.' With a slight, mirthless laugh. 'Come on, let's get this muck off.'

The sea was shallow, only up to their waists for a long way out. They plunged into it and swam about, diving under to clean their hair. 'This stuff,' Jack said, 'sticks like... you-know-what.'

He stood up, swilling water over himself, rubbing his body with the palms of his hands, as she swam over to him with a couple of powerful strokes and stood very close to him.

'Turn around,' she said.

He obeyed and she splashed him, rubbed his back, moving her hands over his shoulders and arms. 'You're very muscular,' she said, feeling the hard laterals as he leaned forward with his hands on his knees.

'I suppose it's the work I do. Rowing, hauling crab-pots.'

She came very close to him, ran her hands up his spine, thinking, what's the matter with him? What's wrong with him? What was wrong with herself, she thought. Her hands were over his hips. Couldn't he understand? She would restrain herself no longer.

'Oh Jack,' she cried in exasperation.

She crushed herself against him, both hands clasping tight, with her breasts on his back and her wet pubic hair brushing the muscles of his buttocks. As he stood up she dropped her hand and held him, with her head on his shoulder, feeling him grow.

She let him disengage himself and turn to face her. She told him with her eyes, in the red moonlight, what she wanted.

He suspected she might be using him but, despite his doubts, he responded, exaggerating his accent, 'I 'ope that you d'knaw what you're doin'.'

She fell against him and let the tears flow as he caressed her wet hair. 'You might think I'm promiscuous, Jack, but I'm not. Not in an immoral way.' Her voice was barely audible over the murmur of the gentle surf. 'It's affection that I need,' she whispered, 'love. And I have to take it from where I can find it. I never had it at home. My parents, to be blunt, are incapable of showing affection... love. It's not their fault, but if I tried to show them love they, especially my father, would see it as revealing weakness, dependency. I can't be forever strong, relying only on myself.' Then a slight shake of her head against his shoulder. 'I simply cannot do it.' She could feel him, still aroused against her, and watched his eyes with apprehension as he drew away and took her by the hand.

'Up on the beach,' he said. 'By the driftwood log.'

Chapter Fourteen

So began a week on the shore of the Red Sea, Al Bahr al Ahmar, a week that Jack later remembered as the most delightful of the whole incredible experience. Yet, in retrospect, there were so many incidents that should have warned them of their predicament. Although they were but a few kilometres from the main coastal road and the small, walled city of Zabid, they were in an area seldom visited, for there was nothing there to interest any Yemeni. The campsite was almost completely devoid of the noise and intrusions of the modern world. Each morning broke in still, windless tranquillity, and they rose at dawn to search the palms and beach for migrants. The lagoon was a shallow hectare of brackish water, fringed on the landward side by the palms and a strip of reeds and sedges. Two flamingos, seen on the first morning, made intermittent visits, flying lazily in and out with their extraordinary long necks and legs protruding from a ball of black and pink. African palm swifts were seen over the trees. The dunes behind the trees were like a crumpled counterpane, irregular and capricious, formed by diverse and varying winds. From the top of the highest crest there was nothing to be seen but sand, stretching away to the hinterland in a haze of uncertainty.

Each morning they saw, along the beach towards the rocky promontory in the distance, men putting to sea on logs or floats, sitting astride them and carrying nets across their knees. They paddled in a wide circle, shooting the nets, and then drew them to shore. Muqbel walked over to them one morning and returned with a bag of large prawns, a gift, he said, from the man whose pick-up they had dug from the dunes. When the catch was ashore and the nets cleared, a small two-stroke motorbike appeared, driven by a boy, and the fish were taken to the town. An hour after dawn the makeshift boats lay hauled out on the almost tide-less beach, the men had gone and they were not seen again for the day. Presumably there was a village somewhere beyond the bluff.

'Habashi,' Muqbel said. 'Mush muheem.' Black men, Abyssinians, not important.

The birding was done in the mornings and evenings, for at midday a fierce breeze arose, drawn by the thermals rising from the Tihamah, and drove at them a searing heat. The palm trees bent their backs to it, the waders on the shore sought shelter in the lee of driftwood and shells. The birders slept through the heat, wrote notes, lay in the shade of the trees, or watched Alison snorkelling along the reef before the waves rose and obscured the clear water. There was no driven sand on the beach for the surface was damp, saturated with salt. They found a dead turtle, some corpses of oiled birds, unrecognisable in the black tangles of tar and flotsam. The onshore wind brought a passage of birds along the coast, which were watched from the shadow of the trees. They saw crested and lesser-crested terns, white-cheeked and saunder's terns, some gull-billed and a brown booby.

'It's good 'ere, innit?' Eddie said as they lay on their camp beds watching and counting the passing birds.

'We're not here to extend our life-lists,' Stanley said, testily.

'You speak for yourself, mate,' Eddie said.

Apart from minor incidents of this nature, the atmosphere among the party was reasonably amicable. Jack was determined not to allow Stanley to rile him and cause a row in front of Alison. Eddie evidently no longer cared a damn for Stanley and his opinions, while Mike seemed oblivious of even the slight incidents which did arise. He, like Jack, spent long periods writing notes, apart from the obligatory daily records entered into the log by Stanley every night. The others remarked that Stanley had not been seen making separate notes of his own.

'He ain't havin' mine,' Eddie said.

Before dawn on the third day they were awakened by the sound of Muqbel departing with the vehicle. Stanley leapt from his bed, shouting in alarm, but their driver had taken the vehicle along the beach and out of sight among the dunes before they could stop him.

'I hope you realise,' Stanley said, after Mike had tried to reassure him by saying that Muqbel was probably bored and had gone off to the village, 'that we'll have one hell of a job getting out of here with no vehicle and, more importantly, that he has all our cameras, film, money...' he was beginning to 'sk sk' in his throat with temper '...to say nothing of passports, food and water, in the back of that bloody Toyota.'

'We'll have to live on shrimps,' Eddie said, referring to the prawns brought by the fishermen. 'They'll just suit you.' He laughed at the implied insult to Stanley's height.

'Stupid moron!' Stanley said.

'You what?'

'You're not exactly the most brilliant brain I've ever met,' Stanley sneered.

Eddie calmed himself and laughed, refusing to be antagonised by Stanley's sarcasm.

'He's left the food,' Mike said, 'and a container of water. He's probably gone off for more. We are getting low.'

Stanley seized the opportunity to assert his authority over Mike. 'I am perfectly aware of that,' he said. 'As I am aware that our remaining funds, in that now-absent vehicle, are also getting low.'

Mike refused to be drawn. There was no reason to concern themselves with money. The expedition was more than adequately financed, in his opinion, although the thought had occurred to him in one of his less charitable moments, that he would rather the surplus were in his own hands as treasurer, than those of their noble leader.

'And if the stupid bugger gets stuck,' Stanley said in order to have the final word, 'I'm not wasting my time digging him out.'

After the morning routine of checking the birds, eating breakfast and clearing up the mess, Jack began to wonder what had happened to Muqbel. They were putting a lot of trust in him, after all. He left the campsite and went along the beach to be free of Stanley for a while. Alison soon followed him.

'That little man,' Jack said, 'has a gift for riling people such as I have seen in no other, but why does he do it?'

'I think he's disturbed. What made you join his team in the first place?'

'Ah, well. What made you?'

'Yes, OK,' she conceded. 'Point taken.'

'I had no intention of coming with him. I was thinking of coming on my own when he wrote and asked me to join his team. If I didn't come with him I knew he would claim all credit for the discovery of the migration for himself. He thought my smattering of Arabic would be useful. I wasn't sure about it, yet there was no point in coming alone when there was an expedition organised. After going to Oxford to meet the others, I decided I would come, although none of the original team were there. He said two chaps, called Harvey and Cook had proved themselves unsuitable, so he had chosen more competent people, me and Mike. It was obvious that Stanley didn't like me and this, ironically, was one of the factors which influenced my decision. If he could overcome personal dislikes in favour of the overall efficiency of the party, I thought, then he ought to make a good leader. That was a daft assumption, wasn't it? And then, when we were all ready to go, it was nearly cancelled when we heard the news that the situation was worsening here, with the short war between North and South.'

'That seems to be over,' Alison said.

'That's what Stanley said. Just a local punch up. A guy called Manton had already chickened out, for no reason, he told us. What was he worried about? Stanley didn't want to cancel the expedition and be obliged to return all the funding, most of which was spent anyway. Mike asked about being a man short. Stanley said that it had been taken care of. One doesn't organise a team like this without reserves, he said. He'd already arranged for Eddie to get a visa in case anyone dropped out. I had to give the bloke credit for his organisation, young as he is. I remember Mike saying something like: we can always pack up and come home. At least we'll see the country. Let's proceed as planned.'

'As planned,' Stanley had said, evidently very pleased at the outcome of the meeting. 'Precisely as planned.'

'You were conned,' Alison said. 'None of the original team would come with him. It's obvious.'

'You think so? Maybe we were blinded by enthusiasm.' He thought about it. 'Yeah. You're right. Bloody conned.'

They walked over to the lagoon, keeping to the shade of the palms, for the beach was a shimmering glare of blinding white sand. A whiskered tern dipped and twisted over the lagoon. At the edge of a pool, among the sedges, they saw a small party of waders. Jack looked at them for some time in silence.

'Stints,' he said. 'One is certainly a little stint, but the others look like long-toed.'

He steadied his binoculars against the trunk of a palm.

'Too much heat haze. Let's get a bit nearer.' They backed off and circled through the trees to emerge almost at the edge of the lagoon. He looked carefully at the diminutive birds. 'Yes,' he said. 'Definitely one immature little and four long-toed, sure of it.'

'Are they unusual here?'

'We don't know. They haven't been recorded in Yemen before, but that doesn't mean much. No one else has been here to look for them. Even if they are annual visitors they may only be here for a week or two during the migration, like the eagles. Sure they're long-toed,' he said.

'You sound anything but sure to me.'

'Ha. Yes. I'm sure enough, but I have to convince other people.'

'Have you seen them before?' she asked, expressing the same doubt that he anticipated from elsewhere.

'Yes. In Saudi Arabia. Nobody believed it. Not until they saw the photographs.' He grinned and added, 'Neither did I.'

'Why don't you photograph these?' she said. 'They're close enough.'

'We can do better than that. We can catch them.' She looked at him doubtfully. 'With nets, mist nets, after dark,' he said.

'What's a mist net?'

'Show you later. Come on, let's leave them to settle in.' He led her back into the shade of the palms. 'There's another stint, even more difficult to identify, called red-necked. I reckon they come through here occasionally. I saw one or two in Saudi Arabia.'

'You surprise me. Saudi Arabia hardly seems the place for water birds.'

He explained the paradox. In such a vast region of desert, any surface water attracted migrant birds. One of the best birding areas used to be a sewer running from the city of Riyadh before they had a treatment plant. Flocks of waders gathered along it, together with herons and egrets, stilts, terns and wild duck. At times, the water following the wadi opened out into a series of wide lakes, with the shore teeming with water birds.

'You must be frightfully keen, to watch birds on an open sewer.'

'This was several miles outside the city. By the time it had travelled down the wadi the natural biological breakdown had turned it into clear water.'

'If you say so.'

They stepped from the shade of the palms into the sun, which was like an unseen furnace in the sky above them.

'I think we ought to stay in the shade,' Jack said.

'Yes, rather.'

They sat at the base of a palm. Beneath the trees nothing but hard, fallen palm leaves, like enormous ferns, and bare sand. 'This must have been an incredibly beautiful country in Sheba's time,' he said, thinking of the ancient, vanished forests.

'More like Ethiopia, I dare say.'

Her shirt, like his, was wet with un-evaporated sweat in the humid air. The afternoon breeze began to rise, stirring the palms overhead. If they went into the sea, their bodies would be caked in salt and hold more moisture than ever. He slumped against the trunk and felt a trickle of sweat run from his chest. *Frightfully keen*, he thought to himself. *Yes, rather. I dare say.* The clichés of the middle class which they nurtured as good English. *Awfully good.* Phrases he would be too self-conscious to use.

Was she as much a snob as her father? She certainly had not been a snob after their swim.

'Have you been to Ethiopia?' he asked.

'Daddy was in Addis for a while.' She lay back on the ground. 'God, it's hot.'

Perhaps that had been an analgesic to alleviate the pain of the souk. Perhaps she had used him. Her tears of relief had been totally unexpected, yet had released the tension from both of them as they lay clasped together under the red moon, letting the salt water dry on their bodies.

'Your father…' he began.

'Yes?'

'What kind of man is he?' The pink bureaucrat, devious, condescending, was an unlikely parent to this frank, athletic girl lying in the shade beside him. 'To tell you the truth,' he continued, hoping he would not offend her, 'he was not at all helpful when we arrived. Not that we had any right to expect favours. Yet he seemed quite a different man when he came to Cecil Hayward's.'

'He wanted something,' she said, as if that explained her father explicitly.

'Wanted something?' He wasn't following her reasoning.

'Yes. He wanted to get rid of me for a few days, so he used you.' Her eyes were closed against the glare filtering through the palm fronds overhead. 'I don't mind. I used him, he used you, and now you must use him.'

'For our visas?'

'Yes. He calls it diplomacy. You can call it what you like.'

'I see.' He did not see. How could a man survive in such a false existence? 'But what's he really like, when he's himself?'

'I don't know.'

'But you must know. You're his daughter.' He found her answer incredible. How could a family live together in ignorance of each

189

other. Perhaps she was diplomatically implying 'mind your own business' but if that were the case, she would have to say so.

'What about your mother?' he demanded. 'What's she like? What does she think of him?'

'I have no idea.'

He was exasperated by her indifferent and evasive answers, but was silent. What did it matter? After enjoying sex together for a few days they would go back to Sana'a and she would be gone from his life forever. In a few weeks she would be unable to remember his name. He meant nothing to her. They were from different worlds and she was making it clear that he was not permitted to go exploring in hers. He thought he heard fan-tailed warblers singing in the distance. *'Met this bird-watcher fellow...'* she'd say. She had used him. It was in the nature of these people.

'Jack,' she said, sighing with the heat, 'he's never himself. There is no "self". He reacts to situations and becomes whatever he thinks is demanded by them. His character has been subjugated by his career, his school and before that by his parents. There were a couple of pillars of society for you. It's not his fault.'

He was happy to note that it was she who had implied that the man had faults. 'But, your mother? Surely...'

Alison was getting impatient with him. 'The same. Just the same. It's what they are. Haven't you noticed that they never call each other by name? It's always "dear", or "my darling". They just can't be close to anyone. Can't you see that?'

'No,' he said. 'It's all beyond me.'

'Perhaps you should pay as much attention to people as you do your birds.'

'I thought I did.'

'Not to that Yemeni girl. The way she looks at you.'

He too lay on his back and closed his eyes. She's talking rubbish, he thought. Yemeni women do not look at foreigners, not in the way she's implying. Bee-eaters calling again. Somewhere, up above the heat and haze, swifts were screaming. He opened an eye, and a hot shaft of sunlight forced its immediate closure. Their thighs were touching.

'Your parents managed to produce you,' he said. 'I suppose they were themselves when that happened.'

Alison Courtenay was half-asleep. She had no inclination to go on interminably discussing her parents.

'Jack,' she said, dreamily, 'my parents have lived together for thirty-two years and have never heard each other fart.'

His involuntary laugh left him choking. He rolled over to look at her. She had not the faintest ghost of a smile on her lips.

'He'll get your visas,' she said. 'Never fear.'

Muqbel returned as they were preparing the evening meal. They heard, and then saw, his taxi coming along the beach. He had a passenger. Hamid. His face was uncovered and his single-toothed smile visible through the windscreen. 'You were right,' Jack said to Alison.

Stanley looked suspiciously at Jack, as if he had been kept uninformed. Muqbel made no attempt to explain Hamid's presence until Alison asked, 'What are you doing here, Hamid?'

'He on holiday,' Muqbel said.

Muqbel had also brought fresh water and a bunch of qat leaves. Hamid shared the meal with them, squatting on his haunches with his skirt tight over his bony knees. They were all a little disconcerted at his presence, especially after Jack explained to Stanley and the others that Alison had recognised him as the driver of the pick-up. Stanley grumbled that he should have been informed, that he had never trusted Muqbel and reminded them that the expedition was here against his advice. Alison assured him that Cecil must have sent Hamid to ensure that they came to no harm. Eddie declared that Hamid was OK. He put his arm around the little man. 'You're OK, ain't cha, mate?'

Stanley was not too sure of that. Why had he not revealed himself when his truck was stuck in the sand dunes? He was up to something. 'Watch your bloody kit,' he said.

Eddie laughed and reached for his camera. Hamid stood to

attention in front of him and pointed to his camera with a bony finger. 'Sura,' he said. 'Sura Hamid.' Picture of Hamid.

Eddie lined Hamid up against the campsite and vehicle and took a photograph. Then Hamid insisted on a picture of them all together. 'I'd like one of those,' Jack said. 'And we ought to have one of just the expedition members.'

Eddie took it by means of the delayed action shutter reverse on his camera. 'It's the only photo we've got of the four of us together,' he said. 'I should have thought you'd want loads of pi'tures of the expedition, Stan.'

Stanley scowled. He had forgotten to pack his camera. 'Don't call me Stan!' he said.

Hamid, through Muqbel, expressed his thanks for the meal they gave him, and made no move to leave. He smiled around his eremitic tooth at each of them as he watched the routine of the camp and the calling of the evening log. Occasionally he spoke to Muqbel, very quietly, almost in a murmur, and Muqbel answered in similar tones, as if in deference to the other's age.

When the log was finished, Hamid addressed Stanley directly, using his head, arms, hands and eyes to compensate for any lack of expression in his voice. He gesticulated in languid motions of his hands and arms, towards the sea, the distant village and the motion of the sun in the heavens.

Stanley nodded, in utter incomprehension, though Jack and Mike, with increasing interest, understood most of what was being said.

'Muqbel translated the monologue as simply, 'Go island. Sambuk sadiq Hamid.'

'When?' Jack asked.

'Bukrah.' Tomorrow.

What an opportunity! Most of the islands in this part of the Red Sea had never had a European set foot on them, much less bird watchers.

Eddie was immediately enthusiastic. 'What abaht it, Stan?'

Perhaps it was the implied acknowledgement of his leadership that induced Stanley to agree to the proposition. They would go to the island in the boat of Hamid's friend. The following morning the long, slim line of the sambuk's bow slid over the coral reef onto the white sand. Hamid cut the outboard engine and jumped with surprising alacrity, thigh deep, into the sea to haul the keel up on the beach. He's done that before, Jack thought.

The early morning air was still, humid but not yet hot, for the sun was barely above the palms. The sea was flat calm and, after loading their gear, they were gliding out over the reef within ten minutes. Muqbel stood on the shore, watching them go.

There was again some doubt about the wisdom of this adventure registering in Mike's eyes as they watched Muqbel's figure shrinking in the distance beyond the wake. No one knew where they were and they didn't know where they were going. Should anything go amiss, they would disappear without trace. He looked at Jack with a wry smile. It was too late now for second thoughts.

Jack checked the sambuk over with his seaman's eye. Some of the planks were split, and the paint was all but peeled away by the heat of the sun. She rode well, and had been designed for speed under sail in calm waters, so the long water-line enabled a reasonable rate to be maintained from a comparatively small engine. He noted that the outboard was new and had started at the first pull of the cord.

They had no notion of where Hamid was taking them. He steered towards the horizon, and presumably their destination, without reference to chart or compass. Jack, from habit and inbred instinct, took note of marks ashore and the islands to port and starboard. Occasionally, when Hamid was not looking, he checked their direction, using the sun and the hands of his watch. Align the hour hand with the sun and bisect the angle from twelve o'clock to give north and south. Hamid took most of the trip to explain that he was going to retrieve some fishing gear from an island, which the fishermen in the village used as a base during certain seasons, or during cycles of abundance. Jack was not sure which, from Hamid's rotating arm, but he got the idea eventually. Hamid was a different man out here, he noted. He had that look in his eye, of constantly yet casually watching the sea, the horizon, the sky, that Jack shared.

193

What, Jack wondered, was an experienced seaman doing working as a flunkey for Cecil Hayward? But then... what were experienced seamen doing washing dishes in guesthouses at home? Jack dismissed his suspicions. It was a mad world, no matter where you lived. He decided that he liked Hamid and kept him supplied with cigarettes.

There was a head wind, which showered them with spray over the bow. They travelled slightly north of west for three and a half hours and passed a few small islands but saw no other boats. Estimated speed six knots... say eight miles, or thirteen kilometres an hour. Twenty-eight to thirty miles. It was a long way for a boat like this.

The island which was their destination eventually rose from the sea like a gigantic wedge of cheese. There were sheer cliffs at the north end, and a long, irregular slope running down to the south, where the landing place was a sheltered beach among the rocks. They could stay for four hours, Hamid told them.

He loaded a few items of fishing gear within the first half-hour of landing and, when he had stowed them, made a makeshift shelter from bits of driftwood and sat on a pile of nets, watching the five Westerners explore the island. Mike observed that the stuff he'd put aboard was so dilapidated that it was, 'Hardly worth coming for, actually.'

'Not worth the petrol,' Eddie said. Stanley remarked that if the crafty old bugger thought he was going to screw them for bringing them out here, he was dead out of luck.

'Ought to give him something,' Mike said.

'You lot can have a whip round for the driver if you wish, but count me out.'

The best birds seen were a pair of sooty falcons, with a dependent juvenile, indicating breeding on the island. Several red-billed tropicbirds wheeled over the cliff face where brown boobies sat, like gannets on a northern isle. The island was only one kilometre long and half as wide, so soon explored, being bare and featureless on the slopes, although they found a few wheatears and some unidentified warblers hiding in the scanty vegetation.

After their initial exploration, they returned to the beach for a brew-up and saw Hamid emerge, carrying a full water container, from a natural declivity among a jagged outcrop halfway up the slope. The water was spilling over his skirt.

'There must be a well,' Mike said. 'Probably explains why they use this island in preference to any other. Very convenient.'

'And the landing is on the lee side,' Jack pointed out. 'Or at least it is at this time of year.'

They went exploring again after their refreshment, and Hamid climbed back into the shade on his rotten nets. The wind, which had arisen during the morning, was less fierce than that on the mainland. While being hot, the day was tempered by the breeze and the surrounding clear water. Jack went along the coast to check a party of white-eyed gulls and a flock of terns fishing offshore. The sea became green and inviting over the white sand of the beach and, past a promontory of rock, he came upon a small sheltered cove, just a few metres wide, where the water was motionless, clear, cool and enticing. Alison was approaching from the opposite direction and he stopped to watch her before she became aware of him. She looked at the water, glanced around at the wall of rock shielding the little cove. Jack walked on, grinning.

'Why not?' they said, and stripped off their clothes. The clear water soon cooled them and afterwards, lying on their backs on the white sand under the shelter of the overhanging rocks, they were at first cold as the water evaporated rapidly from their skin, but soon the heat of the sun in the cloudless sky brought globules of moisture oozing from their pores again.

'That was jolly nice,' Alison said, and Jack roused himself from a daydream in which he was steering the sambuk under full sail – in the old way before the advent of outboard engines – into a stiff tropical breeze, alone on an empty ocean.

'I haven't been skinny dipping for years,' she laughed. 'Now three times in three days.'

He was lying on his back with his hat over his eyes. 'It's nothing to write home about,' he said.

'Golly, no.'

Her accent irritated him. Yet he liked her more as a person as he got to know her. She can't help her upbringing, he thought to himself, and smiled as he opened an eye and caught her looking at his body. He turned over to look at her and she rolled over onto her side.

'I suppose we're all right here,' she said.

'Apart from us,' he said, 'there is no one on this island except for three bird watchers and Hamid. Hamid is staying in the shade, and the bird watchers are studying boobies.' He watched a trickle of sweat run from above her breast into a tangle of silky hairs protruding from her armpit. 'And so am I.'

Stanley and the others stayed with their own boobies and sooty falcons long enough to ensure that the juvenile was too young to have flown from elsewhere, so that the birds could be recorded as definitely breeding on the island. Mike was relieved to find Stanley and Eddie behaving amicably towards each other and that Stanley was evidently pleased with the day's adventure.

Another new species proved breeding, Stanley thought, two more probables and a totally new area to be described by his expedition, to say nothing of close views of seabirds from the boat. The only mildly annoying incident of the day had been the disappearance of Pengelly and the girl for over an hour. He assumed they were together, and hoped that Pengelly had the sense to keep out of danger – from falling off the cliff, or going into the sea. He couldn't believe there was a likelihood of anything amorous developing between those two. Women of that class were only interested in men of their own social status and Jack Pengelly would be a fool to waste his time thinking otherwise. If she were interested in any of them, for reasons other than personal expediency, it would be Mike. No doubt about that.

The day was at its hottest when they returned to the boat. Mike felt sunburn developing on his face and there was no shade on the open rock of the island's surface. Hamid greeted them with a toothy grin and rose to dismantle his shelter. He saw only three of his five passengers and looked towards the peak of the island, where Alison and Jack were approaching the outcrop where they assumed the well to be located. To everyone's amazement Hamid found a powerful, bellowing voice and his gesticulations became wild and violent. There was no doubt that he was warning them to keep away from the well and return to the sambuk immediately. Jack, instead of obeying, pointed to the well and mimed the act of drinking. Hamid became frantic and insisted that they come away at once. He jumped overboard and ran towards them.

Jack said, 'Keep your bloody hair on, sadiq,' but halted to await the approach of their aged boatman.

Hamid, with his skirt held above his bony knees and his breath whistling through the gaps around his solitary tooth, was smiling again when he reached them, although he was adamant in refusing to let them approach the well. He took Jack by the hand and, with profuse apologies and Alison following, led him to the shore.

'What was all that about?' Eddie said before Stanley had an opportunity to remonstrate with Jack for yet again wandering off on his own.

'God knows,' Jack said. 'I can't understand it.'

'I think I know,' Alison ventured.

Stanley screwed up his lips in doubt and, after allowing her time for an explanation, which was not forthcoming, said, 'Well?'

'It's something Nadirah, the girl at Wadi Bana warned me about. Contaminating their water supplies with, well... excretions. I mean... excreta.'

Stanley regarded her with scorn. Mike cleared his throat as Hamid hooked his tooth over his upper lip and looked from one to the other of them.

Eddie said, 'You mean, shit.'

Jack said, 'What did she say, exactly?'

'She said that we should be careful where we drop the excrement. That's what she said. You did ask.'

'You didn't mention it to me,' Stanley said.

'Of course not. I assumed it would not be necessary.' She glared at him defensively and Stanley registered a satisfied smirk.

'If the well is the only water supply on the offshore islands,' Mike said, 'it's hardly surprising they should be so particular.'

'Why were you going to the well?' Eddie asked in his usual bold manner. 'There's plenty of water in the boat.'

'We wanted to wash the salt off,' Jack said. 'Besides, the water in the sambuk is warm. Why else would Hamid take the trouble to fetch more from the well himself? He's not daft, you know.'

Hamid climbed into the boat and invited them aboard with a grin and a bow. Eddie was the last in, after helping Alison over the high stem. He went to the stern, where Hamid was opening the fuel valve on the outboard, and sat down. He pulled the wet shirt from the sweat on his chest and said, 'Bleedin' 'umid 'ere, init 'amid?'

Hamid sucked on his tooth and pulled the starter cord. The engine again fired immediately, on the first pull.

Chapter Fifteen

Cecil Hayward was not particularly worried about the absence of his watchman. He had always recognised that the 'advice', given by the hosts, that such a person was advisable in these uncertain times, was merely a device for providing employment and extracting valuable foreign currency from the numerous expatriates in the country. Hamid slept so soundly and frequently, after stealing small quantities of dope from his employer, that his presence would have offered but little deterrence to a determined burglar. His most useful attribute was his ability to procure the necessities of life from the souk at a price far below that which Cecil could have obtained for himself. Hamid's previous absences had been frequent and apologised for in the most humble terms. This time, Cecil determined, a small deduction from his wages might induce the miraculous rejuvenation of his many ailing relatives, scattered, it seemed, throughout the country.

The whereabouts, on the other hand, of Alison Courtenay and the bird watchers, was a matter for rather more concern. They were not at Mukha and had not been seen or heard of by any of his contacts since leaving Sana'a almost a week ago. Several visitors to the British freighter in the port, returning with their allocation of bottles, had reported that they had never reached there. The ship was waiting for clearance of paperwork before sailing for Suez and the UK with a small cargo of coffee, cotton and dried grapes. He thought of going down there himself and would have done so, for he found it informative to note the amount of military presence and the efficiency of the road blocks en route, but certain matters in the capital needed his personal attention, so he asked Fred Stirling to look out for them and keep in touch by radio.

Fred and the surveyors were leaving for the Tihamah and he gave Cecil the map references of his proposed campsites for the following weeks. Whereas Fred regarded Harry Courtenay as an incompetent buffoon, he recognised Cecil as being extremely efficient beneath the effeminate mannerisms. There was a mutual respect between them, although Fred was aware that Hayward functioned efficiently only by reason of his exploitation of field men like himself. The remarks of Stanley Carter, when he suggested that the surveys were for military purposes, were too near the truth in some respects, and he was all too well aware that his work provided unique opportunities for espionage. He resented the frequent hints from men like Courtenay that 'bits and bobs' of information on 'this and that' would be useful for 'completing the picture, adding the pigments as one might say,' or some such ambiguous suggestion. If they wanted him to spy then they would have to come out and say so. His job was making maps. What they were used for was beyond his control. Cecil had never bothered with the misadventures of wandering expats before and Alison Courtenay was the responsibility of her father, so Fred was suspicious of Cecil's motives.

'Of course,' he said. 'I'll look out for them, but I doubt if they'll come wandering in to any of my campsites.'

Cecil was happy with that. He could not ask for more. Fred could not send his men off searching unless there was certain cause for alarm. Sometimes Cecil, like his superior, thought things would be far more satisfactory if the various departments of his government came under one command while serving abroad. He had learned that Jack Pengelly had been in the souk on the day of the shooting. He had also learned that Abdullah was there at, or about, the same time. He had ascertained that the bull's head was not a fake. He had not ascertained why, or how, it had come into the possession of Jack Pengelly, and this was his prime concern. Some people were too curious by far, my darlings, and were a danger unto their inquisitive selves. So let us hope that our Cornish ornithologist was busy peering into the life of the lesser rock sparrow rather than the greater machinations of the world of politics. Pengelly himself presented no real problem but Alison, through her father, was another matter.

Harry was a difficult man. Should any mishap occur to Alison because of Harry's ignorance of events in his own back garden, then he would become troublesome. Cecil had no doubt of that. One reason for Harry being so difficult was that he was intelligent but untalented. He had no flair, poor dear, and his intelligence required constant patronage. He went back to the embassy and into Harry's office. Sooner or later he might have to be told of negotiations now proceeding which were not for general distribution. True, but not at this delicate stage. No doubt Harry would consider himself slighted for being kept in ignorance of matters known to colleagues both senior and junior, despite assurances that these matters were in hand long before his arrival on the scene. He would also express doubts about certain transactions being negotiated outside official channels, while revelling at being among the privileged elite privy to the information. A difficult man.

'Hello Harry,' he said. 'Any news of Alison?'

There it was, Harry's brief expression of suspicion before his mirthless smile. 'Not a peep,' he said.

'Peep?' Alison said. 'What's a peep?'

She was making an effort, during their last days at the beach, to be pleasant to Stanley. He was always eager to expound upon any subject, seeing the request for information as an opportunity to assert himself.

'It's the American name for small waders,' he said. 'We call them 'stints' which is a far more satisfactory term.' He waited for further questions, but none were forthcoming.

Eddie said he intended using the name 'peep' whether Stanley liked it or not. They were all sitting in the shade of the palms at noon. While they had been on the island, Muqbel said, he had found the way out through the dunes. The wind they had encountered with the dust storm had obliterated the tracks they should have followed in. Each time the sands shifted it became necessary to negotiate a new route, but the habashi in the villages understood the movements of the sands and had shown him a clear way out to the road. He was exceptionally cheerful and kept smiling to himself during the evening meal.

At the roll-call of species that night, Jack halted Stanley at long-toed stint, and informed him of the birds he had seen on the lagoon. To Jack's astonishment Stanley did not dispute the record but implied that Jack should have informed the others immediately, to confirm it. 'They've been recorded from Saudi Arabia, so there's no reason why they should not occur here.'

Whenever Stanley made such a casual announcement, Mike thought, it was always for some devious reason. He suspected that he was about to humiliate Jack in some way while pretending praise for his discovery. He tried to prevent trouble by asking, 'Do we know they occur in Saudi Arabia?'

'I do keep up with the literature,' Stanley said.

'Nothing has been published on the subject,' Jack challenged.

'There's Harvey's paper,' Stanley said, trying, unsuccessfully, to sound casual.

'Harvey?' Jack cried. 'Where did he record them?'

Stanley smirked openly. 'In central Arabia,' he said. 'On a sewage outfall near Riyadh.'

'Christ!' Jack spat. 'That's my record. I found those birds, identified them. Harvey said they were little stints, the bastard. But that's not what I meant. Where did he publish the record?'

The supercilious smirk broadened on Stanley Carter's face. 'In *Garzetta* of course, where else. The *Journal of the Ornithological Society of Central Asia* is, after all, the only publication covering the area.'

'I've not seen it,' Mike interrupted, 'and I'm a member.'

'And me,' said Eddie.

'The latest issue,' Stanley said, 'had not been distributed when we left the UK. They had, however, been printed and naturally I made it my business to obtain a copy. One does not venture forth on a major expedition without being fully informed.'

'Let's have a look at it,' Jack said.

Stanley fetched the magazine from his pack and, still smirking, gave it to him. 'If you were on the ball you'd have your own copy,' he said.

Jack ignored that and turned to the list of contents. He flipped the pages and began reading aloud, *Observations on the stints of Arabia*, with Mike and Eddie reading over his shoulder.

'The bastard!' Jack exploded after reading the paper through. 'He couldn't tell a stint from the ass-end of a duck. This is all other people's work and a lot of it is mine. The bastard. Not even a credit. I suppose he told you of my suspicion about the eagle migration. That's where you got the idea for the expedition, was it? I can see why you all dismissed my theories so readily and asked me to come on this trip too. Afraid I would come alone, eh? An outsider muscling in on sacred territory, was that it? Was the Establishment afraid of being eclipsed by a bungling amateur bringing the ornithology of a whole country to the attention of the world? A country which they had totally ignored for half a century. That was too ripe a plum to fall outside the scientific circle, by Christ.'

Eddie laughed aloud. 'Take it easy Jack, mate. You ought to know better than to tell anyfink to a professional ornifologist.'

'He's not a professional,' Mike said. 'He's a bank clerk, I believe.'

'Maybe he is now. But get a few papers published, make your name and then apply for the jobs. That right, Mr Carter?'

'I am a professional,' Stanley said.

Mike read through the paper while Stanley set about brewing tea. Stanley was evidently in a jovial mood or he would not have undertaken the task voluntarily.

'It's a very informative paper,' Mike said when he had carefully re-read it. 'And he gives you some credit. He acknowledges you under *Additional information supplied by*.'

Jack scowled, moodily, and caught Alison looking at him.

'There is still no evidence of any eagle migration through Yemen,' Stanley said as he suddenly found a job clearing up the mugs from around the camp.

'It's here,' Jack said. 'It's damn well here. And I intend to find it. But one thing's for certain. I keep my findings to myself from now on. God dammit, I'll get them published in Holland.'

Stanley interrupted him. 'All observations and research you undertake during this expedition are to be published under the name of the expedition. That's a condition you all agreed to before I brought you on this trip. So don't forget it.'

Alison was studying his face as he took the copy of *Garzetta* from Mike. She saw that it would prove impossible to enforce such a rule, should they all rebel. He was obviously aware of this and was determined not to let it happen.

'Do you mean under the name of the expedition or under the illustrious name of Stanley Carter?' Eddie asked, with more than a hint of sarcasm.

'Everyone will get the credit due to them,' Stanley said. 'Though I doubt that much will come in your direction.'

'What do you mean by that?' Eddie demanded.

'Well, you have to admit that you're not exactly proving yourself God's gift to ornithology on this expedition.'

Eddie rose from the camp bed and grabbed Stanley by the lapels of his shirt. 'Listen mate,' he said though his teeth, 'any more of that and I'll let you have some of this.' He held his other hand in front of Stanley's face.

'Mister Jack,' Muqbel said, not understanding the confrontation, his eyes full of apprehension.

'Come on, Eddie,' Jack said. 'Cut it out.'

He glanced at Alison, whose eyes had not left Stanley's face throughout the incident. He had revealed to her that megalomania in his devious character which the others had suspected from the first days here.

Eddie thrust Stanley away with contempt and sat on his bed. Stanley returned to the administration of the cups. He began humming and whistling one of his tuneless corruptions of the classics. 'Everyone for tea?' he asked. 'Sugar, Eddie?'

Eddie gazed at him incredulously. 'Bloody little twat,' he said.

'Yeah, I take sugar. Six spoonfuls.'

'Perhaps we might catch up with the log...' Mike ventured.

'Right,' Stanley said, settling himself among his papers. 'Where were we? Stints... we'll have to trap some and measure them. It's the only way to be scientifically certain of their identity.'

Jack exchanged glances with Alison.

'Those who stint...' Mike said in an attempt at a joke that was lost on all of them.

'It is written...' he said: '*Woe to those who stint the measure.* I don't know about measuring the stints. Ha ha.'

They all looked at him in utter incomprehension.

'It's in the Koran,' he explained lamely. 'Surah eighty-three.' And he quoted,

Woe to those who STINT the measure;
Who when they take by measure from others, exact the full;
But when they mete to them or weigh to them, minish—
What? Have they no thought that they shall be raised again
For the great day.

He smiled, with his smooth face briefly creasing into wrinkles, while they stared at him open-mouthed until Eddie said, 'You ought to remember that, Stanley.'

Jack turned to Muqbel and said, in Arabic, 'Mister Mike speaks from the Holy Koran.'

Muqbel was even more astonished. 'Mister Mike know Holy Koran? In the name of Allah!'

'Mister Mike is a learned man,' Jack said. He used the term *Hakim*.

'Mister Mike Muslim?'

By now, nothing irritated Stanley more than hearing Jack conversing with Muqbel in their broken English and Arabic, a language of which he still knew not a single word. 'Shall we get on?' he said.

Jack winked at Muqbel, saying, 'We'll speak later.'

That night they set the nets over the lagoon in an endeavour to trap the birds. Mike explained to Alison how the nets worked, and showed her the fine nylon mesh and shelf strings which caused the nets to hang in pockets along their whole length. The net was so fine that it was almost invisible when set against dark scrub or in the shadow of trees. They used the hard midribs of palm fronds for support poles.

'Why wait until night?' Alison asked. 'If the nets can't be seen.'

'Because waders don't fly into bushes or under trees. They also have exceptionally good vision, especially for seeing obstacles over water, and they keep over water whenever they can. You notice the birds we disturb along the shore, for instance. They never circle around us by flying over the beach. It's always over the sea. Waders would see the nets over the water during the day. The stints are staying on the fresh water of the lagoon, another indication that they're long-toed, incidentally, and will be back later. We can be sure of that.'

He was wrong! They caught nothing but a few moths. Someone suggested they preserve them. But they could not do everything. After a futile two-hour wait, the others left Jack and Alison to take the nets down.

'I hope there are no snakes here,' Alison said.

'So do I. There are carpet vipers and puff adders in the country. The black cobra is a nasty one: attacks without provocation.'

'Now he tells me.'

They were smelling of the mud from among the reeds. Jack was up to his knees in water.

'Something else they have, worse than snakes, bilharzia. We wouldn't go anywhere near this water if we had any sense.'

'It's brackish. Does bilharzia occur in brackish water?'

'I don't know, but I'm going to wash it off.'

'Along the beach?'

'Right. The moon is rising.' Jack led the way back to camp where the others were washing off the mud before turning in. 'We're going in the sea.'

They took their towels and went along the beach where cascades of phosphorescence spilled along the shore as tiny wavelets broke in the windless night. The palms were still, black silhouettes against the rising moon. They found that the silence, as they left the sounds of the camp behind, enveloped them in a cloak of intimacy. The faint music from Muqbel's radio was lost. Waders called as they flew out to sea, moving to Africa. They walked to the end of the trees where a thin, thorny scrub meandered uncertainly along the dune's edge, unconvinced in its struggle for life that there was sustenance here even for its own drought resistant roots. They saw the hermit crabs setting off for the shoreline in search of the dead and rotting, their trails scratched into the sand like tracks of tumbrels. Far back, along the beach, the last light from the camp was soon extinguished. They reached the bleached log, with its smooth and warm surface, and removed their clothes in silence before walking hand in hand to the sea, where they swilled each other with the warm phosphorescent light. They sat astride the log, facing each other as they dried their hair while the moon rose up, high over the dunes, and sent its sparkling light to join the phosphorescence in play along the glittering shore. They lay on their backs on the towels, watching the stars twinkling overhead through a thin mist, high in the sky. Strands of cloud passed the face of the moon, like gossamer on an autumn field. There was a sudden roar as a larger wave broke along the shore, and the night was still again. Alison turned to him and their bodies touched.

'I would have thought that you'd prefer Mike.'

She did not answer and he was silent, thinking he had offended her by encroaching too far into her private thoughts, until he heard her speaking in a voice so quiet as to be almost inaudible

'I shall be obliged marry someone just like Mike,' she said, 'a good honest reliable husband, and be thoroughly frustrated for the rest of my life.'

He thought that was what she said. He was not sure, until she slipped her hand between his thighs and said, 'Right now, I want you. I want you!'

They slept like children until an alien sound infiltrated Jack's subconscious mind and he half woke, listening with eyes still shut, deliciously aware of her body beside him.

Perhaps, he thought, it was our shared experience. Our shared moment of terror that brought us together. These things happen in a split second, when we are unaware. Love can be instant.

The sound was nearer, vaguely familiar and predictable over the lapping of the waves. He opened his eyes. Close to the shore, and approaching along its line, was a boat. Jack kept still, suspicious of something irrational in what he had been hearing. Alison slept.

The boat was a sambuk, like the one they had gone to the island in, but larger, and was being propelled silently by four men manning long, sweeping oars. In the bow, stood a fifth man, clearly outlined in the reflection from the moon, which was now overhead, and glinting brilliantly on the sea.

The long, slim craft was gliding like a ghost ship, with an even motion from the four skilled oarsmen propelling her effortlessly through the silver sparkle. There was no clank of rowlocks, no squeak of protesting leather against wood, no noise but the faint dip and splash of expertly wielded oars, rising, falling. No voices reached the shore. The oars were muffled, the oarsmen mute. As the craft came closer, the silhouette in the bow kneeled on a thwart, or some item of cargo, and the action of the arms, the shoulders, were unquestionably those of a man unslinging a weapon.

Jack remained absolutely still, thanking God for the shelter of the palm log, for its outline on the beach was predictable, unsuspicious, and would be disregarded. The two figures entwined behind it would be dismissed as flotsam provided there was not the slightest movement to attract attention.

At last the boat was opposite them and began to pass from his field of view, but still he kept still, not daring to move even his head. He was not sure whether he was more terrified than curious, but be still he must. He was reminded of the time when a raven had settled beside him at the summit of Brown Willy, and the movement of his eyes alone had scared it off. Alison stirred, with a murmur in her sleep. The sambuk passed.

'Alison,' he whispered. 'Shh.' He tightened his arms around her. 'Are you awake?'

'Yes,' she said, immediately fully aware. 'What's the matter?'

'Shh. Keep still. There's a boat, can you see it?'

'Yes.'

Even through the tender cushion of her breast, he felt her heartbeat thumping against his chest. Or was it his own heart he was aware of, drumming to its own anxious tune?

'Five men,' she said.

'Five men and a Kalashnikov,' he told her. He rolled over slowly, relinquishing her body to the warm night air, and watched the sambuk gliding slowly in the direction of their companions.

'What do we do—' he was asking the question of himself '—if they attack the camp?'

'They seem to be pulling offshore a little.' She reached for her shirt. Jack had forgotten about his clothes and dressed hastily, with sand adhering to his skin.

'They won't see us now, not from this distance, with the dune behind us,' he said, hoping he was right.

By the time they were dressed, the sambuk was evidently heading offshore, as if avoiding the campsite, and they waited until it was lost in the darkness towards the headland and the fishermen's village before they made their way back through the palms.

'Just a minute,' he said as they approached the clearing.

'What?' she whispered. 'What can you see?'

'Nothing. I must have a skeet.'

'Oh, a pee.' She managed a laugh. Easing some of the tension. 'Me too. It must be the excitement.'

'Yes.' He aimed at a tree trunk, while she lifted her skirts and squatted.

'I wish you hadn't told me about the snakes,' she said. 'You know, if the men in the boat pulled offshore to avoid the camp, it must mean they know we're here and didn't want us to see them, right?'

'Right,' he agreed. He wondered how many women could do that with such indifference. It must be her self-confidence, that self-assurance of her class. 'But, why didn't they keep offshore all the way down?' he said. 'Maybe we are not the only reason for the stealth and muffled oars. How far across the lagoon is the edge of the reef? Did you see it while snorkelling?'

'Oh, at least fifty metres before the drop into deep water. It probably varies. Off the bluff, down by the village, it might extend much further out.'

'I was thinking how close a patrol boat, a large launch say, could get in.'

'It would be very risky over the reef,' she said, 'unless the crew were very familiar with the coast. The bottom is very irregular. Some of the coral is only just below the surface at low tide.'

'There's not much tide in the Red Sea,' he said. 'So any patrol boat, or any boat with an outboard protruding below the keel, would have to stay well offshore unless the crew knew the coast.'

'Yes.'

She came very close to him in the dark moon-shadow of the palms and put her arms around him. She was trembling and he held her close, sinking into the sanctuary of her own strong, yet infinitely tender, body.

'Don't worry,' he said. 'It's probably nothing to do with us.'

It was, he knew, a great deal to do with them, although he had no idea what. 'The fellow with the Kalashnikov,' he said, 'was Abdullah. And one of the oarsmen looked like Hamid.'

As they came into the campsite, Mike woke and shone a torch onto his wristwatch. Jack asked him to put it out and, as the others woke, grumbling, he told them what he and Alison had seen. He was amazed that it was still before midnight, forgetting for a moment the early sunsets of these latitudes. They discussed the advisability of staying there and came to the conclusion that to be seen fleeing would be worse. Better that they knew nothing, had seen nothing, so they would stay for the next day, as planned, and leave at dawn on the following morning.

Muqbel had been listening to their conversation. 'Fish man boat,' he said. 'Not to make the terribles.' He smiled and returned to his Toyota to sleep.

'Fishing with a Kalashnikov?' Mike said when Muqbel was out of hearing. 'You did see one, you say.'

'Yeah,' Jack said. 'And I'm pretty sure it was Abdullah holding it.'

'Did you see it?' This to Alison.

'Not the gun. They'd gone past before I woke.'

There was no doubt that in the pause that followed there was a certain speculation as to the exact manner of her wakening. Stanley Carter, who had said little, and now felt reassured by Muqbel's comment, said, 'You saw a fishing boat, being rowed along the coast ,and flew into a blind panic.'

'No lights, muffled oars, no conversation among the crew? Come on!'

'And no bloody Kalashnikov. Typical Celtic over-reaction.'

Jack let it pass. 'Maybe,' he said.

Stanley withdrew his head into the folds of his sleeping bag and soon his snores reverberated between the trees. Jack expected to lie awake for hours worrying and thinking about the events of the day and the previous days, but he woke with the sun on his face to find he had slept soundly and well until late in the morning.

From his bed he watched the native fishermen come, as usual, and set their nets far down the beach. He saw Alison watching them with raised eyebrows as she drank from a large mug of tea. He guessed what she was thinking. Something that had occurred to himself. It was odd that the fishermen had not visited the campsite for, in his experience, the curiosity of local people had brought the inevitable cluster of onlookers wherever foreigners made camp in remote areas. The people here had not even walked along the beach. Maybe they had been ordered off. On the other hand, he thought, Yemen while undeveloped was hardly remote. Over the millennia the country had suffered the consequences of exploitation on a scale almost without parallel, and it was one of the most densely populated countries of the Middle East. Only the barren desert, over the mountains, and these hot humid dunes of the Tihamah were without hordes of people. Some, like these fishermen on their floats, even eked out a miserable existence on this desolate shore. Perhaps they had seen foreigners enough.

Chapter Sixteen

Alison made a point of dividing her time among the men on the final day. She was aware of the jealousies a woman could rouse in such a situation and wished to avoid any recriminations for the deteriorating relationships she saw among the members of the expedition. She and Jack all but ignored each other while in the company of the others and by mutual, albeit unspoken, consent, they continued the deception. They probably fooled no one, she thought. She spent as long as tolerable in the company of Stanley and encouraged Mike to be at ease when alone with her. His background was the most like her own after all, but he was too studious and his humour too contrived. Eddie, stripped to the waist as usual, tried to show off his muscles and went swimming with her in the heat of the day, although she could not resist outstripping him in a powerful crawl over the coral reef.

While the four birders were out checking some larks that Stanley had found among the dunes, Alison sat with Muqbel, drinking tea. She found him remarkably at ease, neither servile like the servants her parents employed, nor chauvinistic like some of the foreign diplomats she met through her father. Muqbel, she guessed, looked neither up nor down to anybody. She asked him if he was married. Yes, he was, and after tomorrow, Inshallah, he would see his family. He showed her some dog-eared photographs of his wife and himself at their wedding. She was a beautiful doe-eyed girl in traditional Yemeni dress standing beside Muqbel, who was clothed in a sparkling white futtah, with a broad embroidered belt and a jewel-encrusted dagger at his waist. He showed her another snap of the same girl holding a small child, while another clung to her skirts in the manner of shy children the world over.

'They are very beautiful,' she said.

Muqbel smiled, and carefully placed the photographs back in his pocket. 'Shukran,' he said. 'Thank you.'

She liked him. He was the first Yemeni, she realised to her shame, that she had ever spoken to. 'Where do you live?' she asked. 'You live in a nice house?' – imagining some ghastly shack in the back streets of Ta'izz.

'I show,' he said, and produced the photographs again. He thumbed through them and selected a coloured print. It was of a tall stone building, three stories high, perched on the edge of a steep wadi running through a village somewhere in the mountains. The windows were outlined in white plaster. The door was intricately carved. 'I make,' he said.

He told her he had earned the money to pay for the building of his house while working on construction sites for British and American companies in Saudi Arabia and Dubai, sending instalments back and paying for the house as it was built. He had learned English at a night school run by a Palestinian refugee and by persistent attempts at conversation with the expatriates. As his English improved, he became indispensable as an interpreter among labourers on the sites and commanded a high salary. He understood, as everyone exploring a new language, considerably more than he could speak, which, in the one-way conversation of instruction regarding work, was of little impediment. After eleven years away from home, returning annually for a month, everything was paid for, he told her: his house, this expensive Japanese vehicle, his bride, all paid for. Did they still do that, she wondered.

Alison was somewhat disconcerted to realise that, even by Western standards, Muqbel was a comparatively wealthy man. He was still not thirty years of age. She herself had nothing that was not of her father's gratuity.

The birders spent the day as usual, checking the palms and scrub for migrants and counting the passing sea-birds when the hot wind of the afternoon drove them into shade. Stanley had dismissed the incident of the silent sambuk as a normal occurrence wildly exaggerated by Jack, yet the relaxed atmosphere of the previous days had changed to an uneasy desire to move on. Although no one said anything, they frequently trained their binoculars along the beach, or climbed the high dune to ensure that no one was approaching the camp unseen. They had settled down for the final species check and daily log when Muqbel, who had been checking over the vehicle, backed it out of the clearing.

'Come back, one hour,' he said, and drove off along the beach.

He returned late. Although it was of no consequence, Stanley found this another reason for condemning the bloody-mindedness of all Arabs. He was predicting the loss of half their equipment when they heard the roar of his approaching motor. 'Stupid git,' Stanley said, covering his own unreasonable outburst.

They rose early on the final morning and breakfasted in the dark. The moon had long dropped below the horizon, leaving the beach black and the palm trees indistinct. Muqbel stowed the gear: rucksacks, bedrolls, camp beds, gas cooking stove. There was less space than previously and they saw that he had stacked five wooden crates beneath all their own stuff.

'I take for friend,' he said. 'All plenty seat.'

Despite their early start, the sun was rising as they left the campsite. Leaving the clearing in the cool morning air was like leaving the seclusion of a familiar sanctuary, a home they would never see again and remember with nostalgia.

'It was nice, camping there,' Alison said.

They disturbed a few waders as they drove south along the beach. The village, where the fishermen lived, was little more than a cluster of round huts made from palm fronds and grass, with a couple of ramshackle shacks of corrugated iron. The fishermen watched them pass without a word or wave. They were darker skinned than the people of the hills and wore tall hats of woven straw. Similar in shape to the traditional hats of Wales, Mike pointed out.

'They don't seem very friendly,' Eddie said.

Jack agreed. 'Most unusual, that is.'

Stanley grunted, 'Unpredictable lot.'

Muqbel found the way through the sands without difficulty. Only once were they obliged to stop and climb a dune to find the track, which meandered among the chaos to an area of poor cultivation. After that they followed the tyre tracks which led to a village shaded by tall palms. At the first garage, Muqbel filled the petrol tanks and a spare jerry can, checked the tyre pressures and insisted on replenishing two of their water containers.

'You would think we were about to cross the Empty Quarter,' Stanley grumbled, as anxious to be moving as ever.

Outside Zabid, Muqbel stopped again, pulling into a roadside cafe where he ordered tea, which he insisted on paying for. He then drove steadily for the hundred kilometres or so along the featureless Tihamah road and reached Mafrak al Mukha before noon. He would not stop at the shop where they had seen Abdullah, although the heat was now intense and they were all dry throated from the hot air circulating inside the vehicle. They drank water from the containers but it was tepid and unrefreshing

Jack eventually became desperate for a stop. 'Lazim abule,' he said, 'wa'l bint kaman.'

Muqbel said sorry, but there was nowhere for the bint to piss just here. There were too many askari. And in English, 'One half hour.'

Forty minutes later, he pulled into the same derelict building where they had sheltered from the dust storm.

They alighted from the vehicle and Jack dashed to the trees. Alison followed him. It was sweltering hot. Muqbel clambered back into the driver's seat and drove to the shade of a large clump of acacias a hundred metres further off the road.

Whereas they had been travelling southeast, down the Tihamah, they were now heading northeast towards the wall of mountains in the distance. Nearer at hand, the acacia trees grew in scattered clumps along the foothills, some on the parched slopes, others in depressions where a few extra drops of moisture gathered in the fitful rains. The trees provided a thin but welcome shade and hid them from the road. Eddie set up the stove to boil the kettle, hot tea being more refreshing than tepid water. Stanley lined up the mugs and waited. Mike leaned against the shady side of an acacia after brushing away the thorns. 'I'm all in,' he said.

Jack led Alison to the seclusion of the trees, where they did what was necessary, and from there to the top of the nearest foothill, where they found some shade beneath an overhanging rock. He hoped she didn't want to talk, his mouth was too dry. He brought his binoculars to his eyes and peered through the shimmering haze rising from the barren undulations receding into the distance. He found moisture in his mouth to gulp at what he saw. Sitting down, he steadied his binoculars by resting his elbows on his knees. Then he turned them to the pale glare in the sky... back to the foothills.

'Christ!' he said. 'Look at that!'

'What is it?' Alison demanded in alarm. 'What can you see?'

He ignored her and ran back to the others, slithering over the rocks, and was unable to speak when he reached them, pointing to the hills as he gasped for breath.

'Eagles!' he eventually croaked as he leaned against the Toyota. 'Steppe eagles. Bloody hundreds of them.'

They ran back to the hill with him, oblivious for a few excited moments of the heat and thirst, and followed his pointing finger as he collapsed at the base of the hill where Alison stood waiting in alarm.

'What's happening?' she cried as they rushed up the hill towards her.

'Eagles! Eagles!'

There they were. There they were at last. Back along the line of hills, rising slowly on huge languid wings, they saw them. No one spoke. They watched in awe as the great birds spiralled up and up on the rising thermals, turning out in majestic loops and gliding in loose formation, in line ahead, along the edge of the plain. They had found them!

From the great plains of Russia they had come, over the Kyzyl Kum and Kara Kum, skirting the Hindu Kush and over the most inhospitable, barren regions of the world before crossing the great deserts of Arabia. Now they had gathered here in preparation for the last obstacle at the Bab al Mandab, the Gates of Hell, at the mouth of the Red Sea, before ascending the mountains of Ethiopia and descending into the plains of Kenya. Some approached and flew silently overhead into the painful glare of the sun, while the majority followed the hills and used the rising thermals to full advantage, with barely a flap of wings. Some rose on the thermals until they were mere specks in the distorting sky and became impossible to discern. Others were seen sweeping low in long glides to join the dust and debris rising on the first swirling spiral of another thermal, before peeling off the top and commencing another in the series of long, effortless glides into Africa.

As they watched, the birders saw other species. 'There's some black kites with them. Look, imperial eagles. That's a short-toed. See over there... storks, sparrowhawks. Listen to the bee-eaters. They're white-cheeked. How many buzzards?'

'There's another lot over there,' Mike said. Even he was unable to conceal his childlike excitement; all thought of fatigue vanished. 'They're moving along the line of mountains. Keep losing them in the haze. More, if anything, than there are here.'

They found, after settling to assess the movement, that there were indeed two lines of birds. One, the nearest to them, was a mixture of species, whereas the second, following the edge of the mountains, seemed to consist entirely of steppe eagles. The distortion in the heat haze made it impossible to see anything smaller at that distance, and even the large birds kept appearing and disappearing in the haze.

'There's two or free 'undred in view at a time,' Eddie said. 'It's almost impossible to count em.' He turned to Stanley, who had been remarkably quiet, and dug him in the ribs with his elbow. 'Bloody good 'ere innit?' he said.

'Of course *sk sk* it's bloody good here. I did assume something like this, or I wouldn't have brought you.'

Alison had never seen four grown men exhibit such childish exuberance, and their excitement was contagious. She found herself laughing with the rest of them. 'How wonderful for you.' Thinking how surprised her father would be.

'Eagles eagles,' they kept chanting. 'We found them.' And Mike repeated, 'How jolly exciting. I say, how exciting.'

'If it weren't for that dust storm,' Eddie said, 'we'd have seen 'em when we stopped 'ere on the way down.'

'When I found the chanting goshawk.' Stanley reminded them.

The others ignored him and returned to the shade of the acacia trees where they set about brewing fresh tea to replenish the pot made by Eddie and untouched except by Muqbel, who had helped himself and thrown the rest away. He was anxious to be on the road but even Jack, for once, was impatient with him and told him to wait.

In high spirits, they discussed the significance of their discovery and the new questions it raised. Whether they could go to Djibouti the following year and see the eagles arriving on the other side. Was there a return in spring?

'We found the buggers,' Jack said, giving Alison a spontaneous hug. 'We found them. When we get to Sana'a we'll celebrate with some of Cecil Hayward's whisky.' They all agreed to that.

Muqbel said, 'I have whisky!'

There was a stunned silence as the significance of his casual words registered and their jubilance died.

So that was it. The boxes in the Toyota, the sambuk in the night. The presence of old Hamid and the trip to the island with the forbidden well. Muqbel's visits to the village. Whisky smuggling! They had been used, right from the very beginning.

'Oh bloody hell, Muqbel!' Jack said in despair. 'What if you get caught?'

Stanley Carter was speechless with indignation. He was about to recover his voice and proceeded with a series of coughs and gasps to gather his breath before telling Muqbel what a stupid, lying, idle, thieving, drunken bastard Arab he was when Jack forestalled him.

'Be quiet, Stanley. Leave this to me.'

Stanley turned his anger on Jack. 'You shut your mouth. I am running this expedition and I'm not...'

He felt Eddie's huge fist grab his upper arm. The grip was not painful, but struggle would have been futile. He was almost lifted from the ground with the strength of Eddie's single hand. Eddie had a pantomime smile on his face.

Muqbel said, 'No get catch askari.'

Jack heaved a great sigh of despair. Did nothing ever go according to plan in this country...? Eddie released Stanley with a shove. They all sat down on rocks and boxes.

'Askari no see, Mister Jack,' Muqbel said, apologetically. 'Car all asdiqayiy.'

'What the hell is he saying?' Stanley asked.

'He's saying that with us in the car, the soldiers won't stop us and see the whisky.'

Jack sighed again, glanced at Mike and shook his head, ignoring Stanley. He was disappointed to think that Muqbel could use them like this, especially as it had been through Jack's own insistence that they had hired him. They should have known that his charges were too low in a country where the cost of everything was prohibitively high. He had been too eager all along to accompany these foreigners for such a low fee. Stanley had been right about him; that was the hardest thing to bear. He would have to apologise to the little twerp. Yet, he still doubted if Muqbel would deliberately put them at risk, lead them into danger. How much was in it for him, he wondered. People the world over were prepared to pay high prices for the forbidden. Forbidden fruits. A story as old as time. 'Whisky mamnooah,' he said. Whisky is forbidden.

Muqbel shrugged. 'Kulshai mamnooah.' Everything is forbidden.

He smiled, but Jack, in considering their predicament, did not respond.

They were faced with the alternatives of unloading all their gear at the roadside and telling Muqbel to go to hell, or risking travelling through the roadblocks with a wagonload of booze. There was little chance of an empty taxi passing on this remote stretch of road. They were more likely to be picked up by the soldiers and thrown in clink.

'How much whisky?' Eddie said.

Mike thought the question was somewhat fatuous but, on reflection, decided that there might be some correlation between crime and punishment. Sentencing might reflect the amount of whisky handled, as with cannabis in Britain.

'In car, five box,' Muqbel said.

His answer was imprecise. They looked at him. 'Wa kaman?' Jack said, struggling with inadequate Arabic, 'And what else?'

By now, Muqbel was used to Jack's atrocious misuse of his language. He led them to the vehicle where, with actions louder than any words, he indicated the five boxes beneath the bird watcher's equipment. Then, he went forward and raised the bonnet.

When the initial shock wave had passed through them, they stood in a silent, almost reverent, semicircle around the front of the car.

Jack said, 'Good God, Muqbel!'

Eddie whistled and said, 'They could give us ten years for that lot,' as Mike's jaw dropped in amazement.

Padded bottles of Scotch whisky were hung about the wheel arches, the battery, brake fluid and water reservoirs and dangled from the horn, They were among the wires and cables of distributor and brake and were hung in sacks everywhere there was space. Even Stanley was obliged to laugh.

Muqbel stood smiling apologetically, like one whose hoard of hidden presents had been discovered on Christmas Eve. Alison said, 'Imagine going through British customs with that little lot.'

'They'd throw the bleedin' book at you,' Eddie said, while Mike, pragmatic as ever, observed, 'We'll be lucky if they don't explode in the heat and catch the lot on fire.'

They heard the rumbling of a heavy truck travelling up the road in their direction. There was another option open to them. They could unload the whisky and leave it here under a tree, or hidden among the rocks, and force Muqbel to take them on without it. He could return for the whisky later and take his chance without the foreigners for distraction.

'Any more?' Jack asked.

Muqbel shook his head. 'Only small,' he said.

Whose was it? Had he bought it to sell inland himself? Was he part of a gang? Could they plead innocence if the stuff was discovered at a roadblock? 'Is the damned stuff illegal in this country or not?' he asked.

'One requires a permit,' Alison said.

'We ain't got no permit,' Eddie said, and Stanley glared at him for stating the obvious.

Jack knew what Eddie was thinking. Their involvement might be dismissed as unwitting and innocent or, on the other hand, it might be construed that they were using Muqbel's vehicle and their own bird-watching activities as part of a predetermined plan to undermine the morals of the country and the Holy Islamic religion. Laws, as recognised at home, did not apparently exist here. Their fate might well be in the hands of a minor official who could simply relieve them of their burden and send them on their way, thanking a Providence which had dropped such a windfall in his hands. It was just as likely, however, that their activities would indeed be used as an indication to the people of the corruption prevalent in the West and they all be thrown in jail 'to encourage the others'. The sensible thing to do was to ditch the stuff and carry on.

'Everyone drinks whisky here,' Alison said. 'Cecil Hayward, my father, plenty of Yemenis. It can't be such a terrible crime to take a few bottles to Ta'izz. I'm sure it's only a matter of permits or something.'

All right for you, they told her wordlessly, with their eyes. You have a diplomatic passport. No Yemeni jail for you. Another thing... was there duty to pay on illegal imports? Probably, if someone felt like imposing it. One thing was for sure and that only. It was illegal for a Yemeni to transport alcohol from the coast to some destination inland, otherwise there would be no necessity for Muqbel's deception. What were they to do with him?

Mike was examining the sacks. One was already dangerously worn from rubbing against the engine block. Another was ominously near the fan-belt. Mike pulled it away and re-tied the string. He rearranged the bottles hanging from the radiator. 'We'll have to secure them better than this,' he said, 'and try to stop them clinking.'

They looked at each other. Mike had made the decision. They began grinning, then laughing. Why not? To hell with it. Why not?

Muqbel sighed with relief. He couldn't see why they had been so angry. There was no danger for them. The soldiers would not search a taxi full of foreigners, he was sure of it. He took water from one of the containers he had insisted on filling at Zabid and poured it over the sacks. A cloud of steam rose from the engine.

They passed beneath the second line of soaring eagles half an hour after bundling into the Land Cruiser. These birds were flying much more steadily than those over the hills and were, it seemed, utilising the force of the onshore winds, which were deflected upwards by the foothills and escarpment. The birders would return, they declared, and spend time here, counting and recording. Assuming their visas were extended.

They began the long, grinding ascent up the road to Ta'izz, past millet fields and the stone and pebble-strewn wadis washed clean of soil by the floods from the denuded mountains. They saw weaverbirds and hornbills again. They saw the gigantic nest of a hammerkop, like a miniature haystack or the dome of a gargantuan wren's nest, perched on the top of a pinnacle of rock. They were all in high spirits. The sheer coincidence of Muqbel stopping almost directly beneath the flight-line of the eagles was incredible. A mile or two away, indeed a few hundred yards away, on days when the distortion of heat and haze combined with the rising dust, and they would never have seen them.

They asked themselves why they had not thought of the obvious: that the birds would use the thermals rising from the Tihamah rather than the cold air of the mountains? No matter. They had found them. Stanley was grinning and whistling a dry, tuneless warble from which there occasionally issued a recognisable phrase from the immortal works of Ludwig van Beethoven. Despite his cheerfulness, however, Stanley Carter was aware that the return journey of his expedition had been successfully subverted by Muqbel, their Arab driver. He would not forget it.

They were climbing the first of the steep inclines, ten kilometres from the village of Hadjah, when the engine cut. There was just enough space to back off the tarmac onto the verge, from which a tumble of boulders dropped fifty metres into the wadi. Muqbel tried restarting the engine with the key, but there was not a spark of life. 'Mumkin karhabayi,' he said. Maybe electrical. 'Aw benzine.' Or petrol. 'Mush quais benzine.'

'The petrol is no good,' Jack said. 'Might be more dirt in it.'

The road was deserted for a moment. There was silence in the wadi and on the slopes to their right. It was a brittle silence of expectancy. Their voices echoed indistinctly, as from the depths of a cavern. No birds sang. They must open the bonnet. 'Perhaps,' Mike offered, 'the heat is evaporating the petrol. We need to let the engine cool.'

None of them had alighted from the vehicle, as if reluctant to admit that the bonnet must, of necessity, be opened.

Eddie looked back down the empty road. 'Never a cop when you want one,' he said. 'You have tools?'

Muqbel nodded. He got out and opened the bonnet. Stanley went with him while the others stayed in their seats, looking anxiously along their limited view of the road. Stanley threw a broken bottle down into the wadi. It smashed with an absurdly loud smash and tinkle against the boulders in the stream. There was the smell of steaming whisky. A truck came into view and ground painfully past them under an overload of quarried stone. Muqbel closed the bonnet as the truck driver called a greeting from his cab, and climbed back into the driver's seat as Stanley sat beside him. He turned the ignition key and the engine fired instantly. He shrugged with an apologetic smile and drove out onto the road, passing the truck with a beep of the horn.

'What was the trouble?' Alison asked.

'The engine was pissed,' Stanley said.

It hiccupped a couple of times and seemed to sober up, for they drove on for fifteen kilometres or so without incident.

The soldiers were waiting at the top of an incline, where the road levelled out on a bend before dropping away into another wadi.

Everything would be moving slowly here as it reached the top of the hill. It was a good place for a checkpoint, no doubt about that.

The soldiers waved them down. They stopped. The engine ticked over erratically.

The soldiers were apparently in an amiable mood; only one NCO was carrying a Kalashnikov. Jack tried to understand the questions put to Muqbel after the 'Salaam alaikum' and 'Wa alaikum salaam'.

'Who are your passengers?'

'Only five foreigners. To Sana'a. They have been swimming in the sea and looking at birds.'

'Crazy people. Let me see their passports.'

They handed them over to him. He was young, good-looking, with a neat moustache, intelligent. He put his head through the window and looked around. He checked their passports, evidently literate, and read through both the English and Arabic of the official stamps. With Alison's, he took much longer, opening the maroon cover and carefully checking the photograph before going through it page by page. Jack felt the sweat trickling down his back. Eddie looked at him, expressionless, as the engine misfired and spluttered back to life. The soldier turned back to Alison's photograph, which was three years old. 'Very beautiful,' he said in English. He gave the passports back to Stanley and the vehicle documents, or whatever they were, back to Muqbel.

He stepped back and waved them on with a smile. 'Welcome to my country.'

Muqbel released the handbrake and gently pressed the accelerator. The engine died like a consumptive in a fit of coughing. The ignition key failed with the kiss of life. The young soldier looked sympathetic, standing with his hands on his hips, the Kalashnikov slung carelessly over his shoulder. One of his subordinates, evidently something of a mechanic, came to the vehicle's front. There was slight forward movement as the heavy Land Cruiser rolled towards the slope in the road. It stopped. Perhaps there was a stone under a wheel. The two soldiers were joined by a third, a fourth, chewing qat. He of the mechanical aspiration placed his hand upon the bonnet.

'Too hot!' he said. 'Let her cool down. Open the bonnet.'

'Perhaps,' said another, 'the petrol is dirty. Open her up and let's have a look at the filter.'

Muqbel was risking the battery by turning the heavy starter motor with no sign of response.

The mechanic banged gleefully on the hot metal. 'Open her up, in the Name of Allah, and let's have a look.'

'It is nothing, O friends,' Muqbel said. 'She will start in a moment.'

'Get out and push,' Mike said. Eddie was already climbing from his seat.

'Give us a push, brothers,' Muqbel said.

The three junior soldiers pushed the wheel over the stone, and the car rolled painfully slowly back on to the smooth tarmac. He of the good looks, education and Kalashnikov, stood watching, his smile gone. Stanley and Eddie climbed back in and they sat helplessly waiting for the forces of gravity and the will of Allah to accelerate the speed of their departure. Muqbel wiped thin beads of sweat off his brow with the corner of his head-cloth.

The NCO stepped forward and looked into the back of the vehicle. He looked at the wooden boxes and came again to the window. 'Stannah shwai,' he said. Wait a bit!

With a neck-jarring, bottle-clinking jerk, the Toyota stopped and jerked forward with the engine roaring full throttle as Muqbel released the clutch, glanced in the mirror and said, with a wave, 'Masallamah.' He whistled through his teeth as the vehicle accelerated away. 'He very nice man,' he said.

Black clouds followed them up to Ta'izz and burst into a downpour as they reached the villa of Cecil's friend. There was still no one there. Muqbel said he would leave the vehicle in the walled garden for the night. They were all too tired and emotionally exhausted to care what he did. Alison asked him if he were not going home to see his family. He would go by taxi, he said. There was another roadblock on the way. He took one bottle and ten minutes after arriving at the villa he was gone.

'Tomorrow I come.'

They were thankful that the hot water system was working, and they all spent an inordinately long time in showering themselves free of the salt, dust and sweat of the preceding days. They were faced with the prospect of cooking, which none of them relished. Eddie suggested they all go down into the city and eat a meal in a Yemeni restaurant to celebrate finding the eagles. Everyone agreed enthusiastically except for Stanley, who said that expedition funds did not run to such extravagance. Mike, for once, argued with him, saying that from his calculations there should be plenty of money remaining in the kitty.

'Not if we spend it eating in Arab restaurants,' Stanley insisted. Besides which there was the risk of infection from such places. God knows what the kitchens of these places were like.

Jack, remembering some of Stanley's attempts at washing up, pointed out that the Yemenis were very clean people.

Eddie was too exasperated to argue. 'You please yourselves,' he said, 'but I'm going dahn tahn.'

Mike and Jack would do the same and pay for their own meals. Alison agreed to go with them, as she had never had the opportunity to experience Yemeni life while living with her parents.

Stanley was to be left alone. There would be all the cooking and the washing up to be done. Something tipped from a tin. He wanted a good meal, he was hungry, but if he gave in to them they would see it as a further abnegation of his authority, which he saw as steadily diminishing due to circumstances beyond his control and the undisciplined irresponsibility of his team. Such as this very business of going in to the city. Yet, if he stayed here in the villa alone, at this time of celebration, he would place himself apart in the hour of triumph. Should they unite against him, his leadership would be effectively ended and he saw that after the events of the day they were at the point of rebellion. There was but one course open to him. At least he would not be spending his own money and he was, after all, soon to be a famous man, for leaders of successful expeditions invariably commanded respect in the academic world.

There was good reason to celebrate. He smiled affably and said, 'Well, there was to have been a celebration dinner on our return to England. I suppose we might as well have it tonight.'

During the meal, which was somewhat inhibited by the presence, in civilian clothes, of the NCO from the checkpoint, Stanley took mental stock of the situation. The editors of *Garʒetta* would give prominence to his paper and, with a bit of luck, leadership of another expedition would follow. The sponsors would be happy that they had invested in him and could be touched for a grant in the future. He might well get a feature in one of the colour supplements if he pulled a few strings. That should bring in a bob or two and might lead to the odd lecture. There might even be a book in it. He had also done well in the choice of team, he decided. Look at them! Eddie. He was not likely to write anything up. Too lackadaisical, no competition there. Jack Pengelly, the Cornish bloody pixie, lacking the drive and ruthlessness of an achiever, would always be an also-ran. As for Mike, he was the ideal expedition man, unassuming and quietly efficient. Like many of his type, he had no ambition of his own. It was always advisable to avoid those with dominant personalities on these ventures. No prima donnas. Pick the ones who would do what they were told and blend into the scenery afterwards. All that remained to be done was the collecting of the specimens. Their labels in the British Museum would also bear his name.

After the meal they took a taxi back to the villa, watched by the suspicious NCO, opened one of Muqbel's bottles from under the bonnet and, after several nightcaps, fell into a contented sleep.

Chapter Seventeen

The air cooled perceptibly as they wound their way up the steep winding road that skirts the slopes of Jebel ad Dami. Broken crash barriers edging the hairpin bends indicated the fate of the careless, the reckless and those whose brakes had failed. Muqbel was driving with exceptional care, for which his passengers thanked the contents of the bottles under the bonnet. There had been one or two splutters of protest from the engine during the first half-hour, after which it recovered from its hangover and resumed its quiet, confident drone.

As always, they kept checking the slopes and wadi bottoms for birds. Gradually, they lost the tropical African species, such as chanting goshawks, rollers and babblers, and passed through the zone of banana trees and euphorbias at the roadside. They ascended once more into the high-altitude habitat of fan-tailed ravens and Yemen serins. At Ibb, they were overtaken by rain, which was lost again as they descended briefly into the upper reaches of Wadi Sahul, in the shadow of Jebel Nu'man.

They were grinding up the steep, tortuous stretch below the Sumarah Pass when Mike said, 'How long to Sana'a, Muqbel?'

Muqbel was concentrating hard on his driving, changing gear without jolts. He was concerned that there might be a roadblock at the pass. During daylight they normally allowed traffic through unchecked and restricted their searches to unpredictable times at night. The further he drove from his own area of Ta'izz, the more tense he became.

'Wadi Bana,' he said. 'We go Wadi Bana,' as he glanced at the skyline of rock overhanging the road.

Stanley turned on him. 'We have to get to Sana'a,' he said. 'Not Wadi Bana.'

Muqbel shot him a quick glance that left them all in no doubt that they were going to Wadi Bana, come what may. He was in no mood for persuasion or discussion. Before they approached the pass, he pulled the vehicle off the road, and they all got out to stretch their legs.

'All men look birds,' he said, and left them while he climbed the boulder-strewn mountainside to where he could see the road ahead.

'Muqbel,' Jack called after him. 'Time for chai?'

Muqbel waved assent, and they took the kettle and burners to a flat rock near the cliff. While waiting for their driver to complete his reconnaissance, they watched the griffon vultures utilising the currents of hot air rising from the hot plains in the far distance below.

'We should have known,' Mike said, 'where the eagles would be after watching these vultures. They're using the same air movements.'

'It's easy to be wise after the event,' Stanley grunted.

He was secretly seething with anger at being obliged, yet again, to obey the orders of Muqbel. The others, in their ignorance of the Arab mind, could not see that the man had taken the expedition over. No leader could accept such a situation and Stanley was quietly determined to be rid of Muqbel, no matter what the others said.

In the distance the sky was abruptly divided by a line of heat inversion between the hot, purple, moisture-laden obscurity of the lower altitudes and the clear blue sky of the mountains. They were in brilliant sunshine but there was a chill in the wind. A pair of Palestinian sunbirds sipped nectar, like humming birds, from flowers growing in the cliff. Down in the wadi, smoke rose from a small village. It was perched on a spur of rock halfway down the precipice and approachable only on foot. Two women were laying fodder on a roof to dry, ducking beneath a television aerial. The only sound was of the light wind passing through the scrub at the summit, until they heard the distant and unmistakable clatter of a helicopter. They saw it emerging from behind the mountains in the distance, hover over a village and disappear in the distant haze above Jebel Raymah.

'Bloody fings,' Eddie said.

Alison suddenly said, as if reminded of some fear deep in her subconscious, 'Why did that sambuk come from the north?'

'The what?' Her question was too obscure.

'The sambuk. The boat. My father said there was a shipment of whisky at the port of Mukha. That's to the south of Al Fazah, where we were. The boat came from the north.'

'So what?' Stanley said.

'I don't know. It just seems odd.'

'Perhaps it was hidden on the island,' Mike said. 'Perhaps that's why Hamid kept us away from the well.'

'But, why? Why take it to the island? There must be plenty of places to hide it on the mainland. It seems silly.'

'We don't know that it was on the island,' Stanley said. 'All I do know is, the sooner we get shot of the damned stuff, the better. And the same applies to that scheming driver, wherever he is. We could still get done for it, may I remind you.'

They needed no reminding. The audacity of the previous day, they were all now aware, could have resulted in serious consequences, and Muqbel would have been to blame.

'Where the hell is he?' Stanley asked. He wished to be moving, for the act of travelling in a vehicle implies progress other than that of the physical movement from place to place, and he felt vulnerable while in a state of imposed immobility. He could be heard making that *sk sk* sound at the back of his throat as he scanned the mountain for a sight of Muqbel, who was nowhere to be seen. Eddie raised his eyebrows to Alison in an expression of exasperation. She smiled in sympathy.

Muqbel eventually returned and was as anxious as Stanley to be off. He said there were no soldiers on road and that he wished to get through the pass as quickly as possible.

Five hundred metres of further climbing and they passed through the narrow cutting at the summit and on into the wide expanse of the montane plain of the Qa al Haql. Fifteen minutes later they turned right, off the tarmac, and followed the dirt road into the fertile fields of Achmed Ghanem and his sister, Nadirah.

'Whisky drink for Achmed,' Muqbel said.

Achmed was on the roof of his house. He could see the plain spread before him like a vast, flat panorama between the surrounding ring of hills and mountains. Under the blue, cloudless sky he could see far into the distance, where the road to Yarim and Sana'a ambled through the last of the outcrops before crossing the open plain of the Qa al Balasan. To the west, the escarpment and the heat of the coastal Tihamah; to the east, the slow descent into the parched interior where, two years in three, crops shrivelled to dust. This was the most beautiful and fertile farm in all Arabia. He was sure of that.

He completed the attachment of a length of coaxial cable to a tall aerial. His new purchase from the rogues at Sa'dah was more useful than the guns his sister thought he was buying there. A new ear, he said to himself. A new ear, O sister mine.

Her voice rose from the courtyard, where she was talking to their neighbour's children. Why could she not see that it was for her, and their neighbours, as well as himself that he did these things? This land was theirs. This land was his, and he loved it as other men loved their women. The greater the love, the stronger the bonds that tied them. He looked at the familiar scene. Was this view, from the top of his own house, to be his only view of the world for the rest of his life? Lazim. It must be. But it would be his view, his own view of his own land, and no one, east or west, left or right, would take it from him. It was his and he would die for it.

He came down through the building to emerge from the massive wooden door into the courtyard. Nadirah was swinging one of the children around in circles. Time she was married and had children of her own, he thought.

'The English have returned,' he said. 'I will go and welcome them.'

'Achmed!'

'Yes?'

'Oh nothing. It is not important.' She would learn in good time, she told herself, why her brother had turned from ill-concealed animosity toward the foreigners to a show of friendship and hospitality. She continued playing with the children. 'I want to go to London,' Mustafa said. 'Joharah and Zana are only girls.' Nadirah hugged all three of them, fearful of the future they must face.

Achmed walked down the winding track to the level of the stream, following the path around to where the bird watchers were standing uncertainly beside the Land Cruiser. He greeted them affably, shook hands with them and asked if they had enjoyed themselves on the coast, listening with interest to their recounting of their discoveries. That he considered their exploits in search of birds to be frivolous and typical of the irrelevancies of the Western mind, he kept to himself. They were, after all, but poor tourists who lived in tents like Bedouin, and it would be pointless to dampen their enthusiasm by explaining that the migration of the eagles had been known to his people for generations. It was part of their national character to believe their knowledge and intellect superior to any Arab. He smiled politely as Stanley expounded on the significance of the migration route through his country and, as soon as practicable, contrived to speak to Muqbel alone. The two of them went to the stream where Muqbel swilled his face with water.

'Any difficulties?' Achmed asked quietly.

'None.'

'No one had followed them?'

'No. No one.'

'The merchandise is here?'

'Yes,' Muqbel said. 'I want to unload it as soon as possible. It has been a great responsibility for me.'

'Yes. Yes. Drive the vehicle to our steps after dark.' Achmed had little patience with such timidity. 'And the foreigners?'

'They wish for Sana'a and to get the visas for staying.'

232

'So,' Achmed said to them, 'you will go back to your eagles. Then why go to Sana'a? Stay here under my protection. This is a dangerous country for you. There are baboons and leopards, to say nothing of wicked men who would rob you and possibly kill you. Ours is a poor country. Your possessions are treasure to some people here.'

He listened to their explanations regarding the renewal of visas and the necessity of taking Alison back to her father.

'Ah, but it is only two hundred kilometres to Sana'a and the road is good. At least stay for the day and see the beautiful birds of Wadi Bana again.'

He left them and went back to his sister. Just as he reached the top of the track, where their house was perched on the edge of the cliff, the helicopter came roaring over the mountains and sped along the plain, scattering sheep and goats in a cloud of dust. He spat at it and went deep into the shadow of his door. The foreigners would stay. Muqbel would see to it.

From the window of the mafrahj he watched them go behind the hill with their tents and camp beds. The British, he thought. Foolish people. How could they ever have convinced themselves that they ruled half the world? The radio scanner at the other end of the coaxial cable halted at the frequency of the transmission from the helicopter. The pilot had an accent. He was no Yemeni. They were heading back to Sana'a, he said. The transmission stopped and the scanner moved on, its green, pulsating light searching the frequencies of the military and the police. His sister tried to ignore the crackling and intermittent snatches of conversation.

'When are the people coming to cut the corn?'

'Tomorrow. I told you.'

'Oh, my brother,' she sighed.

The sun had set in a dark glow, which rose from the coast in the cool evening. The silence of the night fell upon the plain. There were evenings when, at the calling of the log, they found it hard to believe that incidents of the morning were part of the same day. The clipped accent of Stanley Carter's northern voice read down the list of species to be recorded for the day. Their driver took a bottle from the car, placed it before them with a smile and drove away from the camp to the base of the cliff and the steps leading up to the house of Ghanem. They watched him drive off with no comment from any of them.

Achmed was quite right, Stanley reasoned as he finished totalling the species list, there was no necessity for them all to return to Sana'a. If, he thought to himself, I take the Courtenay woman back to her father tomorrow, I can arrange for the renewal of the visas for all of us. I can take the passports of these idle morons that I misguidedly allowed to participate in my expedition, get Courtenay to pull rank and, at the same time, I can dismiss that blasted Muqbel and employ another driver. This Muqbel had, although his companions did not seem to appreciate the fact, gained the advantage of them and could, if he wished, even blackmail them into further acts of recklessness. The others could stay here and work the marsh and Wadi Bana. The Sumarah Pass was within walking distance if only they expended some energy. Reluctant as he was to accede to any suggestion from an Arab, he had to admit, it was a good idea.

He was somewhat disconcerted to find, despite the presence of all that booze in the Ghanem's house, everyone in agreement with the proposal and after the evening meal he poured whisky into their cups as though he were the host... 'That do you, Eddie? What about you, Mike?'

The night air was chilly after the heat of the Tihamah and they needed all their clothes. There was no fuel for a fire so they sat talking in the cold for a while, discussing the eagles and laughing, now that they were rid of it, at the adventure with the booze.

Eddie and Mike soon went to their tents and sleeping bags for warmth, leaving Alison sat on the ground between Stanley and Jack. Stanley was being particularly amiable, which Jack suspected was for ulterior reasons as yet obscure. He was silent as he listened to his leader talking to Alison. Stanley's conversation bored him. The man was humourless and self-opinionated to the point of exasperation. Anyone else would have the perception to see that he was superfluous and go to his tent and leave the other two on their own. Stanley would have her to himself all day tomorrow, God help her, and he could chat her up then, if that was what he wanted. He reached over and poured more whisky into Stanley's mug, then went to Eddie and Mike and topped theirs up also. Alison refused, with a shake of the head.

They heard noises from the house on the cliff. It sounded like Achmed quarrelling with his sister, Nadirah. Perhaps they were only calling to each other. They laughed.

'Bloody Arabs,' Stanley said, and at last, a little unsteadily, he went to his tent.

Jack moved closer to Alison toying with the idea of holding his mug to hers and saying in the best of Humphrey Bogart voices, 'Your tent or mine, baby?' but something in her demeanour, the way she was hugging her knees and staring at the ground, caused him to refrain.

'You know,' she murmured, 'I believe I shall always remember this week as one of the best times of my life.'

'I certainly will,' Jack said, speaking quietly that they might not be overheard, 'Finding the eagles, discovering you.' He hesitated before continuing, 'Seeing you as no other has, I think.'

'Yes. It wasn't easy. At first. Despite what you may have thought.'

'And despite what *you* may think, our secret episodes also came to mean more to me than just the lust.'

Alison chuckled quietly into her knees. 'I've never felt anything like that before. Perhaps the sheer terror I felt in the souk was a sort of catalyst that enabled suppressed emotions and desires to be released. I feel liberated from myself.'

'I shall never forget you,' he said.

'Nor I you.'

There, in those two brief statements, they had said it. All this was to be relegated to memory. With their disparate backgrounds, although both might wish it otherwise, there could be no future together. The silence of the night enveloped them. Millions of stars shone on their predicament.

Jack put his arm around her shoulders and drew her closer to him. 'I suppose I won't see you again,' he said.

'That's up to you. I'll give you our address in England.'

He kissed her cheek. 'Don't expect me to write. I don't want to remember you as an unanswered letter.'

'As you wish.'

When Muqbel drove the Toyota to the base of the cliff Achmed was waiting with the donkey. Achmed paid Muqbel his due, suggesting that he might find it profitable to transport another load sometime.

Muqbel was non-committal. 'Mumkin,' he said, thinking it might be unwise to push his luck with Allah and the askari for a second time without the benefit of foreigners for cover. 'Inshallah,' God willing, he said, and left Achmed loading the donkey. First, he loaded the animal with the sacks from around the engine. The second and third journeys were with the boxes from inside the vehicle.

Nadirah was sitting at the top of the steps when the donkey struggled up with the final load. She had opened one of the sacks.

'Whisky!' she said. 'By God, what are you doing, Achmed?'

'Be quiet,' he said impatiently. 'Hold the donkey while I unload her. These boxes are heavy. They must be hidden in the cave. Help me with them. No one must know but you and me.'

'Oh!' she cried. 'In the name of the Compassionate, the Merciful, why do you do these things?' But she picked up a sack by the corner, the bottles clinking together inside

'No, the boxes first.'

They lifted them from the animal together and brother and sister carried the boxes to the security of the dug-out cave at the side of the house. The cave was small, with a very narrow entrance. It had been used for storage and, in more recent times, as shelter from attack in the civil war. They slid the boxes through the entrance, and Achmed stacked them at the rear where other, longer boxes lay stacked on a crude shelf. They were carrying the fifth box when Nadirah tripped in the darkness and it fell from her grasp. The lid split from its hinges and the contents spilled onto the ground. No broken glass. Nadirah knelt and felt the bare soil, pushing her brother's hand roughly aside. She picked up a handful of hard, cold, heavy...

'Rassassa!'

The word escaped from her lips in a reluctant hiss. 'Rassassa!' Lead! Bullets!

★ ★ ★

Stanley left with Alison and Muqbel before breakfast, saying that he wanted to avoid the heavy traffic that rumbled along the main road later in the day, but fooling no one. They all knew he would stop at a roadside eating-house, and have a good meal, as soon as he found one. He would pay for Alison's breakfast in the hope that she would mention it to her father, who would probably reimburse him for his generosity and include sufficient to pay for Stanley's indulgence also. He took all their passports and insisted that all equipment be removed from the vehicle, even the water containers, though there was no use for them at the camp, with the clear spring nearby. They were glad to see the back of him but their campsite at the base of the conical hill, with three small tents and a heap of equipment, was bereft of substance by the absence of the solid mass of the vehicle. The camp looked vulnerable in the vast landscape... naked.

The morning was windless, yet the cold crept through their clothes with searching persistence, as if eager to penetrate their very bones before being dispelled by the rising sun slanting its rays between the peaks to the east.

Mike and Eddie were anxious to go through the gorge and down into the lush greenery of Wadi Bana. Jack decided to go alone to the eastern hills and, after the early check around the camp at breakfast time, he set off in the direction of the reservoir he had seen the previous week.

The reservoir was ancient, with a dam of massive stonework

and, to his delight, ringing with the calls of waders. Not bad. He stopped to look through the birds lined up along the shore. Stints again. A couple of littles, Temmincks. And some others... Yes, yes, that was a red-necked stint. And another. The white foreheads... the tertials... the scapulars and coverts... sure of it.

He took out his notebook and felt the familiar glow of excitement as the adrenalin flowed through his body and quickened his brain. He wrote rapidly before the birds were disturbed by two men approaching. They asked him to share tea with them and others working in the fields. Jack declined and, to avoid further interruptions of his bird watching, climbed a little way into the hills, where he found a small track following the contours to the east. After an hour's walking, the track ascended a range of hills between terraced fields which became progressively smaller as he climbed. Eventually he saw a village ahead. It was high up, on a ridge, and to its left there was sheer cliff honeycombed with caves. He checked his map and found he had come to As Saddah, one of the oldest villages in Yemen. He checked the map again. Yes, As Saddah. The site was supposed to have been continuously occupied by all the succeeding civilisations of the country since, possibly, Stone Age man lived in the labyrinth of caves. How he wished he had read more of Yemen. No matter where one's eyes alighted there were thousands of years of discarded history evident in ruins and ancient artefacts. Only Mike had taken the trouble to learn anything about the country apart from its birds. He climbed to the village, which seemed deserted. He was walking on a scree of shards and scattered building stone. On stone which had been cut by some expert hand before the time of Muhammad, before Jesus, perhaps before Abraham, or even Moses. They lay in loose cascades, tumbling down the slopes like the fallen walls of Jericho.

Then, he saw an old couple watching him from the door of one of the houses on the ridge. They stood motionless, eyeing him as if some intruder from another age had entered their isolated land. Feeling that his presence required some explanation, he walked over to them.

'Salaam alaikum.' They exchanged the formal greetings but he had difficulty in understanding their strong accents. Three times they asked where he came from.

'Breetania,' he told them.

The old man smiled and told his wife who told him to ask if the kawahjah was married.

'No,' he said, 'not married.'

She made some joke at Jack's expense. They asked his name. He asked theirs. They were lovely, wrinkled, kind-eyed people, who showed him the shoots of corn pushing through the poor soil of one of their terraces. Very good, he said, and made his peace before departing up the hill.

From the top of the jagged ridge above the village he could see the landscape rolling away to the east in a brown barrenness of dry, infinite hills and mountains. He was at the eastern edge of the highlands, and the country fell away before him in a steady descent to the unimaginable desolation of the Empty Quarter. The area before him was less contorted and steep than the western escarpment but, by reason of its shimmering immensity, far more fearful and impossible to traverse. It was a threatening landscape, and he turned away from it.

A covey of partridges rose with a whirr of wings and planed down to the slopes in a wide, evading circle. He raised his binoculars. Philby's partridges. Another species for his life list.

He smiled to himself, thinking, Philby, Thesiger, Doughty... how the foreigners had attempted to know this land and left it ignorant of their passing. What did the Yemenis name these birds, these so-called Philby's partridges?

He left the ridge and settled to look back at the more fertile plain. The colours and contours of the beautiful scene filled him with a sudden irrational elation, and he skipped joyfully down the scree to the village path, where he stopped in astonishment at seeing Nadirah Ghanem talking to the old couple he had encountered on the ascent. They had obviously been discussing him, for the old man indicated Jack's approach with a friendly wave. Jack decided to avoid them and go back to the barikah but the old man called him over, at the insistence, he was sure, of Nadirah.

'Good morning, Mister Pengelly,' she said. 'I believe you have already met my uncle and aunt.'

Her English was perfect when unhurried, yet delivered with the stylised precision of one who is not totally familiar with the nuances of a foreign language.

'Your uncle?' he said. 'Yes, we had quite a chat.'

She smiled, showing her white teeth.

They invited him to eat at the house, which he declined with apologies, explaining with the help of Nadirah, that he had work to do. Nadirah said she would accompany him back to the barikah, and they bade God's peace upon the old couple and left them standing on the steep scree between the village and the caves, obviously doubting the wisdom of allowing their niece to go off with the foreigner.

'This is just like home,' he said. 'Everybody is related to each other in the villages.'

'The English are too many in the cities.'

He told her, as he had told hundreds of others, that he was not exactly English.

'You speak it very well,' she said, and he dropped the subject.

The thought occurred to him that she might have followed him to As Saddah in order to keep an eye on him. To make sure he was not abusing her brother's hospitality. They walked down the steep track in silence and, when they were on the path following the contour, she said, 'The lady has returned?'

He was perplexed for a moment, as to which lady she referred, and he looked directly at her, intending to interrogate her with a look, but she watched the path ahead as if oblivious of his stare.

'To Sana'a,' she continued, recognising the ambiguity of her statement, perhaps.

'Yes,' he said. He allowed her to lead the way down the track, which led to the barikah, an hour's walk away.

'She is very beautiful,' she said, half turning to him.

'You reckon?' he said.

Then there fell a silence between them not entirely due to the difficulties which might arise should they discuss anything but the prosaic, and Jack sensed that she was taciturn by intent. He caught her looking at him questioningly on occasion. Eventually, the silence became intolerable, charged with tension, though he knew not why. She was so close to him. He could smell a faint perfume, which may have emanated from her own body, so elusive and subtle was it. Yet, she was as remote as tomorrow.

Eventually they were down on the level ground and the afternoon sun was at its height. Although she walked with such grace and ease, apparently without effort, he found himself striding with some exertion and felt the perspiration gathering at his brow. They came to some massive boulders overhanging the path, where she suddenly stopped and sat down in the shade.

'You rest,' she said, although she had not looked back at him in fifteen minutes of steady walking.

He found this very irritating, as if she were trying to prove his inferiority. He said, 'Did you follow me today?'

'I not follow you,' she said. 'Of course not.'

He looked straight into her black doe eyes.

'Yes. I follow you.' There was neither smile nor frown.

'Why?' he asked, equally as blandly.

She shrugged. He opened his water bottle, offered it to her. She declined with a shake of the head. He tipped the bottle and drank deeply.

'Very bad for you,' she said.

He finished gulping the tepid water and said, 'Sure.'

The silence again. Far in the distance, he heard the waders calling and, by habit and quite unconsciously, he identified them as he spoke. 'I don't think she's beautiful,' he said. 'She's very attractive, but not beautiful.' He wanted to say, not as you are beautiful. It was mamnooah, forbidden.

Their eyes turned simultaneously and for the first time they looked at each other directly and enquiringly.

Yes, he was thinking, you are the beautiful one, but was unable to tell her. 'Beauty is in the eye of the beholder,' he heard himself saying. 'And in the eye of the beheld.'

Nadirah was not sure that he meant what he seemed to be saying, or of his motive in saying it. 'You think she is a nice lady?'

'Sure, she's a very nice girl.'

'I think her father is not a very nice man.'

This statement astonished him. What did this Arab girl know of Harry Courtenay? He let it pass. Soon, he'd want a skeet. 'We'd better get on,' he said.

As they approached the barikah, and the disturbed waders began calling anxiously, he stopped to look at them from a distance.

'More of your special Yemeni birds,' he said, half mocking her. She did not accept this challenge but, to his amazement, placed her hand upon his arm, drawing the binoculars from his eyes.

'Jack,' she said.

'Yes?'

'Soon we will be back. Near my house. Achmed will be angry if he see me speaking to you.'

His immediate reaction to that, that she was a big girl now and should have a mind of her own and all the other Western replies, were all totally inappropriate. He said nothing.

'You must go from here,' she said. 'There are bad things here for you.'

No doubt she saw the look of incredulity in his eyes, for she dropped her voice to a whisper in that vast, empty landscape and said, 'I cannot tell you what they are, these things, but your life might be for danger.' She smiled wanly and corrected herself. 'In danger. I know.'

He too smiled, for he didn't believe a word she was saying. If they had outstayed their welcome, she had only to say so. It was, as he ought to remind her, at her brother's insistence that they were here and had not gone to Sana'a with Stanley Carter.

'No. Do not smile. Please. Persuade your friends to go as soon as Mr Carter returns. You are risking too much. For the people here, you are the dangerous.'

'What the hell are you talking abut, Nadirah?'

She was play-acting, he thought, showing herself as the subordinate bint, subject to her brother's command. He would call her bluff. Treat her as an equal.

'What danger can we present to your people, for God's sake? All we are doing is looking at a few birds!'

At the conclusion of this, he was bristling with irritation and was even more annoyed when she looked at him and said, 'You know! Damned kawahjah. The boxes you brought for my brother.'

Oh that, he thought. 'So what?' he said. 'If your brother wants the stuff, you can hardly blame the carriers.' He was not sure she had understood. 'You can't blame us,' he said, 'we didn't even know it was in the car. Your brother used us.'

This had occurred to him as a revelation as he spoke and he considered the significance of it. They had been manipulated since leaving Sana'a a week ago. It was obvious when one thought about it. The knowledge of this made him feel suddenly very vulnerable. He watched her eyes. No! It couldn't be. His suspicion was preposterous. Too many apparent coincidences to have been contrived. Too many people involved... Abdullah, Muqbel, Hamid, Achmed, Harry Courtenay and Alison... for credibility.

'I think you're over-reacting,' he said.

She rounded on him angrily, saying, as she swept back her headscarf with one hand, 'What you know? Damned English? Interfering in none of your damn business.'

'I am not interfering with anything. And I'm not an Englishman. How many times do I have to say it, for Christ's sake?'

'You are a damn kawahjah,' she cried.

'And you are behaving like a typical hysterical Arab bint.'

He had said it, and all his regrets could not recall the words. She turned and ran a few paces on her slender brown legs. Then, with sudden tears streaming down her face, she stopped and confronted him with a steam of abuse gushing from her lips like a flood of poison. She cursed him and brought the wrath of Allah upon him and his descendants. She defiled his ancestry as a lineage of sodomites and whores begat of camels and donkeys. With her voice rising, she condemned him and his kind to the eternal fires of hell.

Jack understood not a word of it and she left him standing on the track in a daze of incomprehension. He followed slowly behind her, until she was lost to view in the distance. When he reached the barikah, he stopped to watch the stints, but could not concentrate and wandered back to camp, seeing nothing but those black, beautiful, tear-brightened eyes and the hate and fear they held.

The other two were back at the campsite after spending the morning in Wadi Bana. They were more relaxed than they had been for days and, sensing that they were enjoying themselves in the absence of Stanley, Jack was reluctant to raise the subject of Nadirah's outburst. Achmed had made them welcome, after all.

Eddie, especially, was in no doubt about his leader's absence. 'I 'ope,' he said, 'he stays in Sana'a till his bleedin' birfday.'

'One finds him a bit much, after a month,' Mike said. The first time he had openly expressed doubt about Stanley's leadership. These middle-class English and their sense of duty, Jack thought, can get on your nerves.

'I'd be quite happy,' Mike added, 'to spend a week in Wadi Bana if we had no transport. It's incredibly interesting. I expect some of the dragonflies are new to science.'

'Don't tell Carter,' Eddie said. 'He'll have 'em stuck on pins.'

'Yes. Perhaps. Ha ha.' Mike was thinking of the future when Wadi Bana would be ruined. 'I think we ought to mount another expedition based on this one wadi, with excursions to check and record the raptor migration. It might be rather fun.'

'I'll come,' Eddie said, 'as long as Stanley Carter ain't on it.' He turned to Jack and said, quite seriously, 'There's something wrong with that bloke. He ain't right in the 'ead.'

'He's bit highly strung,' Jack said.

He decided to say nothing about Nadirah's warning. It was probably just her suspicion that they had brought the whisky with their own intent. A word with Achmed should sort it out. There was no point in letting unnecessary distractions prevent them from enjoying the prospect of bird watching in such fantastic scenery with no Stanley Carter to get on their nerves.

'Let's make the most of it while he's away. Guess what. There's some red-necked stints on the barikah.'

Chapter Eighteen

S tanley did ask Muqbel to stop at a good eating-place. He did pay
for the meals, although from expedition reserves, not his own
pocket. He was quite pleased to be away from his companions for
the journey back to Sana'a. They had begun to get on his nerves
during recent days and he needed a break from them. It was a strain
having to keep pushing them all the time. None of them seemed
committed to the purpose of the expedition, despite which he had
achieved the objective and found the eagles. He could see now, in
retrospect, that he had made a great mistake in mounting a four-
man expedition. They had met with no difficulty he could not have
surmounted alone and a damn sight cheaper. By making use of Fred
Stirling, Courtenay and Cecil Hayward, he could have achieved as
much, if not more, than he had with the spurious assistance of his
three compatriots.

For the long drive back to Sana'a, they all three sat on the bench
seat of the Toyota, Muqbel driving, Alison in the middle and
Stanley on the right. Alison had become confident of Muqbel's
driving and she was able to relax and enjoy the scenery of the
cool, sunlit highlands of the central plateaux. Muqbel was the first
Arab with whom she had come in close contact and she warmed to
him with each succeeding day of their acquaintance. His slender
hands grasped the steering wheel with a sensual strength which she
found reassuring, while his happy smile, flashed at her like a bright
confidence, indicated a contentment with life which she envied. She
would like, she thought, to meet his wife and children.

Stanley, feeling nothing in common with either of them,
disliking one for her class and the other for his race and regarding

himself superior in intellect to both, gazed at the passing scenes in abstraction. He had done it. He kept reminding himself. The raptor migration through Yemen was as significant, if not more so, than the great passages over the Bosporus and Gibraltar. Properly written up, the discovery would ensure his place in the annals of science. His name was made. And now, when their visas were renewed, there was the prospect of another month to quantify the migration and explore the country for its endemics. He had good reason to congratulate himself. He began whistling with satisfaction at his achievements.

His whistling was an exhalation of breath between teeth and tongue, like a draught under a door. The wheezing, which was his interpretation of the Shepherd's Song from the great Pastoral Symphony, jarred on the conversation of the other two with persistent discord.

Alison picked up some of Muqbel's cassette tapes and read some of the English labels.

'Don't put any of that rubbish on,' Stanley said.

She ignored him and turned to Muqbel. 'Do you know any Yemeni songs?'

Muqbel laughed. 'Yes,' he said.

'Will you sing something?'

'I sing wedding song. We have man in village make song for any thing. He make song for my wedding.'

Stanley was seething at this direct rebuttal but, short of inciting open conflict, there was nothing he could do but listen to Muqbel sing.

'A special song for you?' Alison said.

'Oh, yes. It is about my beautiful wife and I am handsome man take care her. Have happy house and many children.'

'How sweet.'

She had used the expression thoughtlessly many times before, and for the first time the banality of it struck her like a revelation. 'I mean... how lovely for you.'

'Oh yes. If no like song, no pay money. Tell man he make another.'

He was evidently very pleased with his wedding song and sang all the verses as she watched his face, trying to interpret words she could not understand. It was a delightful song, and she imagined it sung to the instruments of the villagers, and wished she could have someone write a song especially for her. When Muqbel finished, with a long quavering note, she put her hand on his arm and said, 'That was lovely, Muqbel.'

Stanley *skukked* a couple of times with nervous irritation and said nothing, even when Alison put a tape in the player and, for the first time, listened to Arabic music which she had heard, unheeded, on the periphery of her life for many years.

They came into the dust of Sana'a in the afternoon and Muqbel drove straight to Alison's villa. They unloaded their gear, and Stanley paid Muqbel off.

Muqbel counted the money rapidly, in the Arab way, with the notes slipping through his fingers like flickering leaves in a breeze. It was not enough and there came into his eyes an expression of deep, uncomprehending disappointment. After all they had been through together.

Alison said, 'Pay him!'

There were more favours to be asked, so Stanley paid.

'Shukran,' Muqbel said. 'You want I see tomorrow take Wadi Bana?'

Stanley dismissed him, saying that he didn't know when he was returning.

'I take,' Muqbel said.

Of that, Stanley was sure, there was no chance. As they reached the house, he said, 'These Arabs expect one to bargain, you know. There's no doubt that they respect you for it.'

She led him in and showed him his room for the night. He took advantage of the facilities in the bathroom and enjoyed the luxury of a shower before sitting and drinking his host's whisky while awaiting his return.

Alison, despite treating Stanley with indifference, was in high spirits. She was polite and observed the formalities of hospitality, but kept him at a distance while reflecting on the events of the past week. She came to the conclusion that they had been the most exciting of her life, not least of which were the moments alone with Jack Pengelly. She could not relate those incidents to her parents but, for the rest, was like a schoolgirl returned from holiday keen to tell of her adventures.

The Courtenays came through the door with exaggerated cries of welcome. These were extended to Stanley, who found himself enveloped in Mrs Courtenay's arms. She was glad Alison had offered their guest the hospitality of the house, and fetched a couple of glasses for herself and Harry.

'You're looking so well, darling,' she said. 'What have these boys been doing with you?'

Before Alison could answer, her father said, 'Now come and sit down and tell us all about it.'

Her silver exhilaration was thereby transmuted into the dross of leaden formality. Nevertheless her excitement was too intense to be entirely debased by her father's gift of inverted alchemy.

'Oh', she said, 'it's been wonderful.'

She told them of Wadi Bana and the scenery, the dust storms, of getting stuck in the dunes, the coral reefs and the flamingos. She misinterpreted the smug look on her mother's face when she glanced at her husband at the mention of flamingos, but her parents were obviously delighted that the trip had been so enjoyable for her. She did think they were treating her with a degree of condescension, with over-indulgence, so reminiscent of her many returns from boarding school. She decided to enjoy that too, however, for she had not been the centre of their attention for a long time.

Harry was pleased with himself. He smiled benignly on his young woman of a daughter. A very fortuitous notion, to send her off for a holiday before she returned to England. She was a changed woman.

'And what about your eagles?' he asked Stanley, thinking for the first time that his daughter was no longer a child. Alison a woman. The thought was disturbing.

'We found them!' Alison cried before Stanley could gather his wits to answer. 'Hundreds of them. Oh, it was so exciting. It was even more exciting than smuggling the whisky.'

It was whisky that spattered all over Stanley's spectacles as he coughed into his glass, whisky that flopped from Mrs Courtenay's glass into her lap, and whisky that stuck in Harry Courtenay's throat as he contorted his neck in an effort to sluice it over his epiglottis before exploding, 'Whisky? What whisky?'

In the ensuing embarrassed silence, Harry controlled himself very well. 'You did say, did you not, forgive me if I misheard you, my dear, smuggling whisky?'

He congratulated himself for keeping so cool, calm and collected and waited patiently for an answer.

'Well,' Alison said meekly, all her exuberance gone and once more a child before her father. 'We didn't mean to.'

'Perhaps,' Stanley said in what he considered to be the tone of voice and phraseology that Harry himself might have used in the situation, 'you will permit me to explain, sir.'

'Indeed,' Harry said.

'Firstly, I would like to say that under no circumstances would I knowingly have transported illegal alcohol in a vehicle in which the daughter of an ambassador was travelling under my protection. I use the term ambassador advisedly, sir.'

He had seen the brief expression of impatience cross Harry's face and, more significantly, the smirk of smug superiority that followed.

'For a man in your position, sir, any suggestion of illegal activity by a member of your family would be unthinkable.'

His accent let him down. One cannot employ the stilted phrases of the middle classes effectively without mimicking their bland toneless vowels.

Mrs Courtenay twirled the damp glass in her fingers, wondering what law she was thereby breaking, and smiled weakly as her husband refilled it, along with all the others.

'Quite.' Harry said. He was dreading the full story. He thought they might have been caught by the police, that dozens of bottles were buried beneath the grass of his miserable bit of lawn, or that they had accepted a bribe to smuggle the stuff under cover of Alison's diplomatic passport. He saw Washington disappearing from his future like a receding comet. 'Let me have the whole story, please,' he said.

What was there to tell? Muqbel had shown them the whisky and they had agreed, volunteered, to drive with him through the roadblocks. They could blame no one, although some excuse was called for.

'We Westerners,' Stanley said, 'find it very difficult to penetrate the conniving mind of the Arab and are more easily deceived, I'm afraid.'

'Do you know this driver's name? Where he lives? The number of his vehicle?'

'I can find out,' Stanley said. 'The man will be expecting me to hire his vehicle for the rest of our stay. I can find him at the Bab al Yemen bus and taxi terminus.'

'You do realise, young man,' Harry said, 'that there might well follow ramifications. Serious ramifications.'

'I do indeed.'

Stanley had heard no mention of visas and assumed they would still be forthcoming if Courtenay kept his word and this silly business of a few bottles of booze was not exaggerated beyond all reason. While not actually saying that Muqbel could easily be picked up by the police, he had fed the idea to Courtenay, who could act on it as he wished.

'It wasn't entirely Muqbel's fault,' Alison said. 'We didn't have to stay with him. When I think about it, I think we were all manipulated. I think Abdullah was behind it.'

Her father's pink face faded to a pallid grey. 'Abdullah?' he said in a small, highly-pitched voice strangely not his own. He cleared his throat. 'Who is Abdullah, Alison?' he asked, knowing even before he heard his daughter's description of the man, exactly who he was. To Harry's growing dismay, and Stanley's growing anger, she told them about the incident in the Bab al Yemen souk, which explained the gift of the bull's head and the meeting with the same man while travelling to the coast. Stanley confirmed Harry's suspicion by telling him that this Abdullah was the same disreputable character who had guided Fred Stirling to the house of the Sheikh in the north. There was a profound silence in the room.

Stanley resolved that Jack Pengelly was due for a severe reprimand after becoming involved in a shooting incident with Alison and saying nothing about it. If there was one thing essential for efficient leadership it was that the leader be kept fully informed of all events relating to his organisation. Nothing would have induced him to go to Al Fazah had he known of his subordinate's involvement with this man.

'A sad business, sir,' he said to Harry and hoped it was not too long before he got the visas and could get back and sort Pengelly out. Mike and Eddie would side with him for once.

Alison knew, from her father's demeanour, that there was something he did not know and she kept quiet, unwilling to reveal more. She had been very effectively prevented from the enjoyment of relating her adventures and, if he wanted to know anything else, he would damn well have to ask, whatever it might be.

Mrs Courtenay sat with a fixed, winsome smile, while her eyes opened and closed in synchronisation with the fan revolving in wide sweeps below the ceiling, as if expecting a succession of blows from its fourth, oil-thirsty arm.

Harry decided he must see Cecil Hayward before this damned twitcher could tell a biased account of his daughter's involvement with smuggling. Damned silly affair anyhow. Everyone knew perfectly well that alcohol was freely available and that it was not officially banned from the country entirely, merely to good Muslims who, like good Christians, Harry thought, were pretty thin on the ground where alcohol was concerned. The business of Abdullah was more serious. Alison had been involved, as a witness, in murder. The plaque, any court would assume, was a bribe which had been accepted for silence. If the government, both governments, God, either government, found out, there would be serious consequences. Alison must leave the country immediately. The bird watchers would have to be thrown out as soon as possible. To hell with their bloody visas. He wished the damned lot of them had never crossed his path.

That evening, after a meal eaten in virtual silence while they were all preoccupied with their own thoughts, Harry made excuses and went to his office, where he wrote a memorandum to the Old Man, and then called on Cecil Hayward.

The memo was a summary of Abdullah's known movements during the past weeks, together with speculation on the possibility of subversives using whisky smuggling as a means of financing their activities. He made it clear, in modest terms, that his use of the bird watchers, and the vigilance and daring of his own daughter, were instrumental in gathering such intelligence. As to the advisability of informing their hosts of these matters, he left that to the discretion of his superiors. As well to have these things in writing.

Cecil listened to the story of the whisky with some amusement. 'My dear chap,' he said. 'Hardly anything to upset yourself over.'

'I'm not upset,' Harry said, suspecting that he may have overstated his case. 'But I have doubts about helping these chaps to extend their visas. They appear to draw attention to themselves quite unnecessarily. One would have thought bird watching a somewhat unobtrusive activity, to say the least. I really wonder whether one should use one's influence on behalf of such tiresome people.'

There was something else, Cecil knew from his superior's manner, which Harry had not told him. He found Harry's devious ways amusing and knew why Harry had never made it to the top of his profession. In a few years, Cecil would overtake him and possibly find him working as a subordinate. It had nothing to do with social status, despite Harry's belief to the contrary. Harry so concerned himself with the greater visions, in preparation for his great leaps forward, that the minor irritations of day-to-day administration were invariably delegated to his juniors. Consequently, as the greater machinations were beyond his brief, he was inclined to be out of touch in both directions and spent his days in a void of ill-informed speculation which was the very antithesis of his office.

'What shall we do about the bird men?' Harry asked as he firmly resolved to submit the memo when the time was ripe. 'I promised to arrange their visas. Do you think we should do so, under the circumstances?'

'Where are they now? At your place?'

'One of them is. Carter. Claims to be the leader. The others are down near Yarim.'

'Got their passports? Photographs?'

'Passports, yes. They don't have any photographs.'

Harry had forgotten to tell Stanley about the necessity of photographs for visas. He was about to say that Stanley Carter had forgotten to bring them when Cecil forestalled him.

'Leave it to me,' Cecil said. 'I'll arrange something.'

He always knew when Harry was trying to push jobs in his direction and took secret delight in doing these tasks apparently without effort. He wanted no more of Harry's excuses and he didn't want him floundering around out of his depth.

'Send Carter along to me,' he said. 'I've offered them the use of my villa and he might prove something of a burden to your wife. I'll entertain him for a day or two. Oh, and by the way, Fred Stirling intends to survey the Tihamah as soon as it's cool enough. Perhaps you might remind our hosts that the DOS do have permission. We must be sure the locals in the area know that the work is official, or we'll have the whole team locked up by some over-zealous corporal.'

'It's in hand,' Harry said, and thought there was nothing he would like better than seeing Fred Stirling incarcerated in jail for a couple of months.

Stanley resolved to enjoy his sojourn in Sana'a. He saw no reason why taxpayers' money should not be spent on his entertainment any more than on the next man. No doubt Hayward and Courtenay would claim reimbursement for keeping him for a day or two, a distressed British subject. He had his photograph taken in a dingy, but efficient back-street studio. He went to Kawkaban with Alison and Cecil, who took a day off to drive them in his car. His visa took three days and Cecil assured him that the others' were now merely a formality of filling in forms and the submission of photographs.

'One simply has to resign oneself,' Cecil said, 'to the fact that even the most routine business involves hours, or even days, of procrastination. One can do nothing but comply. You'll see that your exit visa is also stamped. There are advantages to the system.'

'In paying bribes, you mean?'

'Quite. Yours is two hundred and fifty riyals.'

Stanley paid, wishing he had not mentioned money, for he assumed, wrongly, that Cecil was too much of a gentleman to ask for it. He was to return to Wadi Bana, use Eddie's camera to take some black and white mug-shots of the other three, get Muqbel to run them up to Cecil for developing, and Cecil himself would bring the stamped passports back on his way to Ta'izz in a day or two.

'Yes,' Stanley said. 'Fine. Great. Thanks very much. I'll do that.'

Except that he had no intention of using Muqbel. There were hundreds of Toyota Land Cruisers for hire and he was having no more of Muqbel's insubordination and scheming. A new broom would sweep clean. This time he was quite determined; they would have a driver who would do as he was told. On his final day, he packed his rucksack and announced his intention to walk across town to the taxi rank. Cecil gave him a lift and left him, aware that he was being used, and asked for the exact location of the campsite.

The drivers were stupid. None of them spoke English and Stanley knew nothing of their impossible language, while none of them, it appeared, had ever heard of Yarim, or Ibb, or Kitab, or even Ta'izz, for that matter. 'Ingijh' was all he could get out of them as he went from one to the other trying to get transport south. On one occasion, an old man took pity on him and tried to discover where he was going, but the driver grumbled at him and the old man shrugged helplessly and sat back in the vehicle, which had three empty seats. The drivers were openly laughing at Stanley. Some made derogatory remarks and crude jokes at his expense; he did not need to speak the language to understand that. He saw Muqbel leaning unconcernedly from his cab.

'Sabah al kier, Mister Stanley.'

Stanley had no choice. 'Take me to Wadi Bana,' he said.

'Yah, Mister Stanley, lazim I go see friend. I very busy.'

'Well, which of these vehicles are going to Ta'izz?' Stanley waved his arm around the crowded park.

'You ask him,' Muqbel said. 'Maybe all. Maybe none. Maybe ingijh.'

'So that's it. None of them will take me because you've fixed it. They're all your mates, is that it?'

Muqbel tossed his head in a mild Arabic gesture of indifference and smiled apologetically. Stanley controlled his rising temper, opened the door and dumped his rucksack on the seat. 'This taxi,' he said, 'is engaged.'

'OK. Ingijh.'

Ingigze, ingidge, engaged. Even when they spoke English one could only guess at what the hell they meant. Good God. Ingijh!

'I come back,' Muqbel said, 'after one hour. Now I chew qat with friend. You come chew qat, Mister Stanley? Same-same Yemeni man?'

'No! Bugger off. I'll wait.'

He arrived at Wadi Bana tired and hungry late that night. He was in a vile temper, swearing to himself that he would get even with this piss-taking Arab as soon as the opportunity arose. So, after initial overtures of welcome, which were rebuffed, the others ignored him. All climbed into their sleeping bags early to avoid both the cold and each other's company.

When Jack awoke next morning, just as the first streaks of daylight were brightening the sky, he saw Stanley already up and dressed. There was a pot of tea made, from which Stanley was pouring four cups. He placed one at the entrance of each tent and held one in his own cupped hands.

'Morning boys,' he said. ' Bit chilly today.'

Eddie and Mike opened their flaps at this cheerful greeting and immediately fell into a trough of suspicion. All retreated with their mugs into their tiny tents and listened to Stanley whistling his tuneless buzz. They expected him to shout them out, to stop wasting time on such a beautiful morning when there was so much work to be done. Eventually curiosity drove them out, but he gave no indication of the reason for his good humour.

Jack took his usual quick walk around the hill before breakfast and saw that Nadirah was coming down the steep track from the house. She paused when she saw him and waited until there was no possibility of their meeting before going to the spring. They had not spoken since her outburst at As Saddah. He would have liked to go over to the spring and talk to her, carry the water pitcher. Such simple convergence in view of the house was mamnooah, forbidden. He returned to the camp, where breakfast was eaten in constraint, in direct contrast to the cheerful enthusiasm of the past few days. Mike was the most suspicious of Stanley's behaviour. He had come to associate these periods of geniality with some devious scheming at the back of Stanley's mind and, while not mentioning his suspicion, was prepared for some unpleasantness to follow.

They arranged the schedule for the day. Eddie was to look at the hills over towards the Sumarah Pass, Stanley said. Jack to check the reservoir for waders, as that was evidently where his interest lay. Mike could go to the village for supplies and check the plain, while Stanley would stay around the campsite. Mike had doubts about leaving Stanley alone all morning, but they were without rational foundation, so he didn't mention them to the others. 'Where are our passports?' he asked bluntly.

The others looked at him sharply. They were unused to hearing such insistence in his normally placid voice. Stanley also detected a note of suspicion in the question, but he smiled and said, 'I've arranged everything. Don't worry. Haven't you learned to have faith in your leader, Mike?' They waited expectantly and he continued, 'Courtenay made a balls of things, as I expected, but I got Hayward to sort it out. Our visas, permitting another month's stay, will be stamped in our passports as soon as we get some photographs of your faces back to Sana'a. Muqbel will take the film back to Hayward for developing and will bring the stamped passports back on his way to Ta'izz, in a day or two.'

Big Eddie was jubilant. 'We can see most of the country in another month,' he cried. 'Great!'

Jack thought that he would be quite happy to spend another

month right here, near Wadi Bana and the house of the family Ghanem.

Mike said, 'Why did you wait so long? You could have sent Muqbel, or come back yourself for the photographs.'

'Because Muqbel buggered off as soon as we got there and I had to do all the arranging. Use your head!'

Eddie looked at his companions, unconvinced. He fetched his camera, loaded it with film and they posed for a series of passport photos.

'Not me,' Stanley said. 'I've got mine.'

Mike was disconcerted to hear this. They were no longer all in it together. Stanley could stay and the rest of them be kicked out. Stanley was not beyond fixing it that way, Mike was sure. If the others went home early, Stanley would get credit for the whole show, being the only one with the opportunity to count the eagles and see the birds in the rest of the country. And what if he, Mike, had not mentioned passports? He gave the exposed film to Muqbel.

'For Mister Cecil, OK?'

'OK. I take.'

They all dispersed to cover their various areas and met back at the campsite for the usual mid-morning break, a cup of coffee, and to prepare notes. Muqbel's vehicle was absent.

'Is he gone?' Mike asked.

'Yes. He's gone. Can't you see?'

Jack had spent some time working on the waders at the barikah and said he was still of the opinion that some of them were red-necked stints. Stanley reacted to this with remarkably good-humoured scorn, saying that Jack was becoming an expert in unidentified birds. The species were impossible to separate in the field. Jack refused to initiate a serious quarrel over the issue, though he made it clear that it would be equally unacceptable to record them as one or the other while doubt remained. Eddie suggested they all go over there and try to resolve the matter. Stanley declined, saying it was a waste of time, and that he was going down the wadi.

'You chickenin' aht?' Eddie said.

Stanley's good humour evaporated like the spilled coffee that left brown stains in the dust. 'Come on then,' he said, and led the way to the reservoir.

The others followed and, after a hot walk over the fields, they lined up at the water's edge.

'Those birds,' Stanley said, 'are little stints. I can't see why anyone could be so stupid as not to see it.'

There was a long pause, until Eddie said, 'We'll have to trap the little bleeders.'

'Brilliant suggestion,' Stanley said. 'Use nets. Upset the locals and get thrown out. Typical'

'We could do it at night,' Mike ventured, 'when there's no one about.'

'That's the only time to trap waders,' Jack said. 'Be dead easy here, with the shallow water and narrow shoreline.'

Stanley was adamant. 'If there was the slightest doubt of their identity, I would permit trapping. Those birds are little stints.'

Jack's pulse quickened in anger. 'Since when have you been an expert on waders? I'm setting a net for those birds tonight, whether you like it or not.'

Stanley also showed his anger, by those *sk sk* noises in his throat, but he was speechless.

'Tonight,' Jack said. 'All right?' He walked off in the direction of the camp and the others followed.

The afternoon was hot. Black clouds with intense silver linings rose in massive columns over the western escarpment above the Sumarah Pass and obliterated the sun for a while, but they shed their rain in distant thunder and dispersed. The plain remained dry, with occasional swirls of dust among the fields. Both Eddie and Jack had their irritation somewhat mollified when Mike invited them to accompany him to see a bird he had tentatively identified as a pallid harrier, which he had seen flying over the north end of the marsh. They mentioned it to Stanley, who said that the three of them should be able to sort it out between them. He was going down the wadi.

All three were reluctant to broach the subject of their leader's mental stability. Jack because he was still too full of anger, Eddie because he really didn't give a damn about the little git as long as they got their visas, and Mike because the things he was thinking were too calumnious to be uttered uncorroborated. Stanley's name was not mentioned as they sat on a mound watching the elegant, pale, dove-grey harrier gliding like a phantom over the reeds.

'Good 'ere, innit?' Eddie said. They laughed their agreement and enjoyed the day about them.

They arrived back in camp in a more cheerful mood, made yet another pot of tea and wondered what had happened to Stanley. It was not like him to be off on his own for so long.

'I suppose he's all right,' Mike said. 'Not fallen or anything.'

Jack drew on a cigarette and didn't answer. Eddie drained the last of the tea from his mug and announced that he was going to the top of the cliff, between the reservoir and the wadi. Jack asked him not to use his bins while overlooking the Ghanem's house. 'You can look right down on it from there,' he said.

The afternoon drew on. Jack and Mike sat in camp, indolent for a while, and read, made notes, occasionally reaching for their binoculars to check a distant bird. People came to work in the fields, using a camel to draw potatoes from the rich, shallow earth. Beetles and ants scavenged among the crumbs around the tent. A lizard emerged from under a stone.

'I suppose we ought to go and look for him.' Jack said. 'He might have broken his neck – with a bit of luck.'

Mike smiled assent and they went through the gorge, following the stream down into the green wadi. The deepest sections were in shade as the afternoon sun fell away behind the cliffs, although the residual warmth radiating from the rocks delayed the chill of evening. The colours were intensified as the red reflections from the cliffs rebounded in the pools, and the butterflies ascended into the dark ribbon of sky suspended between opposing crags. There was no sign of Stanley and they went down as far as they could get before the wadi dropped steeply into a boulder-strewn gully where the steam disappeared, heard but unseen, in the echoing depths. They called and listened to their own voices answering from the cliffs.

'Surely,' Mike said, 'he hasn't gone down there.'

'Not after all the warnings he's given us about going off alone.'

They stood looking at the chaos before them. Twenty men could fall between those boulders and never be seen again.

'He must have returned earlier,' Jack said. 'Come on. Let's go back.'

They were near the large acacia when Mike stopped. 'That's odd,' he said, and bent to examine a narrow area of trampled vegetation.

'Looks like a mist-net site. A twenty footer would just fit in here.'

'It is a net site,' Jack said. 'That swine Carter has been trapping. For specimens!'

Jack strode purposefully up the wadi. 'Time to sort Carter out once and for all,' he said. 'And after all he said this morning about upsetting the locals. God, he's a devious little sod. I can't stand any more of it.'

'Please don't do anything rash, Jack,' Mike gasped as he strode along behind him.

'Rash? I tell you, if he's killed any of those accentors, I'll bloody well murder him.'

They met Eddie waiting at the narrow gorge at the top of the wadi.

'He's in camp,' Eddie said. 'I saw him from the cliff top. He probably hid in the scrub when he heard you coming. You passed him on the way in.'

Mike looked apprehensively at Jack, then at Eddie. He was outnumbered and could not stop them. They found Stanley Carter sitting on a plastic jerry can, powdering the skin of a Yemen thrush with alum. Its carcass, like a tiny oven-ready chicken, lay on the ground, already being investigated by ants. He smiled as his three subordinates stood around him at the points of an equilateral triangle. Two bird bags hung from the low pole of Carter's tent. Jack picked them up, opened the drawstrings and looked inside. The bags contained another thrush and a pair of Yemen accentors.

Carter ignored him and continued preparing the skin. He inserted a small tweezers into the base of the skull and withdrew the little brain, then two large eyeballs, one at a time. He placed a little cotton wool, well dusted with the white powder, into the cranial cavity.

Jack turned away. He took the bags back down the Wadi and released the birds where they had been trapped.

Slowly, deep in thought, he walked back along the stream, feeling disgusted and dirty. He felt as if his very presence here was an intrusion into the clean, unexploited remnant of a garden called Eden, which man had defiled since the day of his creation. He was ashamed to be part of the forces destroying Paradise. He heard the birds at vespers, their voices soft, harmonious, in tune with the elements and, at the highest turn in the wadi, where he had first seen this beautiful scene with Nadirah, he stopped to listen. He sat on a boulder by the stream and looked back, through the trees, at the last of the sunshine creeping up the cliff like a rising curtain uncovering the night. He fought the tears which obscured his view as he wept for the first man, he who had placed one stone upon another and changed the world, he who had become so satiated with beauty and plenty and hungered and thirsted after knowledge.

He blinked his vision into clarity. There must be knowledge, he supposed, but why obtained so ruthlessly, at the expense of the very life and beauty of the planet? He knew not.

The darkening water glittered over the pebbles and boulders. A bush of yellow flowers nodded to the rushing stream. The sky was reflected in the pools, where the shapes of sudden fish darted, like his thoughts, among the depths.

'Oh,' he said. 'It's so beautiful. So beautiful.' And then, perhaps because the sparkle of the water reminded him of her eyes, or because of envy that she would live and die here while he would never see it again, he said, 'Oh, Nadirah, what a place.'

She heard, and halted on the track where she emerged from the narrow gorge behind him. Her name had never sounded so exotic as when spoken in the heavy accent of this foreigner. It was not as spoken by the English she had known before. He would never speak

Arabic properly, but he made some effort to know the Holy language. There was dejection in his posture as he sat with bowed back and elbow on knee, some anguish in his voice, some element of despair.

She was unable to approach him, though he was but a few paces distant, and unable to retreat, lest he turn and see her and assume, again, that she had been spying on him. She allowed a minute to pass while he sat motionless and then she drew close, silently, on her bare feet.

He turned and looked up at her, as a man in a trance, unaware, it seemed of the moisture in his eyes. 'Hullo,' he said.

'Masah al kier.' Morning of health. A formal greeting. She was saddened by his eyes and, when he reached for her hand, she let him take it, watching him intently. He caressed her slender fingers with his own. There was dried earth around her nails. Her black cotton scarf fell upon her arm, the brown, slender, slightly downy arm. She drew her hand away and he released her, saying, 'You are not still angry with me?'

'No,' she smiled. 'You are only ignorant kawahjah.'

He looked up at her. Her eyes were darkened with kohl. He thought she was wearing lipstick, for her mouth was moist. He was deeply tanned but, against the brown skin of this Arab with her velvet eyes, he felt pale and insipid.

'We walk,' she said.

He rose and followed her once more toward the darkening greenness of the wadi and the acacia tree. She walked with the grace of a desert gazelle, a creature of exquisite fragility, too delicate for his rough touch; she was part of her landscape. Jack felt that merely to brush her limbs with a gentle stroke, or place upon her lips the briefest ghost of a kiss, would bruise her indelibly, as the Western touch would bruise her land. He heard her voice, soft and clear, too muted to echo from the cliffs.

'Will you marry her?'

He didn't know what to say. This woman knew perfectly well that he would not marry Alison Courtenay and she was demanding to hear him reject her. Perhaps she had seen them... who knows what was seen in this country. She was scolding him, censuring him for his Western immorality. He could not deny it and accepted the reproach.

'Alison? No.'

'Why not?'

'We are from different backgrounds. It's not possible.'

He did not want to talk about Alison Courtenay. He could not think why Nadirah had brought him here. He felt obliged to challenge her, in defence of his cultural morality. 'Did you follow me again?'

The blush darkened her brown skin and her eyes blinked, but she did not avert them. She accepted his charge. She had followed him. She knew not why. The effect of her embarrassment was to induce in him such a surge of guilt and emotional conflict that he in turn felt the rush of blood to his cheeks. He released her from the obligation to answer his blunt insensitive question by saying, 'It's different for us. You know it is.'

They watched each other. Who *would* he marry? Who would *she* marry? Someone must love her. How, he asked himself as he thought of the cultural void between them, could any man divide his love between her and three others? It was unthinkable. To love and possess such a woman would be the very essence and ecstasy of life.

In answer to his comment, she lowered her eyes and said, 'It is no different.' And then, after a pause, 'You must not touch me.'

'What? What did you say?'

'We must not the touching of the hands.'

A quick glance and her eyes fell away from him. There was nothing he could find to say. He had barely been aware of touching her and would not have done so, except that he had come to love her country and for that brief lapse she was her country. He looked at her beautiful face and those eyes, and felt his mouth dry up in an irrational fear for her innocence. She eventually looked at him with a stolen glance from under her lashes.

'Poor kawahjah,' she said. 'You know nothing.'

She led him to the tree and they sat on the ground. 'This was my school,' she said. 'This is where I studied for my examinations.'

'It's getting dark,' he said. 'The others will be looking for me.'

'After tomorrow, I shall not see you.'

He assumed that she was leaving or, more likely, that her brother had forbidden further contact with the Westerners. He made no comment.

'I did ask Achmed to send you away.' Her eyes were pools of mystery in the fading light; he could not guess what she was thinking. 'He will come to your tents,' she said.

'Send us away? Why?'

'I try to tell you before yesterday. I think you know about the rassassa.'

'Rassassa? What is rassassa?' An apprehensive recollection of the meaning came to mind.

'For bunduq.' She expelled a breath of exasperation. 'I don't know.'

She acted a charade of outlining a bandolier over her shoulder and positioned finger and thumb as if holding...

'Bullets?' he interrupted incredulously.

'Yes, bullets.' She drew her shawl about herself as if suddenly cold.

'In the boxes?' he asked. 'The boxes we brought from Al Fazah? Full of ammunition? Are you sure?'

'Yes.' She allowed the significance of her words to penetrate his reluctant mind.

'Jesus!' he said. 'That bloody Muqbel. He could have got us all shot.'

'No. Muqbel did not know. Only Achmed and Abdullah.'

There was an infinite sadness in her voice, an acceptance of events beyond her control. She turned to him with a wistful smile. Jack thought of the young, efficient NCO with the Kalashnikov checking their passports and looking into the back of the vehicle.

'Jesus,' he said. 'I hope nobody finds out about it.'

They could be in serious trouble over this little deception, for who would believe that they could be unaware of five boxes of ammunition in their vehicle? He had said that they could all have been shot. The realisation of how true this was sent a tingling shiver of fear over his scalp. How long had the deception been perpetrated? Abdullah, and this girl's brother, must have been manipulating them since they met him at Raydah, nearly a month ago. Nadirah must have known. Was she party to the deception? No, for if that was so it meant they had been manipulated since getting off the plane. Surely that wasn't possible. But what now? How else might they be used as unwitting accomplices to crime?

'Why?' he asked her. 'What are they for, the bullets?'

'How I know,' she demanded. 'For nothing. Achmed says to fight the enemy of Yemen. Who our enemy? Maybe send to the South. I don't know.'

She pursed her lips and after a while said, 'Who our friend? Nobody. We fight each other for your quarrels, not ours. Your quarrels cut our blood. You damn English, Americans, Ruskies, what you care for us? You want only the oils at Marib. You think we are fools.'

'It's not my fault.' He was thinking, there's money to be made there from guns everywhere.

'No? Yimkin, maybe. Oh, I am sorry about you.' She sighed in exasperation. 'I don't know.'

'Where did they get the bullets?' he said.

'Abdullah has friends in many places. Maybe they bought them. I don't know.'

'Is Achmed working with Abdullah against the government?' He had a quick, vague notion of betraying Abdullah, through Courtenay or Hayward, and clearing everyone else.

'You do not understand,' she said. 'He is not against anybody. Just the enemies of Yemen. He not know who they are, even. You have seen my country, Jack. You have seen the remains of our ancient culture, our fine old cities, industrious people. We have now the chance for some prosperity. We are not so stupid that with oils and the dar, oh the harbour, yes, at Aden, and a united Yemen

266

would make us rich. Why are we not always together? Because you guraba, foreigners, divide us with our own dividings. Achmed is still defending his village, like in the old days. He is majnoon, crazy man. I love him very much. You understand?'

'I think so.'

The whole business was too complicated for him. All he wanted was a bit of peace and quiet to watch a few birds, count a few eagles.

'Achmed and Abdullah do bad things for you, I know.'

'And for you, Nadirah. What if the government finds out you have secret weapons?'

'The guns? Here, everybody has guns. What they can do?' She shrugged away any possibility of disclosure.

'I don't know what they can do,' he said, 'or what they know. I am afraid for you.'

The thought occurred to him that she ought to know how to take care of herself in her own country. She had been around. She was no fool, but there was something in her voice, a tremulous precognition of possible results of her brother's actions, which made him uneasy. If she was afraid, how should the foreigners feel?

'Don't worry,' she said, as if reading his mind, 'it is not of your business. But you must tell your friends to leave this place. I am very sorry.'

Chapter Nineteen

Darkness was falling on the plain as Jack reached the campsite. The calls to evening prayer drifted from the mosques in the villages, like remote, mysterious, disembodied voices of another culture, vaguely disconcerting in their insistence.

The others said nothing as he sat and helped himself to tea. Even Stanley Carter, who may have been secretly anticipating violence from his colleague, was silent except for the humming of another tuneless, unrecognisable phrase of music. Eddie had prepared a meal but Jack could not eat. His anger at Carter had not diminished, the image of the little skinless carcass was still unforgotten, but concern over Nadirah's revelation took precedence in his mind. He could deal with Carter later. After thinking the matter over he came to the conclusion that the sensible thing to do, for the sake of everyone else involved, Alison, Hayward, Harry and Nadirah, would be for the birders to leave the country immediately. They should go to Sana'a and get out by the first flight they could get seats on, before they were arrested and shot.

'We have to leave,' he said, and told them about the ammunition in the Toyota and Nadirah's warning.

'Ammunition?' Mike said. 'That's a serious matter.' He remembered that it was he who had made the first suggestion that they bring back Muqbel's cargo of contraband. He hoped the others had forgotten it.

Eddie said, 'Christ aw'migh'y. That's firing squad stuff.'

Or beheading, Mike thought.

Jack might have known that Carter would seize upon this as an opportunity to admonish him for past transgressions, and indeed Stanley had been waiting for such a juncture.

'It's all your fault, Pengelly,' Stanley said, for the benefit of Mike and Eddie. 'Alison told me about your collusion with terrorists in the souk.'

He turned to the others. 'Our Celtic rebel has deceived us into associating with a murderer and gunrunner.'

'Don't be stupid,' Jack said.

He told them about the incident at the Bab al Yemen souk, why they had decided to keep it secret and of his suspicions that they had been used by Abdullah ever since they had met him at Raydah.

'And this lot!' Eddie said. 'Don't forget they were in on it. That bleedin' bint and her brother.'

This thought had occurred to all of them: that Nadirah could have been party to the deception, how unlikely it was that she would have been in ignorance of events in her own household. There was no certainty of anything, but Jack felt sure there was no collusion on her part and was about to speak in her defence when Stanley said, 'I'm pleased to note that you're seeing these people for what they really are, Eddie. You can't trust any of them!' With a meaningful glance at Jack.

They could not leave that night, because they had no transport and, in any case, where could they go? They made preparations for spending an uneasy night. Mike had been characteristically quiet and thoughtful and eventually, when the enormity of their folly in bringing the ammunition from the coast had subdued even Eddie's optimism, he said, 'We should leave as soon as Muqbel gets back with the visas.'

Jack assumed he meant leave both the area and the country. One worrying aspect of the whole business was that, should the authorities discover the gunrunners, too many people had seen them with Abdullah, in too many places, for them not to be implicated. No matter where they went in the country now, they were too conspicuous to elude arrest, or to escape undetected. They were trapped.

'How do we know,' Eddie suddenly asked, 'what was in the bleed'n boxes? That bint could tell you anyfing. Muqbel must have known. How could he load a wagon full of ammo and not know abaht it. I mean, he ain't dahft.'

'Of course he knew,' Carter said. 'I didn't trust him from the start.'

'We'll ask him', Jack said, resisting the temptation to ask if Carter had ever trusted anybody, 'when he gets back.'

'He won't be back.' He adjusted his spectacles with both hands, finally shoving them back up his nose with the right index finger. 'I've sacked him.'

His explosive statement produced exactly the stunned silence he had anticipated. While they were recovering their wits, he fumbled among his belongings and produced the daily log.

'Red-billed tropic-bird, anybody,' he said, 'Persian shearwater, brown booby...?'

'Wotcha mean?' Eddie said. 'Sacked him?'

'Sacked him! That's plain enough.'

'You said,' Jack protested, 'that he was gone to Sana'a for our visas. You can't sack him without conferring with the rest of us.'

'And what about our visas?' Mike said. 'He has our photographs, remember.'

'I said... if only you would listen to what you are told... that he was gone. I did not say where, or under what circumstances. As for conferring, I am in charge of this expedition. I say who is, or is not, to be hired and fired and that includes you. So don't forget it. As a matter of fact, I've been suspicious for some time about the conversations in Arabic Jack's had with that bint in the wadi. How do I know what schemes you've planned together? You Cornish have a long history of smuggling, I believe. Did they offer you a cut on the contraband?'

Jack ignored that. 'Even if our visas are not extended we need exit permits,' he said. 'And how the hell are we to get back to Sana'a with no transport?'

'It is very simple. We go out to the main road and flag down a taxi. Or is even that beyond the wit of your feeble minds.'

It was evident to Mike that this harangue was intended to forestall questioning about sacking Muqbel and effectively getting them stranded here in what had become very inhospitable surroundings. None of them questioned him further. They went through the routine of calling the log. Pallid harrier was new to their list, but even that evoked no enthusiasm. They climbed into their sleeping bags for protection against the cold and, after listening to each other turning restlessly under a sky of chilly indigo, went to sleep in the early hours. It was in the morning, just as the first streaks of dawn had lightened the east and the birds were beginning to sing, when Jack Pengelly felt a slight pressure on his shoulder. Cold air brushed his forehead. He woke slowly, to find Muqbel looking at him in the gloom. His immediate reaction was to start in alarm and call the others.

Muqbel warned him to silence with a gesture, called Jack away from camp with a nod of his head and left. Jack rose and, after hastily pulling on his clothes, left the camp and joined Muqbel on the hill to the south. When they had settled themselves among the security of the boulders, he asked Muqbel what had happened in Sana'a.

'I go Sana'a. Mister Stanley no pay. I work long time. Benzine k'teer. Fulous k'teer. Lazim. Bint Alison make him pay. I bring Mister Stanley back here. He say fuck off. No more money. I wait in night to talk Mister Jack.'

Stanley had told Muqbel he was not paying to bring him back because Muqbel had risked getting them all arrested for smuggling whisky. He had threatened to inform the police if Muqbel refused.

'Tomorrow, I take photo Mister Hayward. Come back. Mister Jack and Mister Eddie pay money.'

Jack laughed, despite his anxieties. He was still not sure of Muqbel's integrity. 'Do you know what was in those boxes we brought back from the coast?'

'Yes Mister Jack. I know!' He shrugged his shoulders helplessly. 'Whisky and some gin and brandy drink. Fulous k'teer. Much money.'

'Rassassa!' Jack said.

'Rassassa…? What rassassa? Rassassa is for gun, Mister Jack. You speak Arabi?'

'Aiwah. Bint Nadirah said the boxes were full of ammunition.'

Jack carefully watched Muqbel's eyes. The man was obviously shaken. His skin paled and his pupils dilated with shock. He left Jack in no doubt of their fate if the soldiers at the checkpoint had searched the vehicle. The man did have a wife and family.

'Abdullah mush quais,' he said.

The sun was coming over the distant mountains. Its warmth would soon wake the others. Jack asked Muqbel to go back to the vehicle, refill the fuel tank, keep it hidden and return to camp in the evening.

'OK.' He drove off with no further mention of the money owed to him, and Jack made no mention of his presence to the others.

They saw Achmed approaching the camp just after midday. He was dressed in a traditional white skirt and a check jacket. His head-cloth was clean and neat, with the corner hanging forward over his shoulder. Jack greeted him amicably and, on impulse, decided it would be prudent to spare him the task of ordering them away from his land by saying they were planning to leave immediately. No one would be embarrassed and Achmed's hospitality untarnished. No recriminations on either side. And no questions asked. No loss of face. He explained that the extension of their visas enabled them to study the birds in other areas of Yemen and, while being grateful for his hospitality, they felt obliged to move on.

Achmed saw through this immediately and, with a slight smile, indicated that he was grateful to Jack for his consideration. There was something in his eyes, which indicated that he thought this foreigner could think like an Arab, if he so wished. He contrived to speak with Jack alone.

'My sister...' he began, but tailed off irresolutely with a shrug and a brief smile. Some things are best left unsaid.

This man Jack thought, put our lives at risk. I should hate him. He scrutinised Achmed's face with unconcealed calculation, examining his eyes for signs of deception or duplicity. He saw neither, only the fierce justification of his actions, in defiance of events which were overwhelming him and his country. Jack saw in him a Cornishman of previous centuries, or a Basque, or a Fleming, or a Kurd of today, desperately fighting for his identity and independence. Some telepathic impulse drew them together in an embrace of farewell.

'Masallamah.' Go in peace, Achmed said.

There was little enthusiasm for expedition work. Jack said nothing of Muqbel's return and listened to the others discussing the best means of getting to Sana'a. Carter was talking as if they could go straight to Cecil Hayward, pick up their visas and carry on birding as if nothing had happened. He made no further mention of dismissing Muqbel or that the photographs would, therefore, not be delivered. Jack found himself hating Stanley Carter for his deviousness and noticed that the other two were pointedly avoiding their leader. He will have to be deposed, Jack thought. And then Mike drew Jack aside. 'There seems little point in staying on,' he said. 'Carter has become impossible and we are all at risk of being arrested by the Yemeni authorities.'

They mentioned this to Eddie, who did not agree. 'I ain't come all this way,' he said, 'to be put off by that little git. And the authorities, whoever they are, might not know anyfing about us and the bleedin' bullets. I say, we stay.'

Jack reminded Eddie that they were too conspicuous to be ignored by any factions in the country, and that there were undoubtedly many people who knew that they brought the bullets up from the coast. They should not underestimate the danger they were in. 'And, in any case, how can you continue working under the mad bastard?'

'He's got the bleedin' money, mate, that's why.'

'Right,' Mike said. He led them over to Stanley without a word. He stood before him and said, 'It might be advisable for me to administer the remaining expedition funds, Stanley. Best thing, I think.'

Eddie and Jack stood solidly on Mike's side, expecting opposition, but there was none.

'If that's what you want,' Stanley said. 'All the traveller's cheques are in my name, however. You'll have to wait until I can cash them at the bank in Sana'a.'

He was too co-operative. It was uncharacteristic. He was up to something, Eddie thought, the scheming little berk. We'll have to watch him, or he'll get his revenge for being given the boot.

Jack wanted to go home... They had found the eagles, and it was too risky to stay. Call it quits and go home.

'What do we do nah?' he heard Eddie saying.

Mike pointed out that there was only one thing they could do, make for Sana'a, either for their visas or a plane. They could decide which after speaking to the embassy staff, Courtenay and Hayward.

The day was nearly over. Nadirah had not been seen, yet Jack had no doubt she had been watching them from the house on the cliff. He would have liked to say goodbye to her and assumed Achmed had forbidden it.

'The sooner we move, the better,' he said. 'Let's cook up our nosh and be on our way.'

'Are we to abandon your stints, then?' Stanley said. 'Finding an excuse to leave their identity unresolved, is that it?'

Mike and Eddie looked at Stanley in amazement. His behaviour was impossible. Because no one wished to continue the antagonism, there had been no mention of the skinned thrush and the stints had been forgotten, yet here he was, deliberately trying to provoke Jack into further conflict.

He ain't right in the bleedin' 'ead, big Eddie thought.

'You seemed inordinately anxious to leave as soon as possible,' Stanley smirked. 'I thought you might have asked to stay one more night, at least, and given us the opportunity to resolve the matter in a scientific manner.'

Jack looked desperately at Mike. Stanley was right, of course, but that was not relevant now. He was inviting conflict over the assertion of leadership.

Jack accepted the challenge. 'Right,' he said. 'We'll trap the birds on the barikah tonight. Before we drive to Sana'a.'

'We'll find it difficult to get a taxi at that time of night,' Mike said. He could see that Jack was quite determined.

'Muqbel is here,' Jack said, 'over there, waiting.'

'More deceit,' Stanley said.

Eddie said, 'I can't cope wiv much more of this. Everybody seems to know somefink I don't.' And they all thought the same.

'We'll pull out of here at dusk,' Jack said. 'Wait a couple of hours and set the nets in the dark. Agreed?'

No one dissented. By the time they had finished preparing and eating and packed everything into the Land Cruiser, they left much later than anticipated. Muqbel was very nervous about trapping after dark and said they should get out on to the main road as soon as possible. He was overruled. Jack thought he saw the silhouette of the Yemeni girl watching them, outlined in the glow of light from the windows of her house, but he was not sure. They took the vehicle along the track that skirted the barikah, drove a little way towards As Saddah, the village of caves, left it there with Muqbel and walked the short way back to the waders, carrying the nets. They settled to wait among the boulders on the slope that ran from the barikah up to the top of the cliff at the entrance to Wadi Bana, opposite the house of the Ghanem family, from whence Eddie had looked down on Stanley hiding with the dead thrush. Everything was quiet. They waited for the village lights to go out. From time to time, various trucks came and went along the tracks and, in the distance, always the stream of headlights on the road to Sana'a. The cold was searching into their clothing before they considered it advisable to set the nets. They gathered up the equipment and set off for the water, saying little, each of them aware that more than the identification of a small bird was dependent on this night's work.

'Why do I feel so bleedin' nervous?' Eddie enquired rhetorically. 'I ain't afraid of the dark.'

The waders were calling as they approached the water. They heard greenshanks, the piping of a ringed plover, and the faint 'trrrt' of the stints. The nets were stretched between poles along the shallow edge of water, where low areas of dry ground emerged from the evaporating surface. They guyed them with string and stones, and retired to wait among the boulders. An aircraft flew overhead. There were few lights in the villages.

'It's nearly two o'clock,' Mike whispered.

The air was clear, still and windless; not a breath ruffled the surface of the ancient reservoir. The peaks of the ranges all around them pierced the skyline like black, jagged claws reaching for the stars in the moonless sky, low and distant across the plain, high and crisp on the hills behind them. The boulders on the slope hung over their heads, dark and threatening, one after the other among the bare rocks that sloped up to the cliff at the top of the wadi. The headlamps of vehicles still passed along the main road, moving steadily, silently, disappearing from time to time behind outcrops of rock or black volcanic cones. The plain seemed to have closed in on them, for in the darkness the mountains and the lights on the road looked nearer, clearer, as if the plain had contracted with the cold. The waders called shrill alarms.

After twenty minutes, Stanley inspected the nets. 'Nothing,' he said.

They settled for another wait, for the birds were now at the far end of the barikah. The bitter air chilled the men's faces, their hands, and crept inside their clothes. They drew their hoods tight under their chins.

The stone, which rolled down from the slope behind them, bounced over their heads and cracked sharply against a rock in front. No one spoke, but, the better for listening, they removed their hoods. No sound was heard.

'Is there someone up there?' Mike whispered when they had been straining their ears for several minutes.

'I reckon,' Jack said, under his breath.

'Could be anything,' Stanley hissed at them. 'Could be just a loose rock, or baboons, or even a blasted leopard. Just be quiet.'

They could hear the waders calling as they circled the barikah, evidently nervous and reluctant to settle, as if sensing danger around the shore. Something's upset them,' Jack said. 'They're too nervous. I don't like it.'

'Perhaps they're going to move on,' Mike muttered, doubtfully. 'They have been here long enough to gain sufficient weight for the flight to Africa.'

'For God's sake,' Stanley hissed between his teeth, 'you're making enough noise to wake the...' There was the sound of splintering glass. It came from the direction of Muqbel's Toyota. 'What's the use? What does that damned Arab think he's doing? He's worse than you lot. I did think you could catch a few waders without scaring them off to the valley of the Nile. You're all useless.'

He had spoken louder than any of them. Jack felt his pulse quicken with anger. 'How do you think we would have managed without him?' he demanded, still keeping his voice down. 'He's done everything for us.'

The aircraft noise returned. They could see its lights flashing over Jebel Al Wafi, to the north.

'It's you,' Jack reminded him, 'who's not catching the waders, as well as us.'

'Sshht!' Eddie said. 'What was that?'

There was a vague shape briefly outlined against the water as something leaped between two stones. The cries of the waders were louder, their alarm calls pierced the darkness in shrill consternation. The shape disappeared in the darkness. Stanley was about to say something, when Eddie grabbed his arm, silencing him. A desert fox loped towards them, dodging between boulders. It broke into a run, passed by, and raced up the slope to the cliff.

'Ah!' Stanley said. 'That's all it was. An expedition of naturalists scared stiff by a fox. Wait till I tell them in The George.'

'Silly, actually,' Mike admitted in shame.

'Quiet!' Eddie said. 'There's something else. That fox was running away from something. It was more scared that we were. Didn't even see us.'

'No doubt you're aware that animals function more by their olfactory than visual organs,' Stanley said. 'Even you will know such an elementary fact.'

'Oh, shut your mouth,' Eddie said, losing his patience. 'Don't be so...'

'They've gone in!' Jack cried in a loud whisper. 'The waders are in the net. Some of them.'

'...damned sarcastic, mate!' Eddie's breath was rapid. He was glaring at Stanley in the dark, waiting for a further derisive remark, which would push him beyond the limit of his tolerance.

Stanley's throat skukked a couple of times in preparation for that further jibe, but he thought better of it when faced by Eddie's bulk. He turned to Mike.

'If the birds are in the nets,' he said, 'we'd better get them out.' He made a move toward the water.

'Wait!' Eddie insisted. 'Listen!'

They heard voices. They heard subdued, indistinct voices, mere murmurings accompanied by an occasional shuffle of feet and a scraping of stone. They came nearer... passed between the bird watchers and the barikah until, silhouetted against the still, unruffled water, were five men. They were five Yemeni men, wearing skirts, head-cloths, perhaps shoes, perhaps sandals, but walking carefully, selecting their way among the rocks, with their backs bent under the weight of heavy boxes. Above their shoulders protruded the unmistakable barrels of Kalashnikov AK47s.

The four foreigners all sank slowly, silently, to the ground. They hid their white faces in their arms, or behind rocks and listened, as they had never listened before, while the voices approached, passed before them and receded, with grunts of effort and the occasional low, conspiratorial laugh. For several minutes after they passed, there was silence. The stars overhead seemed to proliferate by the minute, spreading from the zenith down among the peaks.

'That was close,' Mike said. 'I suppose they are going to the Ghanem's house.'

'Where else?' Jack queried. 'They must have an arsenal up there.'

'The sooner we get the 'ell out of 'ere, the better,' Eddie declared, with a nervous tremble in his voice.

Jack raised himself to his knees and unzipped his fly front. The hiss of his pee striking the stony ground seemed unending. 'I wish,' he said, 'that we knew what the bloody hell was going on round here. Let's pack up the nets and bugger off out of it.'

They left their packs and moved in single file to the barikah and along the water's edge to their nets. The aircraft over Jebel Al Wafi was joined by the *chup-chup-chup* of a helicopter rotor before both faded away to silence. There were only three waders in the net, two green sandpipers and a stint.

'Just release them and let them go,' Mike said as he peered along the drawstrings in the light reflected from the water.

Eddie released one of the sandpipers without difficulty, for it lay passively in the net with no attempt to struggle. He let it go and it stood on the bank, bewildered for a moment, before flying off, calling loudly as Jack tried to free the second, which was badly entangled. Stanley, having passed the sandpipers as he inspected the net, was working on the stint, watched by Mike.

'I'll have to use the torch,' Jack said. 'It's in a hell of a tangle.'

'I think it inadvisable,' Mike said, somewhat apologetically.

'No. Perhaps not!' He felt among the feathers for the tangled meshes, gently easing the head and wings from their grip. 'Ah,' he said, 'it's caught around the tarsus.'

His usually steady fingers were fumbling in their haste, but eventually he freed the bird and let it go. It ran along the shore and was lost in the darkness.

Stanley had released the third bird and stood examining it closely. Eddie and Mike gathered up the nets and stuffed them in bags, tangles and all. They left the guy ropes where they were. Stanley put the stint into a bag and closed the drawstring.

'What are you going to do with that?' Jack demanded as Stanley came past him. He was thinking of Stanley picking the brains from the skull of the thrush.

'I am going to determine whether you are the God's gift to ornithology that you think you are,' Stanley said with unconcealed scorn. 'Prove that your red-necked stints are little stints once and for all.'

'Let it go, old man,' Mike said. 'We don't have time for that now. We could all get shot here.'

'Damn right!' Eddie said.

'Come on, Stanley,' Jack said. 'Let it go.'

'Afraid to have one of your precious, unsubstantiated, amateurish theories put to the test of science?' Stanley asked.

'Let it go.'

Stanley Carter pushed past Jack Pengelly and walked back to their packs, lying among the rocks. The others stood watching him retreat into the darkness.

'Christ!' Jack said. 'I'm going to thump that arrogant little bastard before long.'

'After you with the arrogant little bastard!' Eddie joked.

Jack was too furious to be placated. 'Who the hell does he think he's talking to?'

'You may be right about the stints,' Mike said. 'I think you are, actually.'

Jack looked after the disappearing figure with hatred. 'Come on then. I know I'm right.'

They went to the rocks, where Stanley was reaching into his pack for the *Guide to the Holarctic Waders*. 'Where's the torch?' he said.

'You'll get us all killed, you stupid git,' Eddie protested.

'Ought to be a bit careful,' Mike advised.'

'Unlike amateurs, scientists have always been prepared to take risks in furtherance of knowledge,' Stanley said, glaring at Jack in the gloom.

Jack was well aware that the risks taken by scientists like Stanley Carter were usually in furtherance of their own aggrandisement and any benefit to the sum of human knowledge purely coincidental. 'Let's have a look at it then,' he said. 'Get under the rocks.'

Stanley took the little wader from the cotton bag. He opened the guide at the appropriate page. Eddie shone the torch through a slit between his fingers. Stanley ran his fingers down the text.

'Calidris ruficollis,' he said. 'Identification. Similar to C. minuta... mumble mumble... Ah. Here we are. In juvenile plumage the central tail feathers more rounded than C. minuta, with a narrower fringe.'

He was spreading the tail as the helicopter came roaring over the plain from the peaks to the east. It passed right over them with a deafening scream of rotors and a withering storm of wind and dust. It clattered towards Wadi Bana, from where they heard the roar of explosions and saw a blinding flash of light as the chopper accelerated to rise over the peaks of Jebel Sumarah.

In the silence that followed, more deathly than anything they had heard before in the silence of the mountains, there rose the cries of waders and, from somewhere in the direction of Wadi Bana, the scream of a human being in terror.

A red glow rose into the night beyond the slope. Their faces were illuminated as they gazed up over the boulders in a stupor of shock. Further explosions. Two, three, then the sound of rapid, uncoordinated firing of small arms.

Stanley was having difficulty in breathing. His voice occasionally whimpered like a child as he gasped for breath between the *sk sk* spasms of his throat. Eddie took a couple of paces, as if to run, but turned again to the glow in the sky.

'The light, Eddie,' Mike said.

Eddie switched it off, and they stood in a huddle in the darkness. Mike looked at Jack and they exchanged glances of despair and confusion, seeking leadership from each other. The sound of that scream echoed in Jack's ears. He could not drive it from his mind. There had been the one, long, desperate scream of agony such as he had only heard in the stillness of a Cornish night, when a rabbit died in the jaws of a stoat. It was an agonised, terrifying scream, but he wanted to hear it again. The chilling thrill of it, the rage and terror in it. He wanted to know that the same voice could feel again such pain and despair. The voice had been the voice of bint Nadirah. He did not want her dead.

Over the cliff, at the top of this dark, boulder-strewn slope, there was something that he did not want to see, something he would have to see.

Eddie looked to the sky for signs of further attacks, but the aircraft were gone. There was not even the sound of a distant rotor any more. The sky was silent, beautiful, with more stars still emerging from behind thin cloud.

Mike turned from Jack to Stanley, trying to decide what to do.

Stanley was gazing at the glow in the sky, visibly wincing with every crack and bang of noise from over the hill. His clenched fist still held the stint and its head hung limply between his fingers. Jack saw Mike looking at the stint and the bonds of restraint finally snapped. He took Stanley's wrist brutally in his hand and extracted the bird, crushed to death in Stanley's convulsive grasp. But Stanley appeared completely unaware of his surroundings or what was happening. He continued staring at the red glow, like a small child gazing in wonder at fireworks. Jack spread the tail of the limp body before Stanley's eyes.

'See those tail feathers?' Jack cried. 'See those tertials? See the fringe to the scapulars?'

Stanley was still gazing at the red glow in the sky. Jack grabbed him by the hair and forced him to look at the dead bird until Stanley at last recovered from shock and became aware of Jack addressing him. He saw the corpse before his eyes and reassembled his wits. Mike and Eddie were anxiously watching them.

'A red-necked stint,' Jack seethed. 'A dead red-necked stint. The first dead red-necked stint for Yemen, you bloody little tuss.'

'Another success for my expedition.'

Jack hit him... a poorly aimed blow to the side of the head, which did not even dislodge his spectacles, for Jack was no expert at hitting people. He would have hit him again and made a better job of it, but Eddie's big frame came between them.

'You are dismissed from this expedition,' Stanley said when he had recovered his composure, 'for insubordination.'

'Tuss!' Jack said, using a Cornish obscenity again.

He calmed down. He realised that he was suffering from shock as much as Stanley. They all were. He had reacted irrationally in venting his fear and anger on Stanley, but he had no illusions about his fears, was afraid of what they might find across the wadi and angry because there was nothing they could do. His aggression towards Stanley had been merely delaying behaviour to postpone the necessity of looking for Nadirah, and confronting the devastation across the wadi. The four of them stood among the boulders, in the red glow and deep black shadows, unable to think or make rational decisions. The obvious and immediate course of action was to run to the Toyota and flee from that menacing red glow, with its occasional crack of small arms, as quickly as possible.

Mike finally said it… 'We can't just run away.'

'I suppose we'd better 'ave a look!' Eddie said.

Jack realised he was still holding the dead stint. He threw it away into the darkness. 'Come on,' he said, and began scrambling up the slope toward the cliff. From among the boulders at the cliff top, they could see across the wadi. They were five hundred, perhaps six hundred and fifty metres away from what they saw below them on the opposite cliff. A great column of smoke, illuminated by a red hell beneath it, rose above the house of Ghanem and obliterated the stars in the high, silent heavens. Across the narrow wadi before them, they saw flames licking from broken, white-washed windows like the tongues of vipers, flicking and withdrawing, tasting the stonework in search of the devourable. Fuel heaps in the courtyard and the fodder on the roof were disappearing in a blaze of black, spark-ridden smoke. All the vegetation about the house was burnt away, leaving a few glowing stumps among the stones and the low courtyard walls. The house was becoming encrusted with black, glowing soot, fanned to scarlet in the accelerating draught. As they watched, the roof of the house collapsed into the building and the flames leaped triumphantly into the air with a roar of enthusiasm. A few shots were heard, but they were from ammunition exploding in the heat and they saw neither guns nor men to fire them.

Mike, like a priest forced to utter the most obscene blasphemy in the presence of God, breathed the word that was on all their lips. 'Napalm.'

'Oh no!'

Eddie found himself staring in unashamed fascination at the brilliant, leaping flames. There was so much green among the red, such orange and carmine hellish unstoppable heat. The very stones must be on fire. His eyes glowed with excitement until he became aware that Mike had dropped his head on his arms as he lay on his stomach and was sobbing into the ground, saying, 'The children,' over and over.

Eddie said, 'Oh bloody hell, Jack. What's going on, for God's sake.'

'What's that?' Jack said. And they saw a movement on the edge of the cliff, a little to their right. 'There's somebody there!' He leaped forward, down the incline to the precipice, and grabbed the figure which was crawling forward on its hands and knees.

'Nadirah!' he said. 'Nadirah!'

She seemed not to have heard. He held on to her about the thighs and forced her to stop on the brink. She lay head first down the slope, staring at the flames across the narrow wadi in a daze of incomprehension.

'She was spyin' on us,' Eddie said.

'Achmed?' she queried softly. Jack held on to her, prevented her from crawling further and, with the help of the others, managed to get her into a sitting position.

'You can't go down there,' he said. She didn't know. She didn't understand. 'We must wait,' he said, and added weakly, 'Lazim stannah.' She nodded, staring vacantly at the flames.

Then, unbelievably, they saw movement among those flames. Someone was still alive among the destruction. Nadirah tried to stand and her mouth opened to form a cry of God-knows-what unendurable emotion, but Jack restrained her and put his hand over her mouth.

She bit him and struggled violently like a madwoman. He overpowered her and clasped her in his arms. 'Wait,' he said.

They saw two men, carrying a limp and moribund third, although one of the pair could barely stand. He had bloodstains, glistening in the firelight, running down the front of his white skirt. They could see them well, outlined against the glow. The two carried the third to the low doorway, through which a draught fed the flames, as if to a furnace or an oven. They threw him in.

A scream rose in Jack's throat but was strangled by fear before utterance. They watched the grotesque scene with morbid fascination, unable to turn away. Eddie wiped the acrid taste of spew from his mouth, moved to one side. Of the two, one fell. His bloody skirt hung in charred tatters about his legs. He rose, helped by the other, and together they brought a fourth. By the arms and legs they threw him in. One fell again. He had fallen beside a fifth, whose arm rose feebly in the air and fell back, out of sight. The two knelt beside him. They opened his shredded jacket, re-covered what they saw and gave him a drink from a bottle at his waist. As he closed his eyes in gratitude the one shot him in the head. The other was too weak to lift himself, so the one took the body over his shoulder and threw it, like a sack of coal, into the flames. The other struggled to his feet and the two embraced.

Jack was about to drag Nadirah away to stop her going mad but, in the glow of the flames from across the wadi, so near yet so impossibly far away, he saw the calm light of understanding fill her eyes. He said nothing, afraid to speak or even think.

The one took water from a flask and washed the other's face, his hands, the blackened head-cloth thrown away. They embraced, though the other had difficulty in standing, and the one led him to the door where he stood with his hands clasped in prayer and his eyes raised to the mercy of Allah. The bullet entered his brain and jerked he who was Achmed twisting like a dervish into the oven.

Nadirah gently eased herself from Jack's grasp and began praying softly... 'B'ism Allah al Rachman ar Raheem...' with tears on her cheeks reflecting the roaring horror before them as the thin stream of water in the wadi reflected the glow in the sky.

Jack made the sign of the cross from his forehead and shoulders, which he had never done in his life before, and said, 'God rest their souls!'

The hungry flames fed on the air rushing through the doorway until there was a collapse from within, a floor or some ancient timber, and a shower of sparks sprayed from the doors and windows of the house like a final explosion before he flames began to die.

The lights of vehicles were approaching across the plain. The one replaced the pistol in the holster beneath his jacket. He picked up a bandolier of ammunition, an automatic rifle, and ran down the steep winding track and entered the blackness of Wadi Bana. And his name...it was Abdullah.

There was a small smear of blood on Nadirah's forehead, where she had cut herself as she prostrated herself in prayer. Jack took her hand and led her back to the others.

'Where's Carter?' he asked.

They didn't know. He had not climbed the hill with them and was, presumably, still at the bottom with their gear.

'Did you see?' Mike asked.

'Yes.'

'Why?'

Nadirah sat with them on the ground and watched the flames dying of hunger after feasting their appetite on the house and all it contained. They no longer leapt to the sky in showers of sparks. There was a dull, red glow filling the desolation between the walls, occasionally enlivened by a falling stone, a splitting joist or an exploding cartridge.

'Don't know,' Jack said.

'For the peoples,' Nadirah sighed. 'So they cannot speak. And no bodies for the recognising.'

Ah. Yes... If the bodies were identified or, merciful God forbid, the men had been caught alive, their fellow conspirators, the villages, whole tribes would have been implicated. Reprisals could sweep the country like a plague of death.

'Were the children there?'

'No. At their own house.'

'Thank God for that. But what about Abdullah?'

'Abdullah is alone. He no family. They were killed by the British in Aden.'

'Oh God,' Jack said. 'And what about you?'

'And me. All alone now.' Such terrible things, Jack was thinking, to make a captive bulbul sing.

'So it's only us,' Eddie suddenly said, interrupting Jack's morbid thoughts. 'It's only us who know about it, who know who organised it all, all the ammo and that, and about boats down the coast from the island. It's only us who know that Abdullah's still alive.'

When Stanley Carter watched his crew climb away from him to investigate the explosion which had nothing to do with his expedition, he was finally convinced that they had absolutely no loyalty to the venture and came to an immediate decision. He watched the three of them disappear among the boulders on the slope and then searched through their packs. He found two notebooks, the other would be in the taxi. Whatever happened to his companions, he reasoned, there was no point in letting valuable data be lost to science. The red glow in the sky was from a spectacle that he had not the slightest wish to witness. It was nothing to do with him. His objective in coming to this God-forsaken country was to study its ornithology and, unlike the bungling amateur, his tenacity of purpose would keep him to that objective, regardless of any diversions. He picked up his own pack, made a cursory search for the dead stint, which he could not find, and walked back along the track to the vehicle.

Muqbel was asleep on the back seat. There was a smell of whisky and Stanley's foot brushed a broken bottle. The drunken fool had obviously begun tippling as soon as they left him and he was probably too pissed to have heard the explosion or seen the flames. Since then an hour had passed, however, and, as Stanley climbed into the car, Muqbel opened his eyes.

'What you do, Mister Stanley?' he asked, as if dazed or doped.

'We go Sana'a,' Stanley said. 'The bint's house has been bombed. Look over there.'

Muqbel rose from the seat and saw the red glow in the sky. 'Where Mister Jack?' he said. 'Where Mister Mike and Mister Eddie?'

'We have to go,' Stanley said. 'Listen to the guns. Where's the key?'

Muqbel listened. He alighted from the Land Cruiser and stood watching the smoke rising from the glow beyond the hill. The smell of burning wood, fodder, cordite and other, unspeakable, combustibles occasionally reached his nose. He spat the taste from his mouth, fully awake. 'Mush quais,' he said. No good.

'Give me the bloody key,' Stanley demanded.

Muqbel ignored him. He looked to the sky. 'Mush quais,' he muttered. 'Ba'ad ain, Askari k'teer.'

Stanley knew that there would most certainly be soldiers too much before long, and he wanted to be miles away from here when they arrived. How could he convince this stupid wog of the necessity of getting out of here as soon as possible? If those other idiotic morons wished to risk their necks, just to see a house on fire, that was up to them. Stanley Carter had no intention of getting mixed up in matters which were liable to induce a spell in a Yemeni prison or a bullet through the head.

'Come on then,' he said. 'Let's go back and get them before the cavalry arrives.'

Muqbel saw the lights of vehicles approaching from way over toward the Sumarah Pass. Lights were also appearing in the other villages scattered around the hilltops and spurs of rock jutting into the distant plain. They must fetch the others. They were taking too long. He jumped into the driver's seat, next to Stanley and took the key from his pocket, quite unprepared for the elbow in the ribs and the blow in the stomach, which Stanley thumped into him with all his force. While he was retching for breath, Stanley snatched the key, dumped him through the door and drove off, leaving him bruised and gasping on the ground.

Stanley Carter, deposed expedition leader, drove slowly, with the lights out. He drove around the edge of the barikah and switched on dipped headlights. He went away from the road to Sana'a, in the direction of As Saddah, to the east. He assumed there would be a track skirting the plain, somewhere over near the hills in the distance. He was right. After a long, slow circuit, he came back to the main road near Yarim. He switched to main beam and drove steadily to Sana'a with most of the expedition equipment in the back. He reached the capital in the morning, parked briefly on the outskirts while he rummaged through his companions' belongings, took the money he found in Mike's as being rightly his, and came into the main street as the shutters were being unrolled for morning business. He called at the travel agents near the British Embassy and found there was a seat on the morning flight to Sharjah.

At the airport, one of the taxi drivers apprehended him. Why, he demanded, was Stanley driving this vehicle and where was Muqbel? Stanley pretended incomprehension and, after packing his own belongings in his rucksack, cleaning himself up in the dubious facilities of the airport washroom, he caught the flight to Sharjah, took a taxi through acres of derelict new blocks of flats to Dubai, found there was a seat on the evening jet and, after stopping briefly in Rome, walked through the customs at Heathrow with nothing to declare.

Chapter Twenty

When Muqbel recovered from the blow in the solar plexus delivered by Stanley Carter his first impulse was to run after his vehicle. Seeing the futility of this he went instead to the boulders on the slope, where the three British men and one Yemeni woman were huddling in shock and the dark.

'Mister Stanley take car,' he said.

The significance of this took some time to penetrate their numbed minds, and it was Nadirah who answered, in Arabic, and learned of Stanley's abandonment of his compatriots. She was also the first to appreciate the necessity of getting away before they were discovered by the army, or the police, or whoever. 'Come,' she said when Muqbel had told her of Stanley's actions, 'we must go from this place.'

They followed her, back up the slope, to where they could see again the smouldering ruin of her home, and then around eastwards until they came upon the track Jack had traversed a few days before.

'Where are we going?' Eddie asked.

'To As Saddah, hurry.'

They followed her blindly in the dark, to the ancient refuge in the caves on the cliff, putting all their faith in her decision and guidance. They had no choice. Muqbel came up in the rear. He checked his money belt, just to be sure that Carter had not taken his earnings away. He had his doubts as to whether he was doing the right thing in following these people. His vehicle was his income, without it his family would starve or he would be forced to spend more years away working in a foreign country to pay for another. For the moment, however, he followed Nadirah to the caves with the kawajah. He felt obliged to stay with them, for it was he who had deceived them into being here by agreeing to work for Abdullah and this bint's brother. He was sure they had no money because Mister Stanley had taken it all. Oh God. All the plans for his family gone with that crazy man. And Abdullah crazy man. But, Allah kareem. God is kind.

Nadirah led them along the tracks in weary silence and eventually to the ledges on the cliff at As Saddah and into one of the caves.

'Now sleep,' she said. 'I see my uncle.'

Sleep. Soon it would be dawn. Even lying awake on the bare ground, Jack thought he was living a nightmare. There could be no sleep. The figures in the flames danced before him like a grotesque parody of events he could not accept witnessing. How many dead? Five? Certainly the four men they had seen carrying the boxes and Achmed. Perhaps his neighbour and his children too if they had been in the house overnight. Three more was it? His mind could stand no more of this arithmetic of carnage, and he went out onto the ledge in the cold clear night, beneath a million stars which blinked and twinkled in another dimension.

He left Muqbel sleeping, while Eddie and Mike dozed fitfully in exhaustion and shock. They had sunk into that shallow pool of amnesia where the mind obliterates the horrors of consciousness in merciful oblivion. In sleep there is hope, perhaps, that the most terrifying realities are but black dreams, which fade away upon awakening. Jack heard one of them, Mike, he thought, cry aloud in his subconscious purging. 'No. Oh no!' And found himself shivering from more than the cold. That he was himself in a state of shock required merely the most elementary of self-diagnosis, and he remembered the Boy Scout mnemonic for its treatment... WAR. Warmth, Air and Rest, of which only air, cold and penetrating, was available to him. He left the ledge and huddled among the rocks against the cliff for solitude in which to recover his wits. Such things they had seen. How could men do such things, recover, and go on to do more. He felt weak and too inadequate to cope with the horrors of the world. What they had seen was insignificant compared with events he had read about, heard about, even seen, in the vicarious experience of film and television, and which were about to happen again at the head of the Gulf. Human suffering had become entertainment on screens, to grab our attention for a moment and be forgotten, like a dirty joke.

He heard her weeping. Restrained, stifled sobs came from where she lay on the ground, quite close to him. He went to her and, wordlessly, slowly and purposefully, with ultimate tenderness and assurance, as in a dream-sequence of his most outlandish self-confidence, he gathered her into his arms and rocked her rhythmically to and fro until the sobs subsided. She clung to him and then drew her face away and looked into his eyes with an expression bearing the anxiety of all the great, unanswerable questions we have ever asked ourselves. With an anguished cry of grief she fell on to him and let the tears and tremors rack her body until the trembles died in a spasm of exhaustion, and she slept like a baby in his arms.

When he woke, she was gone. The sun was warm on his face. He stared about him. He could not find himself. The blurred memory of the circumstances which had brought him to wake on this bare mountain slowly cleared. He sat up in alarm, that these terrifying memories might be true. Muqbel was approaching with a wicker basket of food and a large, gaudily coloured vacuum flask. Jack looked at the caves. It was all too horribly true. He followed Muqbel through the entrance and found the others sitting on boxes they had found in the innermost recesses. Muqbel passed around the tea and plates of food like thick porridge. They ate in silence and Jack postponed for as long as he could the enquiry, in a voice, which he was sure conveyed more than his curiosity. 'Where's Nadirah?'

She was with her uncle and returned to the caves late in the day. 'We can stay here,' she said. 'Only little time. I am supposed to be dead, my uncle say. He has been to the village, like all the people, to see the burning of my father's house. All think I am inside.'

She managed a smile. There was nothing in her demeanour to indicate the extent of the grief to which she had succumbed the previous night.

'All think I am dead and you go to Sana'a. They not know your friend go alone.'

'Some friend,' Eddie said. 'I'll murder the bastard when I get my hands on him.'

'Mister Stanley, majnoon,' Muqbel said.

'The people say you foreigners bring rassassa for Abdullah. The askari, they look for you.'

'Oh shit,' Jack said, his worst fears realised. He looked to Mike for guidance.

Mike observed that they were safe here only for a comparatively short period. They could stay concealed in the caves but that was not expedient. Nadirah's relatives would be obliged to buy extra supplies from the village souk and word would soon get around that they were hiding someone, thereby implicating themselves. Two, three days at the most, he said, and they would be forced to move. The essential thing was for someone to get to Sana'a and seek help from the British Embassy. As Mike saw it, the best one to go was Jack, for he had at least some Arabic, and Muqbel should go to recover his vehicle. It would hardly place them in more jeopardy than staying here. The vehicle was probably still somewhere in Sana'a, after all.

Muqbel agreed to that. Nadirah would be here to look after the other two, act as interpreter, and guide them elsewhere if they should be forced to move before Jack's return.

They all considered the proposals in silence for a while and it seemed that no one was to dissent, until Nadirah said, 'OK, but you dress like a Yemeni,' and Muqbel, eager for some action toward the recovery of his vehicle, said, 'Aiwa, lazim,' laughing for the first time since Stanley's departure. 'You Englishman, same-same Yemeni.'

'I am not a bloody Englishman. How many times do I have to say it, for God's sake?' But Jack too was laughing, the high tension of his emotional state seeking any outlet for relief. 'When do we go? Tonight?'

'No,' Nadirah said. 'No tonight. You go now, in day time. I get some clothes.'

She was right. Two men walking across the country was a common sight in daytime; at night they might rouse suspicion or walk into patrols of soldiers and be forced to answer challenges. Their best plan was boldness, and to go blatantly to Sana'a as ordinary Yemenis visiting the city. She brought a patterned skirt for Jack, a check jacket, head-cloth and sandals.

Jack tried to see, in Nadirah's eyes, some reaction to their going, but she avoided his direct gaze and gave no indication of remembering the previous night, when she had fallen asleep in his arms.

They took a few bits to eat and set out to walk, if necessary, to Sana'a. Jack avoided shaking hands, as being too final, and wished his feet were tanned.

It was not until Cecil was at his desk the following afternoon, when he was called in to the large office overlooking the embassy garden, that he was made aware of the contents of Harry's memorandum. He returned to his own office and sat in thought for some time, with his brow furrowed in an uncharacteristic frown. Eventually he rose, running his fingers through the waves of his hair, and went along the wide, dingy corridor to have a word, as directed, with Harry.

There were, and in this lay the difficulty, certain matters of which Harry was in ignorance. Certain matters of which Cecil and the Old Man himself were, officially, in ignorance. Harry had blundered dangerously near discovering things which, for his own good, he would be advised, were he only aware of his discovery, to forget. Harry's memo was in writing, however, and, while it remained so, could not be officially ignored. That was the problem, although, as far as Harry was concerned, he might have written it with invisible ink. There were now certain things, however, of which he must be made aware.

Cecil entered Harry's office, with the hand-written memo in his hand, and left when the tiny shreds lay scattered in the waste paper basket and Cecil had informed Harry of all that Cecil considered Harry needed to know. Things that filled Harry with dread.

'Best thing, Harry,' Cecil said. 'Wouldn't do to have it in writing that Alison was in any way concerned. Best thing, old chap.' He smiled knowingly. 'Best to have a word,' he said. 'Just a quiet word. And now,' he said, in a conciliatory gesture, 'come and have a quiet drink on your way home.'

Tomorrow will tell, Cecil decided when he had entertained Harry for a couple of hours. Harry's little problems would sort themselves out all in good time. Cecil retired at an early hour and he wished to relax in the manner which he found most refreshing for mind and body. While watching Harry drink more whisky than was good for him, he inserted a tape of the Brandenburg Concerto in G, by Johann Sebastian Bach, into his expensive stereo system and lounged back into one of his comfortable cane chairs. He took a cigarette from an inlaid box of crumpled filter tips. He passed the box to Harry, who declined.

'Not now, thank you,' Harry said. 'I must be going. I have to pick up my wife.'

Harry left for home and blundered through the crowded, noisy streets, suspecting that Cecil was laughing at him, suspicious of those cigarettes, but too uncertain to challenge him on either count.

★ ★ ★

Alison Courtenay did not want to go 'home'. She sat in the empty mafrahj of her parents' villa trying to devise some scheme by which she could induce them to let her stay on. For the first time that she could remember, the prospect of England loomed bleak and lonely. She had no 'home'. She had seen, and lived in, seven foreign countries with her parents and, despite the image she projected towards her contemporaries in the UK of a romantic existence in exotic surroundings, she had not enjoyed any of them. That which struck others as being a life of excitement and freedom travelling the world had always been so restrictive, due to the cloying over-protection of her parents, that her life overseas had been a misery of homesickness and longing for the damp, grey streets and multifarious countryside of England. Her parents, indeed all her acquaintances, assumed that her first term at the English boarding school would be traumatic and lonely and treated her accordingly, with even more restrictive attention until it nearly stifled her. During her first term at that bleak establishment there had been no tears, just a tremendous sense of freedom and release. She could remember screaming aloud with a racing throng of girls as they ran joyfully over the playing fields with no parents to suppress their exuberance. To return to England alone, even as a small child, was to escape.

Their enquiries, 'How was school?' 'Making the most of your holiday?' demanded doleful answers which she duly provided as a duty to her parents, while secretly resenting every day of restriction that residing in a foreign country, inhabited by ayahs and nannies, imposed upon her. The realisation, which came gradually as she matured, that her parents' over-protection was covert compensation for the abdication of their responsibilities towards her for most of the year, filled her with no distress, but enabled her to purge her own slight guilt at her indifference to them both. She could not remember her mother ever putting her to bed.

That she should now wish to remain in Yemen was in no way attributable to reluctance to leave her parents, but to her acquaintance with the four bird watchers and a desire to see more of a country of which she had been given a glimpse. There was also, she readily admitted to herself, the desire to be seen as herself. She felt as if she had just come alive and wanted to experience more of a world she never knew existed. Her parents, she concluded, had never had the slightest knowledge of her true personality and she was tired of living a pretence, of trying to be what they thought she ought to be.

She waited for her father's return from the embassy with some trepidation, for she had determined to ask him, today, if she might postpone her return to England and go off with the birders. He was unlikely to agree to either of these requests but, after thinking the matter over, she had concluded that now was the time for the battle of her independence. This issue would serve as well as any other for the first skirmish.

She had not mentioned anything of her intentions to the birders themselves, of course, for she had not made the decision when Stanley Carter left to rejoin his team, and no one had heard from them since.

That her parents entered the house in silence was foreboding of ill temper in one, or both, of them. Their shrill greetings usually grated on her nerves but at least she was assured of their good, if enforced, humour and could respond in kind. Now, there was silence as the door closed with its metallic clatter, and her father went straight to the decanter, a destination usually first arrived at by her mother. He was in a vile temper and was allowing it to show, which was most uncharacteristic, as he prided himself on his ability to conceal emotion which, he felt, was the essential quality in a diplomat. Even now, in his black anger, he poured a drink for his wife and daughter.

'Water?' he demanded to know.

'A little, darling!' his wife timidly informed him.

Alison took the neat drink without comment. She thought she might need it. When her father had drained his glass, she ventured, 'Something wrong, Daddy?'

Her father glared at her and postponed his answer until he had allowed the first effects of the alcohol to steady his equilibrium and he had regained control over himself. Mrs Courtenay sat in some trepidation at the table, trying desperately not to fiddle with her glass or to drink too quickly, both of which actions would, she knew, aggravate her husband's temper.

'I have had,' Harry announced gravely, 'the most disastrous day of my diplomatic career!'

Alison made no comment. Such a portentous statement from her father demanded careful consideration or he would assume indifference to his predicament. Mrs Courtenay remembered other most disastrous days of Harry's diplomatic career and also said nothing. Harry, observing that his words had the effect of dumbfounding his family, went on to explain.

'What I am about to tell you, goes no further than these four walls.'

Mrs Courtenay concurred with a wan smile. 'Of course, darling,' she said.

Harry regarded her in contemplation for a few moments before returning his attention to his daughter.

'A certain Abdullah,' he said, 'a gentleman of your acquaintance,

I believe, has ruffled the surface, has caused ripples, made waves, no less. I would go so far as to say that he has created a gale, a diplomatic storm, indeed!' He paused to relish his metaphors. 'It would appear that the said gentleman has been organising a massive gunrunning exercise. We have it that the Yemeni government have suspected him for some time and have kept him under surveillance in order to determine his source of supply. I have been informed, however, that he and some of his fellow conspirators were involved in a battle with government forces last night, and that considerable amounts of arms and ammunition were destroyed. It would appear, although we have no hard facts, that the man and his accomplices were all killed.'

He paused again, sipped his drink, allowing time for his listeners to comment.

'Killed?' Alison might have been speaking to herself.

'Surely that will please you, darling,' Mrs Courtenay ventured, 'you have said…'

'My dear,' Harry interrupted, 'please allow me some measure of judgement. If that were all, I would be pleased, indeed delighted, to know that the damned fellow has been accounted for at last!' The possible implications of recent events clouded his chubby face with dread. 'I will go so far as to say that, regarding the news of Mr Abdullah, I am delighted.'

Alison remembered Abdullah's dark eyes, the rare smile, the long confident strides as he walked to the mountains. It seemed impossible that he could be dead. She wondered how much her father really knew of him. Trying to emulate her father's skill in the concealment of emotion, ignoring the callous tone of his last remark, she asked, 'Who was he working for?'

Her father turned to her with a furrowed frown of consternation. 'Us!' he said. 'According to the Yemeni government, he was working for us.' He went to the whisky bottle, much to the relief of his wife who accepted a refill with a steady hand. Alison refused. Her father's face was already glowing and he had evidently taken a nip, or two, prior to coming home. Before he managed a sip, he trembled in a spasmodic shiver, which spilled whisky, trickling over his fingers.

Alison thought that if he carried on like this, he would kill himself.

'Who are "us", darling?' Mrs Courtenay asked her husband, trying to understand a situation with too little knowledge at her disposal. 'I mean, who are we? I mean, us!'

'My God,' Harry said. 'If you don't know who the hell we are, how can I begin to explain the mess we're in?'

'I am trying to understand, dear.'

Alison had seen this scene before. Her father, by telling half-truths and imparting disjointed snippets of information, would confuse his listeners and then berate them for not following his reasoning. That this was a ploy to enable him to expend anger that should have been directed at himself was now obvious to her and she was finding his behaviour intolerable.

'When you say, "working for us",' she said bluntly, 'do you mean that he was working for you, personally?'

Harry said, in a voice suddenly distraught, 'My own daughter.'

'Oh, for God's sake, Daddy. Are you going to tell us, or not?' She had never spoken to him so harshly.

'Please dear,' her mother said. 'You father is overwrought.'

'My father is drunk.'

'My own daughter,' Harry moaned. 'Accepting bribes, illegally exporting antiques, accomplice to murder, smuggling ammunition, spying, subversion, abuse of diplomatic status!' He made a great effort to regain his composure. 'And I,' he said, 'have been the unwitting accomplice.'

Mrs Courtenay saw the future fall at her feet like a discarded gown, from which she stepped naked to pick up the rags of obscurity. Alison was still on the offensive but refrained from further attack in view of her wish to stay in the country, fearful that she might have already overstepped the boundary of her father's forbearance, drunk as he was. She still had no idea of how she could possibly be implicated in the crimes her father had listed and was intrigued that the one offence of which she might be considered guilty, whisky smuggling, he had not mentioned.

During the silence following Harry's remarks, he thought that his family finally realised how ill-used he had been, not aware that Alison saw that he was using her to cover his own ineptitude. She saw that he was not to be trusted and tried not to despise him. If he wished to inform them of the true reasons for his despondency, he would have to tell them without prompting or exhortation. She went into the kitchen, made coffee, came back to the mafrahj, placed a cup beside each of her parents, sat down and opened a copy of *Country Life* which she had brought out, with others, to adorn her mother's furniture. Her father's face gradually faded to its normal pink.

'The blame for the whole incident lies squarely on the shoulders of those blasted bird watchers,' Harry said eventually.

No one responded. Alison turned a page and read an estate agent's advertisement for a *desirable gentleman's residence in Oxfordshire with paddock, ten acres, fl cnt htg, 4bth, sept grny flt.* It all seemed so incredibly far away. In the past she would have been yearning for the tedium of English life, with its routines and predictability. Now, all her wishes were to stay here among the parched mountains and dusty cities. With her father in his present mood, it was not a good time to express them, but the right time would never arise. Trying to maintain a steady tone in her voice she said, 'I want to stay on for a while.'

'Of course, darling,' her mother said. 'Stay on where?'

'Here.'

'Here?' Mrs Courtenay said, as if she had no idea where 'here' might be.

'I wouldn't be in your way,' Alison said flatly, letting it be known that she was aware of her parents' desire to see her safely back home and out of their lives. 'The bird watchers are intending to explore the interior of the country next month and I could go off with them!' Despite herself, she found an ingratiating plea creeping into her voice.

Her mother said, 'A month?'

Her father thought carefully before replying, gathering his wits. 'Quite out of the question,' he stated. 'Don't you understand, that your bird watchers are more likely to explore the interior of a Yemeni prison and that you might well be incarcerated with them? You're going home as soon as I can arrange a flight.' Alison's wants, desires and problems were dismissed as settled. He rose to his feet, in order that the full significance of his next words might not be lost, and turned to them with a grave countenance.

'A severe reprimand,' Harry said. 'In all my diplomatic career, I have never received such an admonition.'

His wife paled and clasped her hands in her lap. His daughter registered exactly what he had said, he had never received such a reprimand, and that the statement was merely for effect and could be disregarded. There were times when the officialese of diplomacy turned her father's brain. They waited for him to continue.

'Our hosts,' he said, that being the term used on rare occasions when he permitted himself to confer complimentary characteristics upon the indigenous inhabitants of the country. 'Our hosts have let it be known that we, the embassy, are considered responsible for the actions of our nationals accepting their hospitality. Four British subjects, they allege, have been engaged in subversive activities with the full knowledge, if not the connivance, of Her Majesty's Government, in order to overthrow the legitimate regime of the Yemen Arab Republic. These four are said to have associated with known insurgents and left a trail of murder and destruction in their wake. The Yemenis are demanding that we hand them over as spies and that the UK government admit responsibility for their actions and pay compensation.'

The red glow was suffusing his cheeks again. Alison allowed time for him to calm himself. The allegations were nonsensical, contrived for some diplomatic strategy, as her father must well know. 'And will you,' she asked, 'hand them over?'

'We have no choice!'

He was unable to conceal the smug smile at the thought of such action. 'Considering events in the Gulf,' he said, 'this is a major diplomatic crisis. We cannot allow our compassion towards our fellow compatriots to over-ride our international responsibilities.'

'Where are they now? The bird watchers, Jack and Mike, Stanley and Eddie?'

'Where they are now, is irrelevant. Doesn't matter. They cannot leave the country without exit visas. They cannot survive without money. They cannot be concealed without friends. We do not have to seek them out. Eventually, they must come to us. For help, don't you see?'

Alison regarded her father with a blank stare and heard her mother ask timidly, 'But, I mean, what have they actually done, dear?'

'Done?' Harry said. 'Done? They have created an incident. That is what they have done. An incident! And, because they used the diplomatic immunity of my daughter to help them smuggle ammunition for subversives, they have implicated me, an ambassador of my country.'

'Ammunition!' Alison cried impatiently. 'You keep on about ammunition!' She was forced to ask, for Harry had no intention of explaining his cryptic comment. 'What ammunition?'

Her father restrained himself with difficulty. 'That ammunition,' he said, 'which you brought from Al Fazah, together with a consignment of whisky. *That* ammunition.'

As usual, her father had hoarded the most vital information until the end. He was referring to the boxes in the back of the Land Cruiser. The full implications were at last clear to her. Several seconds elapsed before she responded.

'We didn't know about any ammunition! They could be shot,' she said.

'Quite.'

Of course Harry knew they were unaware of the ammunition. But he would allow them to be arrested. Her father would allow it, for diplomatic expediency. Why could they not simply go to the Yemenis and tell the truth? Ah, the truth. Who told the truth when there were points to be scored, pawns to be moved, faces to be saved. Ah yes. Her mind was racing ahead on two or three simultaneous tracks. Carter had a visa.

'They do have friends in Wadi Bana,' she said.

'Not any more.'

She faced him and waited. Her breathing became involuntarily

302

laboured, her scalp tingled and she felt sudden beads of sweat gathering between her breasts and at the base of her spine, where a cold trickle slipped between her buttocks. She would not, could not, ask him to elaborate. What had happened to Nadirah, Achmed, the children of their neighbours? What, when, why and how? The questions surged through her mind and she suppressed them, afraid of the answers.

'Stanley Carter has an exit visa,' she said. 'You got it for him.'

'Cecil did it. And in any case, he'll be stopped at the airport.'

'Not if he went before the airport was alerted!' She kept her face blank. 'He could be talking to the British newspapers tomorrow.'

She thought her father was going to faint. He reached for the bottle and this time poured only for himself.

'I must go to the airport,' he said. 'Immediately!'

Why? Alison thought, what's the hurry? He answered her questions before she asked them.

'To enquire about Carter and arrange your departure.'

'*You* don't have to do it. Certainly not now. Get someone from the office. Get Cecil.'

'I must go myself. It's very important.' Not Cecil, he thought. Oh my God, what a mess.

Alison thought he was asserting himself over trivia, as usual, and that he was in no fit state to drive or to react rationally. In one of these moods there was no thwarting him, however, and he insisted on going to the airport.

'Well,' Alison said, 'if you insist upon going, I think I'd better drive you.'

'Oh please do,' her mother said. 'Let Alison drive, there's a darling.'

He glared at her but assented, and Alison drove him along the dusty airport road as darkness fell over the city and the black kites and fan-tailed ravens came to roost in the eucalyptus trees.

He was told, and should have known, that flight bookings for his daughter should be made at the office of the travel agent in town, and that there was no information available on individual passengers who may have departed on earlier flights. He became angry and the young soldiers in the departure lounge eyed him threateningly. Alison had never seen him so out of control and was fearful that he might do something to antagonise these enthusiastic guards. She was thankful when she eventually got him out of there and persuaded him he must wait till the morning. She was about to drive away from the airport when she saw Muqbel's Toyota parked among the taxis. She said nothing, took her father home, saw him slumped on a sofa, and slipped out to visit Cecil Hayward.

To avoid the insane traffic of the city centre she walked through the dim alleys and back streets, stepping over pools of water from leaking pipes and avoiding piles of rubbish. As the bell rang somewhere at the end of the wires dangling from the garden wall, a family of veiled women watched her through curious eyes as they glided by. When they turned into an alley she suddenly felt very vulnerable, waiting in the dim, empty street, and prayed that Cecil would answer the bell. She heard the door of the house open, footsteps on the garden gravel and Cecil Hayward's voice calling over the wall.

'Who's there?'

'Alison,' she said.

'Are you alone?' Cecil asked in a loud whisper.

'Yes. For God's sake let me in. What's the matter with you?'

Perhaps, she thought, he is afraid of some retaliation from the Yemenis, but it was unlike him to over-react. She had come to him for stability and guidance. As the gate opened, she pushed her way in.

'What the hell's going on, Cecil?'

'Please come in,' he said. He barred the gate behind her and led the way through his small garden to the house door, which he also carefully locked, and up the terrazzo stairs to the mafrahj, where Jack and Muqbel sat over the remains of what had evidently been a substantial meal.

'Oh, thank God,' she said, and found herself suppressing tears. 'Tell me what's going on,' she cried in mock anger, 'or I'll go mad.'

'We were hoping you could tell us,' Jack said.

'I don't know anything!' She turned to Cecil. 'My father has been to the airport to stop Stanley Carter leaving the country.'

'He's too late. Carter has gone.'

Cecil went to his kitchen to attend to the coffee pot.

Alison turned to Jack. 'What about the Ghanems?'

Jack saw no point in attempting to shield her from the truth, which would inevitably reveal itself.

'Dead.'

'Oh no.'

Jack had not told Cecil that Nadirah had survived the bombing. Indeed, since Muqbel and he had arrived at Cecil's, they had told the others very little. They had arrived feeling tired and apprehensive following the journey from the caves. After walking miles over open country they had headed for the main road, where they had been fortunate in being picked up by a taxi driver who refused the fare when he recognised Muqbel. They had been dropped on the outskirts of the city and came in by way of tracks to the south in order to avoid the checkpoints on the road. Their original intention had been to go straight to see Alison and Harry Courtenay but, as they had arrived in the afternoon, they decided to wait until after dark. Muqbel was leading Jack to some unknown intermediate destination when he found himself outside Cecil Hayward's door. They carefully rang the spiteful bell and Cecil answered immediately. He welcomed them as if expected, led them to his shower and lent them clean clothes before preparing the meal they had consumed just before Alison's arrival. When she had composed herself after the bad news of the Ghanems, they listened to her recital of events since returning to her parents. She turned to Cecil Hayward.

'There's something going on, Cecil. Something more than we know. I can always tell when Daddy's up to something. For God's sake, tell us.'

Cecil poured cups of pure Mukha coffee, ground from beans grown in the upper reaches of Wadi Zebid, and which he himself had picked from last season's crop.

'May I suggest,' he said when he had given himself time to think, 'that we all take stock of the situation in our separate ways and confer again in the morning, with your dear father present.'

'My dear father,' Alison said, 'is drunk at the moment and will probably be drunk again tomorrow.'

'Why do we have to see him?' Jack asked. 'He hasn't been exactly the most helpful person in the past!' He looked at Alison. 'If you don't mind me saying so.'

'Harry is my senior,' Cecil said. 'So I am obliged to refer to him, especially in matters concerning his own family. The situation is rather delicate, dear boy.'

Jack thought he detected a mimicry of Harry Courtenay's pomposity in Cecil's voice and suspected that Alison heard it too, but she did not smile.

She turned to Muqbel. 'Your car is at the airport,' she said, abruptly.

Muqbel's face lit up with relief and he rose from his cushion. 'I go for car.'

'Tomorrow,' Jack said as an expression of alarm passed briefly over Cecil's face.

'Yes,' Cecil said. 'Better not be seen in the city if you can avoid it!' He repeated the observation in Arabic for Muqbel's benefit, although Muqbel had understood his English.

Jack wondered why he was so adamant that Muqbel should appreciate the risk of visiting the airport, which was obvious, and postpone the retrieval of his vehicle. He interrogated Cecil with a look, but Cecil avoided his eyes by looking down at his coffee as he sipped the delicate brew which, he implied, was one of the few consolations for being posted to this backwater of the diplomatic world. He savoured the flavour and smiled at them. 'Delicious,' he said.

Alison asked Cecil if he would escort her home. 'I'm too nervous,' she said. 'I know I am but, after what's happened, I would appreciate it. And you can have a word with Daddy if he's capable. I can't face him alone at the moment!' She looked at Jack with a weak, apologetic smile.

'Sorry.'

As soon as they were through the door, Jack said, 'Right, Muqbel, straight to the airport. Get your car, now.'

'You say tomorrow, Mister Jack,' Muqbel protested.

'You have another key? Indak muftah?' Jack asked, ignoring the protest. 'Can you hide the car somewhere in the city? Somewhere near?'

'Plenty place. House for friend.'

'Right. You get your taxi from airport. Take your taxi to hide. One of your friends bring you back. Try to get back before Mister Cecil. OK? Understand? Fahim?'

'Aiwah.'

'Right, Yallah. Go! Masallamah.'

Muqbel sensed that all was not right among these foreigners. They and he were in trouble together but his vehicle was too valuable to leave lying around at the airport where, sooner or later, it would be under surveillance or impounded by the police. He had nothing to lose by hiding it. He was back in the mafrahj before Cecil, who had difficulty in giving what was, in effect, an order to his superior regarding Jack Pengelly and his friends without breach of petty protocol, which demanded that he oblige Harry Courtenay by drinking his whisky as a social equal until well into the night.

Despite the stupor in which Harry fell asleep, he was, after a brief visit to the embassy, at Cecil's door at eight o'clock the following morning. He brought Alison to take part in the discussion and witness his efficiency as an organiser when given half a chance.

He addressed Jack in an avuncular tone of voice which the latter found exasperating under the circumstances. 'Seems you have been rather naughty.'

'You reckon?' Jack demanded.

This upset Harry at once. He regarded the Cornishman's attitude as insolent and ungrateful. He tried a firmer approach.

'What with taking a terrorist to a secret rendezvous in the north, aiding and abetting the murder of a policeman in the Bab al Yemen souk, smuggling whisky, gun running from the coast...' His voice tailed off in abhorrence at the list of crimes. 'You have rocked the boat, somewhat, wouldn't you agree?' He stared at them in silence.

'You must appreciate,' he went on eventually, 'the precarious footing we maintain here. However, you should be jolly thankful that we are here. We'll do what we can for you.'

There was no suggestion of anger in his voice. There was merely the observation that the British Embassy were, yet again, obliged to smooth over the difficulties caused by incompetent citizens of their degenerating country blundering about in affairs beyond their comprehension.

'Our hosts are disconcerted,' he said. His relaxed insufferability, which was the more irritating for being contrived and an impersonation of those Eton and Balliol mannerisms to which he so aspired, was beginning to annoy Jack.

'You can tell them,' he said, 'that we know bugger-all about any of it!' He opened a cigarette packet. It was empty. 'Oh shit!' he said.

'We did our utmost to put your case, I assure you,' Harry said with deep sincerity.

'What did they say about bombing their own people?' Jack asked. He did not miss the look that passed between the diplomats. Harry took it upon himself to answer.

'Where,' he asked, 'did you obtain the information that they bombed their own people? That's a very serious allegation.'

'Well, who else, for Christ's sake?' Jack cried, losing his temper.

'We have never considered such a possibility,' Harry said. 'We assume outside agencies.'

'Oh, come on! With a helicopter? Outside agencies, my ass!' This was too exasperating. He looked from one to the other. Alison's face was blank.

'You would be best advised not to put such a statement about,' Harry said. He was speaking with the sincerity of a concerned parent after hearing a child utter obscenities in innocence. 'You could do yourself considerable harm, dear boy.'

Too much. Sincerity too much, Jack decided. These two could screw him up with a word. He had come to them for help and all he had received so far was a reprimand for irresponsible behaviour. He needed those exit visas but foresaw the unlikelihood of obtaining them. He and his mates were trapped. They were at the mercy of protocol.

Jack was especially suspicious of Harry. It was unlike him to be so relaxed, to give away 'so much valuable time!' He was here under orders, or at least a quiet request, which amounted to the same thing. He was a devious bastard, Jack decided. Why was it impossible to find out what was going on in this damned country? He had the feeling of being used and didn't know how. Someone was watching him, using him. It was similar to that uncanny knowledge that one was not alone when out on an empty sea sometimes. What was in it for these polite, self-assured guardians of his country's interest? People like Abdullah, he could forgive. He was a rogue and had used the foreigners underhandedly yet maybe he was entitled to, especially as he had meant them no harm, and that they should remain in ignorance of his schemes. People like Courtenay, and possibly Hayward, were another matter. Harry was another rogue, Jack suspected, who would use anyone for the furtherance of his own ends. What these ends were, in the present circumstances, Jack didn't know. It might be no more than a question of losing 'face'. The Yemenis probably knew damn well that the birders had no connection at all with Abdullah or any other faction in the country, yet saw the embarrassment they could cause the British Government by producing evidence to the contrary. The British might realise the diplomatic advantages in pretending to believe the Yemenis and in handing over the 'culprits' for a fair trial. They could then negotiate for an early release from prison, in order to expedite political credibility at home and some minor concession in some other negotiation. It might be all a game. Yes, just a question of 'face'.

How the English were predisposed to impose on other cultures the defects of their own, Jack thought to himself as he watched the faces of the men opposite him. Was it not significant that the first, sometimes the only, words they learn in a foreign language were the expressions of procrastination: mañana, bukrah, ma'lish, yimkin…

tomorrow, tomorrow, never mind, maybe. Face! How they would hold their public enquiries and their private condemnation... bad business, that Yemen affair. Bunch of damned incompetents refused to take advice. Typical of the sort of people abroad these days. Thank God old Harry Courtenay was able to sort it out. Lucky for them he was able to keep their heads on their shoulders. Good chap, old Harry. One of the old school... Which he wasn't. Not quite.

There was silence in Cecil's mafrahj. He rose and placed a tape in his hi-fi. The sound of violins, reproducing the genius of Mozart, filled the spaces in the Islamic architecture of the elegant room.

They listened to the music, watching the fan turn below a small group of obstinate flies intent upon fornication while hanging from the ceiling.

'Well,' Jack said, 'what do we do now? The Yemenis seem to be after us and our visas have expired. Can we shelter in the embassy?'

'Quite impossible,' Harry said with such haste that even Cecil could not suppress a smile. 'You must leave.'

'We don't even have our passports.'

'Cecil has them,' Alison said.

Her father's face twitched around the left eye. 'We were waiting for the photographs,' he said. 'We couldn't renew the visas without them.'

'Yeah.'

The music built up to its orgasmic climax and faded dreamily to a close. There was a long silence, during which none of them looked at each other. They heard the voice of Cecil's new watchman singing in the garden and the sound of water spraying on shrubbery. One of the fucking flies buzzed triumphantly.

'We saw Hamid,' Jack said, 'at Al Fazah.'

Cecil said, 'I think that highly unlikely.'

Jack required all his self-control not to look at Alison. He waited for her comment. It never came. Cecil switched the hi-fi off at the mains. There was something more, Jack thought. There's more to come.

At last, Harry cleared his throat. 'Agggh,' he said. 'Nasty business.'

Jack felt as if he were trapped under water, over a beautiful coral reef, with a green sea-surface deflecting the sunlight above. Between him and the air for which his lungs were bursting was a fine net, a net that he could not see although it was about to drown him. As in a trance, or a state of shock, his mind floundered as he watched Cecil unlock a wall-safe and remove a large manila envelope.

'Your passports,' he heard Cecil say. He took the package. There was more than passports in it. He opened it slowly, suspecting a trick.

It was money, sterling, riyals. His face brightened. 'What's all this?' he said.

'Although we cannot obtain your exit visas now, for obvious reasons, we are able to offer you assistance as DBSs. We're not without sympathy, dear boy.'

Jack's face registered confusion.

'Distressed British Subjects,' Harry said, with an ill-disguised smirk.

'You need all the help you can get,' Cecil said.

'Do we?' Jack said as he fingered the money. 'Yeah, sure.' There was more. There was still something else. He looked at them again, at Alison, who had apparently lost her tongue. He chewed on his bottom lip, wondering what it was all about. 'I must have a skeet,' he said.

The loo wouldn't flush. He took the lid off, saw the cistern was empty. He gave the jammed float a poke. It dropped suddenly, allowing air to splutter and water to splash in his face and eyes.

'Blast!' he said, and returned to the mafrahj, where Harry was shuffling a sheaf of papers.

'We must ask you to sign,' Harry said.

Cecil looked at Harry sharply and was about to comment. He refrained after thinking better of it. Even he was not capable of hiding all his emotions.

'Purely a matter of form, you understand,' Harry was saying.

He separated a sheet of embassy notepaper and scribbled a few words.

As a matter of form, Jack thought, this should be done on just that, the correct form and official receipt. Why was the pedantic old sod being so careless? He signed the paper without reading anything but the total.

'Good God!' he said. 'That's a hell of a lot of money.'

They ignored the remark and Cecil said, 'Cheer up, old dear. Things aren't that bad. Now listen to me!' He sounded like a clucking hen. 'I've been working behind the scenes on your behalf. There's a British ship docked at Mukha, the whisky carrier actually, which has to make a brief call at Hodaidah, before sailing for the UK. You have three days before she sails at exactly 0400 on Saturday. The captain is expecting you. I've arranged for him to pick you up outside the dock just after he departs.'

The Courtenays looked at him with open admiration, Jack with jubilation.

'Now, you'll have to go north of the port and pinch a boat or something, perhaps one of those floats they use. It's up to you, but don't go to the quay, obviously.'

Jack looked at Muqbel, who had understood but little of what had been said, and then back to Courtenay. 'Can he come?' he said.

Courtenay looked at Cecil Hayward, who hesitated.

Jack said, 'He'll be pursued as a terrorist here, while his family won't know whether he's dead or alive. You know what his fate will be if they get him.'

'He can go with you as far as we're concerned,' Cecil said. 'One more passenger won't sink the ship.'

'Can you tell the captain?'

Cecil closed his eyes. 'If you wish.'

'Immigration in the UK will need a cipher,' Harry added.

'Oh, for Christ's sake!' Jack said.

'We are opening doors,' Harry grumbled indignantly. 'You might be grateful.'

Alison saw this statement as another of her father's ploys for saying nothing while purporting to convey matters of great significance. Cecil had done it all, and Harry was trying to cash in on the credit.

Jack rose from his chair and reached across to Harry's cigarettes, in a packet on Cecil's inlaid table. He took a small bundle and put them in his own empty packet. Then, with his eyes watching Harry's, he took another one, which he lit with Harry's lighter. Harry watched him in stony-faced silence.

'Six,' Jack said. 'I've taken six. Want a receipt?'

'I'll trust you,' Harry said.

Harry saw no point in committing himself further. Events were moving to a satisfactory conclusion. Cecil Hayward had evidently taken steps to ensure that the remaining three British bird watchers could leave the country on a British ship and be out of the way in a few days, leaving the dust to settle with no harm to anyone. What more could be done? He would send the cipher to say the Arab accompanying Pengelly was 'of interest' and of Harry's recruitment. Provided nothing untoward occurred in the next day or so, Alison could leave the country under diplomatic immunity, as indeed was her right, and the whole affair could be seen in its true perspective as a minor incident blown up out of all proportion. He rose to his feet, tucking Jack's signed receipt into his pocket, saying he had better get to work as the whole nasty business required constant monitoring, and left them.

Cecil returned from seeing Harry out, ran his fingers through that fair, wavy hair and said, 'Now I'm sure we'd all like some more coffee.'

'Cecil!' Alison said. 'For God's sake, will you tell us what's going on?'

This was getting too much for Jack. He thought everything had just been explained. He looked at them, like one mentally defective, trying to grasp one basic fact too profound for him to comprehend.

'Yes!' Cecil said. 'I will, Alison, darling, but between ourselves, all right?'

Jack assumed that the implied insult to Harry, that he was extraneous to the matter, was not lost on them, yet was astonished to hear Cecil actually state, 'No mention to Harry, OK?'

'OK,' they said.

'Well...' Cecil took a deep, preparatory breath. 'Harry is quite correct in all he has assumed. There is a hell of a rumpus going on here, more serious that he realises. In fact it's no longer just local issue. You're obviously unaware, Jack, of the developments in the Gulf area since you organised your expedition. The whole thing has escalated with most of the countries of Middle East divided over religious and political differences. In my position, I can't name names, or reveal sources, but it seems that revolts are possible in at least four countries.'

'It's all a long way from here,' Jack said.

Cecil glanced at him with some tolerance before continuing. 'If only that were so, dear boy. Distances are no longer of great significance. It's more a matter of time and logistics. It'll only take one defiant, ostensibly neutral, country to take sides and we, that's to say the policing powers, if I may put it that way, will be faced with the choice of letting them do so or stopping them with force, thereby alienating half the world. It's a possibility that we can't permit. Therefore it's imperative to obtain the full co-operation of every country in the region.'

He was evidently unsure how to proceed. 'The Arabs,' he said after some hesitation, 'have always been difficult people to deal with.'

And whose fault is that? Jack thought.

'The point I'm trying to make,' Cecil insisted, 'is that in every Arab country there are factions with fanatical beliefs, whatever they are. The feudal rulers and dictators have been very reluctant to relinquish power, and there are those in their own countries who would gladly see them overthrown. We're entering a very complex and dangerous period, as you can see.'

'Where does Yemen lie?' Jack asked. 'They've already overthrown their feudalism, so they say! So there shouldn't be any problems here. What are you driving at?'

'There are factions here which agree to maintain solidarity only for political expediency. Some would like to support the general Arab cause against Western interference in their affairs, but can't do so against another Arab state supported by the West. What they're all looking for... what they might fabricate... is an excuse to convince the rest of the world that there are ulterior motives for our presence here.'

What a mess, Jack thought, thousands of people stand to be killed. And what for? When it was all over, the oil would flow again and the same men be in control, the top hundred men who ruled the world by strangling it with their purse strings. Millions dead in wars and civil wars... all for nothing now that the bosses had kissed and made up. The Eastern and Western blocs spending untold millions on arms, which could enable their people to live in unprecedented prosperity. The same thing happening in the Gulf. What was it to do with anyone else what the Arabs did? By interfering, it seemed to him, the Western powers were more likely to turn a local squabble into an international war. Why? There was more in this than he'd been told. The oil, in order to be of any benefit, would have to be sold, no matter who was running the country. Who would benefit from that? He doubted if there could have been such a fuss if the Arab states had been little countries in Africa producing bananas. He could not begin to comprehend the avarice of men. But all this implied confidence from Cecil was universal knowledge. He had not yet come to the point.

'Well,' he said, 'none of this affects us.'

'Ah. In that, I am afraid, you are gravely mistaken,' Cecil said. 'It seems that you are going to be made the instruments of the Yemenis' dissent. They say that you were smuggling arms in preparation for another uprising in their country. They want your blood for it, and ours, albeit not so literally, because they claim the weapons are SA80s, and that the ammunition you helped smuggle is of British manufacture. They say there's no way in which the stuff could have been exported from the UK without the knowledge, if not the connivance, of the British government. We, of course, have denied all knowledge and demanded that four British subjects who have disappeared or been killed in the bombing be accounted for immediately. They deny any bombing and say that you're being concealed, either by the embassy or other expats who'll be punished when discovered.'

Cecil paused to ensure that they had taken this in. 'They also maintain,' he continued ominously, 'that there's still a large amount of weaponry hidden in the country and that you, and possibly only you, know where it is.'

This was one of the bits, Jack thought. This was one of the bits that Harry Courtenay didn't know about, but why it should be withheld from him, while his daughter could be told, he could not imagine.

'What do we know about their blasted guns? Or anything else about the intrigues of the country? Why don't they get Abdullah? He's the cause of all the trouble.'

'They got him,' Cecil said, 'in the bombing, and he can no longer answer questions. Now let me make the coffee. I'm dying of thirst.'

So they didn't know it all, then? There came a suspicion that no one was telling the truth, or even knew the truth, about the whole matter. Should Cecil be informed that the birders had actually seen the bombing with napalm? For evidence of that incident, as witnessed by foreigners, might embarrass the Yemenis into co-operation. The birders might have identified the choppers, taken photographs. Some market force in Jack's subconscious warned him not to trade such a valuable commodity as this knowledge for worthless assurances of sympathy. Perhaps when they were out...

His eye fell on his bull's head. Cecil had mounted it on the wall, and a very fine piece it looked. The light was catching the smooth polish of the alabaster. Cecil had not mentioned it. If he thinks I'm intending to leave it here, he has another think to come, Jack thought. Oh, that damned Abdullah. If only they had not been speaking to the antique dealer that day in the souk. If only Fred Stirling had not recruited him as raffeeq. If only they had not gone north with Fred they would never have seen Abdullah... If only, if only...

'Where's Fred Stirling?' Jack demanded as Cecil returned from the kitchen with his brass coffee pot and diminutive Arabian cups.

Cecil's features signified a brief annoyance at this apparent irrelevance, although the logic of Jack's question eventually prevailed. 'Ah!' he said. 'Nothing doing there, I'm afraid. The DOS have managed to convince everyone that they're not implicated in any way by recalling the business near Raydah, when they themselves came under fire from rebels.'

'God, that's a right turnabout. Nobody thought to remind the Yemenis that we were there under fire too, I suppose?'

'Subsequent events were rather more convoluted for you. Fred and his team are quietly surveying the Tihamah and keeping contact by radio, through his wife of course'

'Where is he? We might need him if we are to stay hidden until we can sneak aboard the freighter.'

'Now, my dear chap,' Cecil said.

Jack saw the establishment closing ranks, consolidating its defences behind a shield of protocol again.

'There's nothing to be gained in involving the DOS. The only reason they're being allowed to continue their work is that the Yemenis want the survey finished this year, and the Tihamah can only be done in the clear period between the haze and thermals of summer and the rains.'

Jack knew all this. There was a hint of impatience, an irritation, a resentment in Cecil Hayward's voice which had never been there before, as if Jack was being presumptuous in suggesting that Fred Stirling might help them to escape, to save their lives.

'So,' he said sullenly, 'we're on our own, is that it?'

Alison had been listening to all this, and intervened before Cecil could answer. 'Couldn't they just go to Fred for information? They needn't stay in his camp, and you can keep in touch via Fred's radio. You ought to know what's going on, where Jack and the others are.'

'The Yemenis listen to everything we transmit,' Cecil reminded her. 'Deny it, of course.'

'Oh, come on, Cecil. You know you can fool them any time you like. You do it all the time, with oblique references, back-slang and things, I've heard you on Daddy's scanner. You're past masters at it.'

Cecil smiled and thought about it. Then he took Jack's crumpled cigarette packet from the table and unclipped his fountain pen. 'You have your maps still? No? I'll lend you some.' He wrote six figures on the packet.

'Fred's map reference?' Jack queried.

Cecil widened his eyes, as if to say that he could never divulge such a secret, and poured the coffee.

Alison laughed. 'I'm sure you'll be all right, Jack. You can sneak aboard the ship easily. You've seen what a shambles their army is.'

He had seen the shambles of their ragged uniforms and the slouching behaviour of some of them at the checkpoints. He had also seen the clean, well-oiled weapons they carried with such indifference. And the intelligent eyes of the young officers and NCOs. 'Yeah,' he said. 'We'll make it, I'm sure.'

He eyed the plaque on the wall. The smooth horns were catching the light. The eyes seemed to have closed. He wondered what the writing meant. With a sigh, he pushed himself once more from the chair and fetched the plaque from the wall. Cecil watched him as he returned to the chair and ran his hands over the exquisite curves.

Chapter Twenty-One

Muqbel led Jack Pengelly through the narrow back streets of Sana'a. People ignored them. Jack was thankful for his dark eyes and suntan, his short stature and slight build. He could pass as a Yemeni in the clothes Nadirah had provided, whereas the average Englishman was too tall and heavy. He felt slightly foolish. He carried his own clothes in a rag bundle, reluctant to be without them, yet unable to wear them. The alabaster bull's head was in the centre of the bundle. The money Cecil had given him was in a pouch of his money belt. The passports, with the archaic reassurances on the inside no longer consoling him, were in another. His legs felt free in the loose skirt, but he wished the fluttering of his stomach and the desire to piss every ten minutes would cease, so that he could relax and walk with the easy confidence of his companion. They passed through a maze of buildings in the old stone city until Jack was completely lost, and eventually emerged among the chaos of the new developments on the southern edge of the town. Muqbel led the way to a large iron gate set in a wall topped with jagged fragments of broken glass. He produced a key and, as the gate swung open, they found themselves in a large derelict garden littered with vehicle spares and wooden crates. Over the door of a flat-roofed building hung a faded sign written in English. *Directorate of Overseas Survey*. They were in Fred Stirling's compound.

Jack laughed at the audacity of it. 'That's pushing your luck,' he said.

Muqbel went to a battered-looking Toyota Land Cruiser parked close to the wall, where it could not be seen from outside. Jack hardly recognised it. Its number plates were changed and the bodywork daubed with filler, to imitate crude repairs.

'My friend work Mister Fred,' Muqbel said. 'Car OK. Good place, Mister Jack?'

Jack did wonder how many keys to this compound were drifting around the city, but thought that right now he couldn't care less. It was the last place anyone would look for Muqbel's vehicle and with Fred and his team safely away on the Tihamah, doubly safe. Their equipment was all there still. It would not have been so in London, he thought.

'Go Wadi Bana,' Muqbel said. 'I take.'

Jack put his arms around Muqbel and hugged him tightly, fighting back tears of gratitude.

'What about you, sadiqi?' he said. 'You know they're all after you, don't you? That bastard Abdullah has got us all in a bloody mess.'

'I OK. Now, eat.'

Despite Jack's misgivings, Muqbel led him back into the old city. They went into a crowded eating shop near the taxi rank where, Muqbel insisted, everyone was his friend and there was nothing to fear. Jack was afraid to open his mouth for whether he spoke in English or his poor Arabic, everyone present would know that he was a foreigner. The cafe was open-fronted, without glass, and they sat at a table in the shadowy depths, eating a stew of lamb with round discs of crusty khubs. They drank tea from an enamelled pot, poured into chipped glasses. Jack smoked one of Harry Courtenay's cigarettes, thinking that most of the people present in the crowded room were probably completely unaware of the bombing in Wadi Bana, or at most would have heard unconfirmed rumours. The news would not be broadcast on the radio, that's for sure.

The crowds outside, with people jostling and arguing, the street vendors, the families climbing into taxis and buses, seemed so utterly concerned with their own affairs that the very notions of dissident tribesmen, revolutions, gunrunning, were so incongruous that Jack, once again, found himself contemplating his surroundings with incredulity. The people in the street thinned themselves out by some coincidence of perambulation and, briefly, he could see across to the other side.

'Muqbel!' Jack cried, despite his caution. 'Look! There's Abdullah.'

'Where Abdullah?'

'Shh. Over there. In the white car near the taxis. The Peugeot estate.'

Muqbel stood up. The people had merged again, in a seething good-natured mass. 'No see.'

'I'm sure it was him.'

There was no sign of him now. The crowds mingled, people passed, two men laughed as they entered the door. Jack felt his innards trembling again. He was afraid of Abdullah and what he could do to them. There was no doubt that he was utterly ruthless, a frightening adversary. With a chill travelling down his spine like an infusion of dread, Jack became acutely aware, as he scrutinised the faces of the crowd, that he and Muqbel, together with the others hiding in the caves at As Saddah, were a threat to this man. Only they, among his potential enemies, knew he was still alive. A word from them and he would be hunted down like an animal. Should he ever discover what they had seen on that terrible night then, Jack had no doubt, he would pick them off like troublesome fleas. He longed for the deck of that ship beneath his feet.

'Oh shit!' he said.

'You want shit, Mister Jack? I know good place.'

They left the city in the afternoon. The soldiers were looking forward to their qat and impatiently waved everything through the checkpoints. As Muqbel slowed down, a young soldier, with his cheeks bulging with a wad of half-chewed leaves, hurried them on. 'Yallah. Yallah!' he said. Move. Move!

Muqbel smiled at Jack's sigh of relief as they drove on. He assured him that the soldiers were stupid, often allowing hundreds of cars and lorries through during the day, though checking every vehicle that travelled at night, as if insurgency could only flourish in the dark. Once on the open road they dropped conversation, and each became absorbed in his own thoughts. There was little likelihood of another roadblock before they reached As Saddah and the sanctuary of the caves, but Jack regarded the occupants of every vehicle and every worker toiling in the fields as a potential enemy, an agent of either the government or Abdullah. He felt his stomach burning with acid and his hands occasionally trembling with fear when he thought what might befall them if they missed that boat. He leaned his head back against the seat and gazed indifferently at the passing scene as the breeze from the open window fluttered the corner of his head-cloth. Three white storks, near Al Abbas, caught his eye. There was a short-toed eagle beating steadily south near Nagil Yislah. The distant mountains were purple in the haze. Mountains, always mountains, as ever remote and inaccessible, were all about them as they drove down the central highland plateau of fertile cultivation. It was now dry, shimmering, beautiful. They had been lucky to find the route of the eagles among this geological chaos. Luck! They had found them by sheer luck. By coincidence they had found them, and Stanley Carter would lie, say it was by scientific research and deduction. Let him. What did it matter?

Muqbel reached into the glove box and produced a handful of green qat leaves. He offered some to Jack who chewed them for a while and spat them out. They tasted like privet.

'Mush quais,' Jack said. 'No good,' wishing he had asked Cecil Hayward for some of his hashish.

Muqbel laughed. 'Qat quais,' he said. 'Quais k'teer.'

He played his old tape of Oum Kalthoom, the Egyptian singer, *'Mush mumkin, abda,'* which, together with the heavy drone of the tyres on the tarmac, calmed Jack's mind, drove out the fears and lulled him into intermittent sleep. He woke to street noises in the town of Dhamar.

'Lazim ishtara benzine,' Muqbel said as he pulled in to a pot-holed filling-station. We must buy petrol.

Jack gave him some of the money from Cecil Hayward to pay for the petrol, looking uneasily down the long street with its honking traffic, shouts, blaring music, the hammering of metal, an overburdened donkey.

'Mush quais, Dhamar,' Muqbel said.

'Same-same Indian Queens,' Jack assured him.

An oil-smeared urchin, wearing a skullcap and a skirt that may have once been white, placed the filling nozzle in the tank. He made some joke about the state of the vehicle, with a husky laugh. Muqbel did not smile. He had seen four men, their faces covered with head-cloths, one of whom was carrying an automatic rifle, sauntering up the street towards them. As they came abreast of the garage one of them stopped, and was about to address Jack, sat in the passenger seat, but his companions gruffly called him on. They piled into a white Peugeot estate car and drove off towards Ta'izz.

'Who were they?'

Muqbel shrugged and doubtfully shook his head. 'Who were they?' he asked the boy.

'Guraba,' the boy said. Outsiders, foreigners.

Jack smiled. They probably came from the next village, he thought. Muqbel watched them drive away. 'From Aden,' he said. 'I hear the talking. Like Aden.'

He was quiet as they followed in the direction of the white estate car. He drove slowly with no music playing and, when they were well clear of the town, he turned off the main highway onto an un-surfaced road which led, according to a crumpled sign at the junction, to Rada and Al Bayda, way over to the east.

'Where are you going, Muqbel?' Jack asked, after allowing him to drive some five kilometres along the deserted road.

Muqbel swung the vehicle off to the right and stopped among a stand of acacias in a wadi bed. From the back of the car he produced a large vacuum flask of coffee. He flashed his white teeth at Jack in that now familiar diffident smile.

'I very tired,' he said.

'It's the qat,' Jack told him.

'No. Qat wake up. Same-same coffee. In night, no sleep. All night I thinking. Now see Aden men in Dhamar. I afraid now.'

He drank deeply of the thick, black liquid, hot and sweet, and passed a cup to Jack, who accepted it gratefully and lit another of

Harry Courtenay's cigarettes. Only one left. He should have bought some in Dhamar. He was rich. He gave the last one to Muqbel, who took it with a nod of thanks.

'Shukran, yah achi,' he said. Thank you, O my brother.

The smoke was taken through the window by a warm breeze. There was a Palestinian sunbird sipping nectar from a parasitic plant flowering on the acacias. Jack's hand went to his chest. His binoculars were in the cave at As Saddah. Without them, he felt naked.

'Abdullah, mush quais,' Muqbel said, blowing smoke. He paused uncertainly. 'Mister Stanley, mush quais.'

The depression where he had parked beneath the trees was utterly silent. There was not even a rustle of leaves in the hard, thorny branches. There was no traffic, no animals or music. Any movement in their seats, a rubbing of cotton and upholstery, seemed to echo on the hollow vehicle.

'I afraid my wife, my children.'

'You want to go home?'

'Yes. Mister Jack, I no come to ship with you!' He was apologetic.

Jack took his hand. 'You're a good man, Muqbel. There are not many like you. Go home tonight. Drop me at the caves and go home. I understand what you are saying.'

He was saying, as kindly as he knew how, that they would have to get to the coast without him, or his vehicle. He could not go and leave his family. They would have to get there as best they could. They were not his responsibility.

The sunbird moved off, flying to another group of trees further along the depression. They ought to be going too.

'Shall I drive?' Jack said. 'If you are tired.'

'Mister Jack drive sayarah?' He thought this highly amusing. 'OK.'

'Yeah. It's only about fifty kilometres. Let me drive!' He got out and went round to the other door. Muqbel moved over.

They had gone through Yarim without stopping, and were on the road near the turn-off to Dhumran, where there is an outcrop of rock straddling the road. Jack was getting used to the big vehicle, enjoying its smooth power. The setting sun was yellowing the sky.

Muqbel was asleep in the passenger seat, with his head thrown back in exhaustion. Jack was wondering why Nadirah's family did not own a vehicle. Nowhere to park, perhaps, he thought with a smile as he looked around at the vast, endless empty landscape.

As they approached an outcrop of rock through which the road passed on a rise, a single shot rang out from somewhere, and there was a simultaneous thump as the bullet hit the Toyota's roof. Jack's foot slipped from the accelerator and the vehicle jerked convulsively before he regained control and Muqbel woke to another shot and the instantaneous thump and rip of metal. He cried aloud with an inhalation of breath as Jack dropped a gear and sped through the dust and gravel of the outcrop to be clear of the rocks where, presumably, the sniper was hidden. They heard another shot as, with gravel spraying from the tyres, they drove through the boulders and on to a stretch of open road. Jack flipped up into top gear and spun the speedo over the hundred and fifty ks. He was almost laughing with excitement. He glanced at Muqbel, who said, 'You OK, Mister Jack?'

'Yeah. You?'

Muqbel slid his hand under his right armpit. He brought it out and groaned in despair. Thick, red blood dripped from his fingers. 'Yah Allah,' he said.

'Oh my God!' Jack looked in the mirror. No one was following them. He drove for ten minutes, pulled off at the end of a long, straight section and waited. The road remained deserted until a heavy truck came lumbering by. There was nothing behind it.

'Let's have a look.'

The bullet had come through the open window and slashed Muqbel's back and shoulder where it had been cushioned against the seat. There was a long hole where it had disappeared into the upholstery. No bones had been hit, but the flesh-wound was bleeding profusely. There was no place for a tourniquet. Jack took his shirt from the bundle and tore it in half to make pads to place over the wound. He used Muqbel's head-cloth to tie them in place, glancing down the road occasionally, but there was still no sign of pursuit.

'Oh God,' he kept saying as Muqbel's blood permeated the cloth and smothered his hands. 'Oh Jesus, Muqbel. What the fuck's going on? Christ, what a mess.'

'Nadirah murabbiyat,' Muqbel said.

Oh yes. Nadirah was a nurse.

The night had fallen when they got to her. Jack drove over tracks to the base of the hill and the others came down to help Muqbel up to the caves. He had lost a lot of blood. It was all over the car and Jack's clothes. It was caked in his fingernails and in the creases of his hands.

Muqbel was unable to move his arm without pain, but he would be OK. 'He was lucky,' Mike said. Jack disagreed. The gunman, obviously, had not known that he had changed places with Muqbel and was driving at the time. The shot was meant for him. For Jack. 'They're after us,' he said. 'Abdullah, the Government, the army, the police, somebody, everybody.'

He told them! No visas, no sanctuary, no official help, no anything, except money. Plenty of money. Money to get them out of the way and a ship at Mukha if they could get themselves aboard undetected. He informed them of all that had transpired since leaving them.

'We've got to get to that ship,' Eddie said. 'And the sooner we leave here, the better.'

'What about Muqbel?' Jack said. 'What about Nadirah?'

'That's their problem, mate,' Eddie insisted. 'They got us into this mess.'

Muqbel said, 'I stay. You take sayarah for ship. I say intum yasriq. You are thieves. Try kill me. Shoof!' Painfully, he raised his right arm. 'Look.'

Jack and Nadirah laughed at the audacity of Muqbel's plan. They could all go in Muqbel's Land Cruiser except for Muqbel himself, who would stay here. He would say the foreigners had shot him and taken his vehicle, and the authorities would have to accept it. Whether they believed it or not was another matter. They were not particularly interested in him and might welcome an excuse to eliminate him from the game. The British would drive to Mukha, leave the car for Muqbel to collect when he was fit, and get aboard the ship. 'Are you sure?' Jack asked him.

Muqbel tossed his head. 'Me nobody. Drive taxi. One wife, girl and boy. Who care about me?' He looked from one to another and said, in Arabic, 'Anna la Abdullah!' I am not Abdullah.

He had another thought. 'Maybe you pay some baksheesh for car!' He raised his eyebrows and smiled. 'If Allah wills.'

Jack turned to Nadirah. 'What about you? You can't stay here.'

If they ever found she had not been killed in the raid, then she would be arrested as an accomplice in her brother's crimes. Perhaps put on trial... perhaps not.

'You must come with us!' Jack said.

'Yes. I will come!' She had others to think about. Friends, the old people. 'Lazim!' She smiled.

'I mean all the way. To Britain.'

'Yes, I know. I have friends in Newcastle.'

Eddie said, 'Cor blimey, I might a known!' He turned to Jack. 'Just one fing, mate. I'm gettin' fed up with being taken for a ride in this country.'

'What do you mean?' Jack said.

'What I say, mate. Just what I say.'

They made Muqbel comfortable, although Nadirah warned him that the worst of the pain was yet to come. She gave the old couple a list of medicants to get from Yarim. If the wound became infected Muqbel would probably be dead within a month. Keep it clean, she said. Jack took a wad of notes from his money belt and gave them to him uncounted, in an untidy fistful. Muqbel shook hands with Mike, then Eddie, with his apologetic smile. Jack embraced him, with tears brimming his eyes.

Muqbel fingered the bloodstained folds of Jack's skirt. 'You same-same Yemeni man!' he said. 'Masallamah, yah achi. With peace, O my brother!'

Jack laid his arm over Muqbel's shoulder: 'Fi aman Illah,' he said. In God's protection.

Nadirah spoke rapidly to the old people, who seemed to accept everything impassively. They had seen so much before from their home among the caves. Jack checked that the petrol tank was still almost full from the refill in Dhamar. He checked the oil, water, tyres and, provisioned with a bundle of food, they drove quietly away from As Saddah.

When they were approaching the conical hill at the entrance to Wadi Bana and the men thought the memories might be too much for Nadirah, she told Jack to drive to her house. Eddie protested, but they took her. They were uneasy, both at the delay and the possibility of the police and army being there, yet could understand her desire for a last farewell to a home, albeit in ruins, that she would never see again. She asked Jack to go with her and he followed her up the ancient steps, wishing, irrationally, that he had been invited there before that terrible night.

At the top they were greeted by the smell of burnt wood and the acrid taste in their mouths of other, unspeakable remains hidden under the black debris. Wisps of thin smoke, from a glowing cinder here and there, still drifted about them in the cold night air. Looking back for the reassurance of the vehicle, he could not see it. He could see a shadowy bulk near the outline of the conical hill and, over to the right, the glitter of the stream. It seemed a long way off.

To Jack's perplexity, the girl ignored the heap of ruins and passed to the entrance of a small, blackened cave. She peered at a litter of burned and exploded boxes and discharged cartridges at the entrance. Then, without comment, she squeezed through to reach into a deep recess in the depths. She passed out a leather handbag. Jack recognised it as that which she had clutched on the plane. 'This is like our safe,' she said. 'All valuable things in here. My papers, passport.'

She reached into the recess and pulled out, by the barrel, a Kalashnikov AK47. She passed it back to Jack.

'Take it!' she ordered.

She reached in again, brought out three magazines of ammunition. Jack made no comment. His hands were slippery from the grease from the gun. 'We will clean it,' she said. 'You can use?'

'I think so. Abdullah showed me.'

The cold metal, solid, streamlined and efficient, was reassuring in his hands. He stroked the stock with his thumb.

'Come on, kawajah,' she said in her strong accent, 'let's get the hell out of here.'

They were standing facing each other. He with the gun, she with the heavy ammunition in her arms and handbag slung from her shoulder. He wanted to kiss her and was sure that she wanted to kiss him. He wanted to take her in his arms and tell her that everything was going to be all right. She was so frail.

'Come on,' he said. And led the way down the long flight of steps to the car.

They gave the gun to Eddie, who gleefully set about cleaning it. Mike rubbed the ammunition clean of grease. 'Can't see that it's much use to us, quite honestly. If it comes to the crunch we can never fight our way out with one gun and three clips of ammunition. Might as well give up, actually.'

'We'll see about that!' Eddie said.

When the vehicle was loaded, Jack drove to the tarmac of the main road and was about to turn left when Nadirah said, 'Al yameen.' To the right. He obeyed her without question and turned back towards Sana'a.

'Where are we going?' Eddie asked.

Nadirah turned around to look back at him. 'The soldiers will be at the Sumarah Pass, yes? We cannot go by the big road.'

They agreed. But, where else, how else to get to the coast?

'We go Wadi Rima!' Nadirah said. 'They will not expect you to go north again, or to know the way through the mountain!'

'Give us the map,' Jack said, and Mike passed it forward. It was too dark to read it. 'You know the way?'

'Yes. And I have friends in hospital at Medinat Al Abid. Don't worry.'

They drove north quite slowly. Each time the speedometer exceeded the eighty kilometres mark Nadirah asked Jack to slow down. They went back through Yarim and Dhamar, without incident.

Jack kept a wary eye out for a white Peugeot estate among the cars that overtook them, but there were many such.

There were still people on the streets of the towns, but Jack was wearing the head-cloth and passed unnoticed, with Mike and Eddie lying low on the back seat. There were many Toyota Land Cruisers. Just outside the built-up area of Dhamar, Nadirah peered forward and said, 'Left. Left here.'

They turned off onto a track leading away in the gloom. It was difficult to follow at times when the arc of the headlights was cut by a rise in the ground. After half an hour over open country they began descending into a slight wadi. The track became coarse gravel and, at times, bare water-scoured rock. The incline steepened, the track narrowed between walls of rock and the wheels spun and jumped over the fissures and stones. At times the incline became so steep that the vehicle slithered down almost out of control as Jack fought with the brakes and steering. The darkness about them was absolute. They could see nothing but the walls of rock hemming them in and a void of darkness beyond the rough, uncertain track in the headlights.

'I 'ope you know where you're goin', darlin',' Eddie said.

Jack glanced at Nadirah. She hung on to the handgrip over her head and said nothing. Jack drove on, carefully, letting the heavy vehicle roll over the obstacles under its own impetus as they went deeper into the unknown wadi.

'A good place for an ambush,' Mike said.

'Oh sure!' Jack said. 'That's all we need.'

Eddie twisted his neck out of the window to look up at the cliffs towering above them. 'Dunno about ambush,' he said, 'but it looks like a good place for bald ibises up on these cliffs. I can see stars at the top of 'em.'

'You'll see more stars if you don't keep your head in!' Jack said. 'You're likely to get it knocked off on one of these bends.'

The cliff to their right opened out, that to their left still towered above them in the darkness. They saw water glittering. The track became a stream that they followed for a while before climbing a bank. They crossed a stone bridge and saw before them a line of houses on the right and, opposite them, a series of low huts.

'This is Hammam Ali,' Nadirah told them. 'Drive very slow.'

They were stopped by a man waving a small electric torch. She told the man she was hakim going to the mustashfah at Medinat Al Abid. He climbed in.

'Yallah,' the man said. Go!

'Don't worry,' Nadirah told them.

They did. For another ten kilometres, which took two hours of further descent along the wadi bed before they saw the lights of Medinat Al Abid.

They dropped the man and Nadirah directed Jack to drive up to a slight incline and into the compound of a large, low building. 'Mustashfah,' she said. 'Hospital.'

She led them around the back, through a dimly lit corridor to a room with four beds, a chair a table and a fan turning slowly in the ceiling.

'Sleep,' she said, and left them. It was four a.m. They slept.

Three hours later, in the morning light, Mike was out on a wide veranda looking at their surroundings. They were at the bottom of an enormous wadi. He could see houses here and there at the very edge of the high cliffs towering above them. They were built above the most precipitous faces and, from their white windows, the whole wadi was in view. The houses were isolated in the sky, impossible to approach from below. Heaven knows, Mike thought, how they get up there, much less build on such sites. He could see that, whereas in the past they had been invulnerable, they were now exposed and sitting targets for attack from the air. He saw a train of camels coming down the wadi and called the others out to see. The animals were plodding steadily towards them, with their gentle eyes weeping from irritation by flies and the enormous loads on their backs. They stood watching, as if seeing a visitation from another age or another world manifest itself in the eerie silence of this terrifying landscape. The camel drovers were wild, unwashed, tough-looking men with only their eyes visible through their head-cloths. They looked at the foreigners and turned away, hitching their guns over their shoulders, and passed in a line of unsynchronised rhythm.

A large bird squawked, attracting the bird watchers' attention. 'Hornbill!' Eddie said. 'See it?'

'What a country,' Jack said. ' Twentieth century yesterday, middle ages today. Nearly frozen to death one minute, in the tropics the next.'

The sun was not yet in the valley, but the shadow of the cliff was falling and the brilliant light was already striking the nests of weaverbirds hanging from the telephone wires, strung from tottering poles straggling into the distance. There was not a breath of breeze in the bottom of the wadi and the humidity was already rising. Later, the heat would be unbearable.

Nadirah came out. She said there was food waiting and not to make themselves conspicuous. After eating, they drove away. A small group of people watched them go, peeping from behind the window screens.

Eddie drove, keen to try the vehicle. Nadirah warned him that driving would be difficult and, if it rained, impossible. They were to follow the bed of Wadi Rima, south of the massive Jebel Raymah, down to the coast. They looked at the map. It was vague: just a line indicating a water flow at the base of every deep wadi. How far? A hundred k? Say, sixty miles to the coast road?

'I 'ope you know what you're doin'!' Eddie said to Nadirah as she hung on when the car lurched into the water.

After ten miles, Mike took his turn at driving. Eddie's arms were aching, for his big frame made it more difficult to sit comfortably than a smaller man. The heat enveloped them in a steamy haze. They passed the camels. The drovers seemed more friendly, perhaps with the comradeship of fellow travellers. They invited them to stop for chai. 'Drive!' Nadirah said. 'Do not stop.' Eddie took the gun out from under the seat; he slipped one of the clips of ammunition into place. No one objected.

Water splashing from the wheels hissed and steamed against the hot metal of the vehicle. The men became bathed in sweat, yet Nadirah remained remarkably cool. She said hardly a word and kept watching the track, such as it was, along the stream. Gravel grated under the tyres, threatening punctures. At times the steepness of the banks, or the depth of water, forced them to detour from the stream, which slowly gathered in strength and volume until it was a rushing river swirling at the axles. When Mike tired, Jack took over.

They came to a wide stretch of gravel where the wadi opened out. They disturbed little egrets, saw the nests of hammerkops in the branches of the occasional tree or perched among boulders on pinnacles of rock.

'What a country,' Eddie kept saying. 'What a bleedin' country.'

'Easy from now,' Nadirah said.

Midday, and they had travelled fifty kilometres according to the dial, but over such rough riding it might be ten kilometres adrift. They stopped under a wide-spreading acacia tree for a brew and a chew of unleavened bread just before a helicopter came overhead and flew down the wadi.

'That was lucky,' Eddie said.

'They might not be looking for us, you know!' Mike said.

'P'raps not,' Jack sighed. 'You know,' he said after a while, 'they can see a matchbox from a satellite. If these guys have any sophisticated gear at all, they can see us from ten miles away.'

They considered this until Eddie said, 'Well, yeah. There's gear that can see through walls. There's gear that can do things which scare the life outa yuh, but I doubt if these guys got any.'

'Let's hope not!' Mike said. 'They would undoubtedly be very unhappy to know what is under surveillance in their country. I expect Washington, London and Moscow all know more about what's going on here then the locals.'

Nadirah looked at them with some doubt. She found it impossible to believe what they were saying, yet she knew it to be true. These people, their governments... sometimes their governments didn't even know... thought they had the right to do these things. In their national interests, they said. To spy on anybody and manipulate the world to their own advantage. Why? When they already had everything. 'We stay here,' she said. 'One hour.'

The chopper came back, slowly gained height, followed the wadi for a while, rose with an angry acceleration of its rotors, skimmed the mountain and dropped into the next depression in the tangled hills.

'If they are looking for us,' Jack said, 'how do they even know we're in this area?' The map was too vague, the landscape too vast, for them to know exactly where they were. They reckoned they were at a spot where the last of the tributaries joined the main river, just before the open country of the foothills.

'Hang on!' Jack said. 'Fred Stirling is here somewhere!' He checked the map reference. 'According to Cecil Hayward, he's somewhere here!' He dotted the map with a thorn. 'Near that village, Al Madan. We'll be coming out near Zabid, look, not far from Al Fazah.' Nadirah's rough ride had been a very quick short cut to the Tihamah.

'We can stay the night with Fred,' Eddie said. 'If we can find him.'

It would be getting dark at six-thirty. If they left here at three, they could reach him just before dusk. They would have time for a sleep. Jack closed his eyes.

'We go now,' Nadirah said.

'I thought you said an hour?'

She pointed to the clouds over the mountains. 'I change my mind.'

'Yeah. Right. Flash floods, you mean. Right. Let's go.'

They followed the river, which became a stream, dwindled to a trickle, and was sucked into the gravel and thirsty sand before it ever reached the sea. The heat came at them like a furnace on the wind blowing from the plain. Behind them, streaks of lightning dropped from the dark clouds and rolls of thunder echoed ominously in the wadi. Far away, up among the peaks, the rain fell in black curtains and drenched the slopes with rivulets of erosion. Here, the moisture had passed over into clouds unformed; the sun beat down without mercy from a sky of unbroken blue. They drove on into the heat and passed a small village. It was a cluster of flat-roofed houses with a couple of palm trees shading a roadside shop. They saw the usual glare of advertisements for soft drinks, cool, icy. They drove on.

In a hollow among some low hills, they stopped to drink their tepid water. Mike and Eddie climbed a rise to view the terrain ahead.

The distance was haze and shimmering heat, with barren stretches of dusty ground between green fields of irrigated cultivation, scattered acacias and herds of goats tended by small children. Two villages lay to their right, ahead a third, which must be Al Madan. They were thirty kilometres from the road at Zebid, sixty from the sea and maybe a hundred and fifty from the ship at Mukha. So near, yet oh so far. Mike tried to pinpoint their position on the map. It was too vague.

'There's only one road to Mukha,' he said, 'and that's right past the barracks where we saw the soldiers and gave a lift to Abdullah.'

He gazed over the open country before them. 'You couldn't hide a Dinky toy out there. Unless we drive straight out to the coast... here at Khawkah... and then drive along the shore over the sabkah. The map shows a motorable track.'

'Shouldn't like to rely on that!' Eddie said.

Back at the car, Jack tried to converse with Nadirah, who had been silent all day except for her directions to the drivers. 'Do you think we'll make it?' he asked her.

'How I know?' she replied irritably.

He thought she might break down if pressed and left her to her own thoughts. After dark, they drove slowly over to where Fred's camp should have been. They avoided the villages and parked at the base of a long ridge of low hills. They decided to make sure it was safe to visit the camp by making an initial reconnaissance on foot.

'You never know,' Jack said.

The darkness had fallen about them like a cool, impenetrable curtain and the wind dropped suddenly soon after dusk. The air was still, with sounds carrying from the villages. They heard music, a motorbike, the inevitable barking of dogs. They kept under the thin acacia trees and picked their way carefully, ducking low to see the sweeping limbs against the sky, avoiding those vicious thorns. At the edge of the trees they stopped, listened and hurried over the open ground to the last bluff before the camp.

'You go on, Jack,' Mike said. 'Eddie and I will cover your rear.'

'We should have brought the gun,' Eddie said, as they settled down among the rocks.

Nadirah followed Jack up the slope. The bluff was low, the last of the foothills before the flat, sand-blown plain of the Tihamah. At the top was an outcrop of boulders. They heard voices. They crept forward on hands and knees. The camp was right below them. Jack felt guilty for spying on Fred. They saw the water bowser, Fred's Landrover, the truck, the cluster of tents. They could see the movement of the Yemeni porters and the lights of their lamps. 'There's a car!' Jack said. It was parked beside the truck.

They settled among the boulders to watch. Vague thoughts of scorpions crossed Jack's mind. He kept his hands clear of the ground. They watched for an hour.

'What do you think?' he said.

He sensed, rather than saw, the shrug of her shoulders. She looked down indifferently at the camp. The porters were laughing. Somebody was playing a cassette of Arabic music.

'What I care?' she said. Her chin fell upon her arm, and her hair wisped across her face. 'What I care what you do?'

She was exhausted, he thought. She was very close to him and he could smell the faint, musky perfume on her clothes and her female warmth. Her eyes were shining and there was a glint of a tear somewhere on her cheek. He heard the call of an owl, short, abrupt, like a hoarse frog. Eagle owl? He looked about him at the dim shapes and outlines in the night. Stars were beginning to penetrate the dusty sky.

'If you foreigners not come here, none of this happen.'

His sharp inhalation of breath expressed his exasperation. 'Your bloody brother...' he hissed. 'No. I'm sorry. You're worn out.'

'My brother said I must marry Abdullah. It was his last wish!' There were tears on both her cheeks now. 'I don't know. What I can do?'

The headlights of the car were turned on. The tall, drooping frame of Fred Stirling emerging from a tent was unmistakable. So, also, was the slight, rather effeminate figure of Cecil Hayward. They watched him drive away. His car headlights bounced and twisted amongst the trees and outcrops along the bumpy track and were lost in the distant night.

Jack swore vehemently. 'Come on,' he said, and led her back to the others. At the Toyota, he told them what he had seen. 'Cecil Hayward!'

'I don't understand,' Mike said. 'He could have contacted Fred by radio.'

'Not without being overheard. The Yemenis are not daft, they would have understood his cryptic messages, even if Fred didn't.'

'There's something going on,' Eddie said, 'that we don't know about.'

'There's been something going on, Eddie,' Jack muttered, 'that we've not known about ever since we arrived in the bloody country!' He fumbled in his pockets, remembered he had no cigarettes. 'You!' he said suddenly to Nadirah. 'How do you know what your brother's last wish was? You were on the hill, spying on us when Achmed died. When he was murdered by Abdullah.'

Mike regarded them with a sharp turn of the head. Eddie eyed the back of the Toyota, where the Kalashnikov was resting on the seat.

Nadirah said, blatantly, 'Abdullah told me.'

Mike glanced at his two companions, 'But,' he said, 'you have not seen Abdullah.'

'Oh yes,' she cried. 'Oh yes. I have seen him. You have all seen him. Today.' The men exchanged glances of anxiety. 'Today he drives camels. Last night he was at mustashfah. I have seen Abdullah.'

'You mean to say, one of the camel drivers was Abdullah?'

'Aiwa! Abdullah. Abdullah.' She burst into tears. 'He want to take me away from you. I tell him, go to hell.'

'You'll see us all in hell,' Eddie said.

'What are we going to do?' Jack said.

Mike said, 'We'll have to be extremely cautious.'

Jack thought Mike would turn into a pompous old fart, just like Courtenay. He was fed up with them all. 'Oh Christ!' he said.

They had to eat. They prepared the food and ate in silence, each engrossed in their own thoughts. The new factor in the birders' minds, although none of them said it, was how much they could trust Nadirah. They thought how lucky they were to have got this far without being caught. Too lucky! Mike could not understand why Abdullah should behave in the way he had. He must trust her and have assumed that Nadirah would not tell the foreigners about him. Yet, he could have shot them all in the night and none the wiser. He was a mystery, that man. He must need them alive, at least for the time being. Jack wondered if Abdullah loved Nadirah, if he had loved anybody, ever.

The most exasperating thing was that they had done nothing illegal in this country of their own intent. The first illegal act would be to leave, or attempt to leave, the country without an exit visa. Stanley Carter had been the cause of all the problems in this aspect of their troubles. Now, there was this bint who could slip away and betray them at any time. Betray them? As if they owed allegiance to any of their pursuers. They must get to that ship.

'I've been thinking,' Jack said. He was unaware of their scornful glances. Hadn't they all been thinking? 'That was a hell of a lot of money Hayward gave me.' They looked at him. They had not been thinking of that. 'I mean,' he said, 'much more than we need. I gave some to Muqbel, we have bought food, petrol. There's still a lot left. Much more than we had for the whole trip. A damn sight more than we needed to get from Sana'a to the coast.'

'Well?' Eddie said.

Jack thought about it again. 'Look,' he said. 'You know what the official line of British Embassies is. "We're not nannies. People have exaggerated expectations." That sort of stuff. They just don't give away handfuls of money. I've got a gut feeling that we've been set up. Carter set us up for his own glory as a pioneering ornithologist. Abdullah set us up to smuggle his ammunition. The Yemenis are trying to set us up as an example of Western decadence, or something. I think Cecil Hayward has set us up too. Don't ask me why. I just feel it. All this money!' He had been retrieving it from his belt, and now spread it before them.

'Payment for smugglin' arms,' Eddie said. 'Is that what you're thinkin'?'

It was not what Jack had been thinking, but he thought it now.

That was how it might be construed. 'We would have difficulty explaining away such a large amount of money if it was found on us!' he said.

'Especially if they denied giving it to us!' Eddie said. 'We don't have any proof.'

'Say,' Jack mused, 'just suppose, a British firm was exporting arms illegally. Say it was condoned as long as it was kept quiet. Say someone like Cecil Hayward was in the know, taking orders from someone much higher up. If they were in danger of being exposed, it wouldn't matter who they sacrificed lower down the pecking order.'

This was too far-fetched for Mike. 'I think you're being somewhat hysterical, if you don't mind me saying so. You are talking about the British Embassy, old man!' He ridiculed the whole idea. Forcing them to think again.

After all, for what reason could they possibly want such a convoluted deception? Was there a British interest in stirring unrest in the country, or were they supplying the legitimate Yemeni authorities on the quiet, unknown to other arms manufacturers in their alliance? Perhaps a rogue arms dealer had shipped an illegal assignment with the connivance of someone in high authority. Had some of this consignment 'fallen off a ship' at Hudaydah into the hands of Abdullah's faction? Were the new oil discoveries likely to upset world markets unless civil unrest delayed production until others were prepared to allow it? Was there fear that the combination of vast oil reserves and the port of Aden, owned by a now reunified country, would upset the balance of power in the Gulf and Indian Ocean? Too far-fetched?

Mike was forced to concede that whatever was behind the mystery, the capture of the bird watchers would save face for somebody. The money could imply that they had been paid for smuggling arms. The British, if they were involved, would deny all knowledge at the official level and apologise for the unforgivable behaviour of some of their less responsible countrymen. The Yemenis could delight in telling the world that the British had been up to their old tricks in Arabia, while covering up the dissent among their own populace.

They could all save face if the four were caught and put on trial. The British government might encourage some international civil liberty organisation to take up their case and get them released, which they would be eventually, when the raid on the house was all stale news and forgotten. They would not allow the early release of eyewitnesses to any bombing, whoever had done it. There was no doubt, on the other hand, that three dead men were three silent men.

'Perhaps,' Mike said, 'we should allow for every contingency!' He smiled ruefully. 'Just to be sure.'

'We've got to get on that ship,' Eddie said. 'and she ain't runnin' off to tell tales. She's got to stay with us.'

'She's not going anywhere!' Jack said. 'If they catch her, they'll kill her.'

Eddie eyed her coldly. 'And if she tries to get away, I'll kill her!' They could see he meant it. 'Sorry darlin',' but I ain't spendin' years in a Yemeni jail, or havin' my 'ead chopped off, for anybody!' He patted the Kalashnikov. 'Understand?'

'I understand.'

Jack was still thinking about Abdullah's intent to marry her. He knew she was still suffering from the shock of seeing her brother killed in the raid, however, and would be indifferent to Eddie's threats. What was the point? Abdullah knew where they were. 'Does Abdullah know we saw the guns and the bombing?'

'No,' she said. 'I don't know. How I know?'

'He must know,' Eddie said. 'Why else the shot that almost killed Muqbel? He knows everything.'

'We don't know who was behind that,' Jack said.

'Perhaps,' Mike said, thoughtfully, 'we shouldn't go to Mukha.'

They waited for an explanation.

'Well, to get to the ship we have to pass either the barracks on the road or risk driving down the coastal mud flats. After seeing the dunes at Al Fazah I should think the track marked on the map would be impossible to follow. Then we have to board the ship. How can we be sure of doing that? Let's accept that we could get that far without being discovered. It is possible, yes, but highly unlikely.

Let's suppose that Cecil Hayward had come down here to pass the message through Fred Stirling that all's well, to continue to Mukha as planned. He's probably gone off looking for us by the way because, if we came by the usual road, he'd have passed us. At Mukha we're sure to get nabbed, either by the army or the police. I should have thought that you would have questioned that, Jack. Why didn't you put the point to them?'

'Christ,' Jack said, 'do me a favour. Then what?'

'I am merely assuming that if we are being set up, as you suggest, then whoever did so could tip the Yemenis off. They could clear themselves of any embarrassment. I don't suggest that this is the case, but...'

'But you are talking about your own countrymen,' Nadirah said.

Not mine, Jack thought to himself. Sawsnek bastards.

'The helicopter belongs to yours,' Eddie told her. She conceded with a shrug.

'Right ho, then,' Mike said. 'What do we do? The only other port is Hudaydah, the big one. We could try to get a ship there.'

'I think,' Jack said, 'that we should go into Fred's camp. Tell him we're afraid of getting caught at Mukha. A perfectly reasonable fear. And tell him we are going to Hudaydah to look for another British ship.'

'We'll never get on a ship at Hudaydah,' Eddie protested. 'We'll never get near the bleedin' docks.'

'Right! So we don't go to Hudaydah. We go to Al Fazah. We take Hamid's boat and go out to the island in the Red Sea. The freighter leaves at dawn, the day after tomorrow. We can wait for her, or another. No one will know where we are. We will have disappeared. The British will believe the Yemenis have us and are keeping quiet, and vice versa, and none of them will ask the other. We can be away from all of them!' He looked at Nadirah. 'Even Abdullah won't know where we are.'

'Foolish man,' she said. 'They find car at Al Fazah.'

'Oh. I hadn't thought of that.'

'We'll have to hide it!' Eddie said.

Nadirah smiled for the first tine since the bombing. 'You think you can hide a Toyota Land Cruiser? You crazy?' She had an idea, she said. Send the car back to Sana'a. They could drive to Zebid and As Suayq, the start of track to Al Fazah. She would find somebody in one of the villages who would drive the car to Sana'a alone. 'We pay him. But he do it.' When the car was found it would be assumed that they had all gone back to Sana'a with it.

They would then walk from As Suayq over the dunes and sabkah to Al Fazah. She dismissed their doubt. 'It is easy. Walk maybe ten or twelve kilometres.'

They considered it. 'Right!' they said. 'We'll do it. Have no choice!' And they drove into Fred Stirling's camp.

He told them that Cecil Hayward had been to see him on his way to Hudaydah. They didn't believe that. Fred was being used too, but they couldn't tell him. Perhaps he knew. Fred was nobody's fool and if he seemed unaware of their predicament it might be because there was nothing he could do for them. He asked them to stay the night. Share the evening meal, he said. They declined, thinking it like the Last Supper, and said they would push on to Hudaydah, where they would probably see Cecil. They left Fred clutching his teapot, with its stained cosy, dripping on his fingers.

This time, no one knew where they were going. They were, at last, on their own.

Chapter Twenty-Two

The youth from Al Madan was bright, intelligent, and asked no questions. Nadirah ensured that he saw and knew nothing of the men, and assured them that he could be relied upon to return the vehicle to the taxi drivers in Sana'a, who would see that it was eventually returned to Muqbel. She brought bread, vegetables and fruit from the village, as much food as she could carry and some cigarettes for Jack. Having come this far they were obliged to trust her and the youth, though the glint of doubt was ever in their eyes. They watched the tail-lights fade as he drove away along the road to Bait Al Faqih and the port of Hudaydah. From there he would turn east, go up to the precarious villages perched on the cliffs at Manakah, skirt the mountain of the Prophet's uncle and drop down to Sana'a. Without transport, on the other hand, the birders were marooned. If the plan to escape to the island failed, if they could not find the sambuk, there was no way they could survive unaided. As the tail-lights faded in the distance, Eddie, with a wistful catch in his voice as he watched them go out of sight said, 'They're good mo'ors, them Japanese Landrovers.'

The faint glow from the lights of Zebid lay to the south as they crossed the tarmac and followed the dry, gravely ditch that was the parched remnant of the great inland water-course of Wadi Rima. Between here and the sea, Cecil Hayward's map showed nothing but sand. They hitched their rucksacks on their backs and set out in single file towards the dunes. Although they had slept but little the night before and it was now approaching midnight, they found their energies resuscitated at the prospect of escape, and they were alert and wary as their footsteps fell silently into the sand. Mike led the way, followed by Jack, then Nadirah with the food in a bag slung over her back and her leather bag strap across her shoulder. Eddie came up in the rear, with the barrel of the Kalashnikov protruding above his right shoulder. It was heavy and loaded. Mike and Jack each carried a water container and a clip of ammunition in their packs.

They wound their way through the hollows of the dunes, avoiding the crests, both to remain hidden and to obviate the fatigue of climbing the slithering slopes. They had about twenty kilometres to walk. Twelve miles. It took them nearly four hours of hard slogging to reach the coast and find the grove of palm trees, where they lay down, exhausted, ate some bread and drank some water. They heard waders on the shore. The flamingos were still, tall silhouettes against the glittering lagoon. Bats, pale and large, which they had not seen before, flew about the trees like silent spirits of the night. 'Tomb bats,' Mike called them.

'Great!' Jack sighed as he lay back on the sand. 'A bloody good omen!' The waves, breaking gently on the shore, were soporific, an enticement to sleep off their exhaustion.

'Come on,' Eddie said. 'We'd better move before it gets light.'

They followed him along the phosphorescent beach in the direction of the village, where the fish eaters lived in their round, grass huts. The gun was held before him.

'Walk in the sea,' Jack said, for among the dunes, footprints were obliterated by shifting sands as soon as made, and here, the wavelets licked the shoreline clean and left no trace of passing feet.

The sambuk lay with her bow resting on the beach, with a nylon painter made fast to a rock. Just over the brow of low dunes and the slight promontory of the headland, was the sleeping village. Dogs barked. They were answered by others, slinking outcasts on the fringes of distant settlements. A late moon, rising over the distant mountains, cast a thin light that glittered on the sea. They could see the dunes, like billows of ocean, lit with silver crests. They could be seen, shot at from the rolling sands, but Jack welcomed the illumination, for it would aid his navigation until the rising of the sun. The men dumped their rucksacks aboard the boat and leaned on the gunwale, feeling the blistered wood. Nadirah unslung her leather bag and dropped it on a thwart.

'Right,' Jack said.

They all climbed silently aboard and he cast off. He unlashed the long oars and they pulled away towards the reef, with bright drips of phosphorescence showering from the blades. The dogs, black slinking shapes, came and sniffed the shoreline at their departure point.

When the shore was well out of hearing, Jack went aft to the outboard motor. 'Keep rowing,' he said.

The petrol tank was full, so were the spare cans lying under a plastic sheet. After another twenty minutes of silent progress he turned on the fuel valve, adjusted the choke and held the toggle on the starting cord with his right hand, his left hand resting on the tank. He looked back to the distant shore where the mountains appeared to have moved and were now rising directly from the sea. He pulled the starter. There was an apologetic cough from the exhaust.

'Bloody outboards,' Jack said, thinking that there were probably no tools aboard to use on the engine if the damn thing wouldn't start.

On the second pull the engine fired and he adjusted the choke, dropped the gear lever. There was a swirl of water under the stern and he steered for a distant shape, a dark smudge on the horizon which, as the sun rose over the land behind them, became the first of the offshore islands. The distant shoreline dropped away; the horizon crept up the mountains until they were lost in a haze. There was nothing to be seen but the open sea and the islands they had seen before with Hamid. They grinned at each other. Eddie wrapped the gun in a plastic sheet and laid it on the floorboards.

'Have you been here before?' Mike asked Nadirah.

'No. Never. This first time for me. In boat!' She laughed as spray came over the bow and drenched her face. 'I like it.'

They went from mark to remembered mark, island to distant island, and eventually came to the white beach when the sun was high and scorching in the clear uncluttered blue of the Red Sea sky.

Jack ran the bow up onto the beach. He cut the engine. Silence enveloped them.

'That was a very competent bit of navigation!' Mike said.

'Yeah.' Jack thought so too. He had been afraid all along that he would miss the island. But at least there was no fog here. 'I have to get some sleep,' he said.

'One of us ought to stay awake,' Eddie said, looking significantly at Nadirah.

Mike agreed that this was a sensible precaution, if for different reasons. Fishermen might visit the island for water, or to see who was ashore. They could not hide the boat.

Jack was too tired to argue. He tried to remember how much sleep he'd had since leaving Sana'a. Not much. He wished Eddie would trust Nadirah and see that she was just as much a fugitive as they were.

'Do what you like,' he said.

Eddie took the gun and went to the top of the island, saying he was not tired and would wake them when he was. They let him go. Why not? If that was what he wanted to do, the others were happy to comply.

Jack wanted a skeet. He went over to the cove where he had swum with Alison. Came back.

Nadirah said, 'I go.' She returned after half an hour, by which time Mike was asleep on the beach. Jack waved her aboard the sambuk to share the shade of tarpaulin stretched from the gunwales, and they lay on the bottom boards and slept to the gentle motion of the boat on the almost waveless water of the sheltered beach.

A breeze arose. Mike woke and moved to the shade of an overhanging rock. The breeze stirred the scrub growing in crevices in the rocks, struggling to survive drought and salt. Later, they could replenish their water supplies, cook a meal if they dared risk a fire, and leave this island for the shipping lanes before dawn tomorrow. He was reluctant to climb aboard the boat and sleep in the shade of the tarpaulin with the other two. He was a little surprised that Jack should be so intimate with her, for she might yet betray them. He laid his head on his arms. There was still no evidence that they were being pursued by anyone, as far as he could see. Even the fact that Muqbel had been shot did not preclude coincidence. The sniper could simply have been a robber. There was no proof of anything. Everything was speculation. Mike became alarmingly aware that for some time he had taken Jack Pengelly's interpretation of events as the only basis for decision. This, on reflection, was a most unsatisfactory state of affairs, especially as Jack seemed to have developed some kind of affinity with the Arabs which might prejudice his assessment of events. There was no doubt they were all suffering the effects of shock and fatigue. The sooner they left this island for the shipping lanes the better. It was too late for dissension now, he thought, before sleep enveloped him.

Eddie settled himself among the rocks at the top of the cliff. Brown boobies came and alighted on the ledges. The tropicbirds wheeled and screamed high over the sea, with their long tails whipping in the slip-streams of their aerobatic flight. The sea was deep blue, with white crests rolling before him on the rising breeze. He saw an osprey carrying a fish towards the cliff. It saw him and veered off, heading for the next island beyond the horizon. He could see ships off to the west, steaming up the Red Sea to Suez.

He was so tired that he was afraid to sit comfortably, for he knew he would be asleep in minutes. Still, the only reason he had volunteered to keep watch was to ensure that the bint didn't get her hands on the old AK while they were asleep. There was something odd about her, especially in the way in which she seemed to have recovered from the grief of losing her brother, if he was her brother. They wouldn't be safe until they were on that ship. If it existed. They only had Jack's account of what Cecil-bleedin-Mister-toff Hayward had told him. Sitting here was worse than running away. They could have gone out to the ships today, in Eddie's opinion. Jack said he was afraid of running out of fuel and being in the shipping lanes after dark. He should have taken the risk. Why should Jack Pengelly make all the decisions when Mike was supposed to be the leader since Carter's departure?

After sitting for an hour in a daydream, with his eyes staring vacantly in the direction of the mainland, he rose and walked around the island for exercise and to keep himself awake. He passed Mike, on the beach, looked into the boat and returned to the thin scrub of the slope without disturbing any of them. They were all exhausted. He wandered about the island and back toward the cliff. All the shipping had sailed on. The world seemed very empty. The sea was a void of wind-slashed blue. He thought of the circumstances that had led him here. How keen he had been to be part of the famous Stanley Carter's expedition. He thought of Abdullah, striding through Raydah, frightening the children. How he had persuaded them to visit Al Fazah instead of Mukha. The devilish double deception of the whisky and the ammo. What was he doing with the camel drovers at Madinat Al Abid and, more significantly, what did he have to say to that bloody bint? It seemed more than coincidence that they should both have chosen the same route to the coast. And, another thing, why was Abdullah going to the coast when he would have been safest with the old Sheikh at Raydah, among the tribesmen of the north? God, all that seemed years ago. There was something going on then, and there was something going on now, that they knew nothing about. He was quite sure that the bint was party to it. She had as much to gain from the gunrunning as her brother, for all they knew. He checked his watch. One o'clock. He would have to wake the others and ask one of them to prepare a meal while he had some sleep.

The sea looked a great deal more inviting than the hot rocks as he walked over to rejoin the others. The sun was reflected into his eyes, his feet were hot and he was thirsty. The gun was heavy, the sling cut into his shoulder, as he changed it from one side to the other. For the first time, he wished he had never come on this expedition... and it was nearly over.

Mike had been awake for nearly half an hour, watching a party of lesser crested terns fishing in the shallows, but was too relaxed and indifferent to get up from his patch of shade to fetch his binoculars. He lay with his chin on his arms, refreshed from his sleep but already feeling the debilitating sun creeping around to his back. He saw Jack's head appear above the gunwale of the sambuk.

'OK?' Jack called.

Mike responded with a brief raising of the hand. Nadirah sat up beside Jack. Her hair had become loose and was flowing to her shoulders. She gathered it up and covered her head with her shawl. Mike had to concede that some of these Arab women were quite beautiful, in their own way.

They heard Eddie calling. There was some resonance of urgency in his voice. They couldn't make out what he was saying. Mike jumped to his feet. Jack leaped from the boat. 'What's he seen?' he asked.

'I don't know!' Mike said, irritated at such an inane question when he could have no more idea of what was bothering Eddie than Jack did. 'Perhaps he's seen an ostrich!' He laughed at his one and only joke of the whole trip.

Eddie came running down the slope to the shore. He had unslung the gun and was holding it ready to fire, with a finger hovering near the trigger.

'Bring that bloody bint here,' he cried. 'Get her off that boat, before she leaves us stranded.'

Jack called her. She came ashore, plunging her brown legs into the sea.

'What's the trouble?' Mike asked.

'Get her up to the well!' Eddie jerked his head and the barrel of the gun, in universal body language. 'Move!' he said. 'Now!'

'Oh, for God's sake, Eddie.'

'Get her up to the bleedin' well.'

He shepherded them up the slope to the scrub around the well. There was a deep hole in the ground, cut from the solid rock. Crude steps led down to a wide ledge, from which the well sank deeper into the depths of the island in a smaller black shaft of mystery. A plastic bucket and a coil of rope lay wet on the shelf where Eddie had left them after coming here to quench his thirst.

'You stay there,' he said to Nadirah as he stood with the Kalashnikov pointed at her belly. 'Don't go any closer! Look in there,' Eddie said to his countrymen. 'Go on!'

At the level of the ledge, there was a narrow fissure, which looked at first like a natural irregularity in the rock. Jack took his cigarette lighter and held it at the opening. 'Not too close with that,' Eddie said. The tiny flame illuminated a hewn chamber cut in the rock. It was high enough for a tall man to stand in and about three metres square. Jack, being the smallest, squeezed through the opening to see what Eddie had discovered there.

Stacked along one wall, piled five high, were wooden boxes similar to those they had taken up from Al Fazah. Two were open, their tops leaning against the wall, and inside were packed clips of gleaming bullets. Against the opposite wall stood larger longer boxes containing automatic rifles. They were marked, in English and Arabic, *Machine tools, Gulf Drilling Company*. In the centre of the chamber were smaller boxes, one of which had also been opened. It contained cylindrical hand grenades.

'Christ!' Jack said. He ran his lighter along the boxes. 'All good English make. Enough to equip a small army. What are they doing here?'

'Ask her!' Eddie said, as Jack came out of the chamber.

'I know nothing about this!' Nadirah said as they looked at her accusingly.

'Let's get out of here,' Jack said, 'and up in the fresh air.'

The afternoon breeze was still rising: it was warm and gentle, soft to the skin. Nadirah's hair blew from under her head shawl. They trooped back to the boat, following Eddie, who was at the limit of his endurance. His eyes were bloodshot, and he was trembling slightly.

'Those guns,' Mike said, 'are SA80s, NATO weapons, the same as Achmed was carrying in Wadi Bana that day.'

'What the hell are they doing here?' Jack said.

'That's bleedin' obvious,' Eddie said. 'They're waiting for Abdullah to come and get 'em. That right, darlin'?'

Nadirah looked at him with a scowl, but did not deny it.

'She ain't talkin' to me,' Eddie said. 'You ask her. You're the bleedin' Arab lover.'

'Oh, come on, Eddie,' Mike said. 'Bit strong, old man.'

'And annuver fing,' Eddie cried, 'what's she got in that bleedin' bag she's so anxious to keep wiv her all the time? She could 'ave a bleedin' pistol in there, mate.'

Mike quailed at the thought. She could shoot them all at any time.

Jack said to her, 'You will have to show us, Nadirah,' and without a word she un-slung the bag and handed it over. With a long sigh Jack opened the bag and rifled though its contents. He found her documents, passport with visas stamped, a small amount of Yemeni ryals, some clean underwear, small items of cosmetics and several packets of tampons. 'Women's things,' Jack said. 'Make-up and stuff. Nothing to worry about.'

Eddie calmed down, but kept his eyes on Nadirah. 'Seems too much of a coincidence to me,' he said, 'that she should meet Abdullah on the way here. I think we've been conned again. She was too damn keen to get rid of that bleedin' motor, mate. We're stuck out here like decoy ducks on a bleedin' pond.'

Nadirah was shaking her head. 'No,' she said. 'I know nothing about this. I know nothing. Believe me.'

'You know,' Mike mused, 'we thought that the arms were taken off a ship for forwarding up to Abdullah via Achmed Ghanem at Wadi Bana.'

'Via her brother!' Eddie said.

'Yes, but we only took a few bullets. Abdullah could easily have fetched them himself. Those men were carrying boxes up to the house as if they came from the north, and those camels coming down the wadi at Madinat Al Abid were pretty heavily laden.'

'You mean,' Eddie said, 'that the bullets were just part of a stitch-up? We were meant to be caught?'

'I'm not sure about that. It could have been some devious contingency plan in case we were needed to be implicated, or they could have been just a few rounds for Achmed. No, I'm thinking that this island is the main magazine, and that the arms are taken out of Yemen from here to their final destination by boat. One of the sambuks, perhaps.'

'To where?' Jack asked.

'To where the demand and the price are highest.' Under the circumstances, they all knew where that was.

The sun beat down on them as they leaned on the gunwale of the sambuk and considered their new predicament. There was no way in which they could change their plans except, although no one mentioned it, by leaving the girl here on the island.

Eventually, Eddie said, 'I must get some sleep.'

He began to climb aboard the boat for sake of the shade under the tarpaulin, and Nadirah placed her hand on his shoulder. 'I know nothing,' she said with desperation in her voice. 'Believe me.'

'You believe me,' Eddie said with a tap of his hand against the Kalashnikov. 'If you've led us into a trap I'll blow your bloody head off.' He turned to Mike, as if Jack were not to be trusted. 'Just keep your eye on her. Keep her hands off them fireworks.'

As Eddie was settling down on the floorboards, Mike also clambered aboard the boat.

'What do you want now?' Eddie said. 'I have to get some sleep.'

Mike ignored him and moved one of the fuel cans preparatory to lifting it overboard. For the cooking Eddie thought, good. He lay down under the tarpaulin and jerked up violently when he realised Mike's intention. 'Ho ho!' he laughed. 'Ho ho.'

Jack would have none of it. 'We can't afford to waste the fuel!' he insisted. 'Put it back, Mike.'

Mike reluctantly conceded that he was right. They would need every drop of fuel when out at sea, but he argued that they should destroy the arms. Jack agreed to that. 'We can do it just before we leave, with grenades.'

'We don't know how to use them,' Mike protested. 'We could kill ourselves. I was going to run a trickle of petrol and use it as a fuse.'

'I show you,' Nadirah said. 'Achmed told me.'

They took the water containers with them and went back to the well. They left Eddie slumped under the tarpaulin, oblivious of the activities around him as he slept the sleep of exhaustion. They went down into the cool depths and drew fresh water up in the plastic bucket. When they had filled the containers and taken them to the boat, they returned, reluctantly, to the magazine of arms.

'I don't like this,' Mike said. 'Don't these things become unstable or something? God knows how they've been treated.'

'Don't worry,' Nadirah said. 'It is cool here and very dry.' She seemed to know a lot about arms and ammunition.

Jack went in and passed out the opened box of grenades. He was not so sure about the dryness. Sweat dripped from his brow. It was fear, he decided. They left a couple of grenades at the entrance to the chamber, more spread out along the ledge and took four up into the sunlight. The breeze was now fresh. The parched scrub rustled at their feet. Nadirah reached for one of the grenades. Mike drew it away from her.

'I show you,' she said.

She pointed with her long, delicate fingers at the device lying in his hand. 'You hold like this. With the fingers keep this lever closed. Here is the beginner... what you call it?'

'The firing pin.'

'Exactly. You put the finger in the ring. And with the other fingers, of the other hand, on the lever, keep always closed. OK? With the lever open, you have four seconds only before explode. So, always hold the lever. Pull the pin. Throw. OK?'

'Four seconds!' Mike said.

'Yes. It is plenty time. Count on your watches!'

They looked at the pulsating digits on Mike's watch.

'One second,' Jack counted, 'two seconds, three seconds... four!' It didn't seem like plenty time to him.

'We ought to go up to the cliff,' Mike said. 'To keep watch on the sea.'

On their way up the slope they placed the grenades among the rocks and scrub above but within throwing distance of the well. They were glad to be rid of them. At the cliff top they settled down to wait for the night. They found themselves in the same shady place Eddie had used. There were not many such. They saw the scuffmarks of his boots. 'That Hamid is a crafty old bugger,' Jack said.

'Devious,' Mike muttered. 'A thought has occurred to me,' he said. They had learned to view some of Mike's thoughts with trepidation and waited for him to gather them together. 'If we were caught and searched, the photographs of us and Hamid at Al Fazah and on this island would be enough to see us hanged.'

Eddie was visibly shocked that his photographs might have been the reason for their incarceration in a Yemeni prison. Or something worse. 'Do you think that's why Hamid brought us out here? Just to incriminate us?'

'Just a thought,' Mike said.

'Yeah! Just a thought. I thought Hamid was OK,' Eddie said, looking pointedly at Nadirah, 'but now I don't trust any of 'em.'

'Hamid OK!' Nadirah said.

Jack glanced at her and quickly back to Mike, who was looking at him. So, she knew Abdullah, all about Cecil Hayward, Harry Courtenay, and had now revealed she knew Hamid too. Did she know he was a willing member of the gunrunning gang? Jack successfully stifled a groan and looked toward the shipping lanes. There was not a smudge to be seen.

The sea was whipped up by the breeze and white crests topped the waves, which were being driven towards the base of the cliffs. The boobies, hanging on the rising air above the precipice, inspected the men with their silver eyes, while the sooty falcons called from pinnacles of the pitted limestone. These red cliffs and the green sea, with the distance obscured by haze where the indigo sky paled at the horizon, would be, Jack thought, his last view of Yemen. They could never return, never see again the interminable chaos of the mountains, the terraces creeping about their contours, the lush beauty of Wadi Bana. He looked at Nadirah. She was staring eastwards, in the direction of the mainland, with sorrow in her eyes.

Why, he thought, must people inflict such pain on one another? Was it because of a fundamental doubt in their own avowed convictions? A necessity to corroborate their creeds by witnessing the conversion of others? Some did it by the sword, some with a bowl of rice, some by the sharp stones of circumcision, and others by preserving the ignorance behind the unbreached hymen of enlightenment. By what justification did those who invented deities call upon their own contrived doctrines to castigate the unbelievers? They all seemed determined to force their own culture on the world and those with the most sophisticated technology were, by definition, succeeding in their indoctrination. Even here, especially here, in what was arrogantly referred to as the undeveloped world, the battlefield of ideas was strewn with the walking wounded.

Were they controlled by the memes of Dawkins, with no self-will? Do the memes in schemes fall meanly on Yarim? Teams of memes in gleaming streams seem to teem in our deepest dreams. Words became meaningless. He could not summon the initiative of conversation. Mike too was preoccupied. Nadirah appeared to fall asleep.

The afternoon wore on in a dozing wait for the night. The breeze was dehydrating and he had brought no water. The boat in the distance emerged from the haze and was lost again among the white spray whipping from the waves, like a ghost in mist. It was an illusion, of the seventh wave, the seventh wave of seven sevens, higher than all the others. Gone! Mingled with the racing foam. There it was again. It was coming with the weather, riding the waves with white turbulence swirling under her stern. Jack put his binoculars to his eyes.

Mike followed Jack's line of sight and saw it too, another sambuk, like Hamid's, the one they had stolen. Perhaps it was fishing or going to Djibouti for cattle and rinderpest and would pass and go about its business. It came straight for the island, careening down the crests. It was swallowed in the troughs and surged over the breakers like a graceful bird.

'She's fast,' Jack said. 'Faster than ours.'

A point or two to starboard, and the bow veered to broach the waves, and she fell away to round the island on the south.

'We might be rather conspicuous up here,' Mike said.

Nadirah rose to her feet.

'Get down!' Jack said. 'We'd better tell Eddie.'

They found themselves running down the slope, almost expecting the sambuk to be at the beach before them, although she was still two miles away.

Eddie was for putting out to sea. He said they could shoot anyone who pursued them.

'What if they have guns too? She is faster than us. They could easily sink us with guns from the well. We have only three clips of ammo.' There was no time to argue.

'We'd do better to defend the well and weapons,' Mike said.

'Right!'

They gathered their belongings and took them with them. Whoever landed on the island might not be aware that there were foreigners here. They hurried back towards the well and concealed themselves among the cover where they had hidden the grenades. They had a view down the slope of the island down to the landing place, with the well just below them and slightly to the right. No one could come ashore and approach the weapons in the well unseen. They had no sooner concealed themselves than the boat appeared off the southern rocks. She was fast. The outboard was three times as big as Hamid's. Such a boat could slip across to Djibouti in no time. Such a craft could bring arms from the Dahlak Archipelago, Mersa Fatma, Suakin or Ras Banas. She could go to Ethiopia or Sudan. She could even go down through the Bab Al Mandab and take the guns up the Gulf to Iraq or Iran. Who would know? She could run rings around Hamid's boat at sea.

Eddie lay down in the scrub with the muzzle of the Kalashnikov nuzzling through the cover. To his left, about three metres away among the next cluster of rocks, Nadirah lay flat on her stomach. Jack was quite close to her, perhaps a metre, and the grenades they had brought out of the well lay between them. Mike was in cover at the other end of the line, to Eddie's right, unarmed. They could not rearrange themselves without being seen. They watched and waited. Jack felt himself trembling, and Mike chewed on his lower lip in apprehension, thinking that he should have insisted on going out to sea, fuel or no fuel. Eddie clutched the gun and watched the two men in the boat with a hunter's eye.

The sambuk slid onto the white sand, the engine stopped and the island lapsed again into silence broken only by the breeze blowing through the dry scrub. The two men came ashore and inspected the abandoned boat. The wind whipped their head-cloths about their eyes. They tucked the lashing ends across their mouths and into folds at the temple, leaving only the eyes uncovered, but their was no mistaking the confident self-assurance of Abdullah and the spindly legs supporting Hamid of the single tooth. They spent some time searching the shoreline beside the boat. Footprints in the sand. Three pairs of desert boots and one set of small, bare feet. They came up towards the well and, after a few paces, Abdullah reached into his clothing and there was the little automatic pistol. He came on boldly, without fear, approaching the well.

Eddie slowly slid the Kalashnikov forward until he was looking along the sight. Nadirah turned her head slightly and saw him. The other two kept low and looked at Eddie.

Time became distorted for the next few minutes. There were to be more memories generated in seconds than any of them could recall for years of their normal lives. The memories that still impinge themselves onto Jack's imagination when he sits holding the hand of his wife and they watch the slow, mounting swells surging over the reefs at home. It was as if their brains developed another faculty, the ability to receive and process information at an incredible speed. Such a faculty extended over a lifetime would absorb the experience of a million years.

Abdullah stopped and looked about him. He looked back to the shore, up to the cliff, from side to side. There was a slight movement of his thumb as the safety catch was released. The wind flipped the cloth from Hamid's face. He was grinning, with his tooth hooked over his upper lip. He said something to Abdullah. Abdullah laughed, with a nod of the head. He removed the cloth from across his mouth.

'Yah Nadirah!' he called.

They were afraid to turn their heads to see what she would do. Jack was still looking at Eddie.

'Now!' he would remember saying. 'Now, Eddie. Kill him now.'

He heard a stone turn as Abdullah came forward to the well and glanced into its depths..

'*Now—now—now*! For Christ's sake pull the fucking trigger, you stupid cockney bastard. *Kill him*!'

'Nadirah!' Abdullah called again. 'Nadirah. Yah habibi.' Nadirah. O my darling. In that strong, resonant voice.

She rose and showed herself. Eddie came up with the Kalashnikov pointed at Abdullah's chest. Abdullah was taken completely by surprise at seeing the gun and fired one wild shot before leaping down into the cover of the well. Hamid turned and attempted to flee down the hill, but he tripped and fell.

Eddie turned to Nadirah. 'You bloody stupid bint...'

She was kneeling with a grenade in one hand, looking coldly into Eddie's eyes.

'Why didn't you kill him?' Jack screamed as he turned to Eddie... 'Oh my God.'

Eddie turned the gun on her. 'She warned him,' he spat. 'I told you not to trust her!' He raised the barrel.

Nadirah looked at him with hatred and pulled the pin from the grenade. Mike threw a stone into the well.

'Abdullah!' Nadirah called. She drew her arm back.

Eddie pulled the trigger. Nothing happened.

'The safety catch!' Jack beseeched him. 'Oh my God.'

It was all over Jack thought. If Eddie released the catch and killed her, the grenade would get them anyway. He watched helplessly as Eddie fumbled with the gun and Nadirah released the lever and drew her arm back, her eyes never leaving Eddie's. Mike, at the end of the line, began counting the seconds in horror at what was to come.

'You black bitch!' Eddie cried.

Jack cursed himself for ever believing she would betray her own betrothed. She would kill herself and all of them to save Abdullah. Four seconds... five seconds...

'Abdullah!' she called.

He came up firing blindly and paused to take aim in the confusion, as Nadirah brought her arm forward in a graceful arc and lobbed the grenade into the well.

Jack threw Nadirah to the ground and covered her with his body. Mike barged into Eddie and sent both of them sprawling as a stream of shots sprayed wildly from the barrel of Eddie's AK47 and the island erupted in a roaring explosion. They heard nothing after the first ear-splitting detonation. Debris fell in a silent shower. After the earth ceased its convulsions they lay still, paralysed with fear and the expectation of further explosions. They lay there for five? Ten? Twenty minutes? They never knew how long they lay there.

Eventually, some awareness of their surroundings returned. Jack became conscious of the limp body of the girl beneath him. He rolled off her and on to a painful lump under his ribs. It was one of the remaining grenades. He moved it away, placing it in the shade of a rock, fearful that some vibration of the explosion may have disturbed the mechanism of detonation. He had blood all over his right hand. He could not find where it came from, for he was uninjured. He looked at Nadirah. She was lying on her face, with her body trembling in fear or pain. He could hear nothing but saw Mike and Eddie attempting to raise themselves from the ground. He wiped his hand across the front of his shirt and reached to the girl, gently laying his hand upon her back, and she raised her head to look at him. There was blood running into her black hair from a cut on her scalp. A red smear covered her temple.

'Are you all right?' Jack asked, and his voice sounded distant, as if muffled by fog. Her eyes turned to him. They were cold, black with hatred for what they had made her do.

Eddie had roused himself to his knees and was staring at the scorched, smouldering hole that had been the well. Mike was sitting with his hands over his ears, giggling and shaking his head, shocked to find himself still alive and not believing it. Wondering if he was recovering in the hereafter.

Nadirah sat up, then rose unsteadily to her feet, the blood in her hair already congealing into a sticky tangle. The others watched as she went to the well, walking down the slope with tottering steps.

'Oh no,' Jack said, but they all followed her to see what was in that gaping hole.

There was not even a bit of bone, or trailing entrails in the smoking void. Nothing but black smouldering rubble. They stood in a line gazing into the pit, where an occasional stone fell from the rim. She led them away.

Hamid's body lay where he had tried to rise from the position of his fall. His last tooth was knocked out against a rock, and the back of his head smashed in by shrapnel or a stray bullet from Eddie's gun.

They picked up their packs and went down to the boat. Somebody made a fire. Somebody found the mugs. Somebody made tea. Somebody had powdered milk and sugar. They sat drinking as their hearing returned. They spoke of trivialities. What time should they leave? When would the wind die away? Until somebody said, 'What about Hamid?'

They couldn't leave him there. Somebody might find him, identify him, trace him back to Hayward and Courtenay, and to them. The men glanced at each other. Hamid must disappear. It had to be done. The girl sat staring at the sea. She had done enough.

'I'll do it,' Eddie said. He went back alone, up to the well. They saw him stoop to pick up the little body and then a grenade, but could take no more. They turned their backs and looked over the boat, out to sea.

The explosion from the bottom of the black pit sounded almost benign from down by the beach, a muffled 'crump' which sent a column of dust into the air. Eddie came back. There was a faint bloodstain spreading into the fibres of his shirt from a small item in his pocket.

'To remember him by,' Eddie said, when he saw Mike looking at the stain. 'Poor ol' sod. Weren't his fault.'

They put all their equipment into the fast boat: all the fuel and water, the food, tarpaulins, spare outboard, and they towed Hamid's boat out and scuttled her. They steered for the shipping lanes.

A flock of tropicbirds circled overhead, their breasts tinged red by the setting sun. Eddie glanced up at them, his eyes glazed with tears.

'Poor ol' sod,' he said.

Chapter Twenty-Three

As the swells of the falling tide lifted the stern of his boat, Jack steered for the harbour. The evening sun broke through the clouds to the west and illuminated the sky in a rosy glow. Red sky at night, he thought, the barometer high and steady, promising another day of sunshine and light winds tomorrow. The shoreline was green with no shimmering heat, the dunes across the bay with no palm trees or baking, shifting sand. All that was behind him, although he knew that he might still be a wanted man, here, in his own country. His return had been clandestine and unobserved, but they were certain to summon him, eventually. There was so much unresolved from those days under that desert sky so far away.

He brought the boat alongside the quay and unloaded his mackerel, conscious of those dark eyes always watching him from the quay. He moored up and came ashore to meet the eyes again. They were fearful as he accepted the proffered brown manila envelope and read the summons to London. His quiet resumption of his old life, with no persecution, had been too good to be true. Although, in a way, the letter was a relief, relief from the uncertainty of what they might do to her.

'I sh'll have to go,' he said.

★ ★ ★

The hotel was in Cromwell Road, not all that far from the Natural History Museum. Jack timed his visit so that he could examine some skins and be half an hour late for his appointment with Messrs Courtenay and Hayward. He didn't like London and he didn't like the meeting place in the large foyer of the hotel. It was very plush; double-glazing and heavy velvet curtains muted the grinding roar of traffic outside the window of the opulent bar. An Egyptian barman served him his drink. Half the people in the place were Arabs, and the others looked like oilmen or contractors waiting for a flight to the petrodollars of the Middle East. There were some Saudis in immaculate white thobes and red-chequered ghutrahs. Two large, bearded mullahs with stern faces sat drinking coffee. There were dark-skinned men in expensive suits who could have come from anywhere. It was evidently a hotel used extensively by wealthy people commuting to the Middle East. Some of the few Englishmen sat in silence or spoke in inaudible undertones, timid in their own country. There were no women.

'Do you take Yemeni riyals?'

'Of course, sir.'

'You needn't call me sir, sadiq. I was a working man myself, once.'

'I beg your pardon, sir.'

'Keep the change.'

Jack handed over the last of the money from the embassy. The rate was probably only half the official figure in a dump like this anyway.

'No. Wait a minute!' He removed the cleanest and crispest of the ten-riyal notes from the barman's hand. 'Souvenir,' he said.

The barman smiled politely. It was still a large tip, for an Englishman.

Jack sat in an armchair with his back towards the door, from where he could see the mirror on the opposite wall. Memories of all the events in Yemen were evoked by the impending confrontation with the diplomats. Their invitation, worded as an implied order, to meet them in London had been sent to three of them, Eddie, Mike and himself. Eddie, big tough Eddie, was still attending counselling sessions and in no fit state to meet anybody. PTSD, they called it, didn't they? Shell shock! Mike, all his principles shattered, was too depressed, bitter and resentful even to reply to their letter. Only Jack was here, not for his own sake but for that of Nadirah, the most vulnerable of them all. The events out there were recalled as spasmodic images that he had difficulty in placing in chronological sequence. The memories implied that they were lucky to have escaped alive but when, exactly when, had they been in direct danger from anyone? They had been told they were in danger, being persecuted, and had surmised the same from information received. Information received from the two men he was about to meet. The birders had no direct evidence to suggest that even Abdullah meant them any harm apart from using them to smuggle a few bullets. He and little old skinny Hamid could well have come to the island with the sole intent of preventing Nadirah from leaving; being abducted as they saw it. With a quickening of his pulse and a tremble of trepidation came the realisation that they might have killed them for no reason but their own irrational terror. Was it this that had occurred to Eddie and sent him out of his mind? No, no. It was too much to bear. He checked his watch and looked at the mirror, watching people come and go. He opened a magazine, *British Birds*.

Seven minutes later he saw Harry Courtenay's reflection in the mirror. Then there was Cecil Hayward's.

Harry looked much better in a dark suit; the generous cut and heavy material concealed his flab. His face had paled, lost some of the bright glow from the sun. Cecil, on the other hand, looked older. He was wearing an immaculately cut, light tweed suit and narrow-brimmed trilby, which were slightly out of fashion for all but the upper classes, and somehow incongruous against his dark tan and fair, wavy hair. They looked around the room. Courtenay glanced at the clock behind the bar.

They're so damned certain I'll turn up, Jack thought. He watched Cecil's lips turn down in irritation as he too checked the time on his watch. Jack stayed where he was, thinking they were sure to see his reflection in the mirror, and that there was no hurry. He should have spent more time checking the specimens in the museum and forestalled their deliberate insult. These two would never be unintentionally late; the creases in the backs of their jackets indicated a long wait somewhere out of sight.

They seemed to be looking for someone other than himself, he thought. Yes. Harry's ill-disguised perusal was far too casual for his inquisitive nature. Jack looked around at the people in the room. Was one of these men part of another set-up? Where else in London could an Arab be so unobtrusive, or anyone else for that matter? It was a place in which all were anonymous. None of them indicated involvement as they turned the pages of newspapers or checked documents, totally absorbed in their own affairs. They were all too preoccupied. Everybody is interested in other people in their airspace, however casually, so which one was it? He had anticipated something like this and was sure of it as soon as he entered the hotel. He began thinking they would have a cop concealed nearby, ready to arrest him when identified.

This was absurd, his imagination running riot. He opened *British Birds* and read through the *Recent Reports* for the latest news of misidentified rarities... lesser crested tern, Tichfield. Possible Pallas's sandgrouse (flock) at Portland Bill. Fat chance!

As they passed his chair, he heard Harry say, 'Damned insolence,' and Cecil's 'tut' in reply. There was still that deference to status in Harry's voice and in the way in which he allowed Cecil to take precedence in choice of seat.

As the barman came to take their order Jack rose from his chair and joined them. 'Hello,' he said, cheerfully. 'How lovely to see you. Sorry I'm late.'

The old pink flush suffused Harry's cheeks. Cecil smiled and waved Jack to a chair. The barman approached and stood with his hands behind his back.

'Whisky?' Harry enquired of Cecil. A nod of assent. 'Two,' Harry said. 'Soda. No water.'

Jack drained his own glass and placed it noisily on the polished mahogany table. 'Three,' he said, 'and lots of soda.'

The barman looked expectantly at Harry, who nodded consent, while Cecil looked at Jack with a cold stare he had never seen in his eyes before.

'The Christmas decorations are looking great,' Jack said, 'Thought we might have missed them this year, so late coming home and all.'

'We haven't brought you here to discuss Christmas decorations,' Harry said. 'Where are the others?'

'Where's Carter?' Jack countered.

'Messrs Johns and Jenkin,' Harry insisted.

'Oh, them. Too busy. Couldn't make it. They asked me to give you their regards. How's Alison?'

Harry glared at him.

Their drinks were placed before them, with a siphon of soda. Jack fizzed his glass to the top. Smiled at them. 'Cheers,' he said.

'Now look here, Pengelly...'

'Call me Jack,' he said.

Two Saudis rose and glided from the room; slender, elegant figures with pointed beards. He watched them leave. There was a man sitting near the window; he was a small man, clean-shaven, check jacket, would look well in a Yemeni futtah. Was it he? Or was it the European sitting at the bar, the fellow with the gold Rolex and pockmarked skin?

Jack was convinced that Hayward and Courtenay had summoned him here to implicate him in something he knew nothing about, and he guessed it was in order to exonerate themselves. They watched him in anticipation of his curiosity getting the better of his suspicion. They were waiting for that question, that revealing question, which would entangle him in the meshes of their intrigue. Jack looked at Cecil, smiled. Cecil took his hat off, placed it on his lap. He hasn't said anything, Jack realised. He hasn't opened his pretty mouth. Not even a word of greeting. Oh yes, he was covering his ass with more than his hat.

'My dear Jack,' Harry said, 'let us not beat about the bush.'

'That's right Harry. After all, we are men of the world.'

Jack half folded the ten-riyal note and placed it against his lips. He blew a soft, buzzing note. What will they make of that when they play the tape, he thought. He suddenly remembered the hungry flames, the blood oozing through Muqbel's shirt... blood that should have been his own. They had no proof that it was Abdullah's men who had shot him. It could have been done by anybody's men. The

Queen's men. They were not going to mention the war in the Gulf, Jack thought. Well, neither was he.

'I'll have to be going soon,' he said.

'You do realise... ' Harry began.

'I only dropped in to say thanks.'

Now, Harry was suspicious. 'Thanks? For what?'

'For all the help. Out there. You know. We don't know how to repay you. Eddie made some suggestions, but they weren't practicable, and I thought you wouldn't appreciate them: too vulgar for gentlemen of refinement like yourselves, and Mike too. You know what Eddie's like. We'll think of something, I'm sure.'

He fiddled with the banknote. There was so much he didn't know, but he didn't want to know. There was something these two did want to know, for whatever devious reasons, and he was not telling them if he could help it, even though he had no idea what they were after.

'What did you want to see me for? This meeting was arranged at your suggestion, remember?'

Cecil glanced expectantly at Harry. He looked more handsome with his hat off. His beautiful lips creased into a smile, self-assured, confident. Jack felt a slight tingling of the scalp as he looked at those eyes again. They were so friendly in their open invitation to conversation. They might have been discussing strawberries at Ascot.

'Well,' Harry said, the absence of a suitable cliché leaving him at a loss for words. 'We're interested in hearing of the... of the... the results of your expedition.'

'You should ask Carter. He was the leader.'

Harry was obliged to make a concession. 'But Mr Carter didn't participate in the final research. He did leave somewhat precipitously.'

'Did he, sure 'nuff?'

'Well, didn't he?'

They're trying to get me to say it all. Jack thought. There is a tape recorder, or a bug... or something.

'We don't know what happened to him. I came to you to find out, Cecil, you remember.'

The smile faded from Cecil's eyes at the mention of his name.

Harry said, 'Of course he left early. You know perfectly well!' He paused in regret at this lapse of decorum and began again. 'We're simply interested to know how you got on, old chap. We understand that the last days of your studies were among the most interesting of all.'

'Everything will be published in due course.'

'Published?'

'In *Garzetta*, the ornithological journal.'

'Ah yes.'

They were both visibly relieved. Even Cecil had been unable to conceal a flush of alarm at the implications of publication.

Jack decided the time had come to go on the offensive. 'Our observations included matters other than those ornithological, of course, and these might make interesting reading elsewhere. They might be published in some less prestigious journal!' He was imitating Harry's ponderous speech. 'Foreign, perhaps.'

Harry was beginning to lose control. 'Threats will not help,' he said.

Jack considered this as he looked straight into Harry's eyes. 'Then you'd better not make any,' he murmured.

A uniformed porter came and watered the plants near the window. He smiled with a Mediterranean smile.

'You caused us a great deal of anxiety,' Harry said. 'After all, we do feel responsible for our nationals when they are in trouble abroad.'

'Very reassuring. But what makes you think we were in trouble, Harry? Bird watching is a pretty innocuous pastime. Old ladies do it. Girl guides, brownies, even.'

'You were in trouble out there and you're in trouble here. Now, don't be difficult!' Harry tried an obsequious smile.

'What trouble? First I've heard of it. We had a wonderful time. I'll show you my tick list.'

The thought had occurred to Jack that Cecil Hayward should have been conducting this interview instead of sitting opposite in sleek silence. Harry was out of his depth again and there was trouble somewhere in the offing. If Harry were not such a bumptious fool,

Jack might have felt sorry for him. He was no match for the ruthless elite like Cecil Hayward. Cecil was far more implicated in this business than Harry would ever know. Harry was being used, like the rest of them. Poor Harry. But he thought of the toothless Hamid, of big Eddie's shattered nerves, and his compassion dispersed like the mists of an Arabian morning.

'Where next, Cecil?' he asked, 'Moscow? That's the place to be these days!' He turned to Harry. 'He'll do well, that young man.'

Cecil showed no more response than the cold stare in his delicate eyes. Harry bristled with irritation, for Jack had come too near home. Cecil was for Moscow. Harry was staying on in Whitehall for a little break.

'I have to go soon,' Jack said. 'My girlfriend is waiting at home.'

They almost took the bait, then merely glanced at each other.

'Nice girl,' Jack continued, 'Very dark. Very slender. You know the type.'

His smile concealed the deep fear he felt of the power of these men. What could they do to her and to him, unbeknown to anyone? What were they after? What the hell did they want from him?

'Young men should be very discreet in their choice of associates,' Harry said, ominously. 'I heard of a case the other day, in which a young man became involved with a young lady who proved to be an illegal immigrant. Awful mess.'

'Really?'

'Yes!' Harry drawled. 'She was deported in the end. Best thing all round really. Saved the young man an awful lot of trouble. Illegal entry is a very serious offence, these days.'

'I've heard it said that illegal exit is a serious offence too. Is that right? Still, I suppose she would have been OK if she had a multiple entry visa, if she'd been studying here, or something, nursing maybe. I've been told that people sometimes come ashore illegally at night in Cornwall. I shouldn't think that foreigners would know the coast well enough, myself.'

'We should like to meet your young lady!' Harry said. 'You should have brought her with you.'

'She's very shy.'

Harry produced a silver cigarette case. Jack had never seen a cigarette case used in his life. He declined the offer with a shake of the head and took one from his own crumpled packet.

'Never know what's in other people's fags,' he said. A thin smile curled Cecil's lips. Harry reached across with his lighter. 'Thanks,' Jack said. 'Fine bit of silver in that case. Yemeni isn't it? Made by Yehudi. I have a nice piece of their alabaster, you know. Only an old thing, but worth a bit, so I'm told!' Yes, he thought, Hayward had dearly wanted that bull's head. Well, hard luck!

Nobody in the room seemed to be watching or listening to them. There was always the possibility of a bug, for this was the venue of their choice, the table of their choice. They had access to listening devices so sophisticated that their conversation could be recorded in an office streets away. The awareness of this scared him. A word out of place and they could get him, and Nadirah. Any contrived offence or breach of petty regulation would suffice to have her deported back to Yemen. She would never be seen or heard of again. Despite himself, and the growing suspicion that he had the upper hand over these two, he felt himself getting nervous. He drew on the cigarette. 'I sh'll give them up soon,' he said.

'We can help you, you know,' Harry said.

'I don't want your bloody help. I've had some.'

An impulsive outburst, which Jack immediately regretted. The more he thought of it, the more he became convinced that it was because of Nadirah they had summoned him. They intended using her to pressurise him. But for what? He wished to God they would come out with it.

After an interval of silence, Harry said, 'We're genuinely interested in your observations in Yemen, old man. Particularly your records of raptors.'

Jack looked at him sharply, intrigued by the use of this rather specialised word for birds of prey from one whose knowledge of ornithology was virtually nil. 'You mean the eagles?' he said.

'Shall we say… the predators?'

So. There it was. That was what they wanted. They didn't know that Abdullah and Hamid were dead. They didn't know about the arms on the island. They didn't know who had helped the birders. And they didn't know how much Abdullah had told Nadirah. They knew nothing about events on the ground in Yemen. They were still pursuing Abdullah's accomplices for fear they might reveal the involvement of somebody here, in the UK. They wanted Jack to implicate the bird watchers and thereby exonerate themselves. Nothing had changed in this tangle of subterfuge and inference except that Jack now knew he was in possession of some information they desperately required, but not nearly as much as they feared he had.

'We're primarily interested in habitat,' Harry said. 'Where certain species were found. That sort of thing.'

'We spent little time on the resident species. We were only studying migrants. What a pity.' He registered Cecil's recognition of his old nickname. 'I must have told you.'

It was their state of ignorance which they found intolerable. That someone should possess a scrap of information of which they were unaware.

'But you also found the endemics of particular interest!' Harry was performing well, had done his ornithology homework.

'They're very elusive!' Jack sipped his whisky and put the glass on the table. 'Quite dangerous, some of them. Very sharp claws, you know. Some of them feed on snakes. Did you know that?' He looked directly at Cecil. 'They appear to be unaffected by serpents' venom.' He turned to Harry. 'Where's Carter?' he asked for the second time.

Harry was disconcerted by this sudden change of subject and asked, 'Why are you so anxious to see Carter?'

'I owe him something,' Jack said.

'He'll have to wait for it. He's in Mexico.'

'Mexico?'

Jack was taken aback by this disclosure. 'Mexico! I'm not chasing him to Mexico. I'll pay him when he gets back. Always pays me debts, don't 'ee know. It's me workin' class background and that!'

'Yes. Now, about your predators.'

'They're not mine.'

'No. Quite. Well now, did you find their lair, their, what's the term...?'

'Eyrie?'

'Exactly.'

'No!' Jack refused another drink from the obsequious waiter. 'It was not the breeding season,' he said.

'A roost perhaps? A temporary perch, as one might say?'

'No. Nothing like that. We only saw the resident species as we were passing through their territories. It would require considerable fieldwork to discover the habitats you are interested in. We didn't have the time and, in any case, we were not interested in that aspect of their behaviour. Roosting, I mean.'

'But did you see any signs of interesting territorial behaviour? Any inter, or intra, specific aggression for instance?'

'Probably wouldn't have recognised it without detailed knowledge of the species. You're talking about a very specialised field.'

'Quite.'

Harry was at home in this familiar world of innuendo and double talk, where everything is implied, nothing definite. 'Casual observations would be very acceptable,' he said.

'I'll look through my notes,' Jack said, offering a carrot with which he had no intention of parting.

'If you could write them up, or let us have a copy... We would be extremely grateful for anything that you saw of the indigenous species, however insignificant. We're talking about some very rare birds, as you might say.'

'Couldn't do that, sorry.'

'But why not? You've made some highly original observations. The significance of your fieldwork may have eluded you, my dear chap. Your information is vital to the, ah...' Harry almost forgot himself. '...science, as you might say. You owe it to yourself.'

'Well, you would be amazed at the risks incurred by amateurs in disclosing original research in this country. Yeah. Someone else will nick it and publish first. You become overwhelmed by events which appear to be coincidence, and your discoveries are relegated to mere corroboration by reason of pre-emption and prior publication!' He paused for breath. 'I've had some of that too.'

'But you do intend to publish eventually?'

Jack leaned forward until his face was close to Harry's. 'You're damn right,' he said. 'I am going to write up everything. Every minute, insignificant, little detail. Everything about the predators, the prey, the parasites, the commensals, the bloody symbiosis between carnivores, displacement behaviour, false preening, even the rise of the fabulous phoenix from the ashes. All the boring minutiae of scientific observation. Then I'll get it copied prior to sending to foreign journals.'

Harry drained his glass, glanced at the untouched whisky in front of Cecil. 'Then you do admit to making certain interesting observations,' he said. 'Observations, which might be of considerable interest to, shall we say, certain parties. The scientific establishment. As a scientist, you have a duty to disclose your research, not least to your, as you might put it, sponsors.'

'I'm no scientist. That's Carter's job. He'll write up the official version.'

Jack thought he would have liked to lean forward in that expensive chair and whisper: 'Now look here, Courtenay, you perfidious sod, I have no duty nor obligation to you or…' That was exactly what they wanted, what they expected: that he would lose control.

'I'm only an amateur,' he said. 'Carter's the professional, like yourselves.'

'My dear chap!' Harry actually chuckled. 'We British are renowned for the efficiency of our amateurs.'

'No, Harry. The English like to think of others regarding them as amateurs, muddling through. What you can't accept is the fact that they're right. You do muddle through and your only efficiency lies in covering up the fact.' He reached into his pocket for his cigarettes. 'I have to go soon.' He placed his hands on the arms of the chair in preparation for rising.

They could see he meant it. The Yemeni ten riyal note was still in his fingers.

'Damn it,' Harry said. 'You must help us. You owe it to us for all the help we gave you.'

Jack eased himself back into the chair, watching both of them. He took a sip of whisky and wiped his mouth with the back of his hand. He took a handful of cigarettes from the packet, counted some out and lined them up on the table in front of Harry.

'Six, I believe it was. I even bought the same brand, see!' He flicked the red banknote onto the table between them. 'And there's your change,' he said. 'The rest was spent on local contingencies. I owe you *nothing*.'

Harry became magenta across the cheeks, almost blue around his compressed lips. He leaned across the table, over the scattered cigarettes and money. 'Don't you realise,' he seethed, 'that you and your companions placed the whole of your country's Middle East foreign policy in jeopardy by your irresponsible actions? I'm not prepared to allow you to implicate... '

There was a slight movement of Cecil's point of balance, a slight twisting of the body. He had pressed his foot against Harry's leg.

'Don't know what you're talking about, old dear,' Jack said. 'We were only watching birds.'

He suspected that what had been placed in jeopardy was the careers of these two and the reputation of someone in a high, possibly very high, position. Someone guilty of advancing their own policy and lining their pockets regardless of national interests. Harry was breathing like a man recovering from excessive exertion. He slumped back in his chair and slowly recovered his composure, while the beautiful one took a minute sip of whisky. Their diplomatic facade was crumbling like the ruins of Marib, overwhelmed by the accumulated grains of incompetence and intrigue.

'I really would like to help you,' Jack said, 'but I don't see how I can. All that foreign policy stuff is beyond me. Don't know anything about all that business. I just don't see what you want from me.'

Harry sighed in exasperation. He looked to Cecil, who gave him

373

a slight, almost imperceptible, nod of assent. He's keeping his nose clean, Jack thought. This conversation is most definitely being recorded. He was sure of it. They would have to commit themselves before he divulged a scrap.

Harry Courtenay said, 'Jack, my dear chap!' And paused for thought. 'Certain supplies,' he eventually continued, 'consigned to certain people, have gone astray, been mislaid. Certain people have disappeared. These supplies and these people could cause HMG a great deal of embarrassment at the present time. Now, should you by any chance know the whereabouts of either, we would wish to be informed. That's all!' He smiled. 'Would you like another drink?'

The traces of liquor inside Harry's glass had totally evaporated from the heat of his hand. He was beginning to suffer. Jack ignored the suggestion.

'Certain supplies and certain people could cause a great deal of suffering among my friends in Yemen.'

'But, my dear boy, it is suffering we are trying to alleviate.'

'If certain supplies had never been consigned, some of my friends in Yemen would not have already suffered. I did hear a rumour that consignments of British manufacture fell off a lorry, or a ship, and disappeared. I could ask you where those supplies originated, to where they were consigned, and by whom!' He thought Harry was to be permitted some revelation, as a sprat to catch a mackerel, and hastily added, 'But I won't ask, because I don't want to know.'

He wondered how much Harry knew, even now. Not a lot, probably. Too much had gone over his head. He too had been informed on the 'need to know' principle. Not what he needed to know, so much as what others needed him to know. He had been used as a tool to exploit the bird watchers, to use them in furtherance of what some called patriotism, some nationalism, some... spying, the gathering of intelligence by the ignorant, so that in the whole chain of subterfuge there was no one who had both full knowledge and first-hand experience of the intrigues. Even Cecil Hayward, sitting there fingering his lovely wavy hair, probably didn't know the complete story. The whole business was like a chain of paper in which Jack Pengelly had no intention of becoming a link. He could not see that his knowledge of events in Yemen could benefit his country, rather than some individual in the hierarchy of deceit who had instigated the shipment following some policy of his, or her, own. To hell with them.

'We do have methods, you know.'

'Get away.'

'Oh yes. We have our sources.'

The quick frown of exasperation that spread over Cecil's face as he glanced in irritation at his colleague was not missed by Jack. Harry's interrogation was not going to plan. For the first time since meeting these ambassadors of his country in this expensive hotel he felt free of threat and laughed.

'I have to go now,' he said. 'I have a wedding to arrange.'

'Wedding?' Harry said. 'What wedding?'

'And a train to catch at Paddington.'

Jack rose from the deep recess of the chair. These expensive things were never very comfortable. He couldn't understand it. He stretched, spreading his arms wide. He heard a bone click somewhere in his back.

'Goodbye, Harry,' he said through a yawn. 'If I can help anytime!' His arms collapsed at his sides. 'I've no doubt that you'll be able to find me. Ask anyone at home, they all know where I live. At the top of Teetotal Street. Not your kind of neighbourhood! Though you must realise,' he said, looking straight into Harry's eyes. 'that should you have reason to visit me again, I shall not be free to devote as much time to you as I have today.'

They had both adopted hostile stares as they too rose to their feet. Jack, by the direct quote, had reminded Harry Courtenay of his peremptory dismissal of the birders in Sana'a, and Harry knew it.

'Nice meeting you again, Cecil. Enjoyed our little chat, though it's a shame you couldn't make it on time.' Jack was still not sure what they wanted of him. What he was supposed to say and for whose benefit. He looked at his watch.

Cecil Hayward slipped his hand into the inner pocket of his expensive jacket and withdrew it, empty. He spoke for the first time.

His voice was cold and restrained. The anger he obviously felt was permitted to manifest itself only in the precise incision of his diction as he leaned forward and spoke very softly across the table.

'Pengelly, you came within a hair's breadth of doing untold harm to your country, either by foolishness or treachery. I am not prepared to accept that you're a fool, and the conclusion is that you were not alone in dealing with those factions working against us. You will tell us who they are and what happened to the armaments.'

At this, their first mention of armaments, Jack quailed at the thought that he might be arrested as a traitor here in his own country, as he had quailed in Yemen. He was afraid of Hayward but tried to conceal his fear as those blue eyes pierced his own. They could do nothing without implicating themselves, these two, but they scared him. It was difficult for Jack to accept that this ruthless character, with the hatred in his eyes, was the same man who had been so kind and helpful in Sana'a. He could only assume that Cecil Hayward had been pressurised against his will by higher authority into actions even more subversive than those of which the birders were accused. He was covering his tracks, and was, it seemed, being forced to implicate anybody in order to save his own and some other, more important, skin.

'It was impossible for you to leave Yemen without help. How did you get out?' Cecil demanded. 'Who helped you, Pengelly?'

Jack remembered the days in the open boat, when their survival had depended on his seamanship. He remembered the thirst, Eddie's delirium and tears as his nerves packed up, Mike's incredulity at being betrayed by his own kind. He remembered Nadirah's despondency as the sambuk drifted without fuel or water and they watched the passing ships, all of which assumed they were Arab fishermen and ignored them, until they were picked up by the battered little Liberian-registered freighter bound for Amsterdam. He remembered persuading the scruffy skipper to conceal them as they passed thought the Suez Canal and then to put them ashore at night, under the cliffs at Pedn y Vounder, in Cornwall. The man risked his inflatable dingy, after assurances from Jack that he knew the coast and accepting most of the remaining embassy cash.

He said, 'Helped us? Is that what's bothering you? We were sponsored. There are always plenty of organisations trying to justify their existence by giving away other people's money. Ask Carter.'

He watched their faces. Cecil was evidently resigned to accept that Jack would divulge nothing of those last days out there. Harry struggled to find a final threat, but couldn't think of one as Jack stared him out.

Jack's own little tape recorder in his pocket would have saved all this in case he needed it but, unless he floundered and inadvertently divulged what he knew of the armaments, the island, little old Hamid and the death of Abdullah, they had nothing to implicate him, or her, in anything. Nadirah was safe.

When it was evident that they could think of no further questions, or threats, he left them standing there. 'Masallamah,' he said, 'go in peace.'

Time has passed, yet Jack still remembers every detail of that interview. He is pretty sure they had seen through his apparent indifference to their interrogation. He is also certain that he still has no idea of what intrigues were behind all the manipulations in Yemen. Somebody, somewhere, up there in the higher echelons of the hierarchy, might, even now, still be having the occasional sleepless night in fear of some incriminating revelation coming to light. He bloody well hopes so but, in recollecting it all, as he looked across the bay at a few passing gannets, he saw that the tide had turned.

Nadirah would always pine for her ancient culture, her friends and family still out there, the pure water of her beautiful Wadi Bana, but here she was safe and, she frequently reassured him, happy.

The mackerel were coming into the bay on the first of the flood tide, so it was time to put to sea. He boarded his boat, cast off the moorings and headed out past the headland where it had all began. Over gentle swells there was a Balearic shearwater among the flocks of Manx moving west.

Acknowledgements

The author wishes to thank all the people who helped him during the real quest for the migration route of eagles, which he found while exploring alone in Yemen. First of all, The Winston Churchill Travelling Fellowship which enabled him to spend three months looking for the Eagle migration. Without the help and support from various expatriates from Britain and several other countries, the staff of the Overseas Survey team and of the British Embassy, his mission would have failed. The diplomats were very interested in the search and helped in numerous ways. None of them resembled in any way the two portrayed herein. The Yemeni people also were extremely kind and helpful, offering, despite their poverty, hospitality which we in the west have, sadly, lost. I have a great love of, and admiration for, them.

It was my own innocent and inadvertent involvement with a whisky smuggling incident, while searching for the eagles, that was the basic germ of the whole novel. It is a story extrapolated from a minor event that stimulated the author's imagination. Arabic speakers are respectfully asked to forgive my attempts to transcribe the language into the Latin alphabet.

I am very grateful to Liz Tregenza and John Phillips for their suggestions and patient and meticulous proof reading. Any mistakes herein are all my own.